About the Author

Maya Blake's writing dream started at 13. She eventually realised her dream when she received The Call in 2012. Maya lives in England with her husband, kids and an endless supply of books. Contact Maya: mayabauthor.blogspot.com, X @mayablake and Facebook maya.blake.94

The Tycoon's Affair

July 2025
Tempted by Desire

August 2025
Craving his Love

September 2025
Business with Pleasure

January 2026
Stealing his Heart

February 2026
Playing with Power

March 2026
After Hours Passion

The Tycoon's Affair:
Business with Pleasure

MAYA BLAKE

MILLS & BOON

All rights reserved including the right of reproduction in whole or in part in any form. This edition is published by arrangement with Harlequin Enterprises ULC.

This is a work of fiction. Names, characters, places, locations and incidents are purely fictional and bear no relationship to any real life individuals, living or dead, or to any actual places, business establishments, locations, events or incidents. Any resemblance is entirely coincidental.

Without limiting the author's and publisher's exclusive rights, any unauthorised use of this publication to train generative artificial intelligence (AI) technologies is expressly prohibited. HarperCollins also exercise their rights under Article 4(3) of the Digital Single Market Directive 2019/790 and expressly reserve this publication from the text and data mining exception.

® and ™ are trademarks owned and used by the trademark owner and/or its licensee. Trademarks marked with ® are registered with the United Kingdom Patent Office and/or the Office for Harmonisation in the Internal Market and in other countries.

First Published in Great Britain 2025
by Mills & Boon, an imprint of HarperCollins*Publishers* Ltd
1 London Bridge Street, London, SE1 9GF

www.harpercollins.co.uk

HarperCollins*Publishers*
Macken House, 39/40 Mayor Street Upper,
Dublin 1, D01 C9W8, Ireland

The Tycoon's Affair: Business with Pleasure © 2025 Harlequin Enterprises ULC.

Bound by My Scandalous Pregnancy © 2020 Maya Blake
What the Greek's Money Can't Buy © 2014 Maya Blake
A Marriage Fit for a Sinner © 2015 Maya Blake

ISBN: 978-0-263-41863-7

This book contains FSC™ certified paper and other controlled sources to ensure responsible forest management.

For more information visit: www.harpercollins.co.uk/green

Printed and Bound in the UK using 100% Renewable Electricity
at CPI Group (UK) Ltd, Croydon, CR0 4YY

BOUND BY MY SCANDALOUS PREGNANCY

CHAPTER ONE

Reincarnation. Karma. Sins coming home to roost.

Once upon a time, in the not-too-distant past, if anyone had asked me if I believed in any of those things I'd have rolled my eyes and told them to get real. That life worked on the amount of effort you put into each day.

On love.

Loyalty.

Hard work.

How wrong I was.

Frozen outside the towering glass and steel offices of one of the most powerful men on the globe, my wrists tingling from the phantom handcuffs that might become real before the hour was out, I wondered which deity I'd wronged to bring me to this end.

Did it even matter that the domino effect of sheer rotten luck mostly had nothing to do with me? Was it worth ranting that the sins of the father shouldn't be visited upon the daughter?

No.

The awful truth was, while the majority of what happened to me in the past few years wasn't my fault, this last, shocking misstep was one hundred percent mine.

Sure, I could prove that a collection of things had culminated in that one gigantic error, but the reality was inescapable. The buck, and the blame, stopped with me.

Time to own it, Sadie.

One more minute, I silently pleaded to whatever higher power held my fate in its cruel grip.

But, adding to every other misfortune unfolding in my life, my plea went unheeded.

The two sharply dressed security guards who'd been

eyeing me with increasing wariness through the imposing glass frontage were heading my way. These days the whole world was on edge. I of all people should know that.

The economy had been partly responsible for decimating the family I once took for granted. The family currently hanging by a very fragile thread.

And dressed in threadbare clothes that were at least five seasons old, my troubled expression reflected in the polished glass, I wouldn't be surprised if I was wrestled to the ground and arrested for trespassing. Or worse.

Disturbingly, that possibility gleamed palatably for a second, attesting to my true state of mind. *Really?* I'd rather be arrested than—

'Excuse me, miss. Can I help you?'

I jumped, my hand flying to my throat to contain the heart beating itself into a frenzy. The burlier of the two guards had stepped through the revolving doors without my noticing and now stood a few feet away. Everything about him promised he could switch from courteous to menacing in a heartbeat.

Definitely time to own it, Sadie.

'I...' I stopped, moved my tongue to wet desert-dry lips. 'I need to see Mr Xenakis. Is he in?'

His eyes narrowed. 'You'll have to ask for him at the reception desk. Do you have an appointment?'

I nearly laughed. How could I make an appointment to confess what I'd done?

'Um, no. But—'

'I think you should leave now, miss.' His tone indicated it wasn't a suggestion.

'Please! It's a matter of life or death.'

He froze. 'Whose life?'

I bit the inside of my lip, afraid I'd overexaggerated things a little. For all I knew, the man I'd wronged wouldn't bat an eyelid at my actions. Truth was, I wouldn't know until I confronted him.

'I… I can't tell you. But it's urgent. And private. If you could just tell me if Mr Xenakis is in?'

For an interminable minute he simply watched me. Then he grasped my elbow. 'Come with me, Miss…?'

I hesitated. Once I gave my name there'd be no going back. But what choice did I have? Either confess and plead my case or wait for the authorities to show up at my door. 'Preston. Sadie Preston.'

With swift efficiency, I was ushered across the stunning atrium of Xenakis Aeronautics, through a series of nondescript doors that led to the bowels of the basement and into a room bearing all the hallmarks of an interrogation chamber.

Hysteria threatened. I suppressed it as the guard muttered a stern, 'Stay here.'

The next twenty minutes were the longest of my life. In direct contrast to the speed with which my life flashed before my eyes after the enormity of what I'd done sank in.

The man who entered the room then was even more imposing, leaving me in no doubt that my request was being taken seriously. And not in a good way.

'Miss Preston?'

At my hesitant nod, the tall, salt-and-pepper-haired man held the door open, his dark eyes assessing me even more thoroughly once I scrambled to my feet.

'I'm Wendell, head of Mr Xenakis's security team. This way,' he said, in a voice that brooked no argument.

Dear God, either Neo Xenakis was super thorough about his interactions with the common man or he was paranoid about his security. Neither boded well.

Another series of incongruous underground hallways brought us to a steel-framed lift. Wendell accessed it with a sleek black key card. Once inside, he pressed another button.

The lift shot up, leaving my stomach and the last dregs of my courage on the basement floor. I wanted to throw myself at the lift doors, claw them open and jump out, consequences be damned. But my feet were paralysed with the unshakeable acceptance that I would only be postponing the inevitable.

Besides, I didn't run from my responsibilities. Not like my father literally had when things got tough. Not like my mother was doing by burying her head in the sand and frivolously gambling away money we didn't have. A habit that had veered scarily towards addiction in the last six months.

I stifled my anxiety as the lift slid to a smooth halt.

One problematic mountain at a time.

This particular one bore all the hallmarks of an Everest climb. One that might only see me to Base Camp before the worst happened.

Not a single member of the sharply dressed staff I'd spotted coming and going downstairs roamed this rarefied space, which boasted the kind of furnishings that graced the expensive designer magazines my mother had avidly subscribed to back when money had been no object for the Prestons. The kind that had always made me wonder if the pictures were staged or if people actually lived like that.

Evidently, they did.

The dove-grey carpeting looked exclusive and expensive, making me cringe as my scuffed, cheap shoes trod over it. Lighter shades of grey silk graced the walls, with stylish lampshades illuminating the space and the twin console tables that stood on either side of the immense double doors.

Made of white polished ash, with handles that looked like gleaming aeroplane wings, everything about them and the glimpse of the expansive conference rooms I could see from where I stood screamed opulence and exclusivity. The type that belonged to owners who didn't take kindly to strangers ruining their day with the sort of news I had to deliver.

Sweat broke out on my palms. Before I could perform the undignified act of rubbing them against the polyester weave of my skirt, Wendell knocked twice.

The voice that beckoned was deep enough to penetrate the solid wood, formidable enough to raise the dread digging its claws into me…and enigmatic enough to send a skitter of…*something else* down my spine.

That unknown quality threatened to swamp all other emotions as Wendell opened the doors. 'You have five minutes,' he informed me, then stepped to one side.

The need to flee resurged. How long would a prison sentence be for this kind of crime, anyway?

Too long. My mother wouldn't survive more upheaval. And with our landlord threatening eviction, the last thing I could afford was more turbulence.

With no choice but to face my fate, I took a shaky step into the office.

And promptly lost every last gasp of air from my lungs at the sight of the man braced against the floor-to-ceiling glass windows, arms crossed and fierce eyes locked on me.

If his surroundings screamed ultraexclusivity and supreme wealth, the man himself was so many leagues above that station, he required his own stratosphere. Even stationary, he vibrated with formidable power—the kind that commanded legions with just one look.

And his body…

The navy suit, clearly bespoke, enhanced the bristling power of his athletic build. Like his impressive six-foot-plus height, his wide tapered shoulders seemed to go on for ever, with the kind of biceps that promised to carry any load rippling beneath the layers of clothes. Above the collar of his pristine white shirt, his square jaw jutted out with unapologetic masculinity, and his pure alpha-ness was not in any way diluted by the dimple in his chin. If anything, that curiously arresting feature only drew deeper attention to the rest of his face. To the haughty cheekbones resting beneath narrowed eyes, his wide forehead and the sensual slash of his lips.

He was…indescribable. Because words like *attractive* or *breathtaking* or even *magnificent* didn't do him nearly enough justice.

And as he continued to appraise me, every last ounce of my courage threatened to evaporate as surely as my breath. Because the way he stared at me, as if he found me as fascinating as I found him, sent a spiralling wave of pure, unadulterated awareness charging through me.

For some inexplicable reason my hair seemed to hold singular appeal for him, making me almost feel as if he was touching the tied back tresses, caressing the strands between his fingers.

The snick of the door shutting made me flinch—a reaction he spotted immediately as his arms dropped and he began to prowl slowly towards me.

Sweet heaven, even the way he moved was spectacular. I'd never truly comprehended the term 'poetry in motion.' Until now.

Focus, Sadie. You're not here to ogle the first billionaire you've ever met.

I opened my mouth to speak. He beat me to it.

'Whoever you are, you seem to have caught Wendell in a good mood. I don't believe he's allowed anyone to walk in off the street and demand to see me in…well, *ever*,' he rasped in a gravel-rolling-in-honey voice, sending another cascade of pure sensation rushing over my skin.

Momentarily thrown by the effect of his voice, I couldn't tell if his tone suggested he'd be having a word with Wendell later about that misstep or if the whole thing simply amused him. He was that enigmatic to read. The mystery stretched my already oversensitive nerves, triggering my babble-when-nervous flaw.

'That was Wendell in a *good* mood? I shudder to think what he's like in a bad mood,' I blurted. Then I cringed harder when the meaning of my words sank in.

Oh, no…

His eyes narrowed even further as he stopped several feet away from me. 'Perhaps you'd like to move whatever this is along?'

Impatience coated his tone even as his eyes raked a closer inspection over my body, pausing on the frayed thinness of my blouse, the slightly baggy cut of my skirt following my recent weight loss, before dropping to my legs. The return journey was just as sizzling. Hell, more so.

That stain of inadequacy, of not being worthy—which had dogged me from the moment my father's abscondment-announcing postcard had landed on the front doormat, in shocking synchronicity with the bailiff's arrival on our doorstep eight years ago—flared like a fever.

I didn't need one of my mother's magazines to tell me that this man didn't meddle with the likes of me...*ever*.

It was in every delicious frame of his impeccable body, every measured exhalation and every flicker of those sooty, spiky eyelashes that most women would pay hundreds to replicate. He would date socialites with faultless pedigree. Heiresses with flawless bone structure who listed royalty as close friends.

Not the callously abandoned daughter of a disgraced middle-grade financier and an almost-addicted gambler, whose only nod to the arts was learning how to execute a half-decent jeté in year-five ballet.

'Or do you feel inclined to use your five minutes in melodramatic silence?' he drawled.

The realisation that I'd been gaping at him brought a spike of embarrassment. 'I'm not being melodramatic.'

One brow hiked, and his gaze scanned me from top to toe again before his face slowly hardened.

'You stated that you needed to see me as a matter of life or death, but between the time you set foot in my building and your arrival in my office I've ascertained that every member of my family is safe and accounted for. My employees' well-being will take longer, and a lot of manpower to establish, so if I'm being pranked I'd caution you to turn around and leave right now—'

'This isn't about your present family. It's about your future one.'

He turned to stone. A quite miraculous thing since he was such a big, towering force of a man whose aura threw off electric charges. His ability not to move a muscle would have been fascinating to watch if I hadn't been terrified of the look in his eyes. The one that promised chaos and doom.

'Repeat that, if you please.'

I couldn't. Not if I valued my life.

'I... Perhaps I need to start from the beginning.'

A single clench to his jaw. 'Start *somewhere*. And fast. I'm not a patient man, Miss Preston. And I'm about to be late for an important meeting.'

My rib-banging heart rate shuddered in terror.

My life flashed before my eyes. *Again*.

I pushed away disturbingly bleak images of a life unfulfilled and dreams dashed. Curled my sweaty fists tighter and cleared my throat.

'My name is Sadie Preston...' When that only prompted a higher arch of his brow I hurried on. 'I work...*worked* at the Phoenix Clinic.'

Right until I was summarily fired, three hours ago. But the problem of my unemployment would have to be addressed later. Provided I didn't end up in jail—

My train of thought screeched to a halt as he rocked forward, slid his hands into his trouser pockets and brought muscular thighs into singeing relief. Time pulsed by in silence as the very masculine stance ramped up the heat running through me.

'For your sake, I hope this isn't some sort of misguided attempt to garner employment, because I can assure you—'

'It's not!' My interruption was much more shrill than I'd intended. And I knew immediately that neither it nor my tone had gained me any favours. Hell, his imposing presence seemed to loom even larger in the vast office, his aura terrifying. 'Please...if you would just hear me out?'

'*You're* the one who seems to be tongue-tied, Miss Preston. While *my* precious time bleeds away. So let me make this easy for you. You have one minute to state your business. I advise you to make it worthwhile, for both our sakes.'

Or what?

For a single moment I feared I'd blurted the words, the volatile mix of annoyance and trepidation having finally broken me. But he didn't seem any more incandescent. Simply terribly hacked off at my continued delay in spilling the beans.

'I was fired this morning because...' *pause, deep breath* '...because I accidentally destroyed your...' I squeezed my eyes shut. When I opened them, he was still there, breathtaking and immovable as a marble statue.

Firm, sensually curved lips flattened. 'My what?' he demanded tersely.

Tension vibrated through me as I forced my vocal cords to work. 'I destroyed...your...your stored sperm sample.'

For a horribly tense minute he simply stared at me with utter confusion—as if he couldn't quite comprehend my words—and then that face that defied description tautened into a mask of pure, cold disbelief.

'You. Did. What?'

It wasn't shouted. Or whispered. It was even toned. And absolutely deadly.

I shivered from head to toe, severely doubting my ability ever to speak again as I opened my mouth and words failed to emerge.

Terrifying seconds ticked away as we stood in rigid silence, gazes locked.

'Speak,' he commanded, again without so much as any inflexion in his voice. His lips had gone white with grim fury and he was barely breathing.

I prised my tongue from the roof of my mouth. To do what I'd come here to do. Appeal to his better nature.

Taking a hesitant step towards him, I tried a small smile. 'Mr Xenakis—'

One hand erupted from his pocket in a halting motion. 'Do not attempt to cajole. Do not attempt to prevaricate. I want the facts. Bare and immediate.'

This time his voice had altered. It was a primordial rumble. Like the nape-tingling premonition before a cataclysmic event.

My smile evaporated. 'When I arrived at work this morning...' *late because of my mother and another futile attempt to get through to her* '... I was given a list of samples to dispose of. I... It's not part of my job description, but—'

'What is your *actual* job at the Phoenix Clinic?' The barest hint of an accent had thickened his voice, making him impossibly sexier.

'I'm a receptionist.'

It was the only half-decent paying job I could find that would support my mother and me until I figured out a way to help her out of her dark tunnel of despair and resume the marketing degree I'd suspended so I could care for her.

'And what business does a receptionist have handling patient samples?'

His tone was a chilling blade of reason. He wasn't furious. Not yet, anyway. Right now Neo Xenakis was on a cold, fact-finding mission.

I managed to answer. 'It's not the usual procedure, but we were severely short-staffed today and the list I was given stated that the samples had already been triple-checked.'

'Obviously not. Or you wouldn't be here, would you?' he rasped.

A wave of shame hit me. My error could have been avoided if I hadn't been so frazzled. If I hadn't been worried that my mother and I were about to lose the roof over our heads. If my boss's medical secretary hadn't called in sick, leaving *me* as temporary—and infinitely unlucky—cover.

About to attempt another pleading of my case, I froze when a loud buzz sounded from his desk.

For the longest time he stared at me, as if trying to decipher whether or not everything I'd told him was some sort of hoax.

When the intercom sounded again, he strode to his desk with unbridled impatience. 'Yes?' he grated.

'There's a Spencer Donnelly on the line for you, sir. He says it's urgent.'

My breath caught. He heard it and speared me with narrow-eyed speculation. To his assistant, he said, 'I don't believe I know a Spencer Donnelly. Who is he?'

I stepped forward, earning myself more intense scrutiny. 'That's my boss. My ex-boss, I mean. I think he's calling you to explain.'

And most likely to ensure the blame stayed squarely on my shoulders.

Neo hit the mute button. 'Is he responsible for what happened?' he demanded from me.

'Not...not directly. But he's the head of the clinic—'

'I don't care what his role is. I care about who's directly responsible. Are you saying it was you and you alone?'

My nape heated at the imminent fall of the axe, but seeing as there was nothing more I could do but admit my total culpability, I nodded. 'Yes. It was my fault.'

His nostrils flared as he unmuted the line. 'Take a message,' he informed his assistant, then sauntered back to where I stood.

For another stomach-churning minute he pinned me beneath his gaze. 'Tell me what your intention was in coming here, Miss Preston,' he invited silkily.

His even voice did not soothe me for one second. Whatever his reason for depositing a sperm sample at a fertility clinic, the consequences of my mistake would be brutal.

Alternate heat and cold flashed through my veins. I would have given everything I owned to be able to flee from his presence. But, seeing as fate and circumstance had already taken everything from me, leaving me with very little of value...

'I thought you deserved to hear the truth from me. And also my a-apology,' I said, my throat threatening to close up at the look on his face.

He said nothing, simply waited for several seconds before he elevated that characterful eyebrow, his silent sarcasm announcing that I hadn't actually proffered any apology.

I cursed the heat rushing gleefully into my face at his icy mockery as he saw what he was doing to me. 'I... I'm sorry, Mr Xenakis. I didn't mean to destroy your property. If there was a way to undo it, I would...' I stopped, knowing the words were useless. There was no reversing what I'd done.

'And I'm simply to let you off the hook, am I? Based on you doing the honourable thing by coming here to throw yourself on my mercy?'

What could I say to that? 'I know it's a lot to ask, but I promise I didn't mean to.'

His gaze dropped and I caught the faintest shake of his head as a wave of disbelief flared over his face again. For the longest time he stared at the carpet, his jaw clenching and unclenching as he fought whatever emotion gripped him so tightly.

In that moment, my senses wanted to do the unthinkable and put myself in his shoes—but, no. I couldn't afford to get emotionally carried away.

If, by some cruel twist of fate, there was something wrong with Neo Xenakis's reproductive equipment, wouldn't he have seemed a little...*desolate*, somehow, instead of looking as if he could go toe to toe with Zeus? And win?

Several expressions flitted across his features, too fast to decipher. But when he lifted his gaze to mine once more, chilling premonition swept over me.

Mr Donnelly had known I wouldn't be let off scot-free, which was why he'd insisted I be the first in the line of fire in admitting culpability. The hurried internet search I'd done on the bus ride into the city had left me reeling at the enormity of the adversary I'd unwittingly created with one fatalistic click of the mouse.

Neo Xenakis regarded me with the flat coldness of a cobra about to strike. 'You *didn't mean to*? That applies when you tread on someone's foot. Or accidentally spill your coffee at an inopportune moment. Correct me if I'm wrong, but the Phoenix Clinic has a stringent set of checks in place, does it not?'

I opened my mouth to answer, but he was shaking his head, already rejecting my confirmation.

'Whatever you thought was going to happen with your coming here, I'm afraid it won't be that easy, Miss Preston.'

'What do you mean?'

God, did he want me to beg? Fall on my face and prostrate myself before him?

The weirdest thought entered my head. That however he intended me to pay, it would be welcome. Perhaps even a little...*life-changing*.

When his gaze dropped to my parted lips I entertained the notion, while staring at his mouth, that whatever those reparations were they would be *carnal* in nature. That I would perhaps even...*enjoy* it.

Sweet heaven, Sadie. What's wrong with you?

Dragging my focus from the lush curve of his lips, I met his gaze—only to find the grey depths alight with the same blaze that singed my blood.

Abruptly he turned away, returned to his desk and picked up a sleek-looking tablet. 'Willa, please come in.'

Confusion mingled with those peculiar feelings rioted through me, rendering me speechless as the door opened and a stylishly dressed blonde entered. The woman was more suited to traipse down a runway than give executive assistance. The dismissive glance she threw me before sashaying her way to her boss's desk said she was well aware of her assets.

'Yes, Mr Xenakis.' Unsurprisingly, her voice dripped with sensual interest as she smiled at him.

Curbing my instant dislike for Willa, I listened to them exchange a low-voiced conversation about his upcoming meeting before he rounded his desk.

'Escort Miss Preston to my penthouse. She's to stay there until I'm done with my meeting. If she attempts to leave, inform Wendell.'

My irritation at being discussed as if I wasn't there doubled at the edict he'd just delivered. 'What? You can't... I won't just stay here at your whim!'

The fury he'd kept at bay finally flared into singeing life. 'You've destroyed my property, Miss Preston, making your actions a crime. Attempt to leave and I'll be forced to let the authorities handle it. You have two options. Stay and discuss this further, after my meeting. Or leave and face the consequences.' He strode towards the door, throwing over his shoulder, 'I'll let you inform Willa of your decision.'

Then he was gone.

I veered towards the windows, hoping for a ray of enlightenment. But the typical English weather had greyed in complete alignment with my circumstances.

I couldn't leave. Not unless I wanted to risk worsening my situation.

Neo Xenakis was in shock, still grappling with the news. Would he show mercy when he'd calmed down? Was I better off handing myself over to the authorities and pleading my case with a lawyer through the courts?

With what funds? Even before I lost my job we were barely scraping by. I didn't have the resources to pay a lawyer for even ten minutes of his time!

I was better off waiting. Perhaps talking him round to getting him to return to the clinic to deposit another sample...

Willa's pointed throat-clearing triggered a wince. Turning, I lifted my chin and met her contemptuous stare.

'I'll stay,' I announced, with as much firmness as I could manage, considering my stomach had gone into a thousand-foot free fall.

CHAPTER TWO

Retreat. Regroup.

For the dozenth time in what felt like the longest afternoon of my life, I shook my head.

'You don't agree, Mr Xenakis?'

I refocused on the leader of the Brazilian marketing team gathered around the conference table and wondered what I'd missed while my brain was stuck in that endless cycle of life-altering words uttered by the most captivating creature I'd ever seen.

I'm sorry... I've destroyed...everything.

To think I'd been convinced she was pranking me. Or, even more amusing, that she had latched on to an inventive method of getting my attention, since most feminine ploys left me cold these days.

My steep drop in interest in the opposite sex hadn't gone unnoticed in recent years. Socialites who'd smugly decided they were an integral part of my healing process were scratching their heads, wondering why I'd permanently lost their numbers. Heiresses who'd eagerly and blatantly sought an alliance with the newly *un*engaged Xenakis bachelor were left stunned as every avenue of contact was firmly rebuffed.

It hadn't even been worth the time to inform them that the thrill of the chase had stopped being, well...*thrilling*. That the eighteen months I'd spent sowing every wild oat I could had left me ashen mouthed and even more jaded than I'd been when I woke up in that hospital to the cruellest betrayal.

To think I'd imagined *that* was the worst moment of my life.

The stark reality of Sadie Preston's presence in my penthouse—as per Willa's confirmation, minutes ago—attested to that moment having well and truly been usurped.

Was this how my brother Axios had felt when presented with the noose-like proposition he'd faced almost a year ago?

No, Ax's sentence was finite. It would end...or rather should have been ending in a matter of weeks, had his bride of fewer than twenty-four hours not fled from him and vanished without a trace, leaving him bewildered and stuck in limbo.

Christos. *If he's feeling even a fraction of what I'm feeling now...*

But then the bride he'd acquired hadn't been wanted. Whereas what Sadie Preston had taken from me was... *priceless.*

The dreaded cancer diagnosis which had precipitated my sperm donation in anticipation of radiation might have turned out to be a false alarm when I was twenty-five, but the scars marring my skin beneath my clothes were a reminder of why that visit to the Phoenix Clinic had turned out to be a pivotal, life-affirming event for me. A light in the bleak darkness of the blissful ignorance I'd lived in for almost a year, before the blindfold had been ripped from my eyes almost as ruthlessly as the accident that had attempted to rob me of my life.

Anger and pure, unadulterated disbelief flashed like lightning through my system. I shook my head again, aware that I was attracting bewildered stares from the marketing gurus I'd hired to promote the interests of Xenakis Aeronautics in Brazil.

It had taken a draining amount of mental dexterity to get through my other two meetings, and now a quick glance at the presentation slide brought me up to speed with what I'd missed. Or rather, what *they'd* missed.

'This isn't going to work. Besides being unexceptional, you've aimed it at the wrong demographic.'

The team leader nodded enthusiastically. 'Which demographic were you thinking of, Mr Xenakis?'

I stopped myself from rolling my eyes. Was I required to do *all* their work for them? 'You have the data from the beta test. From what I'm seeing, you haven't bothered to consult it. I'm not seeing any application of the feedback we received from millennials with children.'

My chest clenched as another percussive wave of shock pummelled me. Children. Families. *Fatherhood.*

A state I'd never experience now, thanks to the actions of a redhead whose lips had dripped words of remorse but whose attitude vaunted defiance. Those startling green eyes had dared me to *bring it on* even as her bedroom voice wobbled with apology.

That little chin had been raised in silent combat, displaying the silken skin of her throat and a shadow of cleavage. And as for the other treasures hidden beneath her cheap, threadbare clothes…and that hair I wanted to wrap my fist around…

Theos mou. *Get a grip.*

It was searing shock that had stopped me from instructing Wendell to hand her over to the authorities as soon as she'd confessed her crime.

And shock was the reason she was in my penthouse while I bought myself some time to deal with the earth-shattering news. Besides, as much as I trusted my security chief, some things were private. And this matter couldn't get more private.

Sadie Preston had essentially taken every last shred of hope for my future and trashed it. And the worst thing was that I hadn't known how much the nebulous prospect of fatherhood had meant until any chance of it had been destroyed—first with betrayal and lies, and then with a careless press of the delete button on a computer.

My chest growing tighter, I jerked to my feet, the need to do something clawing through me. 'Ladies and gentlemen, I trust we know which direction we're heading for in the campaign now?' At their nods of assent, I headed for the door. 'You have one week to get it right. Don't let me down.'

Don't let me down.

Was I wasting my breath, saying that? Was I doomed to be disappointed in everyone I put my trust in? Be it in personal stakes or in a supposedly exclusive, top-of-the-range clinic?

My mouth soured as I strode for the lift.

The Brazilian contingent only needed a little guidance—they'd come through eventually. If they didn't, they'd simply be…replaced.

While I… Christos, *I would never be a father.*

I braced a hand against the wall, the weight of reality attempting to crush my shoulders.

So what if in the past I'd had my doubts about my potential effectiveness as a father? Xenakis men were many things, but exemplary fathers they were not. My grandfather had buried himself in work up to the point when he'd dropped dead of a heart attack, trying to save his near-bankrupt family. And long before that, my father had been denied his father's favour, resulting in the neglect of his own family.

While we tolerated each other now, for the sake of the family business, I didn't have a single memory of any bonding experience with my father. Boarding school had taken care of my formative years, followed by a gruelling apprenticeship at Xenakis Aeronautics.

I had respect and loyalty, earned from my position.

But affection? Or, hell, *love*?

In light of the bombshell that had flattened my life three hours ago, even the fake-it-till-you-make-it plan I'd so loftily believed would work with any future offspring had been shattered.

The finger I lifted to press the lift button shook with the force of the loss raking my insides. The moment I was inside the cubicle I attempted to breathe through the anguish, to get myself back under control.

Not even when Anneka had shown her true colours that day in the hospital three years ago had such a sense of deep loss affected me. While her betrayal had been similarly life altering, deep down a part of me had been thankful to have been given the opportunity to cut her out of my life before she truly sank her claws into me. Sure, my male pride had smarted for well over a year after she'd made a fool of me—cue excessive wild oat sowing—but ultimately, I'd escaped her trap.

With this there was not a single upside.

Save perhaps making the culprit pay?

The notion had gathered considerable pace by the time I entered my penthouse.

She stood at the glass window, her attention on the view. At some point between leaving the conference room only minutes ago and now, the sun had decided to shine. It threw a halo over her, turning her hair into living flames. Tendrils had slipped their loose knots, and as I watched she absently tucked a strand over her ear, slid her hand over her nape, then her shoulder, to massage it in firm, circular strokes.

The action sent another wave of tension through me, drawing my attention to her translucent skin, to the perfection of her hourglass figure and the stunning legs framed against the glass. Her other hand was splayed against it as if she yearned for the freedom beyond. Sensing my presence, she whirled around, those endless pools of green going wide at the sight of me.

'Oh... I had no idea you'd returned.'

My lips tightened, and that percussive mix of anger and desolation threatened again. 'I believe it's your lack of awareness that has led us to this point.'

She had the audacity to look hurt. The surrealness of it nearly made me shake my head again—but *enough*. I was done with being confounded. The important thing was how to proceed from here.

Doctors. Specialists. Investigate one final time.

Every option left a trail of displeasure, and the prospect of having my dire circumstances prodded was even more unwelcome than the verdict I'd woken to after a three-week coma three years ago: the severity of my skiing accident meant that I couldn't father children naturally. That my only hope of becoming a father rested on a sperm sample donated years ago, when I'd faced another crisis.

A seemingly miraculous turn of events that was now crushed to nothing.

Sadie Preston fidgeted where she stood, even as that pert little nose started to rise.

Christos, had no one ever taught this creature the concept of true contrition? But she wasn't as calm as she attempted to look. Her chest rose and fell in gathering agitation, and her small feet were curling and uncurling within the cheap flat shoes she wore. The action highlighted the smooth definition of her calves, and against my will I dropped my gaze, the better to absorb it.

When that only prompted a sharp need to test their suppleness beneath my fingers, I turned, made a beeline for my drinks cabinet. A dash of Hine in the crystal tumbler clutched in my hand brought a little clarity.

At the delicate throat-clearing behind me, I squeezed my eyes shut for a control-gathering second. Before I turned, she was speaking.

'I know you only need to look at me to remember why I'm here. What I've done. But I've been thinking... If you wouldn't mind giving me a little information, maybe we can put our heads together and come up with a solution.'

Another urge to laugh this away in the hope that it was some extended acid dream hit me. '*"Put our heads together"*? Why would we want to do that? Are you a doctor?'

Rose-red lips compressed, drawing my attention to yet another tempting part of her body.

The body of your nemesis.

'You know I'm not. I'm just trying to help—'

'I think you've done quite enough, don't you? Imagine we are the last two people on earth. Then be assured that I would rather take my chances with whatever apocalypse I face than accept *your* help.'

Her translucent skin lost a shade of colour. 'Do you need to be so cruel?' she muttered.

Absurdly, that plaintive question sent an arrow of guilt through me. *Theos mou.* What the hell was going on? Was it Upside Down Day? I downed half my drink, hoping the alcohol would burn through the fog.

The hope was in vain. So I approached until we stood half a dozen feet apart. 'Fine. Humour me. How would you propose we "put our heads together"?'

'Well, I was thinking that if you wouldn't mind telling me the circumstances behind your needing to use the Phoenix Clinic the first time around—'

'No, I would not. Next scenario.'

She hesitated, the tip of her pink tongue darting out to wet her lower lip. This time the punch in my gut was purely carnal. Ravenous. Demanding. *Lustful.*

For *this* woman? *Christos*, the world had truly turned upside down!

'Okay. If you're in a position to deposit another sample, perhaps I could contribute financially towards the future storage?'

Bitterness and bleakness lanced me in equal spikes. 'You don't look as if you can afford decent attire, let alone the fees of a clinic that charges upward of six figures. Do you have secret access to a gold mine, Sadie Preston? Or clairvoyant insight to the next set of lottery numbers?'

Her eyes flashed. 'Has anyone ever told you it's a mistake to judge a book by its cover?'

'If I am misjudging you, I'll consider rendering you an apology. Am I?'

She managed to hold my gaze for all of three seconds before her eyes dropped. Against her smooth cheeks, her long, unadorned eyelashes fanned in a seductive curl, highlighting her delicate eyelids. The combination of delicate, defiant and alluring made me grip my glass harder. But, more than that, I wanted her to lift her gaze, to show me those hypnotic green pools once again.

When she did, my breath caught.

I was attracted to her.

This woman, who'd brought me news of an apocalyptic kind, had awakened a libido grown so jaded I'd set it on the back burner in favour of pursuing even more success in the challenging boardrooms of Xenakis Aeronautics.

Was it the heightened bleakness of it all triggering this? And why was I wasting time deciphering it when I had no intention of following through on it?

'No, you're not wrong. I can't afford to foot the bill now. But perhaps we can come to an agreement?'

Here it comes. The age-old proposition.

The idea that she would offer herself to me on a platter drew deep disappointment. Enough to make me down the rest of my drink in abject resignation.

'Enlighten me about this agreement.'

'I'm two semesters away from completing a marketing degree. I've been top of my class every year. I can maybe work for your company from when I'm done? Pay you back that way?'

Surprise jolted me, followed by the familiar echo of wanting something because I'd been denied it. Had I *wanted* her on a platter? More specifically in my bed?

Yes!

I ignored the blaring affirmation, concentrated on what she'd said. So she wasn't just a simple receptionist.

The determination stamped across her face almost made

me believe her. *Almost*. For all I knew she was just spinning tales. Just as Anneka had spun lies around our relationship until an unguarded phone conversation had revealed the depths of her deplorable nature and the lengths she'd been prepared to go to ensure she received an unrivalled payday.

'How old are you?'

The mutinous look that crossed her face said she was debating not answering. Perhaps suggesting I mind my own business. But she realised very quickly that the question pertained to the proposal she was making.

'I'm twenty-five,' she offered, with clear reluctance.

'Most twenty-five-year-olds are done with their education.'

'My circumstances are different. I had to interrupt my education for personal reasons.'

Reasons she clearly wasn't about to disclose. I hid my disgruntlement. For now. 'Why a receptionist? Why not a paid internship in your chosen field?'

Impatience crossed her face. 'With respect, my reasons are private. But what I've said can easily be verified with my university professors.'

Enough. This had gone on long enough. 'You walked in off the street to confess a crime. As admirable as you seem to think admitting your culpability should be, I have zero reason to trust you. Not with my personal property and certainly not with my business. Your offer is declined.'

She inhaled sharply, the action drawing my attention to her chest. To her parted lips. *Christos.*

'So that's it? You're going to throw me to the wolves?'

'For what you've done? Yes, Sadie Preston. That's exactly what I'm going to do.'

Despite his doom-filled decree, he didn't move.

In the hours I'd been stuck in his opulent penthouse, one question had persistently swarmed my mind—why did a man whose every breath and expression spelled out his masculine potency and unapologetic virility need to store a sperm sample?

Eventually, curiosity had got the better of me. And the internet had been breathlessly efficient in providing high-resolution digital answers.

'Is this to be a staring contest?' he mused now, in a bone-dry tone tinged with that note I'd mistaken for bleakness earlier when I delivered my news. 'You're attempting to hypnotise me into reversing my verdict, perhaps?'

'What if I am?' I parried. If he was about to throw me to the wolves, what did I have to lose?

One corner of his mouth twitched with stark amusement. But then his face settled into a hard mask. My heart lurched. With every breath I wished I could go back, take my time, pay better attention—even with Mr Donnelly's unpleasant presence hovering over me.

But it was too late.

The damage had been done.

Neo Xenakis took another step closer, bringing that hard-packed body brimming with tensile, barely leashed power into my space. I wanted to step back, flatten myself against the glass wall, but that would exhibit a weakness I couldn't afford to show.

The internet had supplied ample examples of his shark-like business savvy too. This was a man who relished challenge. He'd never step into the arena with a weaker opponent, and the inevitable victory of his trouncing bigger targets was all the sweeter for it.

Was that why I didn't look away?

Was that why I even dared to clench my jaw and all but urge him to do his worst?

Because I wanted him to conquer me?

White-hot sensation flashed through me, made my nape tingle and my body blaze with the same anticipation I'd felt earlier, even before I knew that he'd entered the room. That misplaced illicit thrill that had ratcheted higher when

I turned around to find him watching me with those hooded eyes containing an indecipherable gleam.

Here it was again, eating me alive when all I needed to do was hold my tongue and continue to demonstrate appropriate contrition.

For how long, though? And then what?

He'd given his verdict. Clemency was off the table. And yet, despite what he'd said about throwing me to the wolves, he seemed in the mood to play with me. Seemed perfectly content to indulge in the staring contest he'd ridiculed moments ago.

'Would it work?' I asked.

Dear God. Be quiet, Sadie. Just shut—

To my eternal shame, my stomach chose that pithy moment to announce its intense hunger.

Neo Xenakis's gaze dropped to my belly at the unladylike growl, then returned to mine with a dark frown. 'When was the last time you ate?'

I shrugged. 'I don't remember. It doesn't matter.'

'It matters if I wish to enjoy my evening drink without your digestive system providing accompanying acoustics.'

Heat burned my face. 'I... I had a coffee this morning.'

His frown deepened. 'That's all you've had all day? It's six in the evening.'

'I know what time it is, Mr Xenakis.'

He raised a brow at my crisp tone. I wasn't about to admit I'd gone into the office with hopes of snagging a stray Danish left over from the early-morning client meeting, only to be confronted by an incandescent Mr Donnelly before I could satisfy my raging hunger. After that, fear and panic had eroded my appetite. Until now, evidently.

Neo Xenakis regarded me with quiet intensity, weighing his decision for a terse moment. Then his lips flattened. 'Far be it from me to send a criminal to the gallows on an empty stomach. Shall I instruct my chef to set another place for dinner, or are you in a hurry to face your crimes?' he drawled.

Bite your tongue, Sadie!

'That depends. Do you intend to torture me for the rest of the evening by recounting just how your wolves are going to tear me apart?'

'You think you know what torture is?' he asked, with a veil of deadly calm that didn't fool me for a second.

I'd inconvenienced him, angered him by necessitating a return trip to the clinic to make a second deposit, when he'd much rather be occupied with other things. Like dating another supermodel.

And he wasn't in a mood to let it go.

'There are only so many times I can say I'm sorry. It's clear you're not going to forgive me or tell me what I can do to make this right. Right now I'm failing to see how joining you for dinner improves my circumstances.'

'It could simply be an act of further character exploration on my part. To tell me which way I should lean in the punishment scales. Unlike you, I don't wish to undertake that task on an empty stomach. But, of course, your options are very much yours to take.'

Oh, how cunning of him. That insidious need to surrender to his will swept over me. I resisted by squaring my shoulders. 'Then I guess that's fine. If that's the only way to progress this...discussion.'

The merest hint of a smile twitched his lips. Then, seeming almost stunned by the action, he scowled.

Not the most enthusiastic response I'd ever had to meal-sharing, but I imagined under the circumstances a beggar couldn't be a chooser.

For another short second he stared at me, as if debating the wisdom of his offer. Then abruptly he crossed the vast, magnificently decorated living room to a dainty-legged console table, picked up a phone and relayed a message in rapid-fire Greek.

Finished, he set his glass down. 'Come.'

The command was quiet, but powerful enough to propel me forward. I told myself I couldn't object because I'd agreed to dine with him. And because I owed Neo Xenakis a few non-confrontational gestures.

Thinking he was leading me to the large, antique-filled dining room I'd spotted earlier during my brief and tentative search for the bathroom, I followed him in surprise into a kitchen fit for the world's most exacting chef.

Every imaginable gadget gleamed in polished splendour atop marble surfaces. On a large centre island, silverware gleamed under strategically suspended ceiling lights. Even the elevated stools looked too expensive for such a mundane activity as sitting.

But when he pulled one back and waited with tight expectancy, I swallowed the unnerving sensation that I was tangling with a supremely affluent and powerful man.

To the stout, rouge-faced chef who entered, I gave a quick smile. With a deferential nod, he started to uncover silver dishes.

Glorious smells hit my nostrils, and I stared at the mouthwatering array.

Exquisitely prepared Greek meze dishes were laid out next to an old-fashioned English shepherd's pie. I didn't fool myself into thinking this consideration had been made because I was joining him on such short notice. If the internet was right, Neo Xenakis was a man of extensive tastes and larger-than-life appetites.

Why that reminder triggered another wave of heat through my system I refused to consider as, with a few words, Neo Xenakis dismissed the chef and reached for the bottle of red wine that stood an arm's length away.

Seeing the label, I felt my eyes widen. Once upon a time, before he'd pulled the rug from beneath our feet with his stark betrayal, my father had been as much of a wine enthusiast as my mother was a magazine fanatic. When I was old enough to take an interest, he had often recited his dream vintage collection. The five-figure-price-tagged Château Cheval Neo cavalierly reached for now had ranked among the top three on my father's wish list.

I watched, slack jawed, as he deftly uncorked the bottle and set it aside to breathe.

Catching my expression, he narrowed his eyes. 'Something wrong?'

I swallowed. 'Nothing that doesn't involve my wondering if you normally share expensive bottles of wine with criminals before sending them to their doom.'

His gaze hooded, he shrugged. 'Satisfying your curiosity isn't on my agenda, so you'll just have to keep wondering. Eat.'

I toyed with refusing the order. But I was starving. And, really, he didn't *have* to feed me. With one quick call he could have Wendell tossing me out. Staying might grant me the opportunity to make another plea for mercy.

I placed two beautifully wrapped vine leaves onto my plate, then added a couple of spoonfuls of Greek salad. About to lift my fork, I paused when his eyes narrowed again, this time on my plate.

'You haven't eaten all day and that's all you're having?'

'Yes.'

He nodded at one of the many platters. 'The *kopanisti* won't keep. Don't let it go to waste.' He picked up serving tongs and caught up a dish of salad, roast peppers and an orange paste laid in between two crisp flatbreads. 'Try it,' he said.

Tentatively, I picked up the large morsel and bit into it. Sensations exploded in my mouth as the orange paste, which turned out to be the most incredible aged feta, combined with everything else immediately became the best thing I'd ever tasted—which in turn triggered a groan of appreciation before I could stop myself.

Perhaps my vivid imagination was playing tricks on me,

but I could have sworn Neo swallowed hard at that moment, and I felt his tension ramping up.

Abruptly, he spooned several more items onto my plate, then reached for the wine bottle. 'Would you like some wine?'

The chance to try the jaw-droppingly expensive vintage, especially considering that my fate hung in the balance, was too much to resist. 'Just a little, please.'

After pouring two glasses, he chose steamed white cod and a spoonful of salad himself, which he polished off with a military efficiency that spoke of fuel intake rather than enjoyment. Then he simply sat, slowly twirling the stem of his wine glass, lifting it occasionally to his lips as he watched me eat.

Self-conscious, and reluctant to broach the ultrasensitive subject of my crime, I stilled my tongue in favour of enjoying the most exquisite meal I'd had in a long time, all the while painfully aware that his gaze hadn't shifted from me.

'Which university?'

I started. 'What?'

'Your marketing degree,' he expounded.

I named it, and again caught the faintest hint of surprise in his eyes as he slotted the information away, his long fingers still twirling his glass.

'Do you like aeroplanes?' he asked abruptly, after another stretch of silence.

'Who doesn't?'

His lips tightened and his gaze dropped to my empty plate, then shifted to the platters of lamb cutlets, grilled meatballs, roasted vegetables and bread.

Sensing he was about to push more food on me, I sat back. 'That was delicious. Thank you.'

He frowned, then lifted the lid off a dish set apart from the main courses. The scent of spun sugar and warm pastry washed over me, almost eliciting another groan. I'd been cursed with a sweet tooth—one that needed constant attention.

'Dessert?' he offered gruffly, pushing the baklava directly in front of me.

The sight of the perfect little squares of delight was too much to resist. At my helpless nod, he placed four pieces on a fresh plate and slid it in front of me, again seemingly content to simply sit back and watch me eat.

Perhaps this was Neo Xenakis's method of torture. To feed me until I burst.

At that mildly hysterical thought, I let my gaze flick up to meet his. Again that spark flared in his eyes, and the charge seized me, causing tingles from my palms to my toes.

'If it wasn't for this wholly unfortunate situation, I'd think you didn't want me to leave,' I mused. Then immediately cursed my runaway tongue.

He froze, his grey eyes turning as turbulent as a lightning storm. His hand tightened around his glass, his fingers turning white.

'I'm sorry. I didn't mean—'

'Perhaps you're right,' he interrupted, his voice low, rough and raw, as if scrabbled from a pit of utter despair. 'Maybe I *don't* want you to leave. Maybe I need you sitting there in front of me as a reminder of what has happened. Of the fact that the nightmare you brought to my doorstep isn't one I can wake up from.'

The utter bleakness in his tone launched a lump into my throat. My fingers tightened in my lap as the need to reach out, to lay my hand on his or cup that rigid jaw, powered through me. I did neither, sensing it wouldn't be welcome.

'Is it really that hopeless? Is there no chance that things can be salvaged?' My question was a desperate one. But the thought that things could really be so dire for a man so incredibly masculine and virile looking seemed unthinkable to me.

'Excuse me?' he rasped icily, his eyes turning almost black with the strength of his emotions.

I pushed my plate away and forced myself to answer before I lost my nerve. 'I… Surely it doesn't surprise you that I'd wonder why a man who looks like you—'

'Looks like me?' he grated.

I wetted suddenly dry lips, suspecting I'd strayed into dangerous territory but unable to locate the road map to take me out of peril.

'You're not blind. You look like the poster-perfect image of virility. Is it beyond the realms of probability that I'd wonder why you'd need to use a facility like the Phoenix Clinic?'

His eyes slowly rose. 'Did you not admonish me for judging *you* based on your outward appearance?'

Even as my face heated, something inside me reacted sharply to the notion that I might have ended this man's line with my mistake. Something that utterly rejected that thought.

'Please answer the question, Mr Xenakis,' I urged, aware of my escalating desperation.

'Why? Are you distressed by the thought that a man who *"looks like me"* might be impotent or infertile?' he drawled.

He was goading me, pure and simple. I should've looked away. Backed down.

'Are you?'

He rose and stepped away from the island. 'Come with me,' he grated.

Something raw and intense pulsed in his tone, warning me that whatever he had in mind would decimate me emotionally.

'And if I refuse? Is this where you threaten—'

He slashed one powerful hand across my argument, his lips flattening into a displeased line. 'A word to the wise, Sadie. If you have any desire for self-preservation left in that body, be wise and stop defying me at every turn. I'm a man who faces adversity head-on. Right now, I'm *this* close to tossing you out the door and letting the authorities deal with your crimes. But, again, the choice is yours. Leave and face the consequences or indulge the man you've so gravely wronged. Which is it to be?' he asked, his eyes pinning me in place.

'I... Fine. I'll do what you want. For now,' I tagged on, simply because that self-preservation he'd mentioned was kicking in wildly, doubling my thundering heartbeat. 'I reserve the right to leave any time I want.'

He left the kitchen without responding.

I followed, striving not to breathe in his intoxicating scent and failing miserably.

Senses jumping, I watched him stroll over to the plush sectional sofa, sit down on it in a deceptively relaxed pose, one long arm lazily stretched out on the top of it. He rested one ankle on his knee, and lifted his wine glass to take a liberal sip.

'If you wish. But why postpone the inevitable? And why annoy me further by forcing me to carve another appointment into my schedule when we can settle this one way or the other tonight?'

Because I needed the headspace to think straight!

But Neo Xenakis would be equally imposing and breathtaking tomorrow—and most likely every day from now until eternity.

So why delay the inevitable indeed?

With legs turned rubbery, and nigh on useless, I approached him.

'Let me give you the broad strokes of the consequences of your actions. I come from a large family. Perhaps not your conventional Greek family, but we adore babies without reservation, regardless of how they were conceived,' he said, his hooded gaze on the contents of his glass. 'Which means that from a relatively young age, certain obligations have been required of me. Obligations I had every intention of fulfilling at some point in the future. Do you understand what that means?'

My nod was jerky at best. 'Something along the lines of keeping the family name going?'

'Exactly so. And I take my duty seriously. So what do you think you owe me for effectively ending my chances of fulfilling my obligations?'

'But…have I really?' I asked, unabashed curiosity getting the better of my tongue.

The turbulent emotion in his eyes receded for a moment, replaced by an equally arresting gleam as his gaze raked my face before resting with quiet ferocity on my mouth.

'I see we're back to that little nugget you can't let go of. Are you asking me if my equipment works, Sadie?' he drawled.

There was a layer of danger to his tone that should have frightened me but instead caused the blood to rush faster through my veins, pushing a flood of colour into my cheeks.

'I can't help thinking…it would help to know if the situation is as dire as all that…'

God. Stop talking.

'And if it isn't?' he rasped. 'Are you hoping that with one simple answer you'll be absolved of what you've done?'

God, we were really discussing his…his…

'No. Maybe. Yes…' I whispered.

'My ability or inability to engage in intercourse is not the issue here,' he said.

'Answer the question anyway,' I blurted, attempting to keep my mind on the important subject at hand and losing the battle in favour of racy thoughts of the exploration of his mouth-watering body first-hand.

Growing stupidly breathless, I scoured his face, his sculpted cheekbones, the hard angles of his jaw, the shadowed enticement of his strong throat and…dear God…the sensual curl of his lower lip, currently curved against his glass as he took another lazy sip.

The way he simply...lounged in his seat, was deceptively calm in a still-waters-run-deep manner. I wanted to dive into those waters, lose myself in them until I was completely sodden.

A different sort of heat pummelled me, low and insistent, charting a path of ravenous need directly between my thighs. Against the lace cups of my bra my nipples tightened, and each breath drew urgent attention to the decadent craving coursing through my body.

'I could tell you—but should I? I owe you nothing. You have no right to answers. But if you truly want to know if I can get it up, I invite you to find out for yourself,' he rasped thickly, his hooded gaze announcing that he knew every single yearning crashing through me.

My tongue thickened in my mouth, and that same acute urge to test where this alternative route would take me rammed unadulterated temptation through my bloodstream.

Sweet heaven. Surely he wasn't really suggesting what I thought he was...? And surely I wasn't truly considering it.

Was I?

CHAPTER THREE

My breath burst from between my lips, the wild, dizzying leap of my pulse a damning testament to the fact that his words had exhilarated me for one blind nanosecond before reason reasserted itself.

He can't truly mean that. He's just toying with you.

Even if he wasn't, the proposal was absurd.

'Is this a joke?'

'Do I look amused, Sadie?' he returned.

No, he didn't. That raw confession in the kitchen returned, and the looming possible result of my actions—that I'd deprived not just him and his immediate family but the larger Xenakis clan of his future descendants—hit me with powerful force.

Helpless despair wove through me, and my chest tightened as I watched him, attempted to see beneath the taut mask of his face. Was this all because he truly didn't want to be alone to confront the dire position I'd put him in?

If so, was this his answer?

I shook my head. 'I... I'm not sure what this is all about.'

He shrugged. 'You want me to provide spoilers for a story you seem very interested in. I invite you to peek beneath the cover. Or are you all bluster?'

'Just so we're clear, I'm not making any so-called reparation in the form of sex,' I blurted. Simply because my imagination was threatening to take flight again, and the look in his eyes was sending my senses into free fall once more.

I grappled them down—hard.

One mocking eyebrow elevated. 'You jump to conclusions with the same careless abandon that I suspect landed you in this predicament in the first place. Perhaps you should wait until you're invited to my bed before you respond in one way or another.'

His censure smarted, regardless of the fact that I'd agreed to give him a little leeway in the perpetrator-versus-victim scenario.

'I'm not stupid, Mr Xenakis. I can read between the lines. And whatever you think is going to happen here, it isn't,' I stressed, although the caution was equally for me as it was for him.

'Has no one told you to quit while you're ahead?'

Many times. But I never went against my instinct.

'I believe in laying my cards on the table.'

Slowly, his relaxed stance altered. His arm dropped from the sofa, his body leaning closer as he pinned me with his gaze. With the width of the sofa between us, he wasn't crowding me. But he didn't need to. His presence filled every square inch of space, proclaiming his power and glory in ways that were hard to define and impossible to dismiss.

'Do you? Well, hear this. If I wanted you in my bed you would come—and willingly. Not because of the unfortunate circumstances you find yourself in.'

'If that's some sort of dare, I promise I won't be taking it,' I stated firmly, despite that insidious temptation striking deep. Deeper. Making my every breath strain, making my nipples tingle and peak and *yearn*.

God, what was wrong with me?

He shrugged again. Drawing my eager attention to the firm, bronzed expanse of his throat. Striking me with a fervent need to place my hand right there...where his pulse throbbed powerfully beneath his skin.

I averted my gaze, but the lingering look he gave me said he'd caught me staring. I needed to get up. Leave. Put some distance between myself and the turbulent temptation that *oozed* out of him. But doing so would send another weakening message. He'd invited me here. I'd lobbed the ball into his court. So I waited for his move.

The muted sound of a door opening heralded the arrival of a butler, bearing a silver tray with more drinks on it. While I was a little startled, Neo looked unruffled, as if nothing unusual had happened to interrupt his normal after-dinner routine.

He accepted a glass of cognac, then glanced at me. 'Nightcap?'

I shook my head, surprised at his cordial tone. Then I snapped my spine straight. I couldn't afford to lower my guard. He still hadn't spelled out the parameters of my reparation. Nor given me a straight answer to my question…

With a few words Neo dismissed the butler. The moment we were alone, he discarded his untouched drink and turned his piercing gaze on me.

My eyes connected with his as if pulled by invisible magnets. As much as I was reluctant to admit it, the man was a superb specimen. His impossibly broad shoulders demanded attention, and the gladiator-like synergy of sleekness and power combined with an animalistic aura impossible to dismiss.

The look in his eyes intensified, sending the distinct message that now we were getting down to the heart of whatever was on Neo Xenakis's mind.

'Come here, Sadie,' he ordered, confirming my frenzied thoughts.

Get up. Walk out. He can't stop you.

But temptation could. It wrapped its sinuous vines around me, hard and fast, left me breathless and speechless.

This was theory testing. Curiosity satisfying. Nothing else.

My life had taken a left turn this morning. Not that things had been rosy before… My mother and her gambling problem, my landlord's growing threats, my jobless state… My life and plans were a world removed from what I'd imagined for myself back in the idyllic days when I had the illusion of a solid family. When a fulfilling career, perhaps eventually a family, wasn't a laughable, ephemeral prospect.

The dismaying sensation in the pit of my stomach that had arrived along with my father's callously dismissive postcard and stayed all these years later, the sensation that mocked and questioned and poisoned my dreams, claimed I was as worthless as my father had deemed me, was very much present now, questioning my audacity to remain here, reaching for this temptation.

Step back, it said. *This isn't for you.*

But I wasn't ready to step back into my life just yet. I craved more time in this peculiar bubble with Neo Xenakis. Just for a little while longer.

Before I could stop the motion, I swayed towards him.

He didn't reach out. Simply lounged against the velvet seat, the king of his shiny castle, awaiting his due. And, like a moth to a flame, I couldn't resist the danger, the excitement, the *otherness* he offered.

One taste. Then I could end this any time I wanted.

One minute, then I could get back to why I was here, perhaps armed with the confirmation that he wasn't impaired in any obvious physical way.

The thought that I was attempting to slot this beneath the banner of *research* drew a hysterical chortle, quickly smothered beneath the pulses of lust swelling through my system.

Before I knew it, my body hovered next to his, almost horizontal on the sofa as I heeded his command.

'Here I am,' I replied in a voice that sounded nothing like mine.

Storm-tossed eyes traced every inch of my face, lingering longest and fiercest on my mouth.

'Yes. Here you are,' he replied.

His warm, cognac-tinged breath washed over my lips, causing them to tingle wildly.

Desperately, I slicked my tongue over them, then again when his sizzling gaze followed the wet path. His next breath emerged a touch harsher, his sculpted chest straining against his pristine shirt. The tingling flashed to my fingers, where the need to explore that mouth-watering expanse lashed harder and faster.

'The invitation still stands, Sadie,' he breathed.

Stay. Explore. *Indulge.*

I lifted my hand until it hovered mere inches from his skin. Until his heat caressed my palm, its gravitational pull tugging me with unrelenting force.

Was I really doing this? Baiting a predator to avoid my own reality?

Snatching a jagged breath, I hesitated.

Eyes even fiercer, Neo shifted. My hand met the hard wall of his chest, rested on the powerful thundering heartbeat. Lust burst through like a hot ray of sunshine through fog, melting away the last of my reservations. I slid my fingers up superbly well-defined pecs, over the tie he'd loosened during dinner, to glide around his neck.

The thought that I was headed in the wrong direction, going up when I should be heading down, evaporated as I explored him. He'd invited this. And I wanted to make sure my investigation was...*thorough.*

His eyes grew hooded when my fingers speared the hair at his nape. Lustrous strands slid through my fingers, and that small act fired up the tempest coursing through me. Enthralled by the sensation, I repeated the caress.

A gruff sound left his throat. His Adam's apple moved in a strong swallow. Had he moved closer or had I? My gaze fell to his full lower lip, so temptingly close. Promising a heady reprieve from chaos, despair and uncertainty.

One tiny, tiny taste.

I strained another inch closer, watched his eyes turn darker, felt his chest expand with a heavy inhalation.

One second ticked by. Two.

Then, with a rush of breath and a growl of impatience,

he breached the gap between us, fused his lips to mine in white-hot possession.

Indecent. *Heavenly.*

Outrageous and masculine and, oh, so powerful.

Neo took control of the kiss, brazenly swept his tongue along the ultrasensitive flesh of my bottom lip before delving in between to taste me. With a whimper of urgent need, I parted my lips wider, welcoming him with the eagerness of a starving woman granted a feast.

But even while his lips clung to mine, his hands remained where they were, maddeningly removed from my body. The challenge was too much to resist. Crawling closer, I wrapped both hands around his neck, drew him deeper into the kiss. Dared to meet his tongue with mine on the next sweep.

His body jerked and another growl left his throat as our tongues found a unique dance of decadent delight, of thrilling desire that built with each ferocious second.

Dear God, he could kiss. Even when he wasn't putting his complete effort into it, even when he wasn't touching me, I was nearly driven out of my mind.

In another heartbeat that was all I wanted. Neo Xenakis's hands on me.

Then I would stop.

Because this was getting out of control.

As if he'd heard my silent plea, he finally dropped his hands from the back of the sofa. They glided over my shoulders, down my ribcage, in slow, sensuous exploration to my waist. After the merest hesitation, he wrapped his large hands around my hips and pulled me with supreme masculine ease into his lap.

No need for any southern exploration.

The unmistakable evidence of his proud manhood was imprinted, hot and thick, against my bottom.

At my muted gasp he broke the kiss and edged me back, long enough to deliver a smouldering look of arrogant confirmation.

'Now you know,' he breathed.

'Y-yes...'

A look flickered through his eyes—one that seemed to ask and answer a question in the same heartbeat. Then he was tugging me back into his body, one hand spiked in my hair, the other on my hip, pinning me to his lower body. It was as if he wanted nothing but his powerful masculinity to occupy my mind now he'd provided the evidence.

As if I could think of anything else. *Feel* anything else.

With only one lover in my past, and a fleeting one at that, sex was still a mystery to me—a land whose borders I'd barely breached before retreating, first out of disappointment and then through the sheer strain of holding the tattered rags of my life together.

Now, presented with this tantalising feast, every past experience paled to nothing. My instinct warned that a man like Neo would have more experience in his little finger than I would in my whole body. That this brief taste was merely a drop in the ocean of what he could deliver to the right woman.

Except I wasn't the right woman.

I was the woman he'd goaded into taking this risky, mind-altering challenge. A challenge whose fire blazed to heights I'd never encountered before.

You can stop. Now.

But his lips were intoxicating. And the way his tongue and teeth and lips commanded mine was intensifying that persistent, needy throb between my legs...

With another moan I locked my hands around his neck, strained even closer to that magnificent body. And gasped when he abruptly pulled back, his hooded eyes darting from my parted lips to clash with mine.

He let out a heavy, unsteady exhale. 'This isn't how I foresaw this meeting evolving,' he rasped.

'Me neither,' I muttered.

He gave a short, jerky nod before his fierce gaze bored

into mine. 'Then perhaps it's best if we draw a line under it,' he invited.

But the slight clench of his fingers on my hip said that wasn't what he really wanted. And when his hold loosened, when I sensed he was about to disengage, I clenched my gut against the lash of disappointment and loss.

'Is that what you want? For me to leave?'

His jaw clenched and that hot gaze locked on my lips. 'The more important question is, are you ready to let go, Sadie? I ask this because you're clinging to me as if I'm the last piece of driftwood in your ocean.'

My arms unlocked from around his neck, slow with a helpless need to stay connected, moved down his chest. At his deep shudder a powerful sensation gripped me, along with a twinge of uncertainty barely born, before it was smashed beneath the colossal hunger clawing through me.

I'd never felt anything like this. And the voice inside telling me I never would again birthed a terrifying need to seize this unique experience.

Everything around me was slowly crumbling to dust. My mother's spiralling gambling. Looming homelessness. The job I no longer had. My own shattered dreams…

A secret fear plagued me in the dead of night. One I'd never admitted to anyone. That perhaps my father was right. That unconditional love was an illusion—an obligation fulfilled only up to a point. Or worse, that *I* hadn't been worthy of the effort.

The urgent need simply to forget for a little while longer hooked me with mighty talons, refusing to let go.

'Say what's on your mind,' Neo insisted.

The raw demand in his voice. The turbulent look in his eyes. The edgy hunger in his face. All of them echoed the deep clamouring inside me perfectly. Like two halves of a magnificent, earth-shaking whole. And really, in the desolate landscape of my uncertain future, where and when would I get the chance to experience anything close to this?

'Maybe I'm not...not ready to let go. Just yet.'

For the briefest moment he hesitated, as if he intended to refuse this...refuse *me*. More than a little panicked at the thought of being thrust back into my dreary life, I clung to his lapel.

Need smashed through his fleeting resistance.

Decadent headiness filled me, swirling in a sense of triumph I knew it was unwise to savour.

Strong fingers delved back into my hair, impatiently freeing the knot. As if he'd uncovered a wondrous sight, his breath caught as he fingered the long strands. 'Your hair is like a living flame,' he rasped, watching the thick tendrils glide over his skin.

The next instant he'd tugged open the button holding my jacket closed, pulled it off and had me back against the sofa, angling his powerful body over mine. I clung tighter to him, revelling in the erotic thrill of his kiss.

A moan ripped free from him as he settled his hips between mine and I felt the full power of his arousal. '*Theos mou*, you're intoxicating.'

And he was far from lacking in the ultimate manhood stakes.

I wanted to return the compliment, but words failed to form beneath the assault of his touch. His tongue boldly stroked mine, coaxed it into a thrilling dance, and all coherent thought evaporated.

We kissed until we grew breathless, only the need for oxygen driving us apart.

Frenzied seconds ticked away as Neo stared down at me. From unkempt hair to parted lips to strained nipples. There was nowhere to hide my attraction to this man—the last man I should've been doing this with.

Whether he felt the same or not became a non-issue as he resolutely levered himself away from me to shrug off his jacket. His tie followed, both tossed away with complete disregard for expense or care.

Hot hands slid around my hips once more, moulded them for an exploratory second before gliding downward, past my thighs and calves to my feet.

He removed and tossed away my shoes. Eyes locked on mine, he conducted the most maddening caress of one foot before digging an expert thumb into the arch.

A melting sensation pooled into my belly, a lusty moan leaving my lips.

For one fleeting moment, his lips twitched, as if he'd gleaned something about me that pleased him.

By the time he was done with paying the same attention to the other foot, my back was arching off the sofa, my whole body caught in waves of pleasure so unique I couldn't catch my breath.

He caught me in his arms, and sensation, earnest and powerful, overwhelmed me. Neo too, if his almost frenzied need to divest me of my clothing, filling the room with decadent sounds that escalated the passion-infused air, was any indication.

In minutes he'd reduced me to my panties and bra, and his hand was exploring every exposed dip and curve.

He lowered his head. At the thought that he was about to put his lips on my skin for the first time, I blindly reached for him, eager to undress him before I lost the ability to perform the function.

The first few buttons of his shirt came undone, giving me a tantalising glimpse of what lay beneath. But when I reached for the next one, Neo tensed, one hand staying mine.

'No,' he rasped, his voice tight.

Before I could question his response, he dropped his head and laid an open-mouthed kiss on the pulse racing at my throat, then counterpunched by grazing his teeth over the sensitive flesh.

'Oh!'

'You like that?'

'Yes!'

His satisfied growl set off cascades of shivers, rendering my nerve endings even more sensitive as he intensified his caress. One hand slid behind my knee, parting my legs so he could mould his lower body to mine, accentuating his lean hips and the powerful outline of his erection. I swallowed, momentarily apprehensive of his overwhelming maleness.

Pausing, his gaze bored into mine. 'Sadie, do you want this?'

The question was grave, and it also held a warning. He was reaching the end of his tether and he wanted to grant me the opportunity of ending this before insanity spun us completely out of control.

I didn't want it to end. I was on that same edge.

I boldly cupped his bristled jaw. He exhaled harshly, his sensual lips planting a hard kiss in my palm even while his eyes demanded an answer.

'Yes,' I replied.

Whatever regrets came later—and I suspected there would be many—I was too far gone, had given too many pieces of myself to heartache, from my father, worry over my mother, despair over life itself, to deny this unexpected slice of heaven. Even if it came in the form of an intense, larger-than-life man who was losing himself in me because of the colossal wrong I'd done him.

'I want this,' I confirmed, glad my voice held firm.

The words were barely out of my mouth when, with a deft flick, he released my bra. Eyes locked on mine, he dragged the straps down my arms. For a taut second after he flung it away, his eyes remained on mine. Then his gaze dropped to what he'd uncovered. A breath shuddered out of him.

'You're exquisite,' he breathed.

Pleasure arched my back, the act snatching his next breath. His head dropped, sensual lips wrapping around one peak to pull the tight bud into his mouth. I cried out as pleasure ripped through me, my senses scrambling further when his tongue swirled in erotic caresses. More decadent sounds fell from my lips. My fingers slid beneath the collar of his shirt to track urgently over his shoulders, to grip his back, eager to hold him to his task.

Neo's caresses grew bolder as he switched his attention to the twin peak. Arrows of need shot between my thighs, dampening and readying me for the ultimate possession. Possession he seemed determined to tease out as he feasted on my breasts for an age, returning over and over to my mouth to demand torrid kisses.

Just when I thought he'd drag the moment out for an eternity he drew down my panties, flinging them away with the same sexy carelessness he'd given my bra.

'I have to taste you,' he said, in that deep, raw voice, gripping my thigh to part me to his avid gaze.

His stare was so potent, so ravenous, I lost what little breath I had left in my lungs. 'Neo…'

'Shh, no talking, *glikia mou*. Quite enough words have passed between us.'

Denied that outlet, I grasped another. I touched, I explored, I kissed every covered muscle within reach, delighting in the slivers of heated olive skin he allowed me.

Right until his bold lips delivered the ultimate kiss between my thighs.

I fell back, boneless, onto the sofa, and another cry was wrenched from my throat as he wreaked wicked havoc between my thighs. All the while delivering rough praise in English and Greek.

How had I even contemplated denying myself this soul-stirring experience? Even at this stage, I knew it paled in comparison with my brief sexual foray back at uni.

Neo tongued my nerve-filled bud and I screamed, the shameless keening urging him into deeper caresses until it all grew too much. Until I had no choice but to surrender to the blistering release that gripped me tight for several electrifying seconds before tossing me into utter bliss.

For endless minutes I drifted, a raw mass of sensation.

But in excruciating increments I became aware of my surroundings, of my fingers clenched in his hair. Of the wide, plush sofa beneath me and the hot body slowly prowling up mine. Of the foil caught between his fingers as he eased back, unzipped his trousers and pulled them and his boxers down.

His shirt remained on, the tails covering the tops of his thighs. Eyes pinned to mine, he glided the condom on with that mask of hunger stamped on his face.

Unable to help myself, I dropped my gaze to his shaft. And again I experienced momentary panic at his sizeable thickness. But, as if he'd willed it away with the sheer force of his attraction, the worry receded as he reclaimed his place between my legs.

Nevertheless, I couldn't suppress my whimper at the first breach.

He froze, teeth gritted, as his turbulent gaze searched mine. 'Sadie...?'

Fear that he would stop, that this insulating little bubble would burst and I would be flung back into dreary reality, pushed me to blurt out, 'Don't stop. Please.'

For heart-stopping seconds he didn't move. Just stared at me with a mixture of edgy intensity and banked lust. Then, as if he didn't want to leave this bubble either, he thrust deep.

Pleasure rolled over me, dissipating the initial sting of his fullness. 'Yes...'

Relief washed over his face, immediately chased away by wickedly ferocious determination. Another thrust. His groan melded with my moan as he slid to the hilt.

'You shouldn't feel this incredible,' he grunted. 'But, *thee mou*, you do.'

His words triggered a weird kind of triumph—a fleeting but overwhelming pride that I was good enough for something, *worth* this moment of nirvana. I sank deeper into sensation, shuddering at the powerful emotions moving in my chest. Then in pure carnal bliss Neo rolled his hips, driving me further out of my mind.

'More. Please.'

A wicked pause, then he seized my arms, dragged them above my head. The movement drew my body taut, enlivening every inch of me with intense awareness as he splayed his fingers between mine and proceeded to give me far more than I'd ever imagined possible.

With every thrust, every glide of his lips over my skin, I was hurled closer to that intense spark I knew would ignite the most sacred bliss I'd ever known.

I wanted to rush it and slow it down at the same time.

I wanted to hold it in my palm and savour it even while I strained for complete annihilation with every cell in my body.

'Please…' I panted, unsure which path I yearned for more.

With a series of piston-fast, mind-melting strokes, the moment arrived. White-hot, searing, intense. I was catapulted into unadulterated bliss, eagerly surrendering to the power and might of it.

His head buried in my neck, Neo gave a muted shout, his body shuddering for endless moments in the throes of his own release.

After the frenzied pace of his possession time slowed to a crawl, as if the power of our jagged coming together, the intensity of the moment, needed reverse momentum to slow and steady it.

Heartbeats slowed. Pulses quieted. Like a powerful drug taking me under, lethargy stole over me. I closed my eyes and drifted, cloaked in a moment's peace before I had to face what had happened.

The moment arrived all too soon.

First came the loss of the searing palm-to-palm contact that had somehow heightened this experience from base act to something…*more*, followed by the complete withdrawal of body heat when Neo rose lithely from the sofa, triggering an acute self-consciousness of my naked state in contrast to his almost completely clothed form.

Then, with his thick curse uttered in Greek, but nevertheless unmistakable, I was wrenched from my insulated bubble.

The living room lights, which had provided seductive ambience during our furious coupling, suddenly blazed too bright, exposed too much, making me blink a few times before I focused on the man frozen in a half turn from me, a look of stark disbelief and something else that looked like furious self-loathing etched into his face.

'I... Is something wrong?' I cringed at my husky sex-hoarse tone.

Neo ploughed his fingers through his hair, turned and stalked down the hallway. Dread dripped torturous ice water down my spine. The frantic darting of my mind was locked in place for several long seconds before I jackknifed upward, my feet landing on the plush carpet as I tried to marshal my thoughts.

It took far too long to find and wrestle my tangled panties on. I was cursing my shaking hands and their inability to straighten my bra straps when brisk strides signalled Neo's return.

My disquiet intensifying, I glanced his way. He ignored me. I told myself to be glad, but my stomach churned harder, the regret I'd anticipated and almost accepted would arrive suspiciously light in place of the hurt and confusion swamping me.

His movements jerky, unlike the smooth, animalistic grace he'd exhibited earlier, he headed for the drinks cabinet, but at the last moment veered away and stopped before the glass wall.

Silence pulsed as he stared out, ferocious tension riding his shoulders.

I dragged my fingers through my hair, shoving it out of

the way in order to secure my bra, and hurriedly punched my fingers through the sleeves of my blouse. I was tugging the sides together when he turned.

If his eyes had been turbulent pools before, they were positively volcanic now. But that fury was aimed more at himself than at me. There seemed to be bewilderment, as if I was a puzzle he'd tried and failed to put together and now loathed himself for attempting.

He stared at me for another unsettling minute, his lips parted, his chest rising and falling as if he detested the very words he was about to utter.

'We have a problem,' he grated.

I was surprised he could speak at all, with his jaw locked so tight and the tendons in his neck standing out.

The feeling of unworthiness returned—harder, harsher. *Not good enough*, the insidious voice whispered. *Never good enough*.

I pushed it and my roiling emotions away for examination later. Much, much later.

'I can tell. Although I'm at a loss as to what it is.'

But even as the firm words tumbled from my lips, the cascade and echo of old hurts was deepening, intensifying.

'If you're about to tell me you regret what happened, please save your breath. We don't need to dissect it now or ever. I'll be out of your hair in a few minutes. You need never set eyes on me again if that's what you—'

'The condom broke.'

The words were delivered like a chilling death knell. I was glad I hadn't attempted to stand, because my legs would have failed me. I was aware that my jaw had sagged, that I probably made an unattractive sight, sitting there half-dressed, with my skirt askew and unzipped and my blouse wrinkled.

He confirmed it with a quick rake of his gaze and a harder clenching of his teeth. 'Get dressed, Sadie.'

I ignored the command for the simple reason that I

couldn't move, couldn't force my brain to stop repeating those three damning words on a loop.

'I... What?' I finally managed.

'Cover yourself,' he repeated tersely.

'Why? My nakedness didn't cause the condom to fail,' I flung back, and then compounded my words with a furious blush as his eyebrows hiked upward in flaying mockery.

I turned my back on him, a much more earth-shaking tremble seizing me as the ramifications landed home. While he'd listed everything I may have deprived him of, Neo hadn't definitely confirmed his inability to father children. So did I face a possible pregnancy on top of everything else?

Dear God...

Motherhood? When my own blueprint of childhood was so flawed?

Somehow, through sheer will to fight this battle on somewhere-near-equal footing, I straightened my clothes, slid my feet into my shoes.

There was nothing I could do about my hair, what with the cheap band I'd used nowhere in sight and my refusal to dig around for it under Neo's heavy, brooding stare. So I took a deep breath, and turned around to face the consequences of yet another wrong turn.

CHAPTER FOUR

Mistake.

Big, colossal mistake.

Disbelief, raw and searing, tunnelled deep, bedded down into my bones with unstoppable force until I had no choice but to acknowledge its presence. To accept that I'd simply compounded one problem with not one but two further mistakes.

For the first time in my life I wanted to find the nearest sand dune. Bury my head in it. But I couldn't.

Because there she stood, a flaming hot testament to the temptation I'd given in to when I should've walked away. Should have heeded my own agency to retreat and regroup instead of arrogantly imagining I could handle this—handle *her*—like a normal business challenge, to be ruthlessly and efficiently dismantled before moving on to the next problem.

The chaos she'd brought upon me wasn't a business problem or even a wider family problem, to be accommodated only so far until it could be slotted under *someone else's problem* when in reality it was deeply, straight-to-the-core *personal*.

It had needed addressing, sure. But only once I'd thought things through. Executed a solution with military precision, as I did with everything in my life.

Not losing myself in the very object of my misery. Not letting go of the reins of my sanity so thoroughly and completely that the world could've burned to the ground and I wouldn't have minded in the slightest if it meant I could continue to enjoy her silken warmth, the intoxicating clutch of her tight heat. To hear those spellbinding gasps and cries fall from her lips as she begged for more.

Acid seared my throat, flooded my mouth, bringing with

it a recollection of the only other time I'd let blind lust get the better of me.

An invitation to some faceless heiress's birthday party in Gstaad I'd almost refused—until a possible business opportunity had been thrown in to sweeten the invitation.

A big deal bagged, followed by a night of hedonistic revelry.

A mistaken conclusion that I'd found a worthy soulmate, even though I'd never truly believed in that sort of flighty fantasy.

When that illusion had seemed to hold true in the clear light of day, for weeks and months, I'd congratulated myself for a wise choice made even in the midst of frivolity and decadence.

A proposal in Neostros, before friends and family, an engagement party to trump them all, and I was all set to buck the Xenakis family trend of backstabbing and buckling underneath the smallest pressure.

Even when suspicions arose…even when I allowed Anneka to talk me into another visit to Gstaad and a reluctant turn on the black ski run ended with me being launched twenty feet into the air and descending via a jagged aspen tree…she hadn't bailed.

Unlike most, who barely remembered their trauma, mine still played out in excruciating detail. I heard her cries as she held my hand and urged me to hold on. And I held on, remaining alert right until the doctors were forced to put me in a medical coma. I embraced even that, knowing she would be waiting for me when I woke.

But those fervent wishes for me to hold on had been born not of love but of callous greed and an unconscionable disregard for loyalty and integrity.

She calculated every move, right up until my eyes opened—literally and figuratively—to the betrayal and falsehoods so deeply ingrained she wore them like a second skin. One she attempted to hide with tears and cajoling until she'd learned that she couldn't fool a Xenakis twice.

I'd made a vow never to be caught in another traitorous web ever again.

Where was that vow an hour ago, Neo?

I stifled a growl at the mocking inner voice. There'd been quite enough growling for one night. One *lifetime*. The cold calculation with which I should have approached this situation finally arrived.

I stared at Sadie Preston. Watched her fidget, like she did in my office.

Then slowly that chin went up, throwing the face I'd framed in my hands and caressed into alluring relief while those green eyes began to spark.

'Are you going to stand there glaring at me all night? Look, I know the news is upsetting—'

Harsh laughter barked out of me, startling her, but there was no help for it. 'You think this is merely *upsetting*? Do you not understand that there's no making this right? No glossing over this?'

'I was just—'

'Attempting to make me feel better? Urging me to look on the bright side? Is *that* what the episode on the sofa was all about?'

Raw colour flared in her cheeks but she dared another step closer, that temper I'd suspected bubbled just beneath the surface rising. 'How dare you belittle it?' she breathed, stunning me with her fierce tone. 'It wasn't just a sordid little episode to me.'

'Wasn't it? If I didn't know better, I'd think you actually *mean* that.'

Another less readable look flashed in her eyes. Lips that had tasted exquisite beneath mine firmed, holding in whatever response she'd intended to utter for several seconds before she shook her head and spoke anyway.

'I know there's nothing I can say or do to alter what's

happened. But I was actually talking about the...the incident with the condom, not what brought me here in the first place.'

Christos, the broken condom. Another intensely unwelcome first in a day of abysmal firsts that needed to be smashed out of existence.

But then you wouldn't have met her.

Skatá! What was wrong with me?

I'd hung on to her when I should have handed her over to the authorities within minutes of her confession. Now was I playing devil's advocate with *myself*?

Never crossing paths with Sadie Preston was a trade-off I could cheerfully accept—and that gritty little knot in my stomach that called it out for a white lie be damned.

So what if my digital little black book hadn't been used for the longest stretch since its inception, and she, with that mystifying allure of defiance and sexiness, would've been a prime addition to it had we met under different circumstances?

Facts were facts. And the simple fact remained: sending her packing should have been my first and only course.

'The accident with the condom is another consequence to deal with. But it should be a fairly straightforward matter. I'll start by assuring you that you have nothing to worry about health-wise.'

She arched one well-shaped eyebrow. 'And I'm to take your word for that? Because you're...*you*?'

The clear censure in her tone grated. 'That's your prerogative. But other than the fact that I abhor liars, a man in my position would be extremely foolish not to take the necessary precautions when it comes to every facet of his life. My last medical check returned a clean bill of health. You're the only woman I've slept with since.'

Her eyes widened a touch, questions glinting in their depths. 'And what about...?'

The inevitable question. I needed to answer and it burned

its way up my throat—a searing reminder of why my association with this woman should have ended many hours ago.

'I'm sorry, but I can't *not* ask, can I?' she muttered.

Her expression morphed into one I'd seen on too many faces of friends and family members. Even those without full knowledge of what had happened in that hospital room deigned to pity me. It was why I'd banned my family from discussing my accident.

'I don't need your pity, Miss Preston. Or whatever that look on your face is supposed to signify. The simple truth is, I cannot father children. The *why* doesn't concern you. It's a proven reality—which makes your offer of a further visit to your previous place of employment null. The only thing I need from you right now is reciprocal reassurance that I'm not at risk after this unfortunate mishap.'

Her expression snapped back to that mixture of fiery irritation, hurt and censure.

She wore her feelings so plainly. She would be an abysmal poker player. So why did I crave to keep staring, keep attempting to read what else she felt within this chaos?

'I tell you this only for reassurance, in light of everything that's happened. Let's call it a courtesy.' She paused, pursed her lips. 'I've had one relationship. It lasted five months, while I was in my second year at uni, and I took every necessary precaution. So you have nothing to fear from me medically either,' she snapped.

A layer of tension released its grip on me, even while questions multiplied in my brain. Questions I batted away because, no, I most definitely did *not* care who that relationship had been with. Or why it had ended. These days not being 'in a relationship' didn't mean a woman was celibate. Did she belong to anyone now?

The urge to know was overpowering enough to force my fists closed, to grit my teeth just so the question wouldn't tumble out.

Thee mou, I was losing it.

Her eyes widened as she stared at me. Evidently, my poker face needed work too. She glanced away, her eyes lighting on the shabby little handbag resting on the entryway console table.

When she headed for it I remained where I stood, not trusting myself to approach her. But staying put didn't mean denying myself one final scrutiny of her body. Now that I'd tasted the passion and beauty beneath her tasteless clothes, my body wasn't in any mood to obey my commands to relegate Sadie Preston to the wasteland where she belonged. Instead, it tracked the supple shape of her calves and ankles, the tempting curve of her backside, the dip of her waist.

Her hair…

My fist clenched tighter. I'd never given much thought to a woman's hair before, except perhaps in the way it framed the overall package. I'd dated blondes, brunettes and everything in between without alighting on any specified preference.

Sadie's hair had trademarked its own siren call. One that had hooked into me, driving me to a new and dizzyingly dangerous edge.

'I suppose you want me to leave?'

I refocused on her face. She'd reclaimed her bag and slung it crossways over her slim torso, dragging my attention to her full breasts. I forced my gaze away from the perfect globes, crossed the living room to the front door to summon the lift.

A draining type of despair, a kind I'd never known before—not even when I stared into the heart of Anneka's cruel betrayal—sapped the dregs of my energy. I held it at bay with sheer willpower.

Barely.

'Neo…'

I pivoted to face her, renewed tension vibrating through to my very bones.

'I don't recall inviting you to use my first name. There's

nothing more to discuss. And, just so you're disabused of any lingering notions of attempting to make this right, let me lay it out for you. There's no way back from what you've done. Short of divine intervention and immaculate conception, you've effectively *ended* me, Sadie Preston. My last hope of ever becoming a father was that sample you destroyed. So I'm confident that you can get it through that stunning red head of yours that if I never see you again it will be too soon. Attempt any form of communication with me for any reason and this stay of execution I'm considering will be off the table and you'll be handed over to the authorities to answer for your crime. Is that understood?'

All colour drained from her face, but that stubborn chin remained high. *Defiant.*

'Perfectly. Goodbye, Mr Xenakis.'

Nine weeks later

'You shouldn't be going to work today, Sadie. You look even worse than you did yesterday. And you were out like a light when I looked in on you before I went to bed. I didn't disturb you because I thought a full night's sleep would do you good, but I can see it didn't.'

I busied myself fetching milk I didn't need from the fridge to make a cup of coffee I didn't intend to drink. All so I could avoid my mother's gaze and the questions lurking therein.

Despite despair and bone-tiredness leaching the strength from my bones, I strove to remain upbeat. 'I can't afford not to go to work. And I'm fine, Mum.' The *I promise* I usually tagged on to the reassurance stuck in my throat. I couldn't promise anything. Because I *wasn't* fine.

I hadn't thought it possible to be this far from fine when I blinked back tears as Neo Xenakis's lift hurled me down to the ground floor after that unforgettable night.

I'd been wrong.

That cloying sense of unworthiness, germinated after my father's desertion and watered by doubts and hopelessness, had trebled overnight, and the enormity of what I'd done both before and after meeting Neo Xenakis had thrown me into a state of raw despair. One that'd grown exponentially with the final notice from our landlord a week ago.

We were on a countdown clock to homelessness.

I hadn't been able to bring myself to tell my mother yet.

But I'd been doing a lot of evading lately.

In between sporadic temping I'd ignored the flulike symptoms leaching my energy, initially attributing my delayed period to the condition. Even after a second period was a no-show, I'd refused to believe that fate would be so brutal. That the unthinkable could truly happen.

Then had come the bracing, inevitable acceptance that I wasn't the victim of lingering flu, or a stomach bug that only attacked in the morning, but that, yes, I *was* capable of conceiving immaculately.

Shock.

Disbelief.

A brief spurt of searing anger at Neo Xenakis and his lies.

Followed by that ever-present tug of despair. That feeling of unworthiness. That cruel little reminder that my own blueprint was flawed.

But even while despair lodged a heavy stone in my chest there also came a quiet, even more bewildering...*elation*. Even though I was twenty-five, working jobs that paid a pittance and on the brink of homelessness with a mother who'd promised me, when I finally broke down and begged her to seek help, to combat her growing gambling addiction but had since regressed—as evidenced by the online betting pages I'd spotted on her phone yesterday.

That crushing list of failings was what had overwhelmed me last night. Made me pretend to be asleep when my mother entered the bedroom we shared.

Elation should be the farthest emotion on my reality spectrum.

A hysterical thought flitted across my mind. Perhaps I should have taken a gamble on myself. I'd be wildly wealthy and down one less problem by now. Because, despite all the odds against it, I'd fallen pregnant with Neo Xenakis's baby after one utterly misguided folly.

A baby…

Sweet heaven…

I can't father children…

The lie had dripped so smoothly, so convincingly from his lips. And I'd *believed* him. Had even hurt for him. When all he'd been doing was cruelly toying with my emotions.

Had he seen my feverish desire to stay anchored, *connected*, for just a little while, and viciously exploited it as some sort of payback? Did the man I'd given myself to, in an act I suspected had involved more than just the physical, bear traits of the father who'd so callously rejected me…?

'Sadie, dear, are you sure you're all right? You've gone as white as a ghost.'

I swallowed the encroaching nausea and a bubble of lurking panic, thankful that my mother hadn't noticed that on top of my pseudo-flu I was also plagued by bouts of vomiting.

'I'm not sick, Mum. Really,' I said, infusing as much warmth into my voice as possible.

'Okay, well…if you're sure. I'm going back to bed. Have a good day at work.'

She left the kitchen after sliding a comforting hand down my back. Absurdly, the gesture made my eyes prickle.

I blinked the tears away, forced myself to revisit the subject that filled me with equal parts anger and dread: relaying the news to Neo.

His last tersely worded warning before tossing me out of his penthouse still lingered, two months on. And I believed he'd meant what he'd said.

Then, of course.

But in light of this life-changing news…

I wouldn't know until I tried. *Again*.

My initial attempts to contact Neo had met a brick wall, with a few snooty receptionists even threatening to block my number if I kept trying to reach their illustrious boss. Apparently Neo had issued word that I was persona non grata.

Initially aggrieved by the realisation, I'd stopped trying to reach him for all of three days, before accepting that this reality wasn't going to go away.

Neo needed to learn of his child's existence sooner rather than later. And answer a few pointed questions in the process…

Since returning to his building and risking arrest or worse was out of the question, I ventured onto social media—only to discover that the Xenakis family were embroiled in the kind of publicity that drove the tabloids wild.

Apparently, in the last few weeks, Neo's older brother Axios had returned from a brief trip abroad with his young wife in tow. A wife whose previous absence had been highly conspicuous, fuelling all kinds of scandalous speculation.

Now, not only had the young Mrs Xenakis returned from her mysterious absence without explanation, she'd apparently given birth while she was away. The reunited family had asked for privacy, but already several shots of a baby boy, Andreos Xenakis, had been leaked to the media. He was a gorgeous baby, who bore all the strong characteristics of possessing the Xenakis DNA.

How was Neo taking the news? And, the more important question, how would he take *my* news?

It was only eight o'clock. My temp job didn't start until ten. That gave me a little time to attempt to reach Neo again.

Distaste at the thought of stalking him online lingered as I powered up my laptop. The first headline I found made my stomach drop.

Xenakis Aeronautics Soars to New Heights in the Far East.

Exhaling shakily, I read the article, calming down when I saw it focused mostly on Axios Xenakis and his spearheading of the airline conglomerate's global expansion. Neo would be taking over the European arm of the company, starting with relocating to Athens with immediate effect.

The article was two weeks old. Which meant Neo might now be even further out of reach.

Suppressing the strong bite of despondency, I scribbled down the numbers of the Athens office, shut down the laptop and rushed to the bathroom just in time to heave.

A quick shower and a judiciously nibbled slice of dry toast later, I picked up my bag and headed for the door—only to pause when my mother called out.

'Oh, Sadie, when you can, do you think you can buy me some data for my phone? I seem to have run out.'

Desolation deadened my feet. The urge to tell her that I was barely holding it together emotionally and financially, never mind providing a conduit for her addiction, tripped on the edge of my tongue. But I was woefully ill-equipped for a replay of the inevitable tears and depression that had dogged Martha Preston's life since her husband's cruel desertion. As much as I wanted to dish out tough love, I could barely hold myself together, and nor could I afford to lose another job because I was late.

Vowing to tackle the subject again that evening, I shut the door behind me.

The morning trundled by in the tedium of filing and answering phones.

After using the first minutes of my late lunch break to calm my nerves, I dialled the number I'd saved.

One minute later I hung up, my ears ringing after a crisp, accented voice informed me that while Mr Xenakis was indeed at his office in Athens, he did not accept unsolicited calls.

No amount of pleading had shifted the receptionist's stance.

In the middle of the busy London park, I gritted my teeth and resisted the urge to scream. Or dissolve into helpless tears. Instead, on a desperate urge, I called up the web page of a budget airline, my heart racing when I saw a same-day return flight to Athens.

It would put further strain on my tight bank balance, and would require even more ruthless financial rationing, but the temp agency had no placement for me tomorrow and I had nothing planned for the weekend besides tormenting myself with the many ways my failed childhood might affect my baby...

Without stopping to debate the wisdom of it, I booked the ticket.

Regardless of his reasons for stating a blatant untruth, I owed Neo the news that he was going to be a father. Just as he'd deserved to know of my mistake at the Phoenix Clinic.

Would he think it was another unforgivable mistake?

Would he walk away even sooner than my father had?

It didn't matter.

No. It matters. It's why you won't stop shaking.

I smothered the voice, shrugging mentally. For good or ill, I was going to beard the formidable lion that was Neo Xenakis in his den one more time.

But this time, I was suitably armed with what to expect.

The seat of the Xenakis airline empire was housed in a sprawling ten-storey building that took up a whole city block in the centre of Athens. Security was twice as tight as in London, but this time I didn't linger outside. The brief, succinct note I'd hastily written in the taxi ride and shoved into an envelope trembled in my hand as I approached the ultramodern reception desk.

Before the efficient-looking receptionist could voice the disdain lurking in her eyes, I held out the envelope. 'It's essential that Mr Xenakis sees this immediately.'

Whatever expression she read on my face halted her answer. Rising, she took the note and walked away.

I retreated to the nearest set of expensive club chairs, arranged to maximise the appreciation of the stunning marble-floored, three-storey atrium that formed the welcoming entry into the world of Xenakis Aeronautics, the words of the note echoing in my head:

Mr Xenakis,
I'm downstairs in your lobby.
   It's in your interest to give me ten minutes of your time.
   I'm certain you'll regret it if you don't.
Sadie

Bold words, which would either grant me an audience or fritter away the mercy he'd shown me by not asking Wendell to break out the handcuffs that day in London.

I looked up to see Wendell heading my way, as if summoned by my thought. My heart dropped, but I refused to look away.

'If you're here to throw me out, you should know that I'll simply turn around and come straight back. Maybe you should tell your boss that?'

His expression didn't change. 'Mr Xenakis will see you now.'

I swallowed my surprise and followed him.

This time, knowing the calibre of the man who waited behind another set of imposing doors, I tightened my gut, sure I could mitigate the effect.

I was wrong.

Being on his home turf had heaped another layer of magnificent appeal upon a man who already held more than his fair share. In the sunlight that filtered through wide, rectangular windows, his dark hair gleamed. A skin-skimming stubble highlighted his strong jaw, and with that sexy dimple in his chin it was impossible to stop the flare of heat that attacked my body, robbing me of vital breath for precious seconds.

The matching jacket to his tailored grey trousers hung on a hook in the far corner of his office, leaving him in a pristine white shirt that moulded his broad shoulders and powerful biceps.

Terrified I was already losing the fight for composure, I hurried to speak. To get this over with.

'Thank you for seeing me, Mr Xenakis.'

Eyes that had been conducting a slow, thorough scrutiny of me rose to fix on my face. 'Miss Preston.' His voice was grave. 'I'm beginning to think you have some sort of death wish. Or do you simply relish testing my patience?'

'Neither. Believe me, this is the last place I want to be.'

His arrogant head cocked. 'I sense the inevitable *but* coming,' he drawled mockingly. 'Although I have no earthly idea what it could be.'

Despite his words, he narrowed his eyes, as if he fully suspected a scam. Or worse.

Say it. Just say it and leave.

I sucked in a breath that went nowhere near replenishing my lungs or giving me the courage I craved. 'I'm pregnant. The baby is yours. I thought you should know.'

Deathly silence echoed in the vast office. Then he inhaled sharply, the white-hot sound sizzling across the large room.

'*Christos*, you *do* have a death wish,' he breathed in sizzling disbelief, and his face, unlike last time, when there'd been shock and bleak despair, was a picture of complete and utter fury.

'I don't, I assure you. But—'

'Then you've taken complete leave of your senses. Be-

cause that can be the only viable explanation for this—'
He stopped abruptly, his hands clenching and unclenching at his sides.

For one mad moment I wanted to say yes. That only a peculiar strain of madness would explain why I couldn't look away from his face, why I couldn't quite catch my breath in his presence.

'The door is behind you. Use it right now or I won't be held responsible for my actions.'

It was a hushed entreaty, perhaps even a final attempt at civility for a man hanging by a thread.

Considering I'd jumped on a plane with little hope of being granted even this audience, I was surprised I'd got this far. But complete dismissal wasn't what I'd expected.

The urge to linger, to make him believe, if only for the sake of telling my baby someday that I'd tried, fired through me—along with the question that still demanded an answer. The question about his false statement, the consequences of which had certainly taken *me* by surprise.

But Neo's face was turning even more ashen, his chest rising and falling in rapid shudders as he remained frozen in place.

'Why?' The question was ragged, torn from his soul.

'Excuse me?'

He prowled forward several steps, granting me a better look at his face. And there it was. That look of desolation.

'Why would you do this? Did someone put you up to it? As a joke, perhaps?' he asked from between whitened lips. 'Or a bet?'

'We don't move in the same circles, Mr Xenakis. Nor am I friendly with anyone who would deliberately cause someone distress with such a prank.'

'Then tell me *why*?'

There was a tinge of desperation in his question. Of bewilderment.

'Because it's the truth!'

He jerked forward again, his throat moving as his eyes drilled into me. 'No, it's not. As I told you in London, I'm incapable of fathering children. Three years ago the best doctors in the world delivered that staggering news. And do you know what I did?'

Numb, I shook my head, my anger at his lies dissipating in the face of the searing emotion in his eyes.

'I found a set of doctors with better credentials than the original set. Guess what? They arrived at the same conclusion. So now do you see how what you're saying is impossible?'

Why?
Where?
How?

Questions flashed through my brain even while I accepted that this wasn't the time or place.

I licked lips gone dry with growing anxiety. 'I can't speak to your experience. All I can tell you is my truth.'

If anything, his fury grew. 'Does this *truth* involve a lapsed memory on your part?'

I shook my head. 'I'm sorry—you've lost me.'

His jaw turned to steel. 'You wouldn't be the first woman to find herself in this situation and devise a plan to pass another man's child off as—'

'Don't you *dare* finish that sentence!'

'Because it's much closer to this "truth" you seek to ram down my throat?'

'Because it's most definitely guaranteed to get you slapped! And while we're throwing accusations around, what about what you said to me?'

'I beg your pardon?'

'You assured me I had nothing to worry about. You said I couldn't get pregnant! That it was impossible.'

'And I have a file of medical reports to back that up. What do *you* have?' he snarled.

'I have that immaculate conception you wished for, apparently. Because three pregnancy tests last week and a trip to the doctor confirms that I'm carrying a baby. *Your* baby!'

He shook his head, started to speak.

I held up my hand. 'It's fine if you don't want to believe me. I don't care.'

'You *do* care or you wouldn't be here. Or be crying,' he grated.

Belatedly, I registered the dampness on my cheek. Hating myself for that weakness, I dashed my hand across my cheek. Only to feel more tears spilling.

'It must be a side effect of being repeatedly labelled a liar. Or... I don't know... Pregnancy hormones. But, no matter what, this was the right thing to do. And now it's done.'

There—you've said your piece. Now leave.

But my feet refused to move.

His eyes narrowed with laser focus. 'If there truly is a baby, does the news distress you that much?'

'*Yes!* You lulled me into a false sense of security, made me think I had the flu when I'm *pregnant*!'

He went a little pale, his movements jerky as he closed the gap between us. 'And what would you have done if I'd told you two months ago that there *was* this possibility, hmm? Considered your options *without* me in the picture, perhaps?'

'Watch your tone, Mr Xenakis. The last thing you should be doing is lounging on that lofty perch and looking down your nose at me. What happened between us was consensual. What happened with the condom was unfortunate. You do *not* have the right to question my character. Considering the way we parted, do you really think I would be here, right now, if that was my intention?'

He seemed lost for words even as his gaze scoured my face, dissecting my words.

'You said yourself you only verified the pregnancy a week ago. That means you're about two months along. It's not too late for other options. Maybe that's your plan? To leverage those options?'

His insult sank in, sharp as a stiletto blade. 'God, you can't help yourself, can you?' I realised I'd screamed the words only after they came out.

He frowned. 'Calm yourself, Sadie.'

'If you want me to calm down, then stop upsetting me—*Neo*!'

He sucked in a deep breath, then another. Then he whirled around, dragging his fingers through his hair. Swift strides put the width of the room between us and I watched him stare out of the window at the Friday afternoon traffic, tension riding his shoulders.

Walking out through the door should've been easy, but again that stubborn need to have him believe me held me rooted to the spot.

So when he abruptly grated, 'Perhaps we should discuss this further. Take a seat. Please,' I glared at his back for all of half a second before stumbling over to one of the twin plush sofas positioned tastefully at one side of his office.

Unlike his stunning but impersonal London penthouse, there were more signs of Neo Xenakis's personality here. Priceless objets d'art were placed next to pictures of what looked like his family, and there was even a framed child's drawing. On the coffee table, a large book on Mayan history was open to a well-thumbed page, and several more Aztec-themed books were piled to one side.

The notion that in another time or place I'd have liked to get to know this stranger whose baby I carried hit me hard.

I was busy pushing the thought away when I heard his deep, low tones. He stood at his desk, speaking in rapid-fire Greek. Done, he returned to the window and stood there for an age.

When he turned around, every inch of his body brimmed with purpose. 'You mentioned that you saw a doctor?'

'Yes...after I took the pregnancy tests.'

'And?'

'Everything's fine so far.'

'This probably won't come as a surprise to you, but to me the possibility of an offspring is not…unwelcome.'

The depth of yearning in his low, deep voice rocked me to my core, softening a knotted place inside me I hadn't registered until his words loosened it. Truth be told, I hadn't allowed myself to think beyond delivering the news. Because when it came down to it, Neo had plenty of other options beyond having a baby with the woman who'd brought chaos into his life. If he was willing to accept—

'If it's mine, that is. And at this point I'm hard-pressed to be convinced it is.'

The soft place hardened, strangled tight by his words. 'You really believe I'd lie about something like this?'

The yearning receded slowly, forced back by the power of his scepticism. And something else. Something dark and grave that took complete control of him, hardening his face into a rigid, implacable mask.

'I'm a wealthy, influential man. Anyone with a competent internet connection can see for themselves what any association with the Xenakis family represents. Believe it or not, you won't be the first woman to attempt to saddle me with a paternity claim. Even when the likelihood is remote.'

He believed it. He truly believed he was infertile.

Despite the anguish dredging through me, a tiny voice urged reason. Urged me to see this from his point of view. How many headlines had I caught from my mother's gossip magazines that shouted about a celebrity vehemently denying alleged paternity? How many women had attempted to scam rich men by dangling a baby in their faces?

I was wasting my time.

Neo wouldn't believe even if I shouted until I was blue in the face.

I rose. 'Your hang-ups are your problem, not mine. I have a plane to catch, so I guess it's goodbye, Mr Xenakis.'

He moved with impressive speed. Before I could take my next breath, Neo had arrived before me.

'That's it? You came to deliver the news and now you're just going to head to the airport and return home?'

I dredged up a smile. 'Let me guess. This is where you expect me to make some sort of demand? Maybe ask for financial support or a McMansion to live in while I carry your child? Well, sorry to disappoint you. I want nothing from you.'

The faint colour tingeing his sculpted cheekbones told me I'd hit the nail on the head.

'Did you not hear me when I said I want this baby?' he asked.

'No, what I heard was you hedging your bets on the off-chance that I'm telling the truth. When you decide whether you want to believe me, I'm sure Wendell will be able to find me—'

'No,' he interrupted. 'That is most definitely *not* how this is going to work.'

'What's that supposed to—'

We both froze when déjà vu arrived in the hideously embarrassing form of my stomach giving the loudest growl known to humanity.

He muttered what sounded like an incredulous Greek oath under his breath. 'Tell me you haven't been neglecting to eat?' he bit out.

Heat consumed my face. 'I'm in the throes of a spectacular experience called morning sickness. Anything I eat before a certain time rarely stays down.'

He frowned. 'Surely there's a remedy for that?'

I shrugged. 'If there is, they haven't found it yet.'

His frown intensified. 'So the answer is what…? To starve yourself?'

'I don't do it deliberately, you know. My flight here was at an ungodly hour this morning.'

An exasperated puff of air left his lips as he glanced at

his watch. 'It's now past noon. Does this mean you haven't eaten all day?'

'I tried to eat something on the plane.'

His lips twisted in distaste. 'Budget airline food?'

'We can't *all* afford to travel on private jets, Mr Xenakis.'

'Neo,' he drawled. 'Call me Neo.'

'I'm not sure I want to call you anything, to be honest.'

'If the child you carry is truly mine there's one title you won't be able to deny me,' he stated with stone-rough gravity, just as a discreet knock sounded on the door.

He responded in Greek, and a moment later an impeccably dressed middle-aged woman entered, holding a package which she handed to Neo. Without glancing my way, she discreetly retreated.

He studied me for a moment, then reached into the bag. Although I suspected what the contents were, I was still shocked when he took out the oblong package.

'You sent out for a pregnancy test?'

'With the full intention of accepting any offence it might cause you, yes,' he stated simply, his fingers tight around the box. 'Will you take the test?' he asked, his tone containing a peculiar note I couldn't fathom.

There was something going on here. Something beneath the surface that I couldn't quite put my finger on. Again, questions surrounding the reasons why he believed he couldn't father children crowded my brain.

Resolutely, I pushed them away and accepted the status quo. For now. 'Only to prove I'm not a liar.'

I held my hand out for it but he hesitated, his jaw working for several seconds before he said, 'You should know that this is merely a preliminary test to confirm your pregnancy. A test for paternity will be necessary when the time is right.'

My hand dropped, something hot and sharp lancing my chest. 'You really are something else—you know that?'

'*Ne*, I've been told.' His stance didn't change.

'If you think I'm going to harm my baby just so your suspicions can be satisfied, you can think again.'

Emotion, heavy and profound and almost sacred, gleamed in his eyes. 'So you've made up your mind? You intend to keep it?' he rasped, his voice shaken.

'You think I flew three and a half hours on a cramped middle seat, next to a passenger with a rabid aversion to good personal hygiene, to tell you I'm pregnant, only to go back and get rid of it?'

Neo's gaze dropped to the hand I'd unconsciously jerked up to cradle my still-flat stomach.

'You think I don't have other things to do? I have a life to be getting on with. A mother who needs me to take care of—' I shut my mouth, but it was too late.

The moment his eyes narrowed I knew he was about to pounce on my unguarded revelation. 'Your mother needs taking care of? What's wrong with her?' he demanded sharply.

'It's none of your business.'

'I beg to differ. If this baby is mine—'

I swatted the rest of his words away. 'Enough with the *if*s. Here—hand it over. I'll take your precious test.'

Grim-faced, he held out the pregnancy test. I took it, then followed the tall, imposing body that hadn't diminished one iota in the drop-dead-gorgeous stakes in the last two months down a wide private hallway adjoining his office to a sleek, dark door.

The bathroom was another stylish masterpiece—naturally. Gleaming surfaces held exclusive toiletries, polished floors echoed my nervous tread and the wide mirror faithfully reflected my wan features.

I diverted my face from it, hurried into the cubicle and took the test.

A little over three minutes later, I stepped out.

He stood, square and true, five feet from the door, his gaze piercingly intent on the stick in my hand. For a single moment—knowing what this meant even if he doubted me, knowing I was perhaps about to change Neo Xenakis's life—something moved in my chest.

Then he ruined it by holding out an imperious hand for the test.

I handed it over.

His gaze dropped to it and he swallowed hard.

He seemed to rock on his feet—a fascinating feat to watch, especially for a toweringly powerful man like him. He didn't speak, only held the stick as if it was a magic wand that had the potential to deliver his most heartfelt wish.

Afraid I would succumb to softening emotions again, I hurried to speak. 'As you can see, it indicates how many weeks along I am. I can give you the date of my last period too, if you want?'

It was meant to be sarcastic. It fell far short simply because I wanted him to believe me. Wanted to take away his doubt once and for all.

Because I wanted to hurry to the part where, despite the evidence, he'd conclude that fatherhood wasn't for him after all. That this was a mistake. That *I* wasn't worthy to carry his child.

He didn't respond immediately. When he lifted his gaze his eyes were a stormy, dark grey, the pupils almost black. 'This is sufficient for now,' he finally said, his voice gravel rough.

Then he turned and walked away.

CHAPTER FIVE

I COULD BARELY walk beneath the staggering evidence of what I held in my hand.

Confirmation that there was a child, possibly *my* child, shook through me with every step back to my office. The circumstances astounded me. Seemed almost too good to be true—the stuff of big-screen melodramas.

Had the woman who'd brought desolation to my door returned with redemption, despite my threat to her the last time she'd been in my presence? Despite the medical evidence I'd been provided with to the contrary?

What were the chances of lightning striking twice? Was I setting myself up for the same kind of betrayal Anneka had dished out so callously?

My jaw gritted, my stomach churning with the need for one hundred percent certainty.

I sucked in a calming breath, recalling what rash decisions had led me here in the first place. My fingers tightened around the stick. Not that I regretted it...*if* it was truly happening.

A bolt of euphoria threatened to overwhelm my calm. Brutally, I suppressed it. Rationalised it.

As Sadie had pointed out, the kit I'd asked my trustworthy assistant to purchase was the highest quality, giving an estimation of gestation. The test announced Sadie was more than three weeks pregnant.

Surely she knew how powerful I was? Knew that any information provided could be easily verified by my security team? Would she be so foolish as to toss out falsities that could catch her out?

A throat was cleared huskily behind me, making me aware I'd reached my desk, opened the secure thumbprint-accessed drawer that held confidential documents and was in the process of dropping the stick into it. I needed that connection, this visual evidence that maybe, just *maybe*, I'd defied science and the odds.

Again, stunned awe shook through me. A child. *My child*. But just as swiftly, a less effervescent emotion rose. A little desperate, and a lot dismaying.

The thought struck me that I had no true compass as to how to *be* a father. I'd gone straight from boarding school to boardroom, my spare moments spent watching my grandfather struggle to hang on to the company, and subsequently witnessed my father and Ax embroiled in a cold battle for the helm of the company.

I'd used my time on the sidelines efficiently—learned everything I needed to excel in my field.

Those lessons hadn't included how to be a father.

'Now that we've established that there's a pregnancy, are we done here?' she asked.

Done here? Was she joking? 'No, we're not done. Far from it.'

'What's that supposed to mean?'

'It means I intend to be involved in this baby's welfare every step of the way. Beginning now.'

I forestalled the questions brimming in her eyes by making a quick phone call.

The moment I was done, she approached.

Shock born of the earth-shattering news she'd delivered had partly blocked off the stunning effect of her appearance. Now, with the flood dammed and a plan of action swiftly slotting into place in order to secure what she insisted was mine, I couldn't stem my reaction to her.

The white sundress was a cheap and simple design, but on her it looked anything but. The scooped neckline gave a tantalising glimpse of the perfect breasts that seemed to have swelled a size bigger with her pregnancy. And her skin, now her temper had subsided, glowed with an additional translucence that triggered wild tingles in my fingers with a need to trace, to caress... *Christos*, to lay my lips against that pulse before stealing another taste of those rosebud lips, currently caught between her teeth as she watched me.

I bit back a growl as my gaze rose to that final monument to her beauty. Two months on, her hair had grown longer, the ponytail she'd caught the heavy tresses into almost down to the middle of her back.

The hunger to set it free, to lose myself in the exotic scent of it, powered through me.

'Explain what that means. Precisely. Because less than twenty minutes ago you were almost apoplectic about my perceived deception.'

I forced myself to throttle back this insane arousal that fired up only with her.

It wasn't for lack of trying that I'd remained dateless since that night in London. Hell, I might even have cursed Sadie Preston a little for the sudden urge to set my useless little black book on fire because not a single woman listed within sparked the kind of flame she did with a mere look.

'You have to be aware that I intend to take every precaution with you?'

Her wary glance confirmed that notion was becoming clear to her.

'I've told you I only came here to give you the news—which I could've done by phone if you hadn't blacklisted me.'

While the accusation grated a little, I couldn't allow it to dissuade me from forging ahead. 'From this moment forward consider that status reversed. You will have access to me day or night.'

Curiously, her breath caught, and I glimpsed something that looked like excitement in her eyes—which, perversely, triggered a stronger chain reaction within me.

Her trite reply attempted to disguise her reaction. 'Others might find that offer beyond tantalising, but I don't think much communication between us will be necessary after today...'

Unbidden, my lips twisted in genuine amusement, causing her words to trail off.

'I fail to see what's funny.'

Wonder. Apprehension. Raw anticipation. Panic. The cascade of emotions was threatening to send me off balance.

'You're carrying my child, Sadie. A Xenakis.'

Her eyes widened. 'So you believe the baby is yours?'

Betrayal's curse bit hard—a timely reminder to exercise caution. But for now I needed to buy myself time. After the accusations I'd hurled at her, and her reaction, these negotiations needed to be handled carefully while still keeping her under scrutiny. Because I didn't intend for history to repeat itself.

'In utero paternity tests carry unacceptable risks. We will wait until the baby is born.'

'And how do you know that?'

I clenched my gut against the searing reminder of how wrong I'd been before, how blind trust had almost decimated me.

'That doesn't matter. What matters is that we're in agreement that the health of this baby is the priority.'

She frowned. 'I don't need you to tell me that.'

'Then you'll stay a little while longer? Have lunch with me?'

Her eyes widened, then grew suspicious. 'Why?'

'You need to eat, do you not?'

Memory darkened her eyes and swept the most becoming blush across her skin. She was recalling what had happened after our last meal together. When her long lashes drifted down to veil her expression, I forced back the wild need to nudge her chin up, to see the evidence of the chemistry that heated the very air around us.

'Doesn't mean I have to eat with *you*,' she murmured.

For some absurd reason I bit back another smile, and the urge to keep tangling with her spiralled through me.

'I won't sully your meal with my presence, if that is your wish.'

Surprise jerked her gaze back to me. 'You won't?'

'I have a few more business matters to deal with. You can eat while I take care of them.'

The knock on the door at that moment drew her suspicion.

'You've already ordered lunch, haven't you?'

I shrugged. 'On the off-chance that you'd agree to stay, yes.'

'There's nothing "off-chance" about anything you do, but nice try,' she sniped.

As she headed to the sofa and I returned to my desk, my smile turned resolute. She had no idea how accurate her words were. How meticulously I intended to seal her completely into my life.

If this child was mine—and, *Christos*, I would burn the world down if I'd been fooled for a second time—then nothing in all existence would stop me from claiming it.

For two hours I attempted to ignore her disquieting presence, to concentrate on laying the groundwork for what needed to be done. But with every appreciative bite of the meal I'd had my chef prepare for her, with every stretch of her voluptuous body as she shifted on the sofa and every flick of her hair over her shoulder, my body reacted with visceral hunger.

A hunger I cursed with every breath for messing with my concentration and control. For being neither circumspect nor discerning about the kind of woman it wanted.

First Anneka, with her wide-eyed innocence that had hidden a grotesquely flawed character. Now this green-eyed siren, who should be the last woman to pique my interest and yet fired me up with one simple defiant look.

'You're glaring at me,' she stated, while glaring right back.

I ended a call that was going nowhere fast, rose and approached her. With each step I knew the path I was taking was the right one. Swift. Precise.

Permanent?

She would resist my plans, of course. I chose to ignore the kick in my gut signalling that I'd relish tussling with her. This was more than base pleasure. This was laying the foundations to secure my heir's future.

Her stunning green eyes widened a touch, and I was gratified to see her gaze rush over me before she attempted to look away.

'Did you enjoy your lunch?'

She shrugged. 'It was fine, thanks.'

Her gaze grew more wary the closer I got. Did she know how enthralling she looked, with her face tilted up to me like that, the satin-smooth perfection of her neck just begging to be stroked?

For several heartbeats after I stopped, she stared at me. Then she visibly roused herself, picked up her purse and rose.

'I should be going. If I'm lucky, I might catch an earlier flight.'

'You're aware we have a lot more to discuss?'

She paused. 'Like what?'

'Like your employment status, for starters. Have you secured another job since the incident at the clinic?'

Her gaze swept away. 'Not a permanent one. I'm currently temping.'

I forced my jaw not to grit. 'Are you going to tell me what you meant about your mother?'

Her chin lifted at that. 'No. It's still none of your business.'

'The welfare of this child is paramount. Nothing is going to stop me ensuring it doesn't come to harm. I wish you to be absolutely clear about that.'

'And you intend to dig your way through my life to do that?' she challenged.

'I intend to take away whatever worries you so that you can concentrate on remaining healthy.'

The answer disarmed her. As it had been intended to. Her lips parted, triggering a shot of heat to my groin.

'You…can't do that.'

'Can't I? How exactly do you propose to stop me?'

Her eyes sparkled with that telling green that spelled the start of her temper. 'A restraining order, for starters?'

I curbed the curious smile that threatened. 'What's to stop me from returning the favour? Or have you forgotten the small matter of your crime?'

Vexation receded, to be replaced by apprehension. 'I'm getting tired of your veiled threats, Mr Xenakis.'

'I said you may call me Neo.'

One elegant eyebrow quirked. 'Oh, I can use your first name now, can I?'

A touch of regret zinged through me. 'You'll have to excuse me for not being at my best that day. I wasn't aware that a tangible part of my future had been affected until I heard your news. It was hard to deal with. Almost as I hard as it was for you to deliver the news to me, perhaps?'

After a beat, she shook her head. 'It wasn't easy, no. I guess it's fair you'd want to put it behind you.'

Memories of the passionate way that day had ended blazed hot and insistent. 'Not all aspects of it. And, as it turns out, it will be impossible to do so now.'

Again awareness flashed in her luminous eyes, before she shrugged and took a few steps away from me.

'It is what it is. Now, I'd really like to make that flight, so if you don't mind…?'

I let her leave, granting us both a moment's necessary reprieve. But within seconds of her walking out, I was back at my desk. A quick phone call to my assistant with a handful of immediate action instructions, and I was heading out through the door.

She was already in the lift, her gaze triumphant as the steel doors slid shut between us. I called the next one, further unsettled by the whisper of a smile that I felt curve my lips. I frowned it off.

This was no smiling matter.

When Ax had delivered the news of his unexpected son I experienced a moment's searing jealousy, even while being overjoyed at his good fortune. But I also witnessed his despair at missing his son's first few months.

Nothing would come between me and every step of my child's growth in its mother's womb. Nor a single moment of its life.

If it's yours.

Seven months. For the chance at fatherhood I believed had been cruelly snatched away by a computer mistake, I would endure the torturous wait.

She rounded on me the moment I stepped out of the lift, the tail of her long hair a swinging, living flame I wanted to wrap around my fist.

'Really? You've instructed your goons to stop me from leaving?' she spat out.

'I have done nothing of the sort. Wendell is aware of my intention to give you a lift to the airport and he merely wished for you to wait for me. Isn't that so, Wendell?' I arched a brow at the stoic ex-military man.

'Precisely, sir.'

Sadie rolled her eyes. 'You two make a cracking comedy duo. Can I leave now?'

'Of course.'

She looked surprised when I held the door for her. How had the male she'd indulged in that brief relationship with treated her? Clearly not well enough, if a little chivalry surprised her. What about her mother?

Registering that I knew next to nothing about the woman

who was possibly carrying my child rankled. Enough to make me grow absent-minded as I slid my hand around her waist.

She started, her breath hitching as she shifted away from my touch and stepped dangerously close the kerb.

I caught her arm, stemming momentary panic. 'Easy, *pethi mou*.'

'I... You startled me, that's all.'

'I merely touched you to guide you to the car.'

Her translucent skin flushed again, the captivating sweep of her long lashes brushing her cheeks as she blinked. 'Well, I wasn't expecting it.'

The car drew up. I waved the driver away and opened the door for her. With another flick of her green eyes, she slid in. I followed, tightening my gut against the punch of lust that hit me at the display of one smooth, shapely leg.

The fact that she seemed determined to secrete herself as far away from me as possible when I joined her triggered a bolt of disgruntlement. Was I really that fearsome?

Yes. You all but slapped on the handcuffs both times she attempted to contact you.

Perhaps I *had* been fearsome—whereas Sadie, both times, had been...brave.

Registering the path of my thoughts, the new respect for her actions, I sheared off the notion. It remained to be seen whether her motives were truly altruistic.

And if they weren't?

The sheer depth of my hollow dread unnerved me. Enough for me to step away from it—leave it alone in a way I'd left nothing alone for as long as I could remember. I wasn't ready to tackle *what if*s. Especially the ever-growing one that demanded credentials as to my suitability as a father. Not yet.

What I *could* do was lay further bricks for the lockdown I had in mind.

'Xenakis Aeronautics is expanding into Latin America—

specifically Brazil and Argentina. But my marketing team are struggling to find traction for our newest marketing venture.'

Interest flickered in her gaze. 'What's the problem?' she asked after a handful of seconds.

'We beta-tested our new airline cabin six months ago, to rousing success, but the take-up fell sharply after three months.'

'What does this new cabin deliver? How is it different from other airline cabins?'

Did she realise she'd leaned forward? That her eyes sparkled with interest and intelligence? Clearly this was a subject she liked. Which begged the question of what had happened to stall her studies.

'They're like suites—one step up from first class, but not out of the realms of affordability for the successful individual.'

'I've seen promotional stuff from other airlines. If your cabins are two-person berths only…'

She paused as I shook my head. 'They range from two to six.'

Her eyes widened. 'That's…amazing. But I bet your team's marketing plan was to target billionaires and oligarchs who have more money than they know what do with?'

She'd hit the nail right on the head. 'Something like that.'

Her pert nose wrinkled in a grimace. 'Which begs the question—why would this oligarch fly in a superclass suite on a premium airline when he could charter his own plane? It'll most likely be for the bragging rights, which will lose their lustre after a handful of flights. I'm confident that's why you're experiencing a drop-off. You need to refine the suites. Since they can accommodate up to six, why not attract an entirely different demographic? Besides the luxury and exclusivity of having a suite to yourself on a commercial airline, the unique design also offers privacy.'

'What would be your plan if *you* were in charge?'

She grew even more animated, her eyes sparkling brighter. 'Oh, that's simple. I'd push hard to attract young, successful millennial families. Believe me, there's nothing worse than having an irate child kicking the back of your seat for hours on a long-haul flight. I can't imagine what it's like for harried parents having to apologise to disgruntled passengers. This will be a win-win for everyone. So why not market the suites to those who will welcome peace and quiet together with luxury and exclusivity? I'm assuming your suites are on the upper deck, like the others I've seen?'

I was a little put out that she knew more about my rivals' products than mine. 'Not only that, the Xen Suites come with premium sound insulation.'

She nodded enthusiastically. 'Just think how much that would appeal to the parents with young families who can afford it. And if you have a loyalty programme in place, where passengers can aspire to use of the suites, then it will boost the uptake even further.'

'The Xen Loyalty Programme is one of the best in the industry.'

'But I bet there's a steep points rise from, say, business class to superior class?'

I shrugged noncommittally.

She gave me a wry look. 'On the basis that I'm right, I'd offer incentives for the target demographic to try the suites for a limited period. I'm confident you'll see a sustained growth.'

'Are you, now?'

About to respond, most likely with a tart rejoinder to my droll tone, she glanced out of the window, then performed a double take.

'Why are we here?'

'You wished to return to England, did you not?' I replied.

'I assume that's your private jet?'

'You assume correctly. We have three hours, give or take,

before we land. A little longer after that to deliver you to your home. We can use that time for further discussions.'

Her enthralling green eyes widened. 'You...you're giving me a lift on your plane?'

'I wish to spare you and the baby the discomfort of a return journey in a cramped middle seat next to malodorous passengers.'

Colour tinged her cheeks, drawing my attention to their smoothness, reminding me of other sensational areas of her body. I shifted, willing the blood racing to my groin to slow.

'But—'

'My pilot is waiting on the steps. That means we have a fast-closing window for take-off. So perhaps we can continue your objections aboard?'

Her lips firmed. 'That sort of defeats the object of the exercise, doesn't it?'

'Are you really that attached to your budget airline seat?'

'Fine. You've made your point.'

'Efkharisto.'

'I don't know what that means.'

'It means *thank you*.'

'Oh. Okay.'

Despite having won this hand, I was reluctant to leave the car...to end the moments of accord we'd shared. Reinforcing my guard, I stepped out, telling myself it was only decent manners that made me hold out my hand to her.

She took it, stepped out and immediately released it.

The balmy early evening air drifted a breeze through the hangar, sliding her dress against her hips as she preceded me up the stairs. That hot tug of lust flamed in my groin, reminding me that the months before and after Sadie's eruption into my life had been the longest time I'd gone without a woman.

The notion that if my plan were to succeed I'd have to endure an even longer spell filled me with unwelcome dissatisfaction as I entered the plane after her.

Most people who were lucky enough to be invited onto the Xenakis jet frothed at the mouth at the no-expense-spared opulence of its interior.

One of four in the fleet of Jumbo Jets used for family and business trips, the Airbus was satisfyingly immense. With upper and lower decks, and filled with sleep, entertainment and business facilities, and even a twenty-seater cinema, it catered to every imaginable taste.

Anneka had loved to travel in this lap of luxury, insisting on the use of the jet several times a week during our engagement. Of course, I'd later found out what those trips had entailed…

Sadie's gaze flitted over hand-stitched cashmere throws, bespoke incorporated furniture and Aubusson carpeting with disarming lack of interest, her feet almost dragging as she contemplated the seats she could occupy, then made a beeline for a detached club chair.

About to follow, I paused when my phone buzzed in my pocket. Catching the attendant's eye, I nodded to Sadie. 'Get Miss Preston whatever she wants to eat and drink. Make sure she's comfortable.'

'Of course, sir.'

With more than a tinge of regret, I answered my phone. Then spent the next two hours putting the finishing touches on my plan to ensure an unbreakable alignment with Sadie Preston.

By the time we landed at the private airport twenty minutes from her North London residence, I was satisfied with my decisions. Enough to be confident that I could counter any argument she might have.

Once I'd dealt with the handful of obstacles still standing in my way.

The first came in the form of Martha Preston—a woman bearing a striking resemblance to her daughter, whose red hair Sadie had obviously inherited.

'You must be Mrs Preston,' I said when she appeared at the door. 'My name is—'

'My goodness—you're Neo Xenakis! Please, come in.' She threw the door wide open, much to her daughter's initial astonishment, then immediate annoyance.

'Mum—'

'Is something wrong?' Martha asked, hurrying down the hallway while throwing wide-eyed looks over her shoulder. 'When you said you'd be gone all day I assumed it was to work, not... Wow... Um... Anyway, welcome to our home, Mr Xenakis.'

'Thank you,' I said, unable to suppress my shudder as I looked around.

This squashed, dilapidated structure wasn't a home fit for anyone, never mind the woman who carried my child. I might not have the right emotional advantages to offer this child, but in this I could offer full benefits. My child would not be spending a second in this place. Nor would its mother.

'Can I get you anything? A drink? We have tea. Or coffee. Or—'

'He won't be staying long, Mum. He has things to do. Don't you?' Sadie enquired pointedly.

Martha Preston ignored her daughter, her smile at me widening. *Kalos*, the mother was going to be a breeze to handle.

I stepped into the even more cluttered living room of this house Sadie wouldn't be occupying for much longer, suppressing another smile even while calculating how quickly I could move.

Magazines of every description covered every available shabby surface, and a gaily coloured sofa was the only bright spot in the dank space. A look passed between mother and daughter before they both faced me.

'I'll take a rain check on that coffee, if I may, Mrs Preston. But I do have a request.'

Green eyes similar to her daughter's widened. 'Of course. Anything.'

Sadie frowned. Opened her mouth.

I beat her to it. Because, really, what was the point in dragging out the inevitable?

'I hope you'll forgive my bluntness, but I would be honoured if you'll give me your blessing to marry your daughter.'

Shock gripped me for a second before I rounded on this towering force of a man who'd gone from complete disavowal of his child to a systematic, head-spinning takeover in the last few hours.

'What? Are you out of your mind?'

'Sadie! Where are your manners? I'd like to think I brought you up better than this. I do beg your pardon, Mr Xenakis. And, please, call me Martha.'

My mother all but simpered at Neo, who inclined his head in gracious forgiveness for my bad manners.

I ground my teeth, partly to hold back my shock and partly with fury at his heartless joke. Because he had to be joking! Or, worse, this was payback for the prank he still believed I was playing on him.

'Please don't make excuses for me, Mum. And while you're at it, forget what Mr Xenakis just said. He didn't mean it.' I fired a telling glare at him, communicating my dim view of his actions.

His expression didn't change from one of intractable determination. For some reason, instead of angering me even more, that sent a sliver of a thrill through me. Until common sense prevailed.

'It's Neo, Sadie. You can't very well keep calling me Mr Xenakis when we're man and wife, can you?' he drawled.

'Since that's not going to happen, it's neither here nor there.'

The trace of the civility I was sure he'd cultivated for my

mother's benefit evaporated, allowing me an even clearer glimpse of the flint-hard resolution in his eyes. Cold foreboding gripped my nape, then slithered down my spine.

While I grappled with it, he turned to my mother with suave smoothness. 'This is a shock, I know. Besides, it's late. I don't wish to keep you up, Martha, but I would be pleased if you'd let me pick up our acquaintance again soon?'

I opened my mouth to counter his words.

The look in his eyes stopped me.

'Of course,' my mother replied, and then, for the first time in a long time, the hazy cloak she clung to, so she wouldn't have to face harsh reality, lifted. Her eyes glinted with steel as she stared at Neo. 'As to your admittedly surprising question—I'll speak to my daughter first. Clearly you two need better communication. When I'm satisfied that this is what she wants, you can have my blessing.'

Her answer didn't cow Neo. If anything, reinvigorated tenacity vibrated from him, filling up every spare inch of the living room.

Inclining his head in an almost regal way, he smiled. 'Very well. May I have a private word with your daughter?'

With a few words and what I expected was a hint of blushing, my mother left the room.

Unable to stand so close to him without losing my mind, or dissolving into hysterics, I hurried across the room, before whirling around. 'I don't know what the hell you think you're playing at, but—'

'I warned you I intended to do whatever it takes when it comes to this baby, did I not?' he said, in the even tone he'd used that day in his office two months ago. The one that announced he was chillingly rational. That every word from his lips had been calculated and calibrated to achieve the result he wanted.

A shiver raced down my body, urging me to stay in the present. To give every scrap of attention to this insane moment, lest I was swept away. 'This is... What are you doing?' I finally managed, when my head stopped spinning.

'Taking steps to secure my legacy.'

'Your *legacy*? You don't even fully accept that this baby is yours!'

He shrugged off the accusation. 'I've given it some thought and I've concluded that for the moment we'll proceed as if the child is mine.'

'Oh, wow. Lucky me.'

My sarcasm bounced off him. 'You got on a plane and travelled two and a half thousand miles to convince me. This is me meeting you halfway.'

'No, this is you bulldozing your way into my life with zero regard for what I want.'

He paused, folded his arms across his wide chest. 'Indulge me, then. Tell me some of what those wants are.'

I opened my mouth to tell him the paramount one. That I wanted him to leave. But with this new level of ruthless determination wouldn't I simply be postponing the inevitable?

'Permit me to start. Do you want a stable home for our child?'

'Of course I do.'

He nodded in that arrogant way that stated he'd scored a point for himself.

'What else, Sadie?' he urged softly. Oh, so dangerously.

I shrugged. 'I want what every normal person wants. To keep a roof over my head and to stop worrying about how to make ends meet.'

He looked around the living room, his face carefully neutral. 'I have several roofs. You will be welcome to any you choose.'

My mouth dropped open, but he was still talking. 'Were you serious about finishing your degree?'

'Of course.'

'There will be nothing standing in your way, should you choose to see things my way. As for your mother—'

'She's still none of your business.'

'Very well. When the time comes, and you confirm my suspicions, that too will be dealt with.'

Everything I wanted. Offered on a platter. Just like that. I gasped as the penny dropped. 'My God, this is why you stalled me in your office all afternoon and offered to give me a ride home? So you could chess move your way into my life?'

He didn't bother to deny it. 'I merely took time to ensure my plan was sound.'

'I'm not a damned charity case!'

'No,' he replied with heart-stopping brevity, as something close to awe flashed across his face. 'But according to every imaginable statistic, what is happening is a miracle. The baby you're carrying is a miracle.' Then that staggering determination returned. 'One I don't intend to let slip through my fingers.'

I wasn't sure whether to be angry or horrified at his calculated move.

'Don't overthink it, Sadie. I've simply come up with a plan to remove any stumbling blocks that will prevent what we both want from happening. You have needs. I can satisfy them. It's as simple as that,' he drawled arrogantly.

If he'd discovered a handwritten wish list crafted by me he wouldn't have been off by even a fraction. But what he was suggesting was unthinkable.

Marriage? I shook my head. 'Even if everything you've listed is true, and I want all of it, why would I bind myself to you?'

'Because I can give you everything you want. All you have to do is marry me.'

I laughed then, because all this insanity needed an outlet. Before I spontaneously combusted. When his eyes narrowed ominously, I laughed harder.

'Is this just a trait of all insanely wealthy men, or are

you cursed with the notion that you can throw your weight around like this and get what you want?'

He didn't answer immediately. Instead he sauntered towards me, his gaze locked on my face as he approached.

'You feel the need to resist and rail at what you see as my overbearing move when this is merely accelerating a necessary and efficient process.'

Laughter dried up in my throat. 'But why marriage?'

'No Xenakis child has been born out of wedlock. I don't intend for my child to be the first.'

'Here's an idea. Buck the trend. This is the twenty-first century. Set your own path.'

'No. I will not. Label me a traditionalist if you will, but in this I will not be swayed,' he replied with deep gravity.

'You forget that for you to achieve that you'll need my agreement.'

'And you will give it. I'm sure of it.'

'Are you? How? Let me guess—this is where you threaten me with criminal charges again unless I bend to your will?'

For the longest moment he remained silent, considering it. Then, astonishingly, he shook his head. 'That incident is in the past. It's time to turn the page. That transgression will no longer be held against you. Regardless of where we go from here, we will not speak of it again.'

Shocked relief burst through me. I searched his face for signs that he meant it and saw nothing but solid honesty.

Where we go from here...

Ominous words that rattled me as he stared at me. As with every second, the urge to consider his offer gathered strength.

To buy myself time, I countered, 'If you're standing there waiting for me to give you an answer, you're going to be disappointed.'

Something crossed his face that looked a little like alarm, but it was gone much too soon for me to decipher it.

'While you wrestle with that *yes* you're too stubborn to say, let's discuss other issues. I believe one has already been tackled?'

The head-spinning encroached. Again, removing myself from his immediate orbit, from the intoxicating scent of aftershave and warm skin that made me want to wrap my arms around his trim waist and bury my face in his neck, I crossed to the small pink-striped sofa we'd managed to rescue from the bailiff's clutches and sank into it.

'I wouldn't hold your breath,' I countered.

An arrogant smile twisted his lips. 'I'd like you to put the marketing plan you outlined into a report for me.'

Excitement of a different kind joined the chaos surging through me. 'Why?' I asked, forcing myself not to think of our conversation in the car on the way to the airport. Of my thrill when I solved his marketing problem. The grudging respect in his eyes as he sounded out my solutions. If he wanted a report, did that mean...?

'Because that will form the basis of your employment with Xenakis Aeronautics,' he said.

I was glad I was sitting down, because I was sure the shock would've floored me otherwise. 'What?'

'Your new role. As my intern starting as soon as we have an agreement.'

More puzzle pieces fell into place. 'All those questions in the car on the way to the airport...you were *interviewing* me?'

He nodded.

'And...?'

'And you presented a sound strategy—one worth consideration. The second you sign an employment contract I'll pass it on to my marketing team—of which you'll be a part. If you wish.'

I did wish. With every atom in my body, I wanted to grasp his offer with both hands.

But all this came at a price.

Neo Xenakis, marketing guru extraordinaire, wasn't handing round internships of a lifetime out of the goodness of his heart. He was bartering my wish list for complete access to my child.

But, even knowing that, I couldn't help pride and satisfaction fizzing through me like the headiest champagne. Regardless of what had led us here, to have the president of marketing for a global powerhouse like Xenakis Aeronautics pronouncing my idea sound was an accolade worth celebrating.

'Thanks, that's…um…a generous offer.'

'You're welcome,' he returned, and then for some inexplicable reason his gaze dropped to my mouth.

A moment later, I realised I was smiling. And he seemed…*fascinated*.

CHAPTER SIX

The moment stretched as we stared at one another, a tight little sensual bubble wrapping itself around us, making it hard to breathe as heat and need and desire filled my body.

This time he was the one who broke contact, his chest expanding on a long breath before he said, 'Which item do you wish to discuss next?'

None, I wanted to say. But, reluctantly buoyed by the promise of utilising my marketing knowledge, I wanted to hear him out. See where he was going with this.

'What do you suspect about my mother?'

He shrugged. 'That she's far too dependent on you—perhaps uses you as an emotional crutch to hide a deeper problem?'

I pressed my lips together, unwilling to betray my mother.

'Whatever those problems are, they'll only grow if ignored,' he said.

With a grimace, I exhaled. 'She gambles online. It's small sums, but—'

'Addiction like that is insidious, Sadie. It needs to be curbed now or it'll become a problem.'

Unable to meet his gaze, I toyed with the hem of my dress.

'Has it already become a problem?' he intuited smoothly.

The answer spilled out before I could stop it. 'Yes. I've spoken to her about it. Asked her to get help.'

His face hardened. 'You might have to be a little more insistent. Ruthless, even.'

'Like you?'

A look flashed in his eyes, but he shrugged. 'If it makes you feel better to think that way, then so be it.'

Temptation swelled higher. I knew I had to tackle my

mother's problem before I lost the only parent I had, but...
'She's my concern. I'll find her the help she needs.'

Neo nodded after a handful of seconds.

I licked my lips, knowing the most important topic still needed to be tackled. 'Let's talk about the baby.'

'Yes,' he replied, his voice deep and heavy, with that yearning that still had the power to rock me.

'How would it even work?'

'Our marriage would simply legitimise my child and formalise any agreement as to childcare when it's dissolved.'

A beginning and an end. So...a temporary marriage. A get-out clause and a possible end to his duties as a father when the appeal wore off?

The sting of abandonment registered, deep and true, those flippant words in my father's letter burning through my brain.

'You're pulling out the stops to get what you want *now*. How do I know you'll even want to be a father when this baby is a reality? That you won't simply abandon him or her?'

The hands he'd shoved in his pockets slowly emerged. Purpose vibrated from him. But there was something else. A fleeting look of *doubt* which evaporated in the next instant as his confidence returned, expanding into the room as he strode forward and sank down in front of me.

This close, the look in his eyes captivated me, made me hold my breath.

'I've experienced what it feels like to believe that fatherhood will never happen for me. The feeling is...indescribable. So perhaps this is one of the things you'll have to take on faith. I *want* this child, Sadie.'

The fervour brimming in his voice...

The implacable stare.

That...yearning.

I believed him. But...

'How long did you see this marriage deal continuing?'

He shrugged. 'For the sake of the child's stability and welfare, its first few years at the very least.'

'Then what?'

'Then we agree to whatever custody plan works in the best interests of our child.'

The response should have satisfied me, but something cold and tight knotted inside me. Neo might be in full negotiation mode, but at least he was laying all his cards on the table.

Unlike my father, who'd stuck around until the going got tough and then bailed, with a cruel little letter addressed to the daughter he'd claimed to love and cherish. His wife hadn't even received that courtesy—only a letter from his lawyer, inviting her to sue for divorce on the grounds of abandonment. It was an option my mother was yet to take, the shock and anguish of the abrupt turn her life had taken still keeping her in a fog of despair all these years later.

Wasn't it better this way? To know what was coming and prepare for it rather than be blindsided by it? Especially when until this morning the possibility that my child was going to start life knowing only one parent had been great? Could I pass up this opportunity on behalf of my child?

Neo leaned forward, bringing his power and his glory and that intoxicating scent into play. With one hand braced next to my thigh, he pinned me in place with his gaze for an interminable moment before he lifted the other hand to rest against my face.

Heat from his palm accelerated my pulse. My unguarded gasp echoed quietly between us, my heart wildly thundering as he slowly glided his thumb over my chin, my lower lip.

My insides were debating whether to flip over or melt when he said, 'It's better that we approach this with civility instead of conflict, Sadie.'

Deep, even-toned words that nevertheless gave me a glimpse of what it would be like to keep fighting him.

Jerking away before I did something stupid, like wrap

my lips around that masculine thumb, I shook my head. 'I need time. To think about this.'

Mutiny briefly glinted in his eyes before he gave an abrupt nod and surged to his full height. After a short pace round the living room, he faced me again.

'I have a family function to attend in Athens tomorrow. A new nephew to meet,' he said, with a hint of something peculiar in his voice.

I couldn't tell whether it was anticipation, yearning or bitterness. Perhaps a combination of the three.

'How old is he?'

'I'm told he's almost four months old.'

Curiosity ate at me. 'How come you've never met him before?'

His jaw clenched for a taut stretch. 'Because no one in my family, including my brother, knew of his existence before a few weeks ago.'

So Axios had been in the dark about his son's existence? 'Why?'

He shrugged. 'The reasons for that will become clear tomorrow, I expect.' His gaze sharpened. 'You have until my return to consider my proposal.'

His words flung me back to the present. 'There was no proposal, as I recall. Only edicts thrown down and expected to be followed.'

'I merely set out the course of action I believe is best. If you have a better proposal I'm willing to hear you out.'

He said that while cloaked in an arrogant self-assurance that nothing I could come up with would beat his. Blatant certainty blazed in the gaze that held mine for a nerve-shredding minute.

Other sensations started to encroach. Ones that had heated me up from the inside when he'd touched my lips just now and made every stretch of skin his gaze lingered on burn with fierce awareness. It was as if he'd reached out and touched me again. Stroked me. Tasted me.

Intensely aware of my breath shortening, of the place between my legs growing damp and needy, I cleared my throat and stood. 'If we're done here…?'

He retraced his steps towards me, moving with lithe, attention-absorbing grace, his darkened eyes scouring my face one more time. From his pocket, he produced a graphite-grey business card, embossed with the iconic dark gold picture of the phoenix etched into every Xenakis plane's tail fin. The card simply read *N. Xenakis* and listed a mobile number.

'My personal cell. Use it whenever you wish.'

His fingers brushed mine as I took it. At my shallow inhalation, his eyes darkened.

It struck me then that there was one subject we hadn't discussed.

Neo was a virile, magnificent specimen of a man. One who wouldn't be short of female companionship, should he wish it. Did he intend this proposed marriage to come with the certain leeway rumoured to happen within marriages of conveniences like this?

Even while my mind screamed that it would be the rational course to take, my chest tightened, everything inside me rebelling at the idea.

So what would your solution be?

I ignored the snide little voice attempting to prod me into admitting the secret yearning that had no place in this transaction. What happened two months ago had been an aberration. One that had produced consequences we needed to prioritise now. There could be no repeat of it.

So why were my feet leaden as I followed him to the door? Why did my gaze avidly catalogue his every feature as he stepped out, turned and murmured, 'I'll be in touch'?

And why, when I tossed and turned and sleep wouldn't come, when I should have been thinking about what was best for my child, my mother, my career, did I keep returning to that ever-growing knot of anxiety over whether Neo would take a lover outside of our marriage...or if there already *was* one?

'Is there something I should know, Sadie?'

I'd expected the question. Frankly, I was surprised my mother had waited till morning to ask. Now she stared at me over her teacup, worry reflected in her eyes.

I took a deep breath. 'I'm pregnant, Mum. I'm sorry I didn't tell you before, but—'

'You wanted to tell the father first?' she inserted gently, with no judgement and no surprise over the news. 'I'm assuming Neo Xenakis is the father?'

'Yes. I told him yesterday.'

Another sip of tea, then with a short nod she accepted my news. 'And that's why he wants to marry you?' she asked, visibly holding her breath.

'Yes.'

A smile bloomed across her face. 'Oh, Sadie, that's so romantic.' Her eyes sparkled, much as they had last night, when she'd opened the door to Neo.

'Please, Mum, don't get carried away. This isn't like one of your magazine love stories.'

'Oh, *pfft*. A man like that wouldn't offer marriage unless he was hell-bent on permanence. But is it what *you* want?'

Weariness dragged at me. 'I don't know.'

Her sparkle dimmed. Nevertheless, she reached across the small kitchen table and laid her hand over mine. 'Whatever you decide, I'll support you, sweetheart.'

My eyes prickled, my heart turning over with the knowledge that I loved my mother too much to remain blind to the dangerous road she was treading with her gambling.

About to broach the subject, I froze when the doorbell rang. With a curiously trepidatious expectancy, I answered the door.

A courier held a large, expensive-looking box in his

hand. 'Delivery for Sadie Preston from Xenakis?' the young man asked, eyebrows raised.

Senses jumping, I signed for it.

In the living room, I set it on the coffee table, a reluctance to open it rippling through me. Because, more than not wanting whatever lay within the square box, I was terrified I would *like* whatever Neo had sent me. An expensive something, judging by the discreet logo signifying the endorsement of English royalty often attached to exclusive items.

When the suspense got too much, I tore it open.

The box was filled to the brim with packets of handmade biscuits, each exquisitely wrapped with a thin silver bow. On top of the first one lay a small white envelope, with a note within that read:

I'm told these help with morning sickness. Be so kind as to try not to forget to eat them.

Rolling my eyes seemed like the perfect counterfoil for the smile that insistently tugged at my lips. The man was insufferable.

And he thinks the baby you claim is his might not be.

My smile evaporated, my heart growing heavy as I plucked out one neatly wrapped packet and opened it. The scent of ginger was oddly pleasant, and not vomit-inducing like most smells these days. Apprehensively, I bit into the biscuit, stemming a moan at the heavenly taste. Experiencing no ill effects, I finished one small pack, and reached for another.

'I see your Greek god means business. I bet he had these flown in on one of his private jets?'

I jumped and turned to see my mum in the doorway, beaming as her eyes lit on the box.

'You know what he does for a living?'

'Of course I know! You'd have to be living under a rock

not to know about the Xenakis dynasty. Rumour is they've surpassed the Onassis family in wealth and stature. Shame what happened to your fella, though.'

I frowned. 'He's not "my fella"—and what are you talking about?'

Like a magician's big reveal, she produced a tabloid magazine from behind her back. 'I went digging the moment I left the living room last night. Aren't you glad I keep all my magazines, instead of chucking them in the bin like you keep pushing me to?'

I didn't answer, because my gaze was locked on the crimson headline.

Neo Xenakis Emerges from Three-Week Coma... Ends Year-Long Engagement.

Ignoring the fine tremor in my hands, I scoured the article, concluding very quickly that while the reporter had one or two facts, the majority of the piece was conjecture. But the bit that read, *By mutual consent, Neo Xenakis and Anneka Vandenberg, the Dutch supermodel, have agreed to go their separate ways* clearly had some truth to it.

The reality that I had very little knowledge about the man I was marrying attacked me again in that moment.

Then the very thought that I was leaning towards acceptance of this temporary arrangement slammed into me hard, making my heart lurch.

I told myself I was remedying the former when I retreated to the bedroom and dialled his number the moment my mother flicked on the TV and grew absorbed in the soap she was watching.

He answered immediately. 'Sadie.'

The deep, sexy growl of my name sent sensation flaring through my body.

Tightening my grip on the phone, as if it would stop the

flow of pure need, I launched straight into it. 'You were engaged before?'

He inhaled sharply, then I heard the sound of footsteps as the background conversation and music faded.

His heavy silence brimmed with displeasure. 'There are aspects of my past that have no bearing on what's happening between you and I,' he said eventually.

Unreasonable hurt lanced me. 'According to *you*. You felt entirely comfortable digging into *my* life. I think quid pro quo earns me the same rights,' I said, despite the sensation that I was treading on dangerous personal ground.

'I furnished myself with details of your past only as far as it pertained to the welfare of my child. But if you must know, yes, the tabloids back then got that piece of information right.'

'What else did they get right? What else do I need to know about you?'

Did you love her? Why did it end?

'You want more personal details, Sadie? Then marry me.'

My breath caught, those two words tapping into a secret well I didn't want to acknowledge. Because within that well dwelt a fierce yearning to belong. But to be worthy of consideration for *myself*, not like in the past, because it suited my father's professional ladder climbing, or because I was carrying Neo's child now.

'Will you marry me, Sadie?' he pressed, his voice low and deep.

'It's nice to be asked. Finally. And thanks for answering my question.'

'No—*efkharisto*,' he breathed heavily.

Yesterday he'd said that meant *thank you*. Surprise held me mute for a second. 'For what?'

'For going the extra mile to tell me about the pregnancy even when I made things…unpleasant.'

'You're welcome. But still…why?'

'Because, as much as my brother is overjoyed at the existence of his son, the time he's missed weighs on him. I wouldn't have wished that for myself.'

'Oh.' I drew in a shaky breath as that unique place inside me threatened to soften.

Silence echoed down the line. When he ended it, his voice was tense. 'Do you have an answer for me, Sadie?'

My heart lurched, then thundered as if I was on the last leg of a marathon. 'That depends…'

'On?' he bit out.

'On whether your status two months ago still holds true. I know this marriage will be in name only, but if I'm going to make someone "the other woman", even for a short while, I'd like to be forewarned.'

The background noise had faded completely, leaving the steady sound of his breathing to consume every inch of my attention.

'You have my word that there is no other woman, and nor will there be as long as this agreement between us stands.'

Even as the knot inside me inexplicably eased, that last addition sent a bolt of disquiet through me. I smashed it down, dwelling on the positives in all of this. My child would be getting the best possible start in life. My mother would receive the help she'd denied she needed. I could concentrate on finishing my degree and finally starting the career I'd yearned for.

But, best of all, the fervour with which Neo wanted his child meant there wouldn't be a repeat of what my father had done to me. No postcard would ever land on my baby's doorstep, with a few words telling him or her that they'd been abandoned in favour of a better life.

So what if every facet of this agreement made me feel surplus to requirements? That, although my child wouldn't suffer the same fate, it felt as if I was reliving the past, and again others' needs had been placed above my own?

I couldn't deny that the benefits outweighed the momentary heartache. I would get over this. As long as I placed some firm rules of my own.

'There will be no sex in this marriage. Do you agree to that?'

A sharp intake of breath. 'What?' he demanded tightly.

'No sex. Or no deal.'

He uttered something long and terse in Greek. Time stretched, tight and tense. Then he growled, 'If that's your wish.'

I squeezed my eyes shut, hoping for a miracle solution that didn't involve committing myself to a far too magnetically captivating man for the foreseeable future.

You've already been given a miracle.

Whatever had happened to make him believe he couldn't father children, our encounter had proved otherwise. We simply needed to make the best of the situation.

'Sadie?' His voice throbbed with authority that said he wouldn't be denied.

With a deep breath, I gave my answer. 'Yes. I'll marry you.'

He exhaled, then said briskly, 'Good. I will be in touch shortly.'

I blinked in surprise at the abrupt end to the call. But what had I expected? Trumpets and confetti?

He's marrying you to secure his child. Get used to that reality.

'Oh, Sadie.' My mother stood in the doorway, unapologetic about eavesdropping or the emotional tears spilling down her cheeks. 'I'm so thrilled for you, darling. You're doing the right thing.'

I wanted to tell her not to get her hopes up. But the words stuck in my throat, as the enormity of what I'd committed to flooded every corner of my being. When she swamped me in a tight hug, I let her effervescence counteract the quiet dismay flaring to life that reeked of what-the-hell-have-I-done?

'He won't let you down. Not like your father did. I'm confident of it.'

Financially? Perhaps not. Emotionally...?

I skittered away from that thought, wondering when my emotional well-being had become a factor. The idea of Neo and me was so out of the realms of possibility it was laughable.

So why didn't I feel like laughing? Why did the solid ground I should be stepping onto suddenly feel like quicksand?

That thought lingered, unanswered, throughout the dizzying set of events that followed.

Neo's almost offhand offer to me of his Mayfair property—*If you want to be more comfortable during the process*—had felt like another silken trap, but with homelessness a grim reality it was a lifeline I hadn't been able to refuse.

The property was a world away from the flat I'd left behind. The four-storey mansion sat on an exclusive street in an exclusive part of Mayfair, complete with a basement swimming pool and a stretch limo. A Rolls Royce Phantom and two supercars gleamed beneath recessed lights in the underground car park.

Within the house itself, every surface held breathtaking works of art and the kind of thoughtful blending of antique and contemporary decor that the wealthy either paid for through the teeth or put together with indulgent passion. Since Neo didn't seem the decorating type, I could only assume a king's ransom had been lavished on this place.

In the five immaculate suites, every last item of luxury had been provided—right down to the whirlpool baths and voice-controlled shower. An executive chef whose specialities included catering to expectant mothers presented herself within an hour of our arrival, then proceeded to whip up samples of exquisite meals for me to try.

And barely twenty-four hours after Neo's superefficient moving team had installed us in his property, the wedding spectacle commenced.

As did my arguments with Neo.

He'd soon found out that *leave it with me* when it came to the wedding wouldn't fly with me.

Three stages of wedding coordinator interviews were cut down to one, a dozen bids from the world-famous couture houses vying for the privilege of creating my wedding dress and trousseau, together with the present and upcoming seasons' day and evening wear, were whittled down from five designers to two.

The moment I'd managed to pick my jaw off the floor when I saw the wedding guest list, and stopped my mother from swooning with delight at the ultra-five-star treatment, I dialled Neo's number.

A heated twenty minutes later, we'd reached a compromise.

The wedding would be small, and the choice of dress mine alone. In turn, he would pick the venue—his private island in Greece—and the date—as soon as possible.

The only thing I didn't quibble over, was even grateful for, was the psychologist who arrived on the doorstep—despite knowing that this was simply another box being ticked by Neo on the journey to getting what he wanted.

The gambling conversation with my mother had been hard and tearful, and her acknowledgement that she had a problem and was still having a hard time dealing with my father's desertion had cracked my heart in two.

'I guess I should look forward now,' she'd said. 'You need me. I have a role as the mother of the bride and then as a grandmother.'

But within minutes of wiping her tears she had reached for her phone and excused herself, and minutes later, when

I'd approached her bedroom, I'd heard the distinct sound of electronic chips tumbling on a gaming site.

Heart heavy, I had retreated.

Neo called out of the blue an hour later. Still a little out of sorts, I answered my phone.

He immediately grew tense. 'Is something the matter?'

I barely managed to stop a weary laugh from escaping. 'The better question is "what isn't?"'

Tight silence greeted me. 'You are not having second thoughts.'

It wasn't a question but more of an edict.

'Am I not?' I taunted, my nerves a little too frayed to play nice. 'I can't promise I won't send the next person who asks me how many undernotes I like scenting my vintage champagne packing.'

'That's all that's worrying you? Or is there something else? The prenup I sent over for your signature, maybe?'

The question was a little too tight, like a dangerously coiled spring, set to explode.

My gaze slid to a copy of the prenuptial agreement a sharply dressed lawyer had hand delivered a few hours before. I frowned at the curious note in Neo's voice.

'What about it? It's already signed, if that's what you're calling about.'

A stunned silence greeted my response. 'You *signed* it?'

'Yes. Why are you surprised?'

'I'm not,' he drawled. And before I could call him out, he rasped, 'Tell me what's wrong.'

I let the subject of his peculiar attitude over the prenup go as I toyed with sharing my worries about my mother with him. The reminder that the baby I was carrying was the only thing Neo was interested in stopped me.

'I'm not changing my mind, if that's what you're worried about.'

He exhaled audibly, making me realise he'd been holding his breath. Had he been prepared to launch another vanquishing skirmish should I have responded differently?

'That's a wise course of action.'

For some reason that response hurt. I smothered the sting. 'Was there something in particular you wanted?'

'Yes. To give you the date for our wedding. It'll happen two weeks from tomorrow. That gives you a week to finalise your affairs before you come to Greece.'

Since the internship was at the head office in Athens, I'd agreed to the move.

'My mother's coming with me. A change of scene will help with her outlook on life.'

'I'm not a monster, Sadie. Regardless of where she chooses to stay, she'll receive the counselling she needs. But you must accept that our agreement includes not overburdening yourself with tasks that are out of your control. I will not allow it.'

I knew he was dishing out the hard truth, and I wanted to hate Neo. But deep down I knew that had circumstances been different, had I been granted other choices, I still would have chosen this. An internship at Xenakis. A chance to live in a different country, experience another culture. All of it.

Except staying within the orbit of this man who turned my equilibrium inside out?

Maybe...

The objections I wanted to hurl at him died in my throat, and exactly two Saturdays later my breath caught, as it had been catching seemingly every other second, as the ten-seater luxury helicopter my mother and I were ensconced in circled over a large island in the middle of the Aegean in preparation to land.

The island was mostly flat, bursting with green and pink foliage and large stretches of stunning white beaches. But on the northernmost point a bluff rose sharply over the water, where towering waves crashed against menacing-looking rocks below.

Magnificent, mesmerising, awe-inspiring—but also dangerous in places.

Just like its owner.

Several small houses, most likely staff accommodation, dotted the right side of the island, after which came extensive stables, a large paddock with thoroughbreds being tended to by stable hands.

The aircraft banked, granting a first view of the resplendent villa and grounds in the mid-afternoon sun.

'Oh, my God,' my mother whispered.

The sentiment echoed inside me.

Spread beneath us was the most magnificent sight I'd ever seen. The sprawling whitewashed villa was divided into two giant wings the size of football fields and connected by an immense glass-roofed living area that could easily accommodate a thousand guests. A sparkling swimming pool abutted the living area, and a tiered lawn went on almost for ever, ending at a large gazebo set right on the beach, complete with twin hammocks set to watch the perfect sunset.

I was still drenched in awe when the scene of the wedding ceremony came into view.

Unlike the spectacle of his brother's wedding—the details of which my mother had delighted in showing me via her magazines—Neo had agreed to a close-family-only wedding. The handful of guests were perched on white-flower-decorated seats, laid out on a blinding white carpet on the vast landscaped lawn. The 'altar' was bursting with white and pink Matthiola, specially imported from Italy, and the florists' gushing use of the flower meant to symbolise lasting beauty and a happy life echoed in my mind as the chopper landed.

The walk from the aircraft to where Neo's family members had risen to their feet felt like a trek across a field of landmines, my pulse leaping with apprehension with each step, the sea-tinged breeze lifting my organza and lace wedding dress, reminding me how far away I was from normal reality.

I was marrying a wealthy, powerful man. One who'd proved he could bend the path of destiny itself to his will. One who was assuming greater and greater occupation in my thoughts.

One who bristled with impatience as my steps faltered.

Beside Neo, a man matching his height murmured to him, a kind of hard amusement twitching his lips. Neo sent him a baleful glare before his eyes locked on mine, compelling me with the sheer force of his dynamism.

Despite our many charged conversations, I hadn't seen him since the night of his skewed proposal. His designer stubble was gone, and the lightning-strike effect of his clean-shaven face stalled my feet completely.

Somewhere along this journey I'd fooled myself into thinking I could handle an association with this powerful man. Now, I wasn't so sure. How could I be when his very presence struck me with such alarming emotions?

The man next to him stepped forward, momentarily distracting me.

Axios Xenakis—Neo's older brother.

He approached, eyeing me with the same piercing Xenakis gaze, unashamedly assessing me before the barest hint of a smile lifted the corners of his mouth.

He placed himself next to me and, with a nod at my mother, offered me his arm. 'As much as I'm enjoying seeing my brother twisting in the wind, perhaps you'd be so kind as to have a little mercy?'

'I'm not doing anything...' I murmured.

'Precisely. You are merely hesitating long enough for him to feel the kick of uncertainty. Believe me, I know what *that* feels like.'

His words were directed at me but his gaze flicked to a dark-haired, stunningly beautiful woman cradling an adorable baby in her arms. They shared a heated, almost indecently sensual look that would have made me cringe had my whole attention not been absorbed by the man I'd pledged to marry. The man who looked a whisker away from issuing one of those terse little commands that irritated and burned but also flipped something in my stomach while getting him what he wanted.

What he wanted, clearly, was for me to honour my word.

One hand twitched, and it was as if a layer of that supreme control slipped as he watched me.

Think of Mum. Think of the baby.

Knowing he was eager to secure his child delivered a numb kind of acceptance over me. Helped propel me to where he stood.

He exhaled, and just like that control was restored.

The ceremony went off without a hitch. Probably because Neo had forbidden any.

In what seemed like a breathless, head-spinning minute I was married to one of the most formidable men on earth. And he was turning to me, his fierce gaze locked on my lips.

It was all the warning I got before he leaned down, his lips warm and dangerously seductive as they brushed mine once. Twice. Then moved deeper for a bare second before he raised his head.

His gaze blatantly raked me from head to toe, his nostrils flaring as his gaze lingered on my belly.

'*Dikos mou,*' he murmured beneath his breath.

'What?'

He started, as if realising he'd spoken aloud, then immediately collected himself. When he circled my wrist with one hand and turned me to face the dozen or so guests, I steeled myself against the fresh cascade of awareness dancing over my body—told myself it meant nothing, was simply a continuation of whatever role he was playing. And when he turned to rake his gaze from the swept-back, loosely bound design the stylist had put my hair into, over my face and down my body, before deeply murmuring, 'You look beautiful...' I told myself it was for the benefit of his family.

Barely minutes later, once the wait staff had begun circulating with platters of exquisite canapés and glasses of vintage champagne, Neo had grown aloof. A fine tension vibrated off him, increasing every time I tried to extricate myself from his hold.

When it grew too much I faced him, thankful that we were temporarily alone. 'Is something wrong?'

His expression grew even more remote. 'Should there be?'

I shrugged. 'You're the one who seems agitated.'

For a tight stretch of time, he didn't speak. Then, with piercing focus, he said, 'I commend you for holding up your end of the bargain, Sadie.'

Despite the backhanded compliment, his expression suggested he was waiting for the other shoe to fall.

I raised an eyebrow, eager to find a level footing with him, despite the cascade of emotions churning through me. Barely a month ago I'd been blissfully unaware that I carried a child. Now, I wasn't simply a mother-to-be, I was the wife of a formidable man from an equally formidable family.

'Does that win me some sort of brownie point?' I asked, more to cover the quaking intensifying within me than anything else—because, despite his expression, the fingers holding me prisoner were moving over my wrist, exploding tiny fireworks beneath my skin.

That touch of hardness tinged his smile. 'Sadly not. You had your chance to win more during the prenuptial agreement signing.' His gaze probed as if he were trying to unearth something. 'Perhaps you regret signing it now?'

I frowned. 'Why would I? There was nothing in there unacceptable to me. It seemed skewed in your favour—just as you wanted it, I suspect?'

He shrugged. 'As with any of my contracts, it seeks to

protect what's mine. But you've signed on that dotted line, so there's no going back.'

'I don't get what's going on here. You *wanted* me to throw a fit over the prenup?' I asked, puzzled. 'Why on earth would I do that?'

He tensed, a flash of disconcertion darkening his eyes before he erased it. 'That was one scenario. But, seeing as you signed it, let's not dwell on it. The deed is done.' His gaze dropped to my belly again. 'Now we wait,' he breathed.

CHAPTER SEVEN

His words seeped deep into my bones, robbed me of breath.

For one tiny minute I'd forgotten that Neo harboured a very large question mark over my baby's paternity. That every term he'd negotiated and every luxury he'd tossed at my feet in his relentless pursuit of possessing the child I carried had come with the unspoken clause that he was hedging his bets. That my word wasn't good enough.

And where I'd have shrugged off the accusation a month ago, these past two weeks had weakened my foundations, wilting me enough that the barbs burrowed through the cracks. And stuck.

Worse, I only had myself to blame—because his endgame, like my father's, hadn't changed.

This time when I tugged my hand away he released me, although his lips tightened for a nanosecond. 'What's the matter?'

Our progression over the lush green grass had brought us to a section of the never-ending garden with luxurious bespoke seats set around beautifully decorated low tables, more in the style of an elegant garden party than a wedding reception.

He stopped at the seats that were set up on a dais and, beckoning one of the sharply dressed waiters carrying platters of food, helped himself to two gold-rimmed plates overflowing with Greek delicacies.

'Why, absolutely nothing,' I answered, plastering on a bright, patently fake smile.

He started to frown. I looked away, only to catch Ax's watchful gaze.

I turned back to Neo. 'Does your brother know why you…why we…?'

'We're married, Sadie. I'm your husband. You're my wife. You'll have to get used to saying it. Try the chicken,' he said, holding out a silver-skewered morsel to me.

The scent of lemon and rosemary wafted towards me enticingly, but I hesitated, refusing to let that bewildered fizzing inside me gain traction. 'You didn't answer my question.'

He dropped the food back onto the plate, his jaw momentarily clenching. 'Why we've exchanged vows today is nobody's business but ours. You have my word that no one will dare to question you on it.'

'Because you've decreed it?'

His eyes hardened. 'Yes.'

'And they obey whatever you say, without question?'

A spine-tingling glint flickered through his eyes. 'I'm in a unique position to demand that obedience, so, yes.'

'And how did you garner such unquestioning loyalty?' I semi-taunted, a little too eager to get beneath his skin the way he so effortlessly got beneath mine.

'By giving them what their grasping little hearts desire, of course. Isn't that the way to command most people's allegiance? Something in return for something more?'

Flint-hard bitterness glazed his words, triggering a burst of alarm.

Something in return for something more.

Wasn't that what my father had orchestrated for himself with his own family? A calculated means to an end?

Neo couldn't have made his endgame clearer. So why was I plagued with the urge to be sure? 'Does that apply to you too?'

The faintest ripple whispered over his jaw. 'We're not talking about me.'

'Aren't we?' I asked.

But when he started to speak, I shook my head to pre-empt him. To mitigate the ball of hurt that far too closely resembled the pain I'd felt at my father's actions.

'I'm not sure what happened to you to make you believe that's how everyone ticks—'

His eyes grew icily livid as he stared me down. 'I do not require your pity. Not now or ever,' he stated through gritted teeth.

Aware I'd touched on a raw nerve, I breathed in, curled my hands in my lap to stop them from reaching out for him. 'It wasn't pity. It was a need to understand—'

'Again, this isn't a lesson in dissecting my character, Sadie.'

Aware we were now drawing his parents' gaze, I took another breath. 'Fine. When will I start work?'

Scepticism and suspicion glinted in his eyes. 'So eager to get down to business?' he drawled. 'Not even time to entertain the idea of a honeymoon? You are aware that, as Mrs Xenakis, you now have the power to command my pilot to take you anywhere in the world your heart desires?'

I forced a shrug, and the uncanny sense that this was some kind of test intensified the chaos inside me. 'As tempting as that is, what's the point? We both know what this is. What *my* heart desires is to get started on my internship and finish my degree.'

The tic in his jaw returned, a little more insistent this time. 'You don't need reminding, I hope, that taking care of yourself and the baby is your number one priority?'

My fingers tightened. 'No, I don't. And you're beginning to sound like a broken record.'

'If you wish me to lay off, then have some food. It will please me,' he tossed in silkily, offering the succulent chicken again.

But my appetite had disappeared.

'If you're so interested in the chicken, Neo, then you have it. I'm going to powder my nose. And, in case you don't get that, it's a euphemism for *I need some space.*'

The briefest flare of his nostrils was the only sign he was displeased. In that moment I didn't care. I walked away, making a beeline for the wide opening of the living room wing. With the glass doors folded back and tucked out of sight, and late-afternoon sunlight spilling in through the glass ceiling onto the stylish grey and white Cycladic furnishings, the inside was a breathtaking extension of the outside.

Despite the chaos reigning inside me, I couldn't help but be affected by the stunning beauty surrounding me. But it only lasted for a minute—then reality came crashing back.

I blindly turned down one hallway, relieved when a half-open door revealed the sanctuary I was looking for. Shutting myself in, I attempted to regulate my breathing as questions ricocheted in my head.

The postcard my father left me had testified to the fact that selfishness and greed were his mainstays. But what had happened to Neo to fuel *his* actions?

Over the last week I'd given in to curiosity and done more internet searching. Very few details had been forthcoming regarding his broken engagement to Anneka. Even the circumstances of his accident were obfuscated. Although about the tall, Dutch beauty herself there'd been reams and reams, prompting in me even more questions as to why two people who'd outwardly looked like the kind of couple romance novels portrayed had parted ways.

I wanted to tell myself I didn't care. Again, my very emotions mocked me. The need to know, to see beneath the surface of the man I'd married, clawed at me.

Ten minutes dragged by. Knowing I couldn't remain hidden in the bathroom for ever, I splashed cool water over my hands, dabbed a few drops at my throat before exiting—just in time to see Callie Xenakis enter the living room, carrying baby Andreos.

She spotted me and smiled. 'I came in here to escape the heat for a few minutes. Won't you join me?' she invited, her movements graceful as she sank into one sumptuous sofa.

For some reason I hesitated, my gaze darting outside

to where Neo stood with his brother. There were similar intense expressions on their ruggedly handsome faces as they spoke.

Ax said something to Neo, his expression amused. Neo responded sharply, his mouth flattening into a displeased line which only seemed to further amuse his brother.

'Do me a favour and leave those two alone for now? Ax's been wanting payback for a while,' Callie said with a grin.

'Payback for what?'

Her stare was wickedly teasing but also contemplative, as if she was wondering whether she could trust me.

After a couple of seconds, she shrugged. 'I'm sure you've seen the papers. Let's just say my marriage didn't get off to a rosy start. And Neo... Well, he enjoyed a few jokes at his brother's expense. And those two are nothing if not competitive.'

I frowned. 'So your husband's ribbing my... Neo about me?' Somehow I couldn't bring myself to call him *my husband*.

Callie laughed. 'Ax thought he'd have to wait years to get back at his little brother. If ever.'

'I'm not sure there's much humour in any of this.'

Her eyes grew even more speculative, and there was an intelligence shining in the blue depths that made me wish for different circumstance for our meeting. I would have liked to be friends with Callie Xenakis.

'I don't think you need telling that everyone's wondering about you. This wedding came out of the blue.'

I firmed my lips, reminded of Neo's claim that our marriage was nobody's business.

As if she'd read my thoughts, Callie waved an airy hand. 'It's no one's business but yours, of course, but... Well, no one expected this from Neo. Not so fast, anyway,' she murmured, then grimaced, her gaze searching mine before she returned her attention to her son.

Sensing that she'd said more than she'd intended to, I

let the subject go, unaware that my gaze had strayed to Neo until he turned his head sharply, lanced me with those piercing eyes that threw fresh sparks of awareness over my skin. Even when his brother spoke again, Neo kept his gaze on me, the ice receding to leave a steady blaze that set off fresh fireworks.

It took monumental effort to pull my gaze free, to suck air into my lungs and turn back to Callie, who was laying her son on the wide seat, keeping one hand on his plump little belly to stop him wriggling off as she picked up a futuristic-looking remote and pressed a button.

Immediately a section of the ceiling went opaque, granting a little reprieve from the sun's rays.

As I moved towards her, her gaze flickered over my dress. 'That's a stunning dress,' she said, a wistful tone in her voice.

I stared down at my wedding gown. The style was simple, the bodice had a wide neck and capped sleeves that gave glimpses of my skin beneath the lace, and the soft layered skirt parted discreetly at intervals to show my legs when I moved. The whole ensemble felt like the softest, most seductive whisper against my skin.

'I... Thank you.'

She smiled, but a hint of sadness crossed her face before evaporating a moment later.

'Can I ask you a question?' I ventured.

'Of course,' she invited.

'What does *dikos mou* mean?'

Her eyes widened, and when she blushed I cringed inside, wondering if I'd committed a faux pas. 'I'm sorry. I didn't think it was anything rude—'

'Oh, no, it's not. It's just that Ax says it a lot. Where did you hear it?'

I bit my lip, still not certain I wanted to divulge it. 'Neo said it after...after we exchanged rings.'

A mysterious little smile played on her lips. 'It means *mine*,' she said.

'Oh...' My heart lurched in a foolish, dizzy somersault before I could remind myself that Neo's hand had been splayed over my belly when he'd said the words. That he had simply been revelling in his possession.

Nothing else.

Catching Callie's speculative glance, I hurriedly changed the subject to one I hoped would distract her: her baby. It worked like a charm—the gorgeous Andreos was almost too cute in his little shorts, shirt and waistcoat combo.

The reprieve didn't last, and the tingling along my nape alerted me that Neo had entered the room a second before my eyes were compelled to meet his. His incisive gaze raked my face as he stalked towards me, his brother a few steps behind him.

Axios made a beeline for his wife and son, catching up a giggling Andreos and tucking him against his side before he wrapped a possessive arm around his wife's shoulders.

Sliding her arm around her husband's waist, Callie said smilingly over her shoulder, 'Welcome to the family, Sadie. I have a feeling you'll find things interesting.'

Before I could ask what she meant by that, Neo closed the gap between us, one strong, lean hand held out. 'My parents are leaving. Perhaps you'd be so kind as to join me to see them off?' he enquired silkily.

That look before, as he stood next to his brother...

The terse, revealing little conversation before that...

The thought of taking his hand now...

My instincts shrieked at me to *beware*. And yet every argument as to why I shouldn't burned to ashes when his hand crept up another imperious notch.

I raised my hand.

He took it, his fingers meshing with mine in a palm sliding that jolted electricity through my midriff before spreading out in gleeful abandon over my body, hardening my nipples, speeding my heartbeat and delivering a mocking weakness to my knees.

I was fighting—and losing—the battle for my equilibrium when we stepped outside and approached Electra and Theodolus Xenakis.

Neo had inherited Theo's height and Electra's piercing eyes. Together they were a striking couple, who regarded me with shrewd speculation.

'Perhaps you and Neo would join us for dinner after you return from your honeymoon? I'd like to get to know my new daughter-in-law better,' Electra said, the barest hint of a smile diluting the near command to a request.

About to reply that there was no honeymoon, I paused when Neo answered smoothly, 'Thank you, Mama. We'll let you know when we're free.'

The tenor of his voice put paid to any more conversation. Within minutes they'd departed, followed closely by Axios and Callie.

My mother, the last one remaining, hurried to me, her face creased in smiles. 'It's been a wonderful day,' she said, and sighed. Then her smile turned teary. 'I can't believe my little girl is married,' she mused. 'If only your—'

'The helicopter's waiting, Mum,' I said hurriedly, before she could drop my father into the conversation. She'd agreed to enter rehab to deal with her gambling and the after-effects of my father's desertion. 'I'll see you when I get back to Athens.'

As for my father—I'd tried to block him out, the part of me that blamed him for contributing to my dire straits giving way to the bone-deep hurt caused by his abandonment and never healing. Even the mere thought of walking away from *my* baby filled me with horror. That he'd done so without a backward glance...

Aware of Neo's narrowed gaze on my face, I dredged up a wider smile, hugged my mother and watched her board the helicopter a minute later.

Then, in the dying rays of the sun, bar the dozen or so staff efficiently cleaning up, I was alone on a Greek island with the man I'd married.

The profundity of it hit me square in the chest. A quick glance showed he was still watching me. Still assessing me with those all-seeing eyes.

'The helicopter is coming back for us, right?'

His gaze grew hooded, his eyes flicking towards the aircraft that was now a speck on the horizon. 'Yes. But not till tomorrow evening.'

My heart stuttered and flipped. 'What? Why?'

'Because, as much as we both know why this event happened, I'd rather not fuel further speculation by spending what's left of my wedding day behind my desk in Athens with my new wife in tow.'

'I thought you didn't care what anyone thought?'

He turned, his hand returning to my waist as he led me back inside the sprawling villa. 'Everyone here today values discretion. Beyond the boundaries of that circle is another matter. You'll learn the difference in time,' he stated.

The quiet force behind his words seeped into me, drawing a shiver.

'You could've told me this before trapping me here,' I said, trying to summon irritation but only finding a bubble of hot excitement that swelled with each step I took inside the vast living room with Neo by my side. The potent whiff of his aftershave triggered a hunger deep inside.

'I thought you'd appreciate the peace and quiet.'

And those who didn't know better would imagine I was spending the night making love to my dynamic new husband?

The thought ramped up the heat inside me, making me grateful when Neo guided me past the grouping of sofas I'd used earlier to another set, facing endless lush greenery just beyond the sparkling pool, before dropping his hand.

'Sit down, Sadie. You'll better enjoy the sunset from this spot.' His voice was low, deep, if a little on the stiff side.

One of the wait staff approached and spoke to Neo in Greek. Without another word he walked away, his shoulders still tense.

Choosing to enjoy the temporary release from his overwhelming presence, and grateful to be off my feet, I kicked off my heels. I was smoothing down the floaty layers of delicate chiffon when a beam of sunlight caught the gems in the band on my finger. I'd been a little shell-shocked during the ceremony, but now I stared at the perfectly fitting diamond-encrusted platinum ring, a quiet sense of awe overcoming me.

I didn't need to be a jeweller to know the ring was near priceless. And I'd been stunned to see that Neo wore a similar band minus the diamonds. What was that supposed to prove? That he intended to take this role seriously, even though he was merely biding his time until his child was born? Or was it something else?

You have my word there will be no other...

My heart lurched, despite knowing I couldn't, *shouldn't* read anything into that.

I was writhing in confusion when his bold footsteps returned. I dropped my hand into my lap, sliding the weighted reminder of our wedding ceremony between the folds of chiffon just as he entered my eyeline.

He was carrying a large tray on which several platters of food had been arranged. 'You'll be so kind as not to argue with me over this again, won't you?' he enquired drolly, despite the implacable determination in his eyes.

As if he'd flipped a switch, my appetite came roaring back, the succulent scents emanating off the tray making my mouth water. 'Not this time, no.'

With a satisfied nod, he set the tray on my lap.

'I should change...'

His grey gaze swept over me, lingering at certain points

on my body, including my bare feet, and igniting the sparks higher. When his gaze returned to mine the glint had turned stormy, the sensual line of his mouth seeming fuller.

'There's no hurry. Eat first. Then I'll give you the tour.'

I polished off a portion of moussaka, then a salad with the chicken I'd rejected earlier, almost moaning at the flavours exploding on my tongue.

Keep talking. It'll dissipate the heat threatening to eat you alive.

'Earlier, you said you didn't care what anyone thought about our reasons for doing this. But you'll agree that, you being who you are, everyone's going to be curious about the woman you've married suddenly out of the blue?'

He gave a tight-lipped nod, his nostrils flaring slightly. 'They'll wonder if there's more than meets the eye. They'll wonder if you're pregnant. *How* you got pregnant.'

The food turned to sawdust in my mouth. 'You mean—'

'Certain members of my family know I can't produce children, yes.'

I pushed my tray away.

He firmly pushed the plate back in front of me. 'The deal was that you'd eat.'

For the baby's sake.

The words hung in the air between us.

I chewed. Swallowed. 'So they'll wonder if I'm a liar?'

His jaw rippled, tightened, but he shrugged. 'Only time will resolve that situation.'

Or you could believe me...

The words stuck in my throat, along with the next mouthful of food that suddenly refused to go down.

'The obvious workings of biology aside, why is it so hard for you to believe this baby is yours, Neo?' The question emerged before I could stop it.

'Because I'm not a man who accepts things at face value. Not anymore,' he said with cold precision. 'And I caution you against attempting to change that. You'll be wasting both your time and mine.'

That stark warning should have killed any softening towards him. Put me on the path back to unfeeling composure. Instead it mired me deeper in a quiet urgency to know why.

The urge was stemmed when Neo summoned a hovering staff member to clear away the tray. About to rise, I stopped, suppressing a shiver when his fingers brushed my inner arm.

'You haven't seen the sunset yet,' he murmured. 'Besides, I have something for you.'

I was torn between the stunning sunset unfolding outside and curiosity as to what he had for me. Neo won out. Only he was in no hurry. He nodded at the view.

I watched, awed, as the magnificent combination of orange, yellow and grey danced over the sparkling pool and the sea beyond, stretching across the horizon until it felt as if the whole world was bathed in splendid colour.

'It's breathtaking.'

'Yes,' he said simply.

The weight of his gaze remained as the minutes ticked by slowly and the sun dropped into the ocean. When I turned my head he was staring at me, that fierce light blazing in his eyes. My heart banged against my ribs.

To cover the flustering billowing inside, I cleared my throat. 'You mentioned a tour?'

He nodded, but didn't move. Simply reached into his breast pocket, extracted a small velvet box and prised it open. 'I should've given this to you earlier.'

The magnificent ring consisted of a large square diamond, with a red hue I'd never seen before, surrounded by two sloping tiers of smaller pure gems. The band was platinum, a perfect match to my wedding ring.

I was aware my jaw had dropped with stunned surprise, but I couldn't look away from the most beautiful piece of jewellery I'd ever seen.

'Do you like it?' he asked, his voice a little gruff.

I tore my gaze away to meet his, and was immediately trapped by a different sort of captivation. The *scorching* sort. 'Can I say I hate it, just so I don't have to wear it?'

One eyebrow rose. He was clearly surprised by my answer. 'I fail to see the logic,' he drawled.

'Wearing something like that in public is just inviting a mugging. Or worse.'

His lips twitched a tiniest fraction. 'Let me worry about that.' He held out his hand in silent command.

I hesitated. 'Neo...'

'Wear it, Sadie. It will invite less speculation. And it will please me.'

Perhaps it was the beautiful sunset and the food that had mellowed me. Perhaps this particular fight wasn't worth it because there was no downside to wearing one more ring when I'd already accepted another, binding me to this dynamic man who made my insides twist with forbidden yearning when I should have been shoring up my barriers at every turn.

I gave him my hand.

The act of Neo sliding another ring onto my finger felt vastly intimate, much too visceral. So much so, I'd stopped breathing by the time the band was tucked securely next to its counterpart. And was even more lightheaded when he wrapped his fingers possessively around mine and tugged me up.

'You won't need them,' he rasped, when I went to slip my feet back in my shoes.

He led me to the south wing, where every bedroom and salon was a lavish masterpiece of white and silver and more stunning than the last, and where a private cinema, study and wine cellar were filled to the brim with extravagances only obscenely wealthy men like Neo could afford.

The north wing contained fewer rooms, mainly an immense private living room dividing two master suites. Both suites were bordered by a tennis-court-sized terrace which housed a smaller semi-enclosed version of the swimming pool downstairs.

The urge to dip my bare toes into the sparkling water was too irresistible. I gave in, gasping in delight, only to look up to find Neo's gaze locked on my mouth.

He didn't look away.

Slowly, heat built to an inferno between us. Until that breathlessness invaded again, threatening to drive me to the edge of my sanity.

I stepped back from the pool, hoping to restore a level head. Because sex wasn't part of our bargain. It was the mind-altering drug that had led us here in the first place.

'So, does this island have a name?' I asked as he slowly advanced.

'Neostros,' he supplied, without taking his hooded gaze from me.

'You named your island after *yourself*? How...narcissistic.'

He shrugged off my words. 'More like the other way around. My grandfather bought this place long before I was born and he named it. My parents were vacationing here when my mother went into labour. I was born in one of the houses on the other side of the island.'

That glimpse into his early life made me yearn for more.

'Is your grandfather still alive?'

His face closed up, but not before a flash of twisted pain and bitterness marred his expression. 'No. He died of a heart attack as a direct result of attempting to dig his family out of hard times.'

Looking around me, seeing unfettered opulence at every turn, it was hard to believe that any Xenakis had ever experienced a minute's hardship. 'Hard times? How?'

Again his mouth twisted cynically. 'Another unfortunate example of someone wanting something more than they deserved. In this case it was my grandfather's overambitious business partner. He ran the business into the ground, then left my grandfather to pick up the pieces—but not before extending to him a business loan with crippling interest rates. The strain was too much for him. It broke my grandmother first. After she died... Well, it broke him.'

'From what I can tell, you come from a very large family. Didn't anyone step up to help?'

Neo lifted his hand and caught up a curl of my hair that had come loose. For a long moment I thought he wouldn't answer me, that he intended his intimate caress to swell higher between us until we drowned from it.

When his eyes eventually met mine, residual bitterness lingered, but the heat had grown. 'I don't want to talk about my family anymore. As you can see, someone did step up. Ax and I did what needed to be done to get back what we'd lost. But in doing so we were reminded over and over again that greed and avarice will push people into deplorable behaviour to the exclusion of all decency.'

I opened my mouth to refute it. His fingers left my hair to brush over my lips, stopping my words before I could speak them.

'If you seek to convince me otherwise...again, Sadie, I urge you to save your breath.'

He's showing you his true colours. Believe him.

'So you choose to operate from a position of bitterness and cynicism?'

A hard light glinted in his eyes momentarily before his expression grew shrewd, almost calculating. 'Don't you? Tell me what happened with your father.'

The sudden switch sent a cold shock wave through me. 'What?'

'You take pains to avoid discussing him even though he's alive. And I've deduced that he's a major reason for your mother's troubles. Why the secrecy? What did he do to you?'

I firmed my lips, refusing to be drawn into the painful

subject. But he'd answered my questions, even though it had been clear he didn't want to discuss it.

'Up until I was sixteen? Absolutely nothing. He was a decent father and I guess a good enough husband—I never heard my parents argue or even disagree about anything major.'

Neo frowned. 'What changed?'

'I came home from school one day to find my mother sobbing hysterically. When she calmed down enough to be coherent she handed me a postcard my father had sent from Venezuela. Only problem was, he was supposed to be on a business trip to Ireland.'

Strangling pain gripped my chest, stopped the flow of words for a moment. Neo's fingers trailed down my jaw to rest on my shoulder and, as weakening as it was, I took comfort from the warmth of his hand—enough to finish the sorry little tale of how my family had broken apart with a few scrawled lines on a cheery little exotic postcard.

'He basically said he didn't want to be married anymore. Didn't want to be a father, and he was never coming back. He'd already instructed his lawyers to file divorce papers. What he didn't warn us about was the fact that he hadn't kept up with the mortgage payments for over six months. Or that he'd cleared out their joint bank account. I was still absorbing the news when the bailiffs turned up two hours later with a court order and threw us out of our home.'

Neo cursed under his breath. 'Where did you go?'

'My mother had some savings. Enough to rent us a flat for a year. It would probably have gone further if...' I stopped, fresh shame and the raw anguish of laying myself bare halting my words.

His hand curled around my shoulder. 'If your mother's gambling problems hadn't started?'

I nodded. 'I got a part-time job, which lessened the financial burden. But Mum's depression grew, and she couldn't hold down a job. I think you get the picture of how things panned out eventually.'

'Did you ever hear from your father? Did he give a reason?'

Anguish welled high, consuming my insides. 'No. He stuck to his word and cut off all ties.'

Neo's lips flattened and his eyes bored into mine with a knowing look. 'So the facts speak for themselves. Wasn't he a senior-level banker?' he asked, shocking me anew with the depth of his knowledge about my life.

'Yes.'

'So he had the type of job that demanded respectability. He was fiercely competitive and ambitious, in a high-pressure job that often required cut-throat ruthlessness. Having a wife and child and a seemingly stable home served his purpose. Most likely got him up the rungs of his corporate ambition.'

'You're not telling me anything I don't know, Neo. Yes, my mother and I were just accessories he used while it suited him, then threw away when he was done. So?'

A tic rippled in his jaw, even as his thumb drew slow circles on my shoulder. Did he even know he was doing that?

'So face the facts.'

Unable to stand the waves of anguish, and that need to lean into his caress, I tugged myself out of his hold.

'Is that some sort of warning, Neo?' Had he sensed that occasional misjudged softening? Was this his way of mitigating it?

'Sadie—'

'Enough. Whatever it is you're trying to prove, save your breath. I know what type of person my father was. What type of person you are. There's no illusion on my part.'

His face tightened and he opened his mouth—most likely to challenge me.

'It's been a long day, Neo. I'd like to go to bed, if you don't mind.'

The glint in his eyes morphed, attaining that hooded, sensual potency that sparked every nerve ending to life. But with that spark came greater warning. An edging closer to that dangerous precipice of longing and softening. Wondering if that ring on his finger meant more than simple evidence of the transaction he'd brokered.

'It's your wedding night, Sadie. Surely you wish to make it a little more memorable than simply retiring to your bed at a few minutes past sunset?'

The weighted question started my heart thudding to a different beat.

'You've been at pains to remind me that this marriage is for the sake of the child I'm carrying. How I spend my time tonight is really none of your business.'

He inhaled slowly, and that animalistic aura wrapped tighter around me. 'Perhaps I wish to make it my business.'

I was struggling to stop my pulse from leaping wildly at that statement when his fingers returned to my throat, their sensual caress enthralling, like a magician conjuring up the most delicious trick.

But wasn't this an illusion? A dream from which I'd wake to disappointment?

With monumental effort I pulled away. 'We agreed that sex wasn't part of this bargain. It's an agreement I intend to stick to. Goodnight, Neo.'

I hurried away, my footsteps stumbling at the dark promise in the heavy gaze on my back. The gaze that compelled me to slow down, turn around, find out if he really meant it. If this wedding night following a wedding borne of facility could be something else.

CHAPTER EIGHT

WHITE.

She needed to wear white every day for the rest of her life.

She was walking away from me, her ethereal dress floating about her like the purest cloud, and all I could think about was how enthralling she looked in white.

Sure, I was irritated. Unsettled by that conversation about her father. By her accusation that I wanted to hurt her by making her face the truth. I knew firsthand the consequences of burying your head in the sand.

In that moment none of it mattered except the way her hair shone like a living, breathing flame against the delicate white lace.

Maddeningly arousing.

Everything about this woman I'd married was temptation personified, urging the unschooled man closer. But I was well schooled in the sort of temptation she offered. And, as I'd accurately guessed, granting her wishes had in turn given me what I wanted.

Like Anneka and every woman I'd known, all that mattered to her was getting what she wanted in the end. I didn't doubt that if I was minded to strike another bargain she would accede to my wish to see her clad in white morning, noon and night.

Or perhaps even nothing at all?

The erection straining behind my fly cursed me for agreeing to the *no sex* rule. Why had I? Because in that moment, binding her to me in any way at all had been paramount?

My dealings with women after my failed engagement and the betrayal that followed had taught me one thing. Sex was only complicated when the parameters weren't set out explicitly. Sadie had proved herself a good negotiator. So why not negotiate on this too?

The thought of experiencing her again, of having her beneath me, that breathtaking face turned up to receive my kisses and that body between my hands, mine to pleasure and take pleasure in, powered me several steps after her before I caught myself. Stopped to stare down at the unusual weight of the band circling my finger.

The symbolism wasn't as easy to dismiss as I thought. I had a wife. One whom I suddenly felt a desperate need to bed.

No, not a sudden need. The lust I thought I'd dulled after that first time in my office had been building since she'd turned up in Athens. Since that potent realisation that she could be carrying my child.

Call me primitive, but the thought that I'd sowed a seed in her womb, against all the odds my doctors were still examining after new tests undertook last week, filled me with a sense of... *possession* I hadn't been able to shake.

I twisted the band around my finger. Would it be so unthinkable to strike another bargain, stake my true claim?

Yes, it would. Because that was the kind of bargain that came with a steep price. The Anneka-shaped kind that left only bitterness and regret in its wake.

I turned, heading away from the direction she'd taken.

Three hours later I was still pacing my suite, the tablet laid out with marketing reports and projections to be analysed abandoned in favour of fighting temptation. Fighting the invasion of Sadie Preston...no, Sadie *Xenakis*... in my brain.

And failing.

With an impatient grunt, I slid open the French doors, stepped onto the private terrace. The breeze cooled my skin but did nothing to alleviate the pressure in my groin demanding relief.

A full moon was reflected on a smooth, serene sea, a

picture of calm in direct opposition to the sensations roiling inside me.

Not only were Sadie's words echoing in my head, other observations about her kept intruding, grating like tiny pebbles on my otherwise smooth and solid belief system. Her reluctance to leave that dingy little flat. Her resistance to the lavishness and extravagance of the wedding planning, when most brides would have been rapturous at having an unlimited budget.

Most of all, her complete lack of concern that she'd be walking away with less than one percent of my wealth when I ended this marriage. That clause in the prenup had been deliberate. A ruthless little test she'd batted away without so much as a quibble.

And her bemusement when I brought it up... It had been so...*different*.

But was I seeing what I wanted to see? Repeating the same misjudgement I'd shown when I'd dismissed Anneka's obvious signs of infidelity and shameless avarice in favour of claiming the child she'd sworn was mine?

Restless feet propelled me towards the sound of water. To the pool Sadie had dipped her dainty feet in earlier, triggering awareness of yet another part of her body I found enthralling.

Thoughts of her feet evaporated when I was confronted by the more erotic vision rising from the moonlit pool.

Her back was to me, the tips of her fingers trailing through the water, and her gaze on the view as she moved towards the shallow end. She'd obviously been submerged moments before, because her hair was wet and pearlescent drops of water clung to her flawless skin.

Another few steps and the water dropped below her heart-shaped behind, revealed the bottom half of a white bikini moulding her curves and stopping my breath.

Thee mou, but I loved her in white...

The sizzling thought froze in my mind when she turned

fully to face the view, presenting me with her magnificent profile. If she'd looked spectacular before, now she was a bewitching goddess. At just over three months pregnant her shape hadn't altered profoundly, but signs of her state were visible in specific areas.

Her belly held the slightest curve and her breasts, lush and mouth-watering before, were fuller, more ripe. My palms burned with the need to cup them, to taste them.

A growl broke free from my throat before I could stop it.

She whirled around, one hand holding that rope of hair I wanted to wrap around my own wrist.

'Neo! I... I thought you were...'

'Asleep?' Hell, was that growly mess my voice?

She nodded a little jerkily, her gaze running over my body as I approached. Did her gaze linger below my belt? The throb there grew more insistent, propelling me even closer to the edge of the pool.

'Did I disturb you?' she asked.

'I couldn't sleep. And from the looks of it neither could you.'

A pulse leapt at her throat as her gaze travelled over me once more, her lips parting as she saw the unmistakable evidence of my arousal.

'Was I right? Does this night feel too...extraordinary to waste on sleep?'

Her head tilted up, her smooth throat bared to my hungry gaze as she swallowed. 'I don't know about extraordinary, but it's not every day a woman gets married. Or it could be I'm just getting used to this place—'

'It's not that and we both know it,' I interrupted, almost too keen to have her acknowledge what was happening.

She stared up at me, her breathing beautifully erratic, her face worshipped by moonbeams. Her fingers continued to twist that rope of hair. The whole picture of potent wantonness shattered another layer of my control.

I wanted to grab. To devour. To claim with a thoroughness that guaranteed we'd taste blissful insanity.

'Are you going to stay in there all night or are you done, Sadie?'

She shrugged lazily, drawing my attention to those decadent drops of water on her shoulder.

Two steps back and I snagged a warm towel. Held it out. 'Come out, Sadie.'

Exquisite defiance tilted her chin, long enough for me to feel the weight of her mutiny.

'Is that an order? Because, newsflash, I'm not in a mood to obey.'

We stayed like that, her gaze daring me. Then she turned her back, dived back under the water and swam two more lengths. Only then did she get out and approach me. Eyes on mine, she placed one foot on the shallow step. Then another.

Her full breasts swayed with her movement, her hips sashaying in hypnotic motions that drove spikes of lust deeper. With every inch of the body she exposed, my hunger trebled.

Wrapping the towel around her was a perfunctory move to enfold her within my arms. The smile tilting her lips screamed her triumph, stated she was in my arms because *she* wanted it.

When she wrapped her slim arms around my neck, I barely stopped myself from growling again. 'You want to know why I'm not in my bed? Why I'm out here, shattering my concentration even further and seeking peace of mind I know I won't find?'

Her gaze dropped from mine to lock on my lips.

'Because I do this to you,' she stated sultrily, rocking herself against my hardness in a way that left no doubt as to my state.

'Because you tempt me more than I've ever been tempted in my life.' I laughed, despite myself. Or perhaps because of the singular thought that it was no use fighting this. That

I didn't even want to. 'Despite my every reserve, I hunger for you.'

She inhaled, sharp and sweet, her pink tongue flicking out to swipe across her lower lip.

I captured it, bit her sensitive flesh in punishment for the cyclone of need it had created in me. When she moaned, I deepened the caress, slanted my lips over hers, claimed that mouth and satisfied a fraction of that hunger, even while it continued to rage out of control.

Tentatively, her tongue darted out to meet mine, and I took possession of it, gliding and tasting in an erotic dance I wanted to repeat all over her naked body. Especially that snug, glorious place between her legs.

Finally, I speared my fingers into the heavy mass of her damp hair to tilt her face higher, drive my kiss deeper. When she opened wider for me I couldn't stop my groan of pure satisfaction.

'Your hair is a work of art, *pethi mou*. Simply exquisite.'

'Neo…'

I backed us up a few steps, until the terrace wall met her back and the soft cushion of her body moulded my front.

'And this mouth. *Christos*, you have the most divine mouth,' I confessed, rediscovering that sensitive spot in her neck where her pulse throbbed before returning to reclaim her mouth. 'I haven't been able to stop thinking about kissing you since that unsatisfactory sampling at the altar.'

My free hand slid down her body, stopping briefly to mould one plump, mouth-watering breast, before travelling lower, to cup her hot feminine centre.

'Haven't stopped thinking about this special place either. Imagining you wrapped tight around me again, taking me inside you.'

She whimpered against my lips. 'I… I shouldn't be doing this,' she murmured, almost to herself.

And I shouldn't crave you this much. And yet here I am…

Through the damp material of the bikini bottom I caressed her, my thumb circling that engorged bead I craved to have between my lips. When the need grew beyond containment I slipped my fingers beneath the stretchy fabric. Touched her where I needed to touch her.

Her knees sagged and she whimpered again. Muttered words against my lips I was too incoherent to absorb.

Which was why it took a moment to realise that the hand curled around my wrist, and the other flat against my chest, were both attempting to push me away.

'Neo…we can't…'

The protest was feeble, the look on her face as I drew back a touch torn between hunger and rebellion.

I fought the voracious need gripping me and started to withdraw my hand.

Her thighs clamped around it, holding me prisoner.

'You say we can't while looking at me with yearning in your eyes. Your body clings to mine while you deny me what I want. What we both want. You think I don't feel how wet you are for me, Sadie?'

Heat rushed into her face. Her thighs parted with an abrupt jerk and she swiftly dropped her hands. 'This… It's just chemistry.'

'There's no such thing as "just chemistry." Especially not when it's this powerful. When it creates this response.'

My gaze dropped tellingly to the tight furling of her nipples, clearly visible against the damp bikini top.

'It means nothing,' she protested. 'Besides, sex is what got us here in the first place!'

The cold compress of her words washed away a layer of blazing arousal. 'And it's a place you don't wish to be? Is that it?'

'Don't put words in my mouth. I may not have been prepared for this baby but I've vowed to give it the best life possible. That doesn't mean I want to mess up my life with sex. So if you're looking for a way to scratch your itch you'll…'

She stopped, her throat moving as she swallowed her words.

'I'll what, Sadie?'

She shook her head, sending wet tendrils flying. I caught a strand, tucking it behind one ear. Her pulse jumped beneath my touch.

'You can't say the words, can you?' I taunted, deriving a little devilish satisfaction from it. 'Did you fool yourself into thinking giving me liberties I didn't want would be easy?'

She turned her face to the side, avoiding my gaze. 'I don't know what you're talking about.'

My grating laughter earned me a ferocious glare. I caressed her cheek, unable to resist touching her even now. 'Do you not? Really? Then let me posit a theory. Perhaps this marriage isn't as clinical as you wish it to be? Perhaps this itch you speak of isn't a one-sided thing?'

Watching her gather her frayed composure was a thing of unwanted awe.

'I'm a grown woman, Neo. With independent thoughts and needs I can choose to indulge or deny. While the last few minutes have been pleasant, it's not worth sullying my life for. So, no, the itch will remain a one-sided thing and no amount of temptation will sway me. Goodnight.'

For the second time I watched her walk away from me, leaving even more chaos behind. Acknowledging that I wanted her much more than I'd wanted any other woman in my life, that I might never have her, disarmed me enough to leave me propped up against the wall long after she and her voluptuous curves and her stubborn defiance had disappeared behind her suite doors.

But when the realisation hit that I, Neo Xenakis, was being denied a woman's attention for the first time in my life, I surged away from that wall, determined to rid myself of this...infernal need.

A teeth-gritting, bracing cold shower restored a little sanity. But with sanity came the acknowledgement that perhaps I hadn't bargained as well as I'd thought for what I wanted.

Because what I wanted was...*more*.

And nothing drove home that realisation harder than the first prenatal scan just days later.

When I heard the strong, powerful heartbeat of my child for the first time.

I couldn't look away from the unrestrained stamp of possession on Neo's face and that flash of uncertainty and apprehension as he stared at the monitor. I might have serious doubts as to his motives in other things, but in this I couldn't dismiss the strength of his feelings. But were they positive? Or calculated?

As the doctor took measurements and studiously recorded details, Neo's gaze drifted feverishly over my face, then down my body to latch onto my belly.

'*Dikos mou,*' he murmured, with even more fervour than he had two days ago.

Mine.

That proclamation moved something in me, and I was glad for the echo of my baby's heartbeat otherwise I was sure he'd have heard my own thundering heart.

Would it be the end of the world to give in to this unrelenting craving?

The thought wasn't easy to dispel, especially now, when he leaned closer, his body bracing mine on the king-sized bed.

Like a flower reaching for the sun, my every cell strained for him, defiantly ignoring my inner protests.

It was almost a relief when the doctor finished the scan and printed off two copies, which Neo immediately took possession of, sliding one into his wallet and handing me the other.

When I reached for it he held on to it for a moment, his eyes pinning mine as his fingers brushed my skin. Something heavy and intense fired up in his eyes—something that should have sent apprehension dancing down my spine but instead left molten heat in my belly, my heartbeat fast enough to match my baby's.

The moment passed.

After Neo's rapid-fire questions provided reassurance that the baby was healthy, the doctor and his technician were dismissed and Neo turned to me.

'How do you feel?' he asked.

'Well enough to start work.'

His mouth compressed and I geared myself for another disagreement.

'The morning sickness has passed?'

I nodded. 'It stopped about a week ago.'

His gaze returned to my belly, stayed for fevered seconds. 'Very well. We'll leave in half an hour.' With brisk strides, he left the room.

I rose, spinning slowly in place, still awed by my surroundings. By the size of the bedroom that would easily fit my previous home twice over. Not to mention the dressing room.

I approached the large, cavernous room decked from floor to ceiling in wood, and tastefully arranged into sections for shoes, handbags, day and evening wear.

Last night, when the helicopter landed in the exclusive neighbourhood of Voula, minutes from the centre of Athens, I'd been too overwhelmed by the hour spent in close proximity to Neo to appreciate the opulence of his tiered mansion.

Unsurprisingly, every square inch dripped with luxury. Cream with grey-veined marble and hues of dark blue and grey was the theme running through each room. Set into its own vast exclusive hillside, it overlooked a miles-long vista, with the Acropolis the jaw-dropping centre of attraction.

The staff of six spoke impeccable English, and after I'd dressed, the housekeeper directed me to Neo's study.

My knock was answered in deep, crisp tones. When I entered his gaze was hooded, loaded with the sort of heavy speculation and calculation that sent another wave of sensation over my skin.

I'd walked away on Saturday night believing that I'd ended that dangerous episode before it had blown up. But with each look, I got the uncanny sensation that we weren't done. That Neo's machinations were merely gathering pace.

Which made walking beside him on the way to his underground garage a monumental task in composure keeping for me. But once we were seated in the black Maserati, the powerful engine speeding us through early-morning traffic, he was all business.

He indicated the stylish briefcase in the footwell next to my feet. 'The briefcase is yours—so is the tablet inside it. I've loaded three marketing reports on it. I want your thoughts on them by midday.'

I grabbed the case, hung on to it as if it would dilute his effect on me.

It didn't even come close.

Our previous interactions had given me a taster of Neo's power, but my introduction to his corporate life provided a mind-bending main course of the sheer formidable force he wielded. For example, the middle-aged woman I'd encountered in his office months ago was one of six assistants poised to answer his every demand.

And his first demand was to have her summon his top marketing executives into his office, where I was introduced as his wife and personal intern—a statement that garnered speculation and brought a warm flush to my face.

But it was his second demand—that I be set up in one corner of his vast office—that drew a protest from me. 'Aren't you worried about whispers of nepotism?'

One eyebrow lifted. 'Not even a little bit,' he tossed away. At my frown he added, 'I don't intend to make this an easy ride for you, Sadie. But by all means, if you're worried about it, then prove them wrong.'

***

In the three dizzying weeks that followed it was impossible not to meet that challenge, to smash it to pieces. Because, while Neo was maddeningly rabid in ensuring I was provided with mouth-watering meals at precise intervals during the day, that my prenatal vitamins were taken like clockwork and my every comfort was catered for, business-wise he was a slave-driver—often lounging back in his thronelike seat while firing questions at me from across the room. He tossed every menial marketing task at me, barely letting me catch my breath before the next project landed on my desk.

And when he wasn't doing that, his gaze rested on me with molten, unapologetic interest.

It was on one such occasion, when I was feeling mellowed from a client's high praise of a marketing analysis I'd put together, that I caught his gaze on me as I rose from my desk.

'What are you thinking?' I asked, before I could curb my curiosity.

The question seemed to startle him. Then his long lashes swept over me. 'White.'

'Pardon me?'

'White suits you. You should wear only that from now on.'

An anticipatory shiver fired through me, because he'd just tossed one of his imperious observations at me. And, oh, how I'd relish batting it away.

'Is this where you say "Jump" and hope I'll say, "Yes, sir…how high do you wish, sir?"'

For some absurd reason his lips twitched with amusement. 'I'd say yes, but we both know you'd never do anything that accommodating. Not without something in return, at least.'

A pang of hurt caught me unawares.

His gaze sharpened on my face, then he grew irritated.

'That was meant to be a compliment, Sadie, not a prelude to a fight. You look beautiful in white.'

'Is that why my wardrobe is suddenly full of white stuff?' The predominantly white outfits had appeared suddenly, with no explanation offered.

He shrugged. 'I was told you didn't seem interested in the whole clothes-shopping process back in London. I made the choice for you. If I was wildly inaccurate, then feel free to amend it.'

Mutiny rose and died almost as soon as my fingers drifted over the soft white cotton dress I'd picked for the office today. The boat-necked A-line design draped over my body without clinging, cleverly disguising the small swell of my belly. And, like this dress, every item in my new wardrobe was a perfect fit.

'It's okay, I suppose.'

He inclined his head in an imperious nod, but not before I caught a look of...*relief*?

Before I could be sure, he was rising, messing with my breathing as he sauntered around to perch on the edge of his desk.

'Come here, Sadie,' he commanded, his voice gravel rough.

'Why?'

His eyes shadowed. 'Because it's time to go over the final details before our meeting,' he said easily.

I wasn't fooled. The fierce gleam in his eye announced other intentions.

But, unable to resist that hypnotic voice, I stumbled over to him. He caught my hips between his hands, positioning me between his spread legs, and as he stared down into my face I struggled to catch my breath. And then the most wondrous thing happened.

I felt the sweetest, most delicate tingling in my belly.

'Oh!'

His gaze sharpened. 'What is it?'

'I just felt...'

Raw, thick emotion arrested his face. 'The baby?'

The hushed gravity of his voice, the depth of yearning in his voice, disarmed me.

'According to all indications you *should* be experiencing the first movements of my child inside you,' he rasped.

'I thought I felt something...a flutter yesterday...but it hasn't happened again—' The fluttering came again, making me gasp. 'Oh!'

His gaze dropped to my belly, and his hand slowly lowered to hover over the small bump. 'I would very much like to touch you, Sadie,' he said, his voice gravel rough.

Shakily fighting back hormonal tears, I nodded. He exhaled raggedly, his warm hand remaining on me for long moments, during which the fluttering was repeated twice more, each time drawing from him an awed gasp.

Stormy eyes rose to mine. 'I said you looked beautiful. That wasn't quite accurate. You look radiant.' One hand rose to caress my cheek. 'Your skin glows with exquisite vitality. I've never quite seen anything like it.'

'It's...it's the pregnancy. Not me.'

'Most women would wholeheartedly bask in such a compliment, but not you,' he murmured, his gaze curiously flummoxed. 'Are you so determined to topple my opinion of you?' he rasped, a touch disgruntled.

'Neo—'

'Hush, *pethi mou*. Let us enjoy this moment,' he suggested, his voice hypnotic.

We stood trapped in that intensely soul-stirring bubble until the ringing phone made us both jump. I hastily stepped back from the exposing moment.

Back to a reality where this pregnancy was the sole reason I had a ring on my finger and a place in Neo's office.

Back to a place where the softening emotions that had been expanding over the past few weeks needed to be shoved back into a box marked *delusional*.

When he reached over to answer his phone I escaped, reciting every reason why resisting temptation and Neo was essential to my equilibrium.

When I returned, half an hour later, Neo's laser-beam eyes focused on the frosted treat in my hand. 'What's that?'

I raised an eyebrow. 'It's a cupcake, Neo.'

'I can see that. I meant *that*.' He pointed his arrogant nose at the thin candle perched in the middle of the frosting.

'It's a candle. Which I'm going to light when I get to my desk and then blow out. Because it's my birthday.'

He went pillar still. 'What did you say?'

'I said it's my birthday today.'

His eyes narrowed. 'If this is a ploy of some sort—'

'You think I'd bother to lie about something you can find out in less than ten seconds?'

The fire and brimstone left his eyes immediately, leaving him looking curiously nonplussed.

'Wow. So much for me thinking felicitations might be forthcoming,' I said.

My waspish tone further unnerved him. Then his lips firmed.

'You scurried away before we were done talking. You do realise you're not doing yourself any favours by annoying me, don't you?'

I shrugged. 'I'm here now, and I don't see a fire, so…'

His eyes widened a fraction, then I caught a hint of amusement. Again I had the feeling that the mighty Neo Xenakis liked being challenged.

Striding over, he took the cupcake from me, set it on my desk and took my hand.

'What are you doing? And, more importantly, why are you separating me from my cupcake?'

He frowned, or least gave an impression of it. But it fell far short of his overriding expression—bewilderment. Perhaps even a little shame.

'You asked where the fire was. Our meeting has been rescheduled to now.'

'What? But—'

'You helped the team land the deal that has brought the Portuguese trade minister here. I don't think you'll want to keep him waiting while you devour a dubious-looking confection from a vending machine.'

'It wasn't from a vending machine. It was from your executive restaurant, which is manned by a chef I hear is on the brink of winning his first Michelin star.'

He simply shrugged and kept moving while he extracted his phone from his pocket. Rapid-fire Greek greeted whoever answered the call, after which he held open the door to the conference room with one eyebrow hiked up.

'You know there's a rule against keeping a pregnant woman from what she craves, don't you?'

My words had been meant harshly. Instead they emerged in a sultry undertone, wrapped in a yearning that was only partly for the cupcake he'd forced me to abandon.

And if I had any doubt that my words had triggered the same thought in him, the darkening of his eyes and the slight parting of his sensual mouth told me we'd skated away from the subject of cupcakes to something more potent.

'I will bear the consequences of it this once,' he rasped, his voice an octave lower. Deeper.

Sexier.

My gaze dropped to the sensual line of his lips and I sucked in a breath.

'The minister is waiting, Sadie. As much as I want to answer that look in your eyes, it won't do for me to start making love to my wife in full view of a potential business associate.'

My wife.

It was the first time he'd referred to me as that since the wedding...

The two-hour meeting passed in a rush of effectively

troubleshooting every last one of the minister's objections. While the team acted in perfect cohesion, Neo seemed intent on lobbing further questions for me to answer, giving a satisfied nod when I did.

Perhaps he wanted to give me a chance to prove my worth, to publicly expunge any hint of nepotism once and for all. Whatever the reason, it left me with a warm, buoyant glow that shrivelled the hard knot of unworthiness that had clung to me and drew a wide smile once the minister left, satisfied.

Perhaps my smile was too wide. Too proud. It certainly triggered something in Neo, and his stride was purposeful as he marched me from the conference room.

'I hate to repeat myself, but where's the fire?' I asked.

'I'm giving you the rest of the day off,' he declared.

'I can't take time off *and* finish the work you've asked me to do.'

He merely shrugged as he stepped with me into the lift and pressed the button for the parking garage, where a valet stood next to his car, keys ready.

'Change of plan,' Neo said, once I was seated and he'd slid behind the wheel. 'There's an event I need you to attend with me tonight.'

'Oh? Do you want to tell me about it so I can prepare?'

While the thought of working on my birthday hadn't disheartened me, because working with Neo was a secret thrill I wouldn't pass up, I wasn't sure I wanted to be thrown into the deep end of an unknown situation.

'Preparation won't be necessary,' he said cryptically. 'But dress formally.'

For the rest of the journey back to the villa he fell into silence, his profile not inviting conversation.

Inside, he excused himself, shutting his study door behind him with a definitive click.

I retreated to my dressing room to face the daunting task of picking what to wear. Eventually, I chose a white gown made of the softest tulle layered over satin. The gathered material swept down from one shoulder and cupped my bust before falling away in a long, elegant sweep to my ankles. I complemented it with light, champagne-coloured strappy heels and a matching clutch, and left my earlobes and throat free—simply because the jewellery I owned was too understated for the gown, and because I still had no clear idea of where Neo was taking me.

As if I'd conjured him up, his firm knock arrived.

I opened the door and suppressed a gasp.

His business suit had been swapped for a dinner suit, a dark silk shirt, a darker-hued tie and bespoke shoes polished to within an inch of their life. With his freshly showered hair slicked back, and his face and that cleft in his chin thrown into relief, it was all I could do to not stare open-mouthed at the overwhelmingly dashing figure he cut.

His return scrutiny was electric, his eyes turning a skin-tingling stormy grey as they sizzled over my body. 'You look exquisite,' he pronounced, managing to sound arrogant and awed at the same time.

The combination melted me from the inside out, and my heart was pounding even before he held out his arm in silent invitation.

I slid my hand into the crook of his elbow, concentrated in putting one foot in front of the other as he led me not to the garage but out through the wide living room doors and down another terrace towards the helipad.

He helped me into the sleek aircraft, then strapped himself in.

'Are you going to tell me where we're going?' I asked.

He slanted me a lazy, shiver-inducing glance. 'You'll see for yourself in a few minutes.'

The aircraft lifted off, flew straight towards the horizon for a full minute, then started to descend again. When it banked slightly to the right to land, I saw it.

The Acropolis.

Lit to magnificent perfection, it was a breathtaking sight to behold. 'We're meeting the client *here*?'

Neo simply gave an enigmatic smile, deftly alighted when the aircraft set down, and held out his hand to me. I'd been in Athens long enough to know that tours took place both day and night. But there was no one around—just a handful of dark-suited men, one of whom looked suspiciously like... *Wendell*.

A sharp glance at Neo showed that enigmatic expression still in place.

My heart thundered harder.

At the Parthenon, I wanted to linger, the beauty surrounding me demanding appreciation. But Neo's fingers tightened.

'You can have a private tour later, if you wish. But not now.'

I discovered why minutes later, felt something sacred break away and hand itself over to Neo without my approval or permission. Because there was no event. No client. Just an elaborately laid candle-lit table set for two in the middle of the Temple of Athena Nike.

Emotion, far too delicate and precious for this man who could be in equal parts hard and bitter and magnetic, swelled inside me. 'Neo, why are we here?'

He stepped forward, drew back my chair. 'You helped land a very big deal for Xenakis today. An achievement worth celebrating,' he said.

And as that warm bubble of *worthiness* expanded inside me, he added, 'Plus, it's your birthday.'

My throat clogged, dangerously happy emotions brimming.

'I spoke to your mother's counsellor at the rehab centre. She didn't think it would be wise to grant dispensation for your birthday. *Syngnómi.* I'm sorry.'

'It's fine. I'm just glad she's getting the help she needs.'

Deep down, while I'd have loved to share this moment

with her, I was selfishly glad I had this all to myself. That I had Neo all to myself, as unwise as the thought was.

It took a few minutes for the shock to wear off, to grasp the fact that he'd had the tours shut down, had his executive chef prepare a sublime meal and transported it to this incredible place. All in a handful of hours.

The impact of his actions threatened to drown me in dangerous emotion. The kind that prompted yearnings that would never be fulfilled. The kind that led to restless, need-filled nights.

In a bid to put some distance between myself and those feelings, I glanced at pillars that whispered with history. 'Was Athena Nike not a fertility goddess?'

Neo inclined his head, his gaze brooding. 'Which makes this location apt, does it not?'

A blush crept into my cheeks, and when his gaze lingered boldly, heat spread fast and hard over my body.

Easy conversation flowed between us as we ate. And when the pièce de résistance was wheeled out—an enormous cupcake-shaped birthday cake, with a single candle set into the pink frosting—I fought back tears as Neo took my hand and led me to it.

'You made a wish?' His tone suggested the idea was alien to him.

'I did. Something wrong with that?' I asked when an involuntary muscle clenched in his jaw.

'Wishes are useless. Reality is what matters.'

Bruising hurt launched itself into my chest. 'It's my birthday. I'm one hundred percent sure you're not allowed to rain on my birthday parade.'

He stared at me for a long spell. Then nodded abruptly. '*Ne*, I'm not. What I *can* do is give you your birthday gift.'

From his pocket, he pulled a sleek, oblong box. Before he could open it, I laid my hand over his.

'I don't need a present, Neo. This...' I waved my hand at the setting '...is more than enough.'

He blithely ignored me and flicked the box open.

Inside nestled a gorgeous necklace. Fiery ruby stones battled with sparkling diamonds for radiance. I couldn't help my gasp.

'You might not want a gift, but it's yours nevertheless,' he stated, in that absolute manner I'd come to accept was simply his nature.

'And you want me to take it because it will please you?' I semi-mocked, using his words from before.

He shook his head. 'Because it will look beautiful on you. Because the rubies match your sensational hair and it would be a shame to keep this thing in a box.'

The compliments burrowed deep inside me, disarming me long enough for him to fasten the necklace, step back and boldly admire it.

'You have a thing for my hair, don't you?' I said.

Expecting a mocking comeback, my heart flipped over when raw need tightened his face.

Before I could draw a breath he was capturing my shoulders, dragging me against his body. 'I have a thing for *you*, Sadie. For all of you,' he breathed, right before his head swooped down.

Helpless to deny the hunger which had been building inside me for weeks, I surged onto my toes and met his fiery kiss. Sensation went from one to one hundred in the space of a heartbeat. In a tangle of limbs we grappled to get closer, to kiss deeper, to sate an insatiable need.

When an abstract sense of propriety finally drove us apart, we were both breathing harshly, and Neo's face was a taut mask of arousal. His hands continued to roam over my body, stoking need, until I feared my heart would bang clean out of my ribcage.

Lips parted in stunned surprise, I watched him sink to his knees, frame my hips between his hands, before leaning forward to kiss the swell of my belly. When he rose again, his eyes churned with thunder and lightning, his hands trailing fire when he cupped my nape and angled my face to his.

'I want you, Sadie. Naked. In my bed, beneath me. Think of the sublime pleasure I can give you and give in to me,' he coaxed, his fingers caressing my throat.

My knees sagged, the heady words finding their target and weakening my resolve. I scrambled hard for it. Because when it came right down to it, what Neo was offering was great sex. But still only sex.

I wanted more. Much more than I'd even allowed myself to dream of.

It was that very monumental need that made me shake my head. 'I can't. Not for a quick tumble that will simply complicate things. Besides, this isn't part of our agreement.'

And it's not enough for me.

His face slowly hardened. 'Be careful, Sadie, that you don't box yourself into a corner you'll regret.'

Those cryptic words stayed with me long after we'd returned to the villa. Long after he'd bade me a curt goodnight and left me at the door of my suite.

Undressing, I caught sight of myself in the mirror and gasped, the effect of the spectacular necklace freezing me in place. I couldn't help but appreciate its beauty. Appreciate the compliments Neo had paid me. Dwell on the look in his eyes before he'd kissed me.

I have a thing for you...all of you...

Had I dismissed his words too quickly? Had he been paving the way for...*more*?

A glance at my bedside clock showed it was only just past ten. My birthday wouldn't be over for another two hours.

Perhaps it wasn't too late to make another wish come true.

CHAPTER NINE

I TOSSED THE covers aside and slid out of bed before I lost my nerve.

My knock on his door elicited a sharp, gruff response. My clammy hand turned the handle and, ignoring my screaming senses telling me to turn back, I nudged it open.

He was reclined in the middle of his emperor-sized bed, his top half bare and his lower half covered by a dark green satin sheet. For several heartbeats he stared at me, a tight expression on his face.

'Come to drive a few more points home?' he asked eventually, his voice taut.

Unable to clear the lump of nerves lodged in my throat, I shook my head.

Slowly, torturously, his gaze roved over my body, lingering at my throat, where the necklace still rested, then my breasts, hips, down my legs, before rising to stop where the hem of my silk night slip ended high on my thighs.

He swallowed hard before his gaze clashed with mine, a turbulence percolating there that triggered a similar chain reaction in me.

'Then what *do* you want, Sadie?' His accent had thickened, throbbing with deep, dark desire.

'What you said, back on Neostros, about me giving you liberty you didn't want to take. What did you mean by that?'

That mask twisted with flint-hard warning. 'Whether you end up in my bed or not, I don't plan to stray. Earlier tonight I thought we could, in time, get to a place where the possibility of renegotiating wasn't unthinkable.'

In time...

Once he was certain the baby I carried was his?

I forced myself to focus as he continued.

'But you shut that down, so I'm not sure why you're here. One thing you should know, though. I abhor infidelity of any sort. If that's what you're here to propose—'

'No!' My heart twisted with dark, rabid jealousy. 'That wasn't... That's not why I'm here.'

'Spit it out, my sweet. There's only so much torture I'll take from my wife. Even on her birthday. Especially when she's standing there looking like my every fantasy come to life.'

His gaze dropped again, this time to the fingers I was unconsciously twisting in front of me. Something eased in his eyes and he reared up from his recline.

At the sight of his sculpted chest, my mouth dried. Then almost immediately flooded with a hunger that weakened me from head to toe.

'Come here, Sadie,' he commanded gruffly.

I shook my head. 'You're going to have to come and get me.'

Expecting an arrogant comeback, I was surprised when his jaw clenched and his fingers bunched on the sheets. For an age, he contemplated me, his gaze weighing mine.

If I hadn't known better I'd have imagined Neo was... *nervous*.

Before the thought could deepen, he swung his legs over the side of the bed and rose.

And for the first time I saw Neo naked. Saw him in his full magnificent glory.

Saw the deep, stomach-hollowing scars that dissected his left hip, then zigzagged their way over his pelvis to end dangerously close to his manhood.

My hand shot up to my mouth, a horrid little gasp escaping me before I could stop it.

Dear God, so *that* was why he believed he couldn't have children?

Neo's head jerked back, his eyes darkening at my reaction. Yet he didn't flinch or cower. Hell, he seemed resolute, even a little proud to show off his scars. He prowled forward, naked and unashamed, his impressive manhood at full mast.

'What's the matter, Sadie?' he rasped when he was a handful of feet away. 'Is this too much for you? Are you going to run from me? Again?'

My gaze flew to his. 'No! What would make you think that?'

His eyes shadowed and he paused for several beats. 'The sight of me doesn't horrify you?' he asked, a peculiar note in his voice.

'Of course I'm not horrified. I'm heartsick that you had to endure that. Who wouldn't be?'

His lips twisted bitterly. 'I've discovered from past…encounters…that there are three reactions to my scars. Horror, pity or stoicism.'

'Well, I don't belong in any of those groups, thank you very much.'

Again his gaze probed mine. 'Do you not?'

'No. And if you keep looking at me like that I'll leave right now.'

'Your words salve me a little…but perhaps I require more? A demonstration of why you're in this room in the first place?' he said huskily. 'If you're not here to torture me, *pethi mou*, then why are you here?'

His voice grew more ragged, his chest rising and falling along with the impressive arousal that was somehow growing even prouder by the second.

I dragged my gaze from his intoxicating body. 'I came to tell you that I've changed my mind. That I… I want…'

God, what a time to be struck senseless. But, really, who could blame me? When he looked this magnificent? When it seemed—powerfully and thrillingly—that I had this effect on him?

'I want the fantasy,' I whispered.

'What fantasy? Tell me what you want, Sadie. Explicitly.'

Nerves ate harder, knotting my tongue.

'Perhaps it would be better to show me, hmm?' he encouraged, his voice a barely audible rasp.

Had he said this with even a stitch of clothing on I would have balked. But with the miles of gleaming olive skin on show, his virility just begging to be explored and every atom in my body screaming for contact, the urge was impossible to deny.

My twitching hands flexed, rose. Brushed over one long, thin, jagged scar.

A sharp breath hissed out.

I snatched my hand away. 'I'm s-sorry. I didn't mean to hurt you.'

He gave a sharp shake of his head. 'It doesn't pain me, Sadie. Quite the opposite,' he grated.

My gaze darted to his face. While his expression was tight with barely leashed control, his eyes blazed with an emotion I couldn't quite name.

'I've never permitted anyone to explore me this way,' he added.

'Really?' Why did that please me so much?

'*Ne*. Continue. Please,' he urged.

Encouraged, I trailed my fingers over the raised skin, tracing the map of his trauma, a little in awe that he'd survived what had to have been a horrific experience.

When I neared his groin the sculpted muscles in his abs tensed, but he didn't stop me. Growing bolder, I stepped into his force field, felt the searing heat of his skin blanket me.

'Will you tell me what happened?' I asked.

He regarded me for several heartbeats, then nodded. 'Later. Much later.' Then, grasping my hand, he growled, 'Don't stop.'

The invitation was too heady to resist.

I explored him from chest to thigh, but avoided the powerful thrust of his erection until, with a growl, he swung me into his arms and strode for the bed.

Laying me down, he divested me of the slip and panties but left the necklace on. Then he stayed by the side of the bed, staring down at me with blazing eyes.

'Our first time was rushed. Understandably chaotic. This time I intend to take my time, learn everything you like. Show you what I desire. Are you willing, *pethi mou*?'

I nodded jerkily, aware that my pulse was racing at my throat.

'Good.'

Boldly, he reached forward and cupped one breast, while the other hand covered the damp heat gathering between my legs. His eyes devoured my every expression as I arched into his touch.

'I want to watch you drown in pleasure. I want to see your beautiful green eyes when you come for me.'

He toyed with one peaked nipple, drawing from me a breathless gasp, then swooped down, twirled his tongue around the tight nub, drew it into his mouth for several hot seconds before he raised his head.

'I want to hear your breath hitch like that when you lose your mind for me.'

His thumb found the needy pearl of my core and rubbed with an expertise that arched my back, made desperate moans erupt from my throat.

'Ah, just like that, *moro mou*.'

'Neo, you're making me... I'm...'

'Give yourself over to me, Sadie,' he grated thickly, urgently. 'Give me what I want and I'll reward you.'

'With...what?' I gasped.

An arrogant smile curved his sensual lips. 'With as much of me as you can take. Would you like that?'

'Yes!'

'Then come for me. Now, Sadie,' he demanded throatily, his clever fingers demanding that ultimate response as his due.

With mindless abandon I handed it over, sensation piling high as he flipped the switch that triggered my release. My screams scraped my throat raw, my body twisting in a frenzied bliss I never wanted to end.

All the while Neo rained kisses and praise on my body, his lips and hands prolonging my pleasure until I was spent. Until all I could do was try to catch my breath as he finally climbed onto the bed, parted my thighs and situated himself above me, arms planted on either side of my shoulders.

Even as my heart raced from one climax, need built again, and the sight of Neo, this powerful mountain of a man whose scars only served to make him even more unique, more potent and desirable, and yet so dangerous to my emotional well-being, rendered me speechless.

Eyes frenzied with need scoured me from head to toe. 'Touch me, Sadie,' he rasped.

Too far gone to resist, I cupped his jaw, gloried in the sharp stubble that pricked my skin, delighted when he turned his face deeper into my touch. I explored him with the same thoroughness with which he'd explored me, until his breaths turned ragged and his stomach muscles clenched with the tightness of his control.

Throwing my legs wider, I let my gaze find his. Our visceral connection thickening the desire arching between us, he surged sure and deep, filling me in places that went beyond the physical. Because as Neo began to move, a kind of joy filled my heart. One that prickled my eyes and made me cling tighter, cry out a little louder.

Because while it was wondrous it was also terrifying, this feeling. Because in those moments when sweat slicked from his body to mine, when he fused his lips to mine with a heavy, passionate groan and stepped off the edge with me, as I touched his scar and felt his pain echo in my heart, I knew this would never, ever be about just sex for me.

When it was over, when I was exhausted but sated, my hand traced the whorls of raised scar tissue, my heart squeezing as I thought of what he'd suffered.

'So was it a helicopter crash or a ski accident? The papers couldn't seem to decide on one or the other,' I said.

He stiffened, then gave a bitter chuckle. 'When have they ever bothered about what's the truth and what isn't?' Silence reigned for a handful of seconds before he added tightly, 'It was on a black run in Gstaad. A run I'd skied many times before. But familiarity and expertise don't mean a thing if there's a lack of concentration.'

I frowned. Neo wasn't the type to court danger by being reckless. The ruthless efficiency with which he'd steered events from the moment he'd learned of his child was testament to the fact that he didn't drop the ball. *Ever*.

Unless... 'Something happened?'

Grim-faced, he unconsciously tightened his hand on my hip. Not enough to hurt, but enough to signal that whatever memory I'd roused wasn't pleasant.

'The company had just started a major international push when Anneka and I got together. She was part of the ski season crowd who worshipped the slopes. I didn't mind so much when she chose to party with her friends without me. But when she told me she was pregnant—'

He stopped at my shocked gasp. 'Your fiancée was *pregnant*?'

His face turned even grimmer, his jaw clenching tight before he nodded abruptly. 'But I began to suspect that she was chasing more than prime snow when she was away.'

'She was cheating on you?'

'I sensed she wasn't being truthful about a few things. But she denied it and I...' His jaw clenched tight for a single moment. 'I chose to believe her. She convinced me to let her stay in Gstaad for a few more days before coming back to Athens. On the morning I was supposed to leave, she wanted to ski on the black run. She was an excellent skier, but she was pregnant with my child and I didn't feel right about letting her go alone. So I went with her. It started snowing heavily almost immediately. I lost sight of Anneka for a moment and lost my concentration.'

He stopped.

'I woke up from a coma three weeks later. Just in time to hear her plotting with her lover about how they would pass off their child as mine long enough to get a ring on her finger and all of my wealth. Within minutes I had no child, a duplicitous fiancée and the dreadful news that my injuries had ended any hope of my ever fathering a child naturally.'

As I was grappling with that, his turbulent gaze found mine.

'Do you understand now why hearing you'd destroyed my one last chance prompted my reaction?'

His stark bitterness threw ice-cold dread over me, keeping me numb for a minute before sensation piled in, puzzles slid into place.

With a horrified gasp I moved away from him, pulling the sheet tight around me. I suppressed another sharp cry as pain lanced me and the weighted certainty that another woman's transgressions had been the measuring rod I'd been judged against all along froze me from the inside out.

'So I'm Project Two Point Zero?'

He frowned. 'Excuse me?'

'You thought I was lying when I said I was pregnant. Then you accused me of trying to foist another man's child on you. Then you thought you'd hedge your bets by marrying me, on the off-chance the child was yours. How are those imagined offences of mine any different from what your fiancée did to you?'

He reared up, his face tightening further. 'For one thing, we're married. And for another, you barely touch the possessions I've showered on you. You don't drive, or ask to be driven anywhere. The thought of going to a social event makes you grimace.'

'So my saving grace is that I'm not a fashion whore and nor do I salivate over the dozen supercars you store in your garage? What makes you think I'm not just biding my time, lulling you into a sense of complacency before I strike?'

One insolent eyebrow rose, as if the idea was amusing. 'Are you? And how do you propose to do that?'

'Give me time—I'm sure I can come up with something.'

'You won't,' he parried arrogantly. 'You want to know how you're different?'

I pressed my lips together, the strong need to know almost overwhelming me.

'The only thing that gets you fired up—truly fired up—is your work. Your eyes light up when you're in the boardroom, challenging men and women with years of experience to better market an idea. Anneka got fired up by shopping until she dropped. The reason she was an ex-supermodel by the time she was twenty-five was because she'd gained a reputation for being unprofessional and lazy—partying and skiing were the only things she lived for. Sometimes I'd go two or three weeks without seeing her because she was too busy flying around in my jet to spend time with me.'

I frowned. 'So what on earth did you see in her? And is it even possible to shop and party that much...?' I muttered.

'Believe me, she gave it a good try. And after a few months we barely saw each other. I was about to break it off when she told me she was pregnant.'

The similarities crushed me harder. Neo and I would never have met again had it not been for the baby.

'You know how else you're different from Anneka?' he said.

I hated these comparisons. Hated the other woman's name on his lips. But I'd started this. And, for good or ill, the need to know more about what had shaped this man who made me terrified for my heart's well-being wouldn't abate.

'Enlighten me. Please.'

He ignored my droll tone, his eyes growing even more incisive as he stared at me, as if the list he was enumerating was necessary to him. Essential, even.

Maybe he needed to scrape together my *worthy* characteristics in order to be able to accept me as the mother of his child? And if he failed? If I wasn't enough? Anguish seared deeper, but he was still talking, so I forced myself to listen.

'You signed the prenup without so much as a quibble. Anneka got a team of lawyers to negotiate every clause—especially the one that stated that should I perish while we were married she would receive one hundred percent of my assets, including the funds I'd set aside for charity. Your attention to detail in the boardroom is exceptional. But I'm willing to bet you can't even remember the details of the financial package in the prenup you signed?'

I shook my head. 'The only part I cared about was what happened to our child,' I replied.

His arrogant smile widened. 'So tell me again how you plan to fleece me?'

I shrugged away the taunt, still consumed with wanting to know why he'd bothered to get together with a woman like Anneka if those were her true colours.

But I knew the answer. She was beautiful, vivacious and he'd thought she was carrying his child. It had become clear over the last few weeks that there was nothing Neo wouldn't do for his child. No sacrifice he wouldn't make.

My heart dipped in alarm and, yes, I felt a bite of jealousy at the thought that the all-encompassing feeling would never extend beyond his child. Not after what he'd experienced at the hands of another woman. Not after what I'd done to him even before our first meeting.

I was simply the vessel carrying what he wanted most in the world. How soon after I served my purpose would I be relegated to the background?

That anguishing thought drove my next question. 'So I'm a step or two up from the previous model—no pun intended. But I still have question marks over my head, don't I?'

'Don't we all?' he drawled.

'No, that's not going to fly. You've just listed the ways

I'm different from your ex, but what does that difference mean to you, Neo?' I pressed, an almost fatalistic urge smashing away my precious self-preservation.

'That remains to be seen,' he replied, and that aloofness I'd fooled myself into thinking was gone for ever resurged, saturating every inch of his perfect face.

'You mean until I prove my *worth* to you? Add the ultimate title of true mother to your child to that list? Maybe *then* you'll stop comparing me to her?'

He shrugged.

Stone-like dread settled in my midriff, depriving my lungs of air. Slowly but unrelentingly, perhaps even since that first night on Neostros, I'd allowed this thing to go beyond doing the right thing for my baby. I'd reached out, taken what I wanted for myself despite the lingering suspicion that my actions would come with emotional consequences.

And now, with this account of what had shaped him, he'd bared my own weaknesses to me.

I started to slide out of bed, froze when he reached for me.

'Where do you think you're going?'

'I'm going to shower. Alone.'

Tension rippled through his frame, his eyes narrowing to ferocious slits. 'We can't go back, Sadie. It's better you're aware of that. That you accept it.'

'You're right—we can't go back. But with your feet firmly stuck in clay you're not going to move forward either, are you?'

Again his silence spoke for him.

'Well, guess what? You may be stuck, but I'm not.'

'Explain that, if you please,' he rasped tightly.

'You're lauded for your sharp brain, Neo. Work it out for yourself.'

When I tugged myself free he released me. And that little act of setting me free, when deep down I wanted him to recapture me, drove the hard truth home.

His actions would always skew towards protecting himself. Towards shoring up his foundations with thick layers that guaranteed everyone else would remain on the outside.

Which was rather a sad and agonising state of affairs, because I very much wanted to be on the inside. So much so that when the composure that had held me together crumbled I let it, allowing the hot scald of tears to mingle with the warm shower jets. The hiss of the water muffling my quiet sobs.

But what I didn't know in those stolen, self-pitying moments was that my agony was only just starting.

Work it out for yourself.

I resented the unnerving panic those five words had triggered.

We were married. We'd made an agreement!

But listing her better qualities had opened my eyes to what I'd known for a while…that Sadie was truly different from Anneka. A wife a husband would be proud to possess.

But…what kind of husband? One who valued her for her brain but was too jaded to look into her heart? Perhaps because his own emotions fell short of fulfilling her needs?

Could I really stop her if she deemed me unfit to hold up my end of the bargain? If the doubts I harboured about my effectiveness as a father grew apparent?

I'd negotiated another deal in my favour by reclaiming her in my bed. One that had given me a yearning for a state I'd never considered before.

Contentment.

Theos mou, the woman I'd married was sensational. She tasted like the purest strain of innocent temptation, which would only get richer when she'd fully embraced her sensuality.

I should be pleased.

And yet, her words had only intensified that hollow sensation I'd woken up with the morning after the wedding. The feeling that had expanded ever since.

Not in a glaring, aggressive way, that could easily be identified and fixed, like a marketing flaw that required sharp intellect and an eye for detail. It had started as a ripple on the surface of a pond, effortless but determined. Unstoppable. Expanding against my will and desire to contain it.

And you need this triple-strength protection, why?

I ignored the wheedling voice, alarmed when I couldn't find any immediate comeback as to why I needed protection against Sadie.

Even more disturbing was the louder voice that questioned whether I was equipped to safeguard what I fought so valiantly for once my child was born. Cynicism and bitterness and being a shark in the boardroom were hardly the cornerstones of fulfilling parenthood...

Would the child I was so intent on claiming eventually resent me?

No. I would do better than the indifferent and bitter hand I'd been dealt. Just as I knew Sadie would too—if only to counteract what her own father had done to her.

The hollow sensation intensified—as if now I'd admitted one craving, several more demanded to be addressed.

Something was missing. Perhaps...within me.

Had I bargained with chips that were flawed? Pushed Sadie into marriage without stopping to examine whether I was the type of husband she wanted? A fit father for our child?

Money. Influence. Power. All things I could offer.

All things she'd rejected one by one without batting an eyelash.

Her question lingered long after she'd disappeared into the bathroom, after the hiss of the shower taunted me with the knowledge that tonight might have been the only pleasure I experienced with her.

And then, like that tree I'd known would be my doom in that moment of clarity right before the accident in Gstaad, when I heard the sharp scream from the bathroom, I suspected things would never be the same again.

When, an hour later, I stood by Sadie's bedside in another hospital, my gut twisting into knots as I stared down the barrel of a metaphorical gun, suspicion became certainty.

CHAPTER TEN

Looks much worse than it is... Everything is fine, Mrs Xenakis. You just need to take it easy.

I repeated the doctor's words to myself as the limo drove us home from the hospital a few hours later.

The ravaging pain shredding my heart had merely been put on hold in light of the scare in the bathroom. It was still waiting in the wings.

And even if I'd fooled myself into thinking it was in any way diminished, the tight, drawn look on Neo's face testified that our conversation in the bedroom had merely been stayed.

That determined little muscle ticking in his jaw said it all. And it had only intensified with the doctor's reassurance that our baby...*our son*...was fine. Thriving, in fact. That the blood I'd spotted in the shower was concerning, but ultimately nothing to stress over as long as I took it easy.

Why that news had triggered Neo's ashen complexion and lockjawed determination only served to expand the stone lodged in my heart.

Had our conversation and the scare merely fast-tracked the inevitable?

We completed the journey home in tight, fraught silence.

When the driver shut off the ignition, Neo strode around to my side, offered his hand in silent command. I took it, stepped out, but when he leaned forward to lift me up I threw out a halting hand.

So soon after everything I'd experienced in his bed, and afterwards, having him so close would be detrimental to my emotional well-being.

The very thing I should've guarded against in the first place.

'I can walk on my own. The doctor said to take it easy. I think that safely includes walking from the car to the villa,' I said, unable to keep the tightness from my voice.

His lips tightened and he stayed close, unbearably surrounding me with his heat as I climbed the stairs to my suite, then perched on the wide, striped divan and watched the staff fuss with a tray of food and soft drinks Neo must have ordered before we left the hospital.

When the housekeeper lingered, Neo dragged an impatient hand through his hair. 'Leave us,' he snapped, authority stamped in his voice that saw his command immediately obeyed. He paced to the door, shut it, then returned, his footsteps heavy and resolute.

I knew what was coming. Unlike that postcard that had torn my world apart, this heartache-shaped wrecking ball I could see coming from a mile away.

'Don't do it. Whatever you're about to say, don't say it, Neo,' I blurted.

He froze beside the bed, then dragged his hands down his face. Even with two-day stubble and shadows haunting his turbulent eyes, he looked sublime.

The man I craved more than was wise for me.

The man I'd fallen in love with as he glared at me from across his office, tossing bullet-sharp questions about marketing and then reproducing a birthday cupcake at short notice in the most stunning setting on earth.

'Do you know what it felt like to see you there on that bathroom floor?' he demanded raggedly, his voice rough to the point of near incoherence.

My pain twisted, morphed, as a new strand was woven into its jagged fabric. 'Every pregnancy carries a risk. The doctor just said that.'

He gave a violent shake of his head. 'It wouldn't have happened if I'd kept my hands to myself! If I hadn't pushed for more!'

'You don't know that.'

'I do. I feel it, Sadie. Right here.' He pounded his closed fist on his midriff, his jaw tight with recrimination.

'You think you're something special?'

He inhaled sharply. 'What?'

'You think we're the only couple who indulge in sex during pregnancy? That you deserve some kind of special punishment for doing something that comes naturally?'

His gaze turned bleak. 'I can't speak for others, but I know what my actions came close to costing me. The way I've been with you, right from the start, herding you into decisions you were reluctant to take—'

'There you go again—seeking the crown of martyrdom. I have a voice, Neo. And, if you recall, you didn't get everything your own way. What makes you think I didn't want it too? That I wasn't in a hurry to fall into bed with you or marry you for my own reasons?'

He shook his head. 'Be that as it may, I set this ball rolling—'

'What? Gave me a roof over my head? A job opportunity that most would give their eye teeth for?'

'You said yourself—those are just things. What you could've lost—'

'But *we* didn't *lose* anything, Neo. Our baby is fine.'

Raw bitterness tightened his face. 'But for how long?'

My heart shredded. 'What?'

'I only negotiated for the short term, Sadie. As unfortunate as the circumstances are, it's a wake-up call. I need to accept that I don't have the tools for the long term.'

My fists bunched as anguish ripped through me. 'I don't buy that either, Neo. But I can't stop you from this path you obviously want to take, so just spare me the suspense and spit it out?'

His jaw worked for the longest time. Then he nodded. 'I'm leaving for Brazil tomorrow. Then travelling in Latin America for the next few weeks.'

'You're leaving.'

It wasn't a question. More absorbing the impact of the wrecking ball.

'Yes.'

'Because I'm *so different* from Anneka?' I taunted sarcastically.

'Yes!' The word was drawn from his soul. Almost as if he was terrified to admit it.

My jaw dropped. 'Neo...'

'You'll be taken care of—'

'I don't want a laundry list of things you're putting in place to ensure I don't lift a finger. I want to know why you promised me better terms and are now reneging.'

'This is for your own good.'

I couldn't help the laughter that spilled out. 'Is it, though? You know what you remind me of, Neo? My father. Always looking for something better! You changed the rules to suit you when you decided you wanted a wife, not just in name, but in your bed. Then you changed them again because you can't handle a little challenge. I've outlived my usefulness to you in one area. So you're shelving me until you get the other things that you want.'

His jaw clenched. 'No—what your father did, he did for himself. What I'm doing is for *you*.'

'Trust me to know my own mind! Believe me when I tell you what's in my heart.'

He lost another layer of colour, but his eyes blazed with quiet fury. 'I've made my decision. But know that besides my absence, nothing changes.'

'That's where you're wrong. *I've* changed. I know my own worth now. I know I want more than this. I won't be bargained with, or put on a shelf to suit you. So if you think your world is going to stay trouble-free because you've laid down the law, think again.'

'What's that supposed to mean?'

I shrugged dismissively, even though it was the last thing I felt like doing. 'I guess we'll find out. Goodbye, Neo.'

He stayed put, his gaze fixed in that way that said he was assessing me for weakness.

And because I wasn't sure how long I could stay put without cracking, I turned away from him, closed my eyes and simply pretended he wasn't there.

I heard the ominous snick of the door a minute later.

Then the tears fell—long and hard and shattering.

It was supposed to work.

The punishing schedule.

The soul-sucking jet lag.

The endless meetings.

Hell, even barking at executives was supposed to make me feel better. To fuel the conviction that I was doing the right thing.

She'd accused me of being like her father. Initially it had provided sustaining anger, and I'd burned in the righteousness of believing myself the exact opposite.

But, as relentless as time's march, the kernel of truth had expanded...like a weird, never-ending concentric circle that echoed its presence in my quiet moments.

First I'd used her to salve the bad news she'd delivered. Then, from the moment she'd announced she was carrying my child, I'd pinned her to me—my last hope of fatherhood and I was determined to have it, regardless of the fact that I lacked the effective tools to be a father. And during the process, I'd hammered out an agreement that bound her to me only until I had what I wanted.

And when I'd decided I wanted more, I'd worked on the problem until she'd fallen into my arms.

Only then had I realised the full impact of *more*. That, while I could give her every material and carnal pleasure she desired, *I* was the one who was too greedy. Too selfish. Because I'd never stopped to think that she would want more too. Or that I was equipped to deal with her demand.

Fate had given me the rudest wake-up call. And, as much

as every moment of breathing turned me inside out, Sadie deserved for me to stay away. She deserved the peace to bear her child without my greedy, demanding presence. Without the wants and needs and longings that clawed at me every hour of every day, sullying her beautiful existence.

So what if the thought of going another minute, another hour, without seeing her face killed me?

You'll simply have to suffer!

My intercom sounded, ripping another curse from my throat.

'I was quite explicit in my desire not to be disturbed.'

Because I deserved at least ten minutes of undiluted torment each hour, even as other minutes provided unending agony.

'Yes, sir, but I thought you should know—'

'Save your breath. Warning him won't do any good.'

I jackknifed up from my position against the dark wall in my office. Took a step forward and steadied myself against the dizzying effect of her.

Two long weeks during which only the security cameras installed at the villa had provided woefully brief glimpses of this goddess who carried my child. During which daily reports of her improved health and blooming pregnancy had sustained my raging hunger for her.

And now she was here.

A vision in white cotton that clung to her bust, her hips and, *Christos*, the magnificent protrusion of her belly. Her hair was twisted into an elaborate crown on top of her head, further proclaiming her celestial status.

It was all I could do not to fall at her feet in sublime worship of her, this woman who held a heart unworthy of her. This woman who'd exploded into my life and claimed a place in it I never wanted back.

God, would I ever get over the impact of Neo Xenakis?

I doubted it.

Or else every single vow I'd taken and every form of punishment I'd devised for myself in a wild bid to stop thinking about him, stop dreaming about him, would have worked.

Instead, each day had brought a bracing kind of hell. A craving that went against all common sense.

I'd driven Callie quite mad with my pathetic stoicism. While I wanted to blame her for appointing herself chief nursemaid, I'd eventually taken pity on her—succumbed when she'd called up the Xenakis jet and arranged an intercontinental flight, along with a doctor, much to the chagrin of her husband.

From Neo's poleaxed expression now, Axios had kept the secret.

The look was morphing, though, the shock wearing off.

His gaze rushed over me and he paled a little before his eyes narrowed. 'What are you doing here?' he bit out.

Despite its tension, the sound of his voice sent tingles down my spine.

I closed the gap between us by another few steps, my heart kicking against my ribs when his eyes dropped to my distended stomach.

'I work for this company, remember? Unless those privileges have been revoked too?'

'You know exactly what I mean. You should be resting. In Athens. Not...not...' He stopped. Frowned.

'Have you forgotten where you are?' I asked. 'You're in Costa Rica...negotiating to buy the country's second-largest airline.'

His frown intensified. 'Thanks for the reminder. My statement still stands.'

'Does it? Perhaps if you'd been at home I wouldn't have needed to cross continents to have a conversation with you.'

His mouth worked and he swallowed noisily. 'Sadie—'

'No.' I took another few steps, then stopped when his aftershave hit me like a brick of sensation. 'You don't get to speak. Not until I've said what's on my mind. And even then, the jury's out as to whether I want to hear what you have to say.'

'This is the third time you've stormed my office since we met.'

'It seems to be the only place where I can get through to you.'

A raw gleam lit his grey eyes before his expression tightened. 'That's not entirely true. But, *parakalo*, whatever you have to say to me, do it while sitting down?'

'And ruin this superb effect I'm having on you?'

His fist tightened with the blatant need to bodily compel me to the sofa. 'What do you want, Sadie?'

'For you to come home. Or give me a divorce.'

He lost another shade of colour. 'What?'

'Two choices. Take one or the other. But I'm not leaving here without an answer.'

'You dare to—'

'Oh, I do. Very much. Because you know what? I've decided there's nothing you can do to me. Sue the mother of your child? I think not. Toss me out of your company? I'll just find another job, because I'm good at what I do. But I don't think you want to lose my professional skills either. Really, all that's standing in our way is *you*.'

His breathing intensified and he looked, shockingly, as if he was on the brink of hyperventilating. 'You think any of this has been easy, Sadie?'

The raw note in his voice caught at that vulnerable spot I'd never been able to protect, ever since our first meeting.

I stepped into his space, uncaring for my own heart, and glared with everything I had. 'You walked away. And stayed away. You tell me.'

'It's been torture!' he yelled. 'I reach for you at night and you're not there. I turn to throw a question at you in the boardroom and find some lame executive staring back at me. You've ruined me for everything! For everyone! You were supposed to bewitch me for a little while. Until I satisfied the craving you triggered. Instead you're all I think about—every second of every day.'

My heart swan-dived right to my toes, then dared to beat its wings faster, to climb and climb and *hope*.

'Keep...keep talking.'

'That night, when you accused me of not moving forward, I couldn't answer your charge because somewhere along the line I'd gone from holding you to a higher standard to recognising that I couldn't meet those standards myself.'

'What are you *talking* about?'

'I've held myself back from giving my all emotionally all my life, Sadie. My grandfather did and look where he ended up. When Anneka told me she was pregnant I immediately offered her my name and my wealth, but nothing else. I knew I didn't love her and, aside from her betrayal and the lesson that delivered, I haven't spared her a thought since I threw her out of my life. But you...'

He stopped, swallowed.

'I spent weeks after our first meeting unable to get you out of my mind. When you turned up in my office in Athens I thought you felt the same. That you'd simply been better at plotting a reconnection.'

'Instead I dropped another bombshell in your life.'

He shook his head, jerked closer until we were breathing the same air. 'Instead you held out your hands and presented me with the most precious gift any man who wishes to be a father could ask for.'

'So you believe our baby is yours?'

'I believed you before we landed back in London that day. A woman who goes to great pains to admit her wrongdoing when she could have run a mile and passed the blame to others is a woman of integrity, in my book. Even when I gave you the chance to pass the blame on to your boss, you didn't.'

'If you knew all that, then why?'

He shrugged, that domineering alpha male rising to the

fore. 'Because I'm a negotiator, Sadie. I played my cards close to my chest to gain the upper hand. I wanted our child, but I wanted you even more. I could've dispatched you back to London, had a security team watch you and swoop in to negotiate terms of custody once the baby was born.'

'But you didn't because you *wanted* me? Past tense?'

'Oh, no, *glikia mou*. Not even close to past tense. It's very present. Very real. So much it scares me.'

Something electric lit up inside me. 'Is that why you're hiding here on the other side of the world? Because you're scared?'

'I'm here because I don't deserve you. As much as I want to negotiate my way back to you, I can't stand the possibility that you'll wake up one day and be disappointed.'

'My God. You've put us through all this suffering because for the first time in your life you're experiencing the very human emotion of self-doubt?'

He frowned. 'Sadie, this isn't a flimsy—'

'You think I wasn't scared to death when I realised I was in love with you? That I haven't wanted to tear my hair out to see if it would bring me a moment's relief from the constant ache of loving you and not knowing whether you love me back?'

His gorgeous lips dropped open in shock. '*Christos*, Sadie. I—'

'I'm a pregnant woman nearing her third trimester, Neo. The next words out of your mouth had better be words I want to hear.'

His arms darted out, caught me to him, as if he was afraid I'd flee when in fact my legs were threatening to stop supporting me.

'Let's get one thing clear. You're never to touch a hair on your head with an aim of tearing it out. Ever. But, more importantly, Sadie…if this madness inside me that yearns only for you, if this heart that beats true only when you're near, means this is love, then I love you. And if it's not, if

I get it wrong somewhere along the way, I know I'll have you there to steer me true. For a chance to be at your side through this life I will leave the negotiations to you, follow your lead. Show me how to love, Sadie, and I will be your apt pupil for the rest of our lives.'

The depth of his promise took the last ounce of strength from my legs. He caught me up, as I knew he would, strode over to the sofa and sank into it.

'Okay, if that's what it takes. Here's your first lesson. You never leave me behind again.'

'I vow it,' he replied, with feeling.

I rearranged myself in his lap, framed his face between my hands. 'You bring any doubts you have to me. We fix and grow and love together. But most of all, Neo, you just open your heart, let me love you and our baby. We'll be the best versions of ourselves we can be for our family and trust the rest to take care of itself. Will you do that?'

A suspicious sheen glistened in his eyes. But he didn't look away, didn't blink it back. He just stared into my eyes and nodded. 'You have yourself a deal, *amorfo mou*.'

'Good. Now, please kiss me. Then please take me home.'

EPILOGUE

'IT'S TIME, NEO.'

Heels clicked closer as my wife entered our bedroom and crossed over to where I stood at the window.

'Our guests are wondering if the two of you are planning to join the festivities—especially since you're holding the guest of honour hostage,' she teased.

I was torn between staring at the vision Sadie created in her white Grecian-style dress and the precious bundle I held in my arms.

With her flaming hair piled on top of her head in an elaborate knot, and the skin I'd explored thoroughly just a few hours ago glowing, Sadie won the attention-grabbing stakes. But only by a fraction.

My son—*thee mou*, would I ever stop being awed by the miracle of him?—three months old and in good health, came a very close second.

'Five more minutes?' I cradled his warmth closer, unwilling to share him just yet.

Sadie shook her head, smiling widely as she approached, her swaying hips wreaking havoc with my breathing.

'You said that twenty minutes ago. I know you don't care what anyone else thinks, but I have a good brownie point system going with your family. I don't want to ruin it.'

'Impossible. Every person out there loves you—they wouldn't been invited to Helios's christening otherwise.'

Her beautiful eyes widened. 'You didn't have Wendell vet them, did you?'

I shrugged. 'Maybe...'

She laughed, and the sound burrowed deep, stirring emotions I hadn't imagined I could experience just a handful of months ago.

But then, so many things had changed since that day in Costa Rica. Sadie had introduced me to the phenomenon of unconditional love, her giving heart and fearless love challenging mine to reciprocate. And the result continued to astound me daily. Even the atmosphere of cool indifference with my parents had began to thaw under Sadie's expert guidance.

She insisted the birth of our miracle son was the reason. I disagreed.

'Well, just to let you know, our mothers are *this* close to staging a break-in to claim their grandson,' she said with a stunning smile. 'I estimate you have about a minute.'

'Then I'll make the most of it. Come to me, *agape mou*,' I murmured, greedy for more of this soul-stirring feeling.

'I love it when you call me that,' she said when she reached me, one hand sliding around my waist, her other caressing Helios's black-maned head. 'He's so beautiful—our little miracle.'

The overwhelming love and wonder I felt was echoed in her voice.

'He's as beautiful as his exceptional mama, but *moro mou*, you're our miracle, Sadie. Without you, our lives wouldn't be this full, mine changed for ever for the better,' I said.

Beautiful green eyes blinked back tears, and when she went on tiptoe to kiss me I met her halfway, revelling in the supreme contentment that this gorgeous creature was mine. That she had given me a son despite my doctors still scratching their heads over tests that showed such a feat was impossible.

Their verdict was that Helios might be the only child Sadie and I would have. But who were they to make pronouncements? I already had the miracle of love and fatherhood. Nothing was impossible.

When we broke the kiss Sadie sighed, resting her head

on my shoulder. 'Okay, Neo. Five more minutes. But I get to stay too.'

As if I would let her go.

'*Agapita*, you should know by now that I wouldn't have it any other way.'

*****

WHAT THE GREEK'S MONEY CAN'T BUY

CHAPTER ONE

'COME ON, PUT your back into it! Why am I not surprised that you're slacking as usual while I'm doing all the work?'

Sakis Pantelides reefed the oars through the slightly choppy water, loving the exhilaration and adrenaline that burned in his back and shoulders. 'Stop complaining, old man. It's not my fault if you're feeling your age.' He smiled when he heard his brother's hiss of annoyance.

In truth, Ari was only two-and-a-half years older, but Sakis knew it annoyed him when he taunted him with their age difference, so of course he never passed up the chance to niggle where he could.

'Don't worry, Theo will be around to bail you out next time we row. That way you won't have to *strain* yourself so much,' Sakis said.

'Theo would be more concerned about showing off his bulging muscles to the female coxes than he would to serious rowing,' Ari responded dryly. 'How he ever managed to stop showing off long enough to win five world championships, I'll never know.'

Sakis heaved his oars and noted with satisfaction that he hadn't lost the innate rhythm despite several months away from the favourite sport that had at one time been his sole passion. Thinking about his younger brother, he couldn't help but smile. 'Yeah, he always *was* more into his looks and the ladies than anything else.'

He rowed in perfect sync with his brother, their movements barely rippling through the water as they passed the halfway point of the lake used by the exclusive rowing club a few miles outside of London. Sakis's smile widened as a sense of peace stole over him.

It'd been a while since he'd come here; since he'd found time to connect with his brothers like this. The punishing schedules it took to manage the three branches of Pantelides Inc meant the brothers hadn't got together in way too long. That they had even been in the same time zone had been a miracle. Of course, it hadn't stayed that way for long. Theo had cancelled at the last minute and was right this moment winging his way to Rio on a Pantelides jet to deal with a crisis for the global conglomerate.

Or maybe Theo had cancelled for another reason altogether.

His playboy brother wasn't above flying thousands of miles for a one-hour dinner date with a beautiful woman. 'If I find out he blew us off for a piece of skirt, I'll confiscate his plane for a month.'

Ari snorted. 'You can try. But I think you're asking for a swift death if you attempt to come between Theo and a woman. Speaking of women, I see yours has finally managed to surgically remove herself from her laptop...'

He didn't break his rhythm despite the jolt of electricity that zapped through him. His gaze focused past his brother's shoulder to where Ari's attention was fixed.

He nearly missed his next stroke. Only the inbuilt discipline that had seen him win one more championship than his brothers' five apiece stopped him from losing his rhythm.

'Let's get one thing straight—she's *not* my woman.'

Brianna Moneypenny, his executive assistant, stood next to his car. That in itself was a surprise, since she preferred to stay glued to his in-limo computer, one finger firmly on the pulse of his company any time he had to step away.

But what triggered the bolt of astonishment in him more

was the not-quite-masked expression on her face. Brianna's countenance since the day she'd become his ultra-efficient assistant eighteen months ago had never once wavered from cool, icy professionalism.

Today she looked...

'Don't tell me she's succumbed to the Sakis Pantelides syndrome?' Ari's dry tone held equal parts amusement and resignation.

Sakis frowned, unease stirring in his belly and mingling with the emotions he refused to acknowledge when it came to his executive assistant. He'd learned the hard way that exposing emotion, especially for the wrong person, could leave scars that never really healed and took monumental effort to keep buried. As for mixing business with pleasure—that had been a near lethal cocktail he'd sampled once. Never again. 'Shut up, Ari.'

'I'm concerned, brother. She's almost ready to jump into the water. Or jump your bones, more like. Please tell me you haven't lost your mind and slept with her?'

Sakis's gaze flitted over to Moneypenny, trying to pinpoint what was wrong from across the distance between them. 'I'm not sure what's more disturbing—your unhealthy interest in my sex life or the fact that you can keep rowing straight while practising the Spanish Inquisition,' he murmured absently.

As for getting physical with Moneypenny, if his libido chose the most inappropriate times—like now—to remind him he was a red-blooded male, it was a situation he intended to keep ignoring, like he had been the last eighteen months. He'd wasted too much valuable time in this lifetime ridding himself of clinging women.

He strained the oars through the water, suddenly wanting the session to be over. Through the strokes, he kept his gaze fixed on Moneypenny, her rigid stance setting off alarm bells inside his head.

'So, there's nothing between you two?' Ari pushed.

Something in his brother's voice made his hackles rise. With one last push, he felt the bottom of the scull hit the slope of the wooden jetty.

'If you're thinking of trying to poach her, Ari, forget it. She's the best executive assistant I've ever had and anyone who threatens that will lose a body part; two body parts for family members.'

'Cool your jets, bro. I wasn't thinking of that sort of poaching. Besides, hearing you gush over her like that tells me you're already far gone.'

Sakis's irritation grew, wishing his brother would get off the subject.

'Just because I recognise talent doesn't mean I've lost my mind. Besides, tell me, does *your* assistant know her Windsor knot from her double-cross knot?'

Ari's brows shot up as he stepped onto the pier and grabbed his oars. 'My assistant is a man. And the fact that you hired yours based on her tie-knotting abilities only confirms you're more screwed than I thought.'

'There's nothing delusional about the fact that she has more brains in her pinkie than the total sum of my previous assistants, and she's a Rottweiler when it comes to managing my business life. That's all I need.'

'Are you sure that's all? Because I detect a distinct...*reverence* in your tone there.'

Sakis froze, then grimaced when he realised Ari was messing with him. 'Keep it up. I owe you a scar for the one you planted on me with your carelessness.' He touched the arrow-shaped scar just above his right brow, a present from Ari's oar when they had first started rowing together in their teens.

'Someone had to bring you down a notch or three for thinking you were the better-looking brother.' Ari grinned, and Sakis was reminded of the carefree brother Ari had been before tragedy had struck and sunk its merciless claws into him.

Then Ari's gaze slid beyond Sakis's shoulder. 'Your Rottweiler's prowling for you. She looks ready to bare her teeth.'

Sakis dropped his oars next to the overturned scull and glanced over, to find Brianna had moved closer. She now stood at the top of the pier, her arms folded and her gaze trained on him.

His alarm intensified. There was a look on her face he'd never seen before. Plus she held a towel in one hand, which suggested she was expecting him not to take his usual shower at the clubhouse.

Sakis frowned. 'Something's up. I need to go.'

'Did she communicate that to you subliminally or are you two so attuned to each other you can tell just by looking at her?' Ari enquired in an amused tone.

'Seriously, Ari, cork it.' His scowl deepened as he noted Brianna's pinched look. Again acting out of the ordinary, she started towards him.

Moneypenny knew never to disturb him during his time with his brothers. She was great like that. She knew her place in his life and had never once overstepped the mark. He started to walk away from the waterfront.

'Hey, don't worry about me. I'll make sure the equipment is returned to the boathouse. And I'll have all those drinks we ordered by myself too,' Ari stated drolly.

Sakis ignored him. When he reached speaking distance, he stopped. 'What's wrong?' he demanded.

For the very first time since she'd turned up for an interview at Pantelides Towers at five o'clock in the morning, Sakis saw her hesitate. The hair on his nape rose to attention. 'Spit it out, Moneypenny.'

The tightening of her mouth was infinitesimal but he spotted it. Another first. He couldn't remember ever witnessing an outward sign of distress. Silently, she held out his towel.

He snatched it from her, more to hurry her response than a need to wipe his sweat-drenched body.

'Mr Pantelides, we have a situation.'

His jaw tightened. 'What situation?'

'One of your tankers, the Pantelides Six, has run aground off Point Noire.'

Ice cascaded down his back despite the midsummer sun blazing down on him. Sakis forced a swallow. 'When did this happen?'

'I got a call via the head office from a crew member five minutes ago.'

She licked her lips and his apprehension grew.

'There's something else?'

'Yes. The captain and two crew members are missing and...'

'And what?'

Her pinched look intensified. 'The tanker hit an outcropping of rocks. Crude oil is spilling into the South Atlantic at an estimated rate of sixty barrels per minute.'

Brianna would never forget what happened next after her announcement. Outwardly, Sakis Pantelides remained the calm, ruthlessly controlled oil tycoon she'd worked alongside for the past eighteen months. But she would've failed in her task to make herself indispensable to him if she hadn't learned to read between the lines of the enigma that was Sakis Pantelides. The set of his strong jaw and the way his hands tightened around the snow-white towel told her how badly the news had affected him.

Over his shoulder, Brianna saw Arion Pantelides pause in his task. Her eyes connected with his. Something in her face must have given her away because before she'd taken another breath the oldest Pantelides brother was striding towards them. He was just as imposing as his younger brother, just as formidable. But, where Sakis's gaze was sharp with laser-like focus and almost lethal intelligence, Arion's held a wealth of dark torment and soul-deep weariness.

Brianna's gaze swung back to her boss, and she wasn't even slightly surprised to see the solid mask of power and ruthless efficiency back in place.

'Do we know what caused the accident?' he fired out.

She shook her head. 'The captain isn't responding to his mobile phone. We haven't been able to establish contact with vessel since the initial call. The Congolese coast guard are on their way. I've asked them to contact me as soon as they're on site.' She fell into step beside him as his long strides headed for the car. 'I've got our emergency crew on standby. They're ready to fly out once you give the word.'

Arion Pantelides caught up with them as they neared the limousine.

He put a halting hand on his brother's shoulder. 'Talk to me, Sakis.'

In clipped tones, Sakis filled him in on what had happened. Arion's gaze swung to her. 'Do we have the names of the missing crew members?'

'I've emailed the complete crew manifest to both your phones and Theo's. I've also attached a list of the relevant ministers we need to deal with in the government to ensure we don't ruffle any feathers, and I've scheduled calls with all of them.'

A look flickered in his eyes before his gaze connected with his brother's. When Sakis's brow rose a fraction, Arion gave a small smile.

'Go. I'll deal with as much as I can from here. We'll talk in one hour.' Arion clasped his brother's shoulder in reassurance before he strode off.

Sakis turned to her. 'I'll need to speak to the President.'

Brianna nodded. 'I've got his chief of staff on hold. He'll put you through when you're ready.'

Her gaze dropped to his chest and immediately shifted away. She stepped back to move away from the potent scent of sweat and man that radiated off his deep olive skin. 'You need to change. I'll get you some fresh clothes.'

As she headed towards the boot of the car, she heard the slide of his rowing suit zip. She didn't turn because she'd seen it all before. At least that was what she told herself. She hadn't seen Sakis Pantelides totally naked, of course. But hers was a twenty-four-seven job. And, when you worked as close as she did with a suave, self-assured, powerful tycoon who saw you as nothing but a super-efficient, sexless automaton, you were bound to be exposed to all aspects of his nature. And his various states of undress.

The first time Sakis Pantelides had undressed in front of her, Brianna had taken it in her stride, just as she'd brutally trained herself to take most things in her stride.

To feel, to trust, to give emotion an inch, was to invite disaster.

So she'd learned to harden her heart. It had been that…or sink beneath the weight of crushing despair.

And she refused to sink…

She straightened from the boot with a pristine blue shirt and a charcoal-grey Armani suit in one hand and the perfectly knotted double Oxford tie Sakis favoured in the other. She kept her gaze trained on the sun-dappled lake beyond his shoulder as she handed the items over and went to retrieve his socks and hand-made leather shoes.

She didn't need to see his strong neck and shoulders, honed perfectly from his years of professional, championship-winning rowing, or his deep, ripped chest with silky hairs that arrowed down to his neat, trim waist and disappeared beneath the band of his boxers. She most certainly didn't need to see the powerful thighs that looked as if they could crush an unwary opponent, or pin a willing female to an unyielding wall…in the right circumstances. And she especially didn't need to see the black cotton boxer briefs that made a poor effort to contain his—

A loud beep signalling an incoming call from the limo's phone startled her into dropping his socks. She hastily picked them up and slid into the car. From the corner of her eye, she saw Sakis step into his trousers. Silently, she held out the remaining items and picked up the phone.

'Pantelides Shipping,' she said into the receiver as she picked up her electronic tablet. She listened calmly to the voice at the other end of the line, tapping away at her keyboard as she added to the ever-growing to-do list.

By the time Sakis slid next to her, and slammed the door, impeccably dressed, she was on her fifth item. She paused long enough to secure her seat belt before resuming her typing.

'The only answer I have for you right now is no comment. Sorry, no can do.' Sakis stiffened beside her. 'Absolutely not. No news outlet will be getting exclusives. Pantelides Shipping will issue one press release within the hour. It will be posted on our company's website and affiliated media and social network links with the relevant contact details. If you have any questions after that, contact our press office.'

'Tabloid or mainstream media?' Sakis asked the moment she hung up.

'Fleet Street. They want to verify what they've heard.' The phone rang again. Seeing the number of another tabloid, she ignored it. Sakis had more pressing phone calls to make. She passed him the headset connected to the call she'd put on hold for the last ten minutes.

The tightening of his jaw was almost imperceptible before complete control slid back into place. His fingers brushed hers as he took the device from her. The unnerving voltage that came from touching Sakis made her heartbeat momentarily fluctuate but that was yet another thing she took in her stride.

His deep voice brimmed with authority and bone-deep assuredness. It held the barest hint of his Greek heritage but Brianna knew he spoke his mother tongue with the same stunning fluency and efficiency with which he ran the crude-oil brokerage arm of Pantelides Shipping, his family's multi-billion-dollar conglomerate.

'Mr President, please allow me to express my deepest regret at the situation we find ourselves in. Of course, my company takes full responsibility for this incident and will make every effort to ensure minimal ecological and economic distress. Yes, I have a fifty-man expert salvage and investigation crew on its way. They'll assess what needs to be done... Yes, I agree. I'll be there at the site within the next twelve hours.'

Brianna's fingers flew over her tablet as she absorbed the conversation and planned accordingly. By the time Sakis concluded the call, she had his private jet and necessary flight crew on standby.

They both stopped as the sleek phone rang again.

'Would you like me to get it?' Brianna asked.

Sakis shook his head. 'No. I'm the head of the company. The buck stops with me.' His gaze snagged hers with a compelling look that held hers captive. 'This is going to get worse before it gets better. Are you up to the task, Miss Moneypenny?'

Brianna forced herself to breathe, even as the tingle in her shoulder reminded her of the solemn vow she'd taken in a dark, cold room two years ago.

I refuse to sink.

She swallowed and firmed her spine. 'Yes, I'm up to the task, Mr Pantelides.'

Dark-green eyes the colour of fresh moss held hers for a moment longer. Then he gave a curt nod and picked up the phone.

'Pantelides,' he clipped out.

For the rest of the journey to Pantelides Towers, Brianna immersed herself in doing what she did best—anticipating her boss's every need and fulfilling it without so much as a whisper-light ruffle.

It was the only way she knew how to function nowadays.

By the time she handed their emergency suitcases to his helicopter pilot and followed Sakis into the lift that would take them to the helipad at the top of Pantelides Towers, they had a firm idea of what lay ahead of them.

There was nothing they could do to stop the crude oil spilling into the South Atlantic—at least not until the salvage team got there and went into action.

But, glancing at him, Brianna knew it wasn't only the disaster that had put the strain on Sakis's face. It was also being hit with the unexpected.

If there was one thing Sakis hated, it was surprises. It was why he always out-thought his opponents by a dozen moves, so he couldn't be surprised. Having gained a little insight into his past from working with him, Brianna wasn't surprised.

The devastating bombshell Sakis's father had dropped on his family when Sakis had been a teen was still fodder for journalists. Of course, she didn't know the full story, but she knew enough to understand why Sakis would hate having his company thrown into the limelight like this.

His phone rang again.

'Mrs Lowell. No, I'm sorry, there's no news.' His voice held the strength and the solid dependable calm needed to reassure the wife of the missing captain. 'Yes, he's still missing, but please be assured, I'll personally call you as soon as I have any information. You have my word.'

A pulse jumped in his temple as he hung up. 'How long before the search and rescue team are at the site?'

She checked her watch. 'Ninety minutes.'

'Hire another crew. Three teams working in eight-hour shifts are better than two working in twelve-hour shifts. I don't want anything missed because they're exhausted. And they're to work around the clock until the missing crew are found. Make it happen, Moneypenny.'

'Yes, of course.'

The lift doors opened. Brianna nearly stumbled when his hand settled in the small of her back to guide her out.

In all her time working for him, he'd never touched her in

any way. Forcing herself not to react, she glanced at him. His face was set, his brows clamped in fierce concentration as he guided her swiftly towards the waiting helicopter. A few feet away, his hand dropped. He waited for the pilot to help her up into her seat before he slid in beside her.

Before the aircraft was airborne, Sakis was on the phone again, this time to Theo. The urgent exchange in Greek went right over Brianna's head but it didn't stop her secret fascination with the mellifluous language or the man who spoke it.

His glance slid to her and she realised she'd been unashamedly staring.

She snapped her attention back to the tablet in her hand and activated it.

There'd been nothing personal in Sakis's touch or his look. Not that she'd expected there to be. In all ways and in all things, Sakis Pantelides was extremely professional.

She expected nothing less from him. And that was just the way she wished it.

Her lesson had been well and truly learned in that department, in the harshest possible way, barring death—not that she hadn't come close once or twice. And all because she'd allowed herself to *feel*, to dare to connect with another human being after the hell she'd suffered with her mother.

She was in no danger of forgetting; if she did, she had the tattoo on her shoulder to remind her.

Sakis pressed the 'end' button on yet another phone call and leaned back against the club seat's headrest.

Across from him, the tap-tap of the keyboard filled the silence as his assistant worked away at the ever-growing list of tasks he'd been throwing at her since they'd taken off four hours ago.

Turning his head, he glanced at her. As usual her face was expressionless save the occasional crease at the corner of her eyes as she squinted at the screen. Her brow remained smooth and untroubled as her fingers flew over the keyboard.

Her sleek blonde hair was in the same pristine, precise knot it had been when she'd arrived at work at six o'clock this morning. Without conscious thought, his gaze traced over her, again feeling that immediate zing to his senses.

Her dress suit was impeccable—a black-and-white combination that looked a bit severe but suited her perfectly. In her lobes, pearl earrings gleamed, small and unassuming.

His gaze slid down her neck, past slim shoulders and over the rest of her body, examining her in a way he rarely permitted himself to. The sight of the gentle curve of her breasts, her flat stomach and her long, shapely legs made his hands flex on his armrests as the zing turned stronger.

Moneypenny was fit, if a little on the slim side. Despite his slave-driving schedule, not once in the last year and a half had she turned up late for work or called in sick. He knew she stayed in the executive apartment in Pantelides Towers more and more lately rather than return to... He frowned. To wherever it was she called home.

Again he thanked whatever deity had sent her his way.

After his hellish experience with his last executive assistant, Giselle, he'd seriously contemplated commissioning a robot to handle his day-to-day life. When he'd read Brianna's flawless CV, he'd convinced himself she was too good to be true. He'd only reconsidered her after all the other candidates, after purporting to have almost identical supernatural abilities, had turned up at the interviews with not-so-hidden agendas—ones that involved getting into his bed at the earliest opportunity.

Brianna Moneypenny's file had listed talents that made him wonder why another competitor hadn't snapped her up. No one that good would've been jobless, even in the current economic climate. He'd asked her as much.

Her reply had been simple: 'You're the best at what you do. I want to work for the best.'

His hackles had risen at that response, but there had been no guile, no coquettish lowering of her lashes or strategic crossing of her legs. If anything, she'd looked defiant.

Thinking back now, he realised that was the first time he'd felt it—that tug on his senses that accompanied the electrifying sensation when he looked into her eyes.

Of course, he dismissed the feeling whenever it arose. Feelings had no place in his life or his business.

What he'd wanted was an efficient assistant who could rise to any challenge he set her. Moneypenny had risen to each challenge and continued to surprise him on a regular basis, a rare thing in a man of his position.

His gaze finally reached her feet and, with a sharp dart of astonishment, he noted the tiny tattoo on the inside of her left ankle. The star-shaped design, its circumference no larger than his thumb, was inked in black and blue and stood out against her pale skin.

Although he was staring straight at it, the mark was so out of sync with the rest of her no-nonsense persona, he wondered if he was hallucinating.

No, it was definitely a tattoo, right there, etched into her flawless skin.

Intrigued, he returned his gaze to the busy fingers tapping away. As if sensing his scrutiny, her fingers slowed and her head started to lift and turn towards him.

Sakis glanced down at his watch. 'We'll be landing in three hours. Let's take a break now and regroup in half an hour.'

Despite the loud whirr of her laptop shutting down, he noticed her attention didn't stray far from the device. Her attention never wavered from her work—a fact that should've pleased him.

'I've ordered lunch to be served in five minutes. I can hold it off for a few more minutes if you would like to look over the bios of the people we need to speak to when we land?' Her gaze met his, her blue eyes cool and unwavering.

His gaze dropped again to her ankle. As he watched, she slowly re-crossed her legs, obscuring the tattoo from his gaze.

'Mr Pantelides?' came the cool query.

Sakis inhaled slowly, willed his wavering control to slide back into place. By the time his gaze reconnected with hers, his interest in her tattoo had receded to the back of his mind.

Receded, but not been obliterated.

'Have lunch served in ten. I'll go take a quick shower.' He rose and headed for the larger of the two bedrooms at the rear of his plane.

At the door, he glanced back over his shoulder. Brianna Moneypenny was reaching for the attendant intercom with one hand while reopening her laptop with the other.

Super-efficient and ultra-professional. His executive assistant was everything she'd said on the tin, just like he'd explained to Ari.

But it suddenly occurred to Sakis that, in the eighteen months she'd worked for him, he'd never bothered looking *inside* the tin.

CHAPTER TWO

'I NEED TO get to the site asap once we land,' Sakis said in between bites of his chef-made gourmet beef burger.

Brianna curbed her pang of envy as she forked her plain, low-fat, crouton-free salad *niçoise* into her mouth and shook her head. 'The environment minister wants a meeting first. I tried to postpone it but he was insistent. I think he wants a photo op, this being an election year and all. I told him it'd have to be a brief meeting.'

His jaw tightened on his bite, his eyes narrowing with displeasure. Brianna didn't have to wonder why.

Sakis Pantelides detested any form of media attention with an almost unholy hatred, courtesy of the public devastation and humiliation Alexandrou Pantelides had visited on his family two decades ago. The Pantelides' downfall had been played out in full media glare.

'I have a helicopter on standby to take you straight to the site when you're done.'

'Make sure his people know my definition of *brief*. Do we know what the media presence is at the site?' he asked after swallowing another mouthful.

Her gaze darted to his. Green eyes watched her like a hawk. 'All the major global networks are present. We also have a couple of EPA ships in the area monitoring things.'

He gave a grim nod. 'There's not much we can do about the Environmental Protection Agency's presence, but make sure security know that they can't be allowed to interfere in the salvage and clean-up process. Rescuing the wildlife and keeping pollution to a minimum is another top priority.'

'I know. And...I had an idea.' Her plan was risky, in that it could attract more media attention than Sakis would agree to, but if she managed to pull it off it would reap enormous benefits and buy back some goodwill for Pantelides Shipping. It would also cement her invaluable status in Sakis's eyes and she could finally be rid of the sinking, rock-hard feeling in her stomach when she woke in a cold sweat many nights.

Some might find it shallow but Brianna placed job security above everything else. After everything she'd been through as a child—naively trusting that the only parent she had would put her well-being ahead of the clamour of the next drug fix—keeping her job and her small Docklands apartment meant everything to her. The terror of not knowing where her next meal would come from or when her temporary home would be taken from her still haunted her. And after her foolish decision to risk giving her trust, and the steep price she'd paid for it, she'd vowed never to be that helpless again.

'Moneypenny, I'm listening,' Sakis said briskly, and she realised he was waiting for her to speak.

Gathering her fracturing thoughts, she took a deep breath.

'I was thinking we can use the media and social network sites to our advantage. A few environmental blogs have started up, and they're comparing what's happening with the other oil conglomerate incident a few years ago. We need to nip that in the bud before it gets out of hand.'

Sakis frowned. 'It isn't even remotely the same thing. For one thing, this is a surface spill, not a deep sea pipeline breach.'

'But...'

His expression turned icy. 'I'd also like to keep the media out of this as much as possible. Things tend to get twisted around when the media becomes involved.'

'I believe this is the ideal time to bring them round to our side. I know a few journalists who are above-board. Perhaps, if we can work exclusively with them, we can get a great result. We've admitted the error is ours, so there's nothing to cover up. But not everyone has time to fact-check and the public making assumptions could be detrimental to us. We need to keep the line of communication wide open so people know everything that's going on at every stage.'

'What do you propose?' Sakis pushed his plate away.

She followed suit and fired up her laptop. Keying in the address, she called up the page she'd been working on. 'I've started a blog with a corresponding social networking accounts.' She turned the screen towards him and held her breath.

He glanced down at it. '"Save Point Noire"?'

She nodded.

'What is the point of that, exactly?'

'It's an invitation for anyone who wants to volunteer—either physically at the site or online with expertise.'

Sakis started to shake his head and her heart took a dive. 'Pantelides Shipping is responsible for this. We'll clean up our own mess.'

'Yes, but shutting ourselves off can also cause us a huge negative backlash. Look—' she indicated the numbers on the screen '—we're trending worldwide. People want to get involved.'

'Won't they see it as soliciting free help?'

'Not if we give them something in return.'

His gaze scoured her face, intense and focused, and Brianna felt a tiny burst of heat in her belly. Feverishly, she pushed it away.

'And what would that something be?' he asked.

Nerves suddenly attacked her stomach. 'I haven't thought that far ahead. But I'm sure I can come up with something before the day's out.'

He kept staring at her for so long, her insides churned

harder. Reaching for his glass, he took a long sip of water, his gaze still locked on her.

'Just when I think you're out of tricks, you surprise me all over again, Miss Moneypenny.' The slow, almost lazy murmur didn't throw her. What threw her was the keen speculation in his eyes.

Brianna held his gaze even though she yearned to look away. Speculation led to curiosity. Curiosity was something she didn't want to attract from her boss, or anyone for that matter. Her past needed to stay firmly, irretrievably buried.

'I'm not sure I know what you mean, Mr Pantelides.'

He glanced down at the laptop. 'Your plan is ingenious but, while I commend you for its inception, I'm also aware that keeping track of all the information flowing in will be a monumental task. How do you propose to do that?'

'If you give me the go-ahead, I can brief a small team back at the head office to take over. Any relevant information or genuine volunteer will be put through to me and I can take it from there.'

The decisive shake of his head made her want to clench her fist in disappointment. 'I need you with me once we get on site. I can't have you running off to check your emails every few minutes.'

'I can ask for three-hourly email updates.' When his gaze remained sceptical, she rushed on. 'You said so yourself—it's a great idea. At least let me have a go at trying to execute it. We need the flow of information now more than ever and getting the public on our side can't hurt. What do we have to lose?'

After a minute, he nodded. 'Four-hourly updates. But we make cleaning up the spill our top priority.'

'Of course.' She reached for the laptop but he leaned forward, took it from her and set it down beside his plate.

'Leave that for now. You haven't finished your meal.'

Surprised, she glanced down at her half-finished plate. 'Um...I sort of had.'

He pushed her plate towards her. 'You'll need your strength for what's ahead. Eat.'

Her gaze slid to his own unfinished meal as she picked up her fork. 'What about you?'

'My stamina is much more robust than yours—no offence.'

'None taken at all.' Her voice emerged a little stiffer than she intended.

Sakis quirked one eyebrow. 'Your response is at variance with your tone, Miss Moneypenny. I'm sure some die-hard feminist would accuse me of being sexist, but you really need it more than I do. You barely eat enough as it is.'

She gripped her fork harder. 'I wasn't aware my diet was under scrutiny.'

'It's hard to miss that you watch what you eat with almost military precision. If it wasn't absurd, I'd think you were rationing yourself.' His eyes were narrowed in that unnervingly probing way.

Her pulse skittered in alarm at the observation. 'Maybe I am.'

His lips tightened. 'Well, going without food for the sake of vanity is dangerous. You're risking your health, and thereby your ability to function properly. It's your duty to ensure you're in the right shape so you can fulfil your duties.'

The vehemence in his tone made her alarm escalate. 'Why do I get the feeling we're talking about more than my abandoned salad?'

He didn't answer immediately. His lowered lids and closed expression told her the memory wasn't a pleasant one.

He settled back in his seat, outwardly calm. But Brianna saw the hand still wrapped around his water glass wasn't quite so steady. 'Watching someone wilfully waste away despite being surrounded by abundance isn't exactly a forgettable experience.'

Her grip went slack. 'I'm sorry...I didn't mean to dredge up bad memories for you. Who do you...?'

He shook his head once and indicated her plate. 'It doesn't matter. Don't let your food go to waste, Moneypenny.'

Brianna glanced down at the remnants of her meal, trying to reconcile the outwardly confident man sitting across from her with the man whose hands trembled at a deeply disturbing memory. Not that she'd even been foolish enough to think Sakis Pantelides was one-faceted.

She recalled that one moment during her interview when he'd looked up from her file, his green eyes granite-hard and merciless.

'If you are to survive this job, I'd strongly urge you to take one piece of advice, Miss Moneypenny. Don't fall in love with me.'

Her response had been quick, painful memory making her tongue acid-sharp. 'With respect, Mr Pantelides, I'm here for the salary. The benefits package isn't too bad either, but most of all I'm here for the top-notch experience. To my knowledge, love never has and never will pay the bills.'

What she'd wanted to add then was that she'd been there, done her time and had the tattoo to prove it.

What she wanted tell him now was that she'd endured far, far worse than a hungry stomach. That she'd known the complete desolation of coming a poor second to her mother's love for drugs. She'd slept rougher than any child deserved to and had fought every day to survive in a concrete jungle, surrounded by the drug-addled bullies with vicious fists.

She held her tongue because to speak would be to reveal far more than she could ever afford to reveal.

Curiosity gnawed at her but she refused to probe further. Probing would invite reciprocity. Her past was under lock and key, tucked behind a titanium vault and sealed in concrete. And that was exactly where she intended to keep it.

In silence, she finished her meal and looked up with relief as the attendant arrived to clear away their plates.

When the phone rang, she pounced on it, grabbing the familiarity that came with work in an effort to banish the brief moments of unguarded intimacy.

'The captain of the coast guard is on the line for you.'

Sakis's gaze swept over her face, a speculative gleam in his eyes that slowly disappeared as he took the phone.

With an inward sigh of relief, Brianna reached for her laptop and fired it up.

Sakis's first glimpse of the troubled tanker made his gut clench hard. He tapped the helicopter pilot on the shoulder.

'Circle the vessel, would you? I want to assess the damage from the air before we land.'

The pilot obliged. Sakis's jaw tightened as he grasped the full impact of the damage of the tanker bearing the black and gold Pantelides colours.

He signalled for the pilot to land and alighted the moment the chopper touched down. A group of scandal-hungry journalists stood behind the cordoned-off area. From painful experience, Moneypenny's suggestion to bring them on-side rankled, but Sakis didn't dismiss the fact that in this instance she was right.

Ignoring them for now, he strode to where the crew waited, dressed in yellow, high-visibility jumpsuits.

'What's the situation?' he asked.

The head of the salvage crew—a thickset, middle-aged man with greying hair—stepped forward. 'We've managed to get inside the tanker and assessed the damage with the investigation team—we have three breached compartments. The other compartments haven't been affected but, the longer the vessel stays askew, the more likely we are to have another breach. We're working as fast as we can to set up the pumps to drain the compartment and the spillage.'

'How long will it take?'

'Thirty-six to forty-eight hours. Once the last of the crew get here, we'll work around the clock.'

Sakis nodded and turned to see Brianna emerge from the hastily set-up tents on the far side of the beach. For a moment he couldn't reconcile the woman heading towards him with his usual impeccably dressed assistant. Not that she had a hair out of place, of course. But she'd changed into cargo pants and a white T-shirt which was neatly tucked in and belted tight, emphasising her trim waist. Her shining hair made even more vivid by the fierce African sun was still caught in an immaculate knot, but on her feet she wore weathered combat boots.

For the second time today, Sakis felt the attraction he'd ruthlessly battened down strain at the leash.

Ignoring it, he turned his attention to the man next to him. 'It'll be nightfall in three hours. How many boats do you have conducting the search?'

'We have four boats, including the two you provided. Your helicopter is also assisting with the search.' The captain wiped a trickle of sweat off his face. 'But what worries me is the possibility of pirates.'

His gut clenched. 'You think they've been kidnapped?'

The captain nodded. 'We can't rule it out.'

Brianna's eyes widened, then she extracted her mini-tablet from her thigh pocket, her fingers flying over the keypad.

One corner of her lower lip was caught between her teeth as she pressed buttons. A small spike of heat broke through the tight anxiety in his gut. Without giving it the tiniest room, Sakis smashed down on it. *Hard.*

'What is it, Moneypenny?' he asked briskly after he'd dismissed the captain.

Her brow creased but she didn't look up. 'I'm sorry, I should've anticipated the pirates angle...'

He caught her chin with his forefinger and gently forced her head up. When her gaze connected with his, he saw the trace of distress in her eyes.

'That's what the investigators are here for. Besides, you've had a lot to deal with in the last several hours. What I need is the list of journalists you promised. Can you handle that?'

Her nod made her skin slide against his finger. Soft. Silky. Smooth.

Stási!

He stepped back abruptly and pushed the aberration from his mind.

Turning, he moved towards the shoreline, conscious that she'd fallen into step beside him. From the air, he'd guestimated that the oil had spread about half a mile along the shore. As he surveyed the frantic activity up and down the once pristine shoreline, regret bit deep.

Whatever had triggered this accident, the blame for the now-blackened, polluted water lay with him, just as he was responsible for the missing crew members. Whatever it took, he would make this right.

The captain of the salvage crew brought the small boat near and Sakis went towards it. When Brianna moved towards him, he shook his head.

'No, stay here. This could be dangerous.'

She frowned. 'If you're going aboard the tanker, you'll need someone to jot down the details and take pictures of the damage.'

'I merely want to see the damage from the inside myself. I'm leaving everything else in the hands of the investigators. And, if I need to, I'm sure I can handle taking a few pictures. What I'm not sure of is the situation inside the vessel and I won't risk you getting injured under any circumstances.' He held out his hand for the camera slung around her neck.

She looked ready to argue with him. Beneath her T-shirt, her chest rose and fell as she exhaled and Sakis forced himself not to glance down as another spike of erotic heat lanced his groin.

Theos...

The unsettling feeling made him snap his fingers, an irritatingly frantic need to step away from her charging into him.

'If you're sure,' she started.

'I'm sure.'

By the time she freed herself from the camera strap and handed it over, her face had settled once more into its customary serene professionalism.

Her fingers brushed his as he took the camera and Sakis registered a single instance of softness before the contact was disconnected.

Taking a deep breath, he started to walk away.

'Wait!'

He turned back. 'What is it, Moneypenny?' His tone was harsh but couldn't stop the disturbing edginess creeping over him.

She held out a large yellow jumpsuit. 'You can't get on the boat without wearing this. The health and safety guidelines require it.'

Despite the grim situation, Sakis wanted to laugh at her implacable expression as she held him to account.

'Then by all means...if the guidelines require it.'

He took the plastic garment, shook it out and stepped into it under her watchful eye. He glanced at her as he zipped the jumpsuit and once again saw her lower lip caught between her teeth.

With more force than was necessary, he shoved the small digital camera into the waterproof pocket and trudged through the oil-slicked water.

An hour later, the words of his lead investigator made his heart sink.

'I retired from piloting tankers like these ten years ago, and even then the navigation systems were state-of-the-art. Your vessel has the best one I've ever seen. There's no way this was systems failure. Too many fail-safes in place for the vessel to veer this far off course.'

Sakis gave a grim nod and pulled his phone from his pocket. 'Moneypenny, get me the head of security. I want to know everything about Morgan Lowell... Yes, the captain of my tanker. And prepare a press release. Unfortunately, the investigators are almost certain this was pilot error.'

Brianna perused the electronic page for typos. Once she was satisfied, she approached where Sakis stood with the environment minister. His yellow jumpsuit was unzipped to the waist, displaying the dark-green T-shirt that moulded his lean, sleekly muscular torso. She'd never thought she'd find the sight of a man slipping on a hideous yellow jumpsuit so...hot and unsettling.

He turned, and she held her breath as his gaze swept over her. The crackle of electricity she'd felt earlier when their fingers had touched returned.

Abruptly she pushed it away. They were caught in a severely fraught set of circumstances. What she was experiencing was just residual adrenaline that came with these unfortunate events.

'Is it ready?' he asked.

She nodded and passed the press release over, along with the list of names he'd requested. He skimmed the words then passed the tablet back to her. Brianna knew he'd memorised every single word.

'I'll go and prep the media.'

She headed for the group of journalists poised behind the white cordon. As she walked, she practised the breathing exercises she'd mastered long before she'd come to work for Sakis Pantelides.

By the time she reached the group, she'd calmed her roiling emotions.

'Good evening, ladies and gentlemen. This is how it's going to work. Mr Pantelides will give his statement. Then he'll invite questions—one from each of you.' She held out a hand at the immediate protests. 'I'm sure you'll understand that it'll take hours for every question you've jotted down to be answered and frankly we don't have time for that. Right now the priority is the salvage operation. So, one question each.' Control settled over her as her steely gaze held the group's and received their cooperation.

Yes, that was more like it. Not for her the searing, jittery feelings of the last few hours, ever since she'd looked up on the plane and caught Sakis's gaze on her ankle tattoo; since he'd touched her on the beach, told her not to worry that she'd missed the pirates angle. Those few minutes had been intensely...*rattling*.

The momentary heat she'd seen in his eyes had thrown her off-balance. At the start of her employment she'd taken pains to hide the tattoo but, after realising Sakis took no notice of what she wore or anything about her, she'd relaxed. The sensation of his eyes on her tattoo had smashed a fist through her tight control.

It had taken hours to restore it but, now she had, she was determined not to lose it again.

There was too much at stake.

Feeling utterly composed, she glanced over to where Sakis waited at the assembled podium. At his nod, she signalled security to let the media through.

She stood next to the podium and tried not to let his deep voice affect her as he started speaking. His authority and confidence as he outlined the plans for the salvage mission and the search for the missing crew belied the tension in his body. From her position, she could see the rigid outline of his washboard stomach and the braced tension in his legs. Even though his hands remained loose at his sides, his shoulders barely moved as he spoke.

A camera flashed nearby and she saw his tiniest flinch.

'What's going to happen to the remaining oil on board?' a reporter asked.

His gaze swung to where the minister stood. 'For their very generous assistance, we're donating the contents on board the distressed vessel to the coast guard and army. The minister has kindly offered to co-ordinate the distribution.'

'So you're just going to give away oil worth millions of dollars, out of the goodness of your heart? Are you trying to bribe your way out of your company's responsibilities, Mr Pantelides?'

Brianna's breath stalled but Sakis barely blinked at the caustic remark from a particularly vile tabloid reporter. That he didn't visibly react was a testament to his unshakeable control.

'On the contrary, as I said at the start, my company assumes one hundred per cent liability for this incident and are working with the government in making reparations. No price is too high to pay for ensuring that the clean-up process is speedy and causes minimum damage to the sea life. This means the remaining crude oil has to be removed as quickly as possible and the vessel secured and towed away. Rather than transfer it to another Pantelides tanker, a process that'll take time, I've decided to donate it to the government. I'm sure you'll agree it makes perfect sense.' His tone remained even but the tic in his jaw belied his simmering anger. 'Next question.'

'Can you confirm what caused the accident? According to your sources, this is one of your newest tankers, equipped with state-of-the-art navigation systems, so what went wrong?'

'That is a question for our investigators to answer once they'd finished their work.'

'What does your gut feeling say?'

'I choose to rely on hard facts when stakes are this high, not gut feelings,' Sakis responded, his tone clipped.

'You haven't made a secret of your dislike for the media. Are you going to use that to try and stop the media from reporting on this accident, Mr Pantelides?'

'You wouldn't be here if I felt that way. In fact—' he

stopped and flicked a glance at Brianna before facing the crowd, but not before she caught a glimpse of the banked unease in his eyes '—I've hand-picked five journalists who will be given exclusive access to the salvage process.'

He read out the names. While the chosen few preened, the rest of the media erupted with shouted questions.

One in particular filtered through. 'If your father were alive and in your place, how would he react to this incident? Would he try and buy his way out of it, like he did with everything else?'

The distressed sound slipped from Brianna's throat before she could stop it. Silence fell over the gathered group as the words froze in the air. Beneath the podium, out of sight of the media's glare, Sakis's hands clenched into white-knuckled fists.

The urge to protect him surged out of nowhere and swept over her in an overwhelming wave. Her heart lurched, bringing with it a light-headedness that made her sway where she stood. Sakis's quick sideways glance told her he'd noticed.

Facing the media, he inhaled slowly. 'You have to go to the afterlife to ask my father that question. I do not speak for the dead.'

He stepped from the podium and stood directly in front of her. The breadth of his broad shoulders blocked out the sun.

'What's wrong?' he demanded in a fierce whisper.

'N...nothing. Everything is fine.... Going according to plan.' She fought to maintain her steady breathing even as she flailed inside. Needing desperately to claw back her control, she searched blindly for the solid reassurance of her mini-tablet.

Sakis plucked it out of her hands, his piercing gaze unwavering as it remained trained on her. '*According to plan* would be these damned vultures finding another carcass to pick on and leaving us to get on with the work that needs to be done.' From his tone, there was no sign that the last question had had a lasting effect on him, but this close she saw his pinched lips and the ruthlessly suppressed pain in his eyes. Another wave of protectiveness rushed over her.

Purpose. That was what she needed. Purpose and focus.

Swallowing hard, she held out her hand for her tablet. 'I'll take care of it. You've chosen the journalists you want to cover the salvage operation. There's no need for the rest to hang around.'

He didn't relinquish it. 'Are you sure you're all right? You look pale. I hope you're not succumbing to the heat. Have you had anything to eat since we got here?'

'I'm fine, Mr Pantelides.' He kept staring at her, dark brows clamped in a frown. 'I assure you, there's nothing wrong.' She deliberately made her voice crisp. 'The sooner I get rid of the media, the sooner we can get on with things.'

He finally let her take the tablet from him. Hardly daring to breathe, Brianna stepped back and away from the imposing man in front of her.

No. No. No...

The negative sound reverberated through her skull as she walked away. There was no way she was developing feelings for her boss.

Even if Sakis didn't fire her the moment she betrayed even the slightest non-professional emotion, she had no intention of letting herself down like that ever again.

The tattoo on her ankle throbbed.

The larger one on her shoulder burned with the fierce reminder.

She'd spent two years in jail for her serious error in judgement after funnelling her need to be loved towards the wrong guy.

Making the same mistake again was not an option.

CHAPTER THREE

SAKIS WATCHED BRIANNA walk away; her back was held so rigid her upper half barely moved. His frown deepened. Something was wrong. Granted, this was the first crisis they'd been thrown into together, but her conduct up till now had been beyond exemplary.

Right up until she'd reacted strongly to the journalist's question. A question he himself had not anticipated. He should've known that somehow his father would be dredged up like this. Should've known that, even from beyond the grave, the parent who'd held his family in such low, deplorable regard would not remain buried. He stomped on the pain riding just beneath his chest, the way he always did when he thought of his father. He refused to let the past haunt him. It no longer had any power over him.

After what his father had done to his family, to his mother especially, he deserved to be forgotten totally and utterly.

Unfortunately, at times like these, when the media thought they could get a whiff of scandal, they pounced. And this time, there was no escaping their rabid focus...

The deafening sound of the industrial-size vacuum starting up drew his attention from Brianna, reminding him that he had more important things to deal with than his hitherto unruffled personal assistant's off behaviour, and the unwanted memories of a ghost.

He zipped his jumpsuit back up and strode over to the black, slick shoreline. Half a mile away, giant oil-absorbing booms floated around the perimeter of the contaminated water to catch the spreading spill. Closer to shore, right in the middle of where the oil poured out, ecologically safe chemicals pumped from huge sprays to dissolve as much of the slick as possible.

It's not enough. It would never be enough because this shouldn't have happened in the first place.

His phone rang and he recognised Theo's number on his screen.

'What's happening, brother? Talk to me,' Theo said.

Sakis summarised the situation as quickly as he could, leaving out nothing, even though he was very aware that the mention of kidnap would raise painful, unwanted memories for Theo.

'Anything I can do from here?' his brother asked. The only hint of his disturbance at being reminded of his own kidnap when he was eighteen was the slight ring of steel in his voice when he asked the question. 'I can put you in touch with the right people if you want. I made it my business to find out who the right contacts are in a situation like this.' His analytical brain wouldn't have made him cope with his ordeal otherwise.

That was Theo through and through. He went after a problem until he had every imaginable scenario broken down, then he went after the solution with single-minded determination—which was why he fulfilled his role as trouble-shooter for Pantelides Inc so perfectly.

'We've got it in hand. But perhaps you could cause an outrageous scandal where you are, distract these damned paparazzi from messing with my salvage operation.'

'Hmm, I suppose I could skydive naked from the top of *Cristo Redentor*,' Theo offered.

For the first time in what felt like days, Sakis's lips cracked in a smile. 'You love Rio too much to get yourself barred from the city for ever for blasphemy.' His gaze flicked to where Brianna stood alone, having dispersed the last of the journalists. She was back on her tablet, her fingers busy on the glass keyboard.

Satisfaction oozed through him. Whatever had fractured his PA's normal efficiency, she had it back again.

'Everything's in hand,' he repeated, probably more to reassure himself that he had his emotions under control.

'Great to hear. Keep me in the loop, *ne*?'

Sakis signed off and jumped into the nearest boat carrying a crew of six and the vacuum, and signalled to the pilot to head out.

For the next three hours, while sunlight prevailed, he worked with the crew to pump as much sludge of out the water as possible. From another boat nearby, the journalists to whom he'd granted access filmed the process. Some even asked intelligent questions that didn't make his teeth grind.

Floodlights arrived, mounted on tripods on more boats, and he carried on working.

It was nearing midnight when, alerted to the arrival of the refresh crew, he straightened from where he'd been managing the pump. And froze.

'What the hell?'

The salvage-crew captain glanced up sharply. 'Excuse me, sir?'

But Sakis's gaze was on the boat about twenty yards to his left, where Brianna held the nozzle of a chemical spray aimed at the slick, a distressed look on her face as she swung her arm back and forth over the water.

The first of the changeover crew was approaching on a motor-powered dinghy. Sakis hopped into the small vessel and directed it to where Brianna worked.

Seeing him approach on a direct course, she changed the angle of her nozzle to avoid spraying him, her face hurriedly set in its usual calm expression. It was almost as if the bleakness he'd glimpsed moments ago had been a mirage.

'Mr Pantelides, did you need something?'

For some reason, the sound of his father's name on her lips aggravated him. For several hours he'd managed not to think about his father. He wanted to keep it that way. 'Put that hose down and get in.'

She turned the spray off, eyes widening. 'Excuse me?'

'Get in here. *Now*.'

'I...I don't understand,' she said. Her voice had lost a little of the sharpness and she looked genuinely puzzled as she stared down at him.

He saw the long streak of oil across her cheek. Her once white T-shirt had now turned grimy and slick and her khaki cargo pants had suffered the same fate.

But not a single hair was out of place.

The dichotomy of dirt, flawless efficiency and the bleakness he'd glimpsed a moment ago intrigued him beyond definition. The intrigue escalated his irritation. 'It's almost midnight. You should've left here hours ago.' He manoeuvred the dinghy until it bumped the boat, directly below where she stood on the starboard side.

From that angle, he couldn't miss the landscape of her upper body—more specifically, the perfect shape of her breasts or the sleek line of her jaw and neck as she glanced down at him.

'Oh. Well...I'm here to work, Mr Pantelides. Why should I have left?'

'Because you're not part of the salvage team, and even they work in six-hour shifts. Besides this—' he waved at the nozzle in her hand '—is not part of your job description.'

'I'm aware of what my job description is. But, if we're being pedantic, you're not part of the crew either. And yet here you are.'

Sakis felt a shake of surprise. In all her time with him, she'd never raised her voice or shown signs of feminine ire. But in the last few minutes, he'd seen intense emotion ream over her face and through her voice. Right now, Sakis had the distinct feeling she was extremely displeased with his directive. A small spurt of masochistic pleasure fizzed through him at the thought that he'd unruffled the unflappable Miss Moneypenny.

'I'm the boss. I have the luxury of doing whatever the hell I want,' he said softly, his gaze raking her face, secretly eager for further animated reaction.

What he got was unexpected. Her shoulders slumped and she shrugged. 'Of course. But, just in case you're worried about the corporate risks, I signed a waiver before coming aboard. So you'll suffer no liability if anything happens to me.'

Irritation returned, bit deeper. 'I don't give a damn about personal liability or corporate risks. What I do give a damn about is your ability to function properly tomorrow if you don't get enough sleep. You've been up for over eighteen hours. So, unless you have super powers I'm not aware of, put that hose down and get down here.' He held out a hand, unwilling to examine this almost clawing need to take care of her.

She didn't put the hose down. Instead she handed it over to a salvage crew member. Finally, she faced Sakis.

'Fine. You win.' Again he saw the tiniest mutinous set to her lips and wondered why that little action pleased him so much.

He was tired; he *must* be hallucinating. He certainly wasn't thinking straight if the thought of getting under his executive assistant's skin held so much of his interest.

She swung long, slim legs over the side of the boat and dropped into the dinghy. The movement made the vessel sway. She swayed with it, and threw out a hand to steady herself as Sakis turned.

Her torso bumped his arm and her hand landed on his shoulder as she tried to find her feet. His arm snagged her waist, encountered firm, warm muscle beneath his fingers.

Heat punched through his chest and arrowed straight for his groin.

'*Stasi!*'

'I...I'm sorry,' she stammered, pulling away with a skittishness very unlike her.

'No harm done,' he murmured. But Sakis wasn't so hot on that reassurance. Harm was being done to his insides. Heat continued to ravage him, firing sensations he sure as hell didn't want fired up. And especially not with his PA.

A quick glance showed she'd retreated to the farthest part of the small dinghy with her arms crossed primly around her middle and her face averted from his. He tried not to let his gaze drop to her plump breasts...but, *Theos*, it was hard not to notice their tempting fullness.

With a muttered curse, his hand tightened on the rudder of the dinghy and steered it towards shore.

This time she didn't refuse his offer of help when they stepped into the shallow water. After making sure the vessel was secure, he followed her onto the floodlit beach.

When he neared, he caught another glimpse of distress on her face.

'What's wrong? Why were you on the salvage boat? And, before you trot out "nothing", I'd advise you not to insult my intelligence.'

He saw her hesitate, then shove her hands into her pockets. This time, he couldn't stop himself from staring at her chest. Thankfully, she didn't notice because her gaze wasn't on him.

'I was talking to the some of the locals earlier. This cove was a special place for them, a sanctuary. I...I felt bad about what's happened.'

Guilt lanced through him. But, more than that, the rare glimpse into Brianna Moneypenny's human side intrigued him more than ever. 'I'll make sure it's returned to them as pristine as it once was.'

Her gaze flew up and connected with his, surprise and pleasure reflected in her eyes. 'That's good. It's not nice when your sanctuary is ripped away from you.' The pain accompanying those words made him frown. Before he could probe deeper, she stepped back. 'Anyway, I assured them you would make it right.'

'Thank you.'

She started to walk towards the fleet of four-wheelers a short distance away. Their driver stood next to the first one.

'I reserved a suite for you at the Noire. Your case was taken there a few hours ago and your laptop and phones are in the jeep. I'll see you in the morning, Mr Pantelides,' she tagged on.

Sakis froze. *'You'll see me in the morning?* Aren't you coming with me?'

'No,' she said.

'Why not?'

'Because I'm not staying at the hotel.'

'Where exactly are you staying?'

She indicated the double row of yellow tents set up further up on the beach, away from the bustle of the clean-up work.

'I've secured a tent and put my stuff in there.'

'What's wrong with staying at the same hotel I'm staying in?'

'Nothing, except they didn't have any more rooms. The suite I reserved for you was the last one. The other hotels are too far away to make the commute efficient.'

Sakis shook his head. 'You've been on your feet all day with barely a break— Don't argue with me, Moneypenny,' He raised a hand when she started to speak. 'You're not sleeping in a flimsy tent on the beach with machines blasting away all around you. Go and get your things.'

'I assure you, it's more than adequate.'

'No. You say I have a suite?'

'Yes.'

'Then there is no reason why we can't share it.'

'I would rather not, Mr Pantelides.'

The outright refusal shocked and annoyed him in equal measures. Also another first from Brianna Moneypenny was the fact that she wasn't quite meeting his gaze. 'Why would you *rather not*?'

She hesitated.

'Look at me, Moneypenny,' he commanded.

Blue eyes... No, they weren't quite blue. They were a shade of aquamarine, wide, lushly lashed and beautiful...and they met his in frank challenge. 'Your room is a single suite with one double bed. It's not suitable for two, um, professionals, and I'd rather not have to share my personal space.'

Sakis thought of the countless women who would jump at the chance to share 'personal space' with him.

He thought of all the women who would kill to share a double bed with him.

Then he thought of why he was here, in this place: with *his* oil contaminating a once incredibly beautiful beach; *his* crew missing; and the tabloid press just waiting for him to slip up, to show them that the apple hadn't fallen far from the tree.

The sick feeling that he'd forced down but never quite suppressed enough threatened to rise again. It was the same mingled despair and anger he'd felt when Theo had been taken. The same sense of helplessness when he'd been unable to do anything to stop his mother fading away before his eyes, her pain raw and wrenching after what his father and the media had done to her.

'I don't give a damn about your personal space. What I do give a damn about is your ability to fire on all cylinders. We discussed this—you being up to standing by me in this situation we find ourselves in. You assured me you were up to the task. And yet, for the last ten minutes, you've shown a certain...mutiny that makes me wonder whether you're equipped to handle what's coming.'

Her outrage made her breathing erratic. 'I don't think that's a fair observation, sir. I've done everything you've asked of me, and I'm more than capable of handling whatever comes. Just because I disagree with you on one small issue doesn't make me mutinous. I'm thinking about you.'

'Then prove it. Stop arguing with me and get in the jeep.'

She opened her mouth; closed it again. When she looked

at him, her eyes held a hint of fire he'd seen more than once today. The fire *he'd* tried—and failed—to bank fired up deep in his groin.

'I'll go and get my things,' she said.

'No need.' He exchanged glances with the driver and the young man headed towards the row of tents. Sakis leaned against the jeep's hood. 'You can fill me in on the results of your social media campaign while we wait.'

He saw how eagerly she snatched at her tablet and suppressed another bout of irritation. Whatever was causing this abnormal behaviour, he needed to nip it in the bud pretty darned quick. The crisis on his hands needed all his attention.

'I've found six individuals who I think will be useful to us. One's a professor of marine biology based in Guinea Bissau. Another, a husband and wife team who are experts in wildlife rescue. They specialise in disaster rescue such as this. The other three have no specialities but they have a huge social media following and are known for volunteering on humanitarian missions. I'm having all six vetted by our security team. If they pass the security test, I'll arrange for them to be flown over tomorrow.'

'I'm still not convinced bringing even more focus on this crisis is the best way to go, Moneypenny.' His insides tightened as he thought of his mother. 'Sometimes you don't see the harm until it's too late.' He thought of her devastation and misery, the incessant sobbing, and finally the substitution of food with alcohol when it'd hit home that the husband she'd thought was a god amongst men, the man she'd thought was true to her and only her, had had a string of affairs with mistresses around the globe, some of whom had dated back to before he'd put his wedding ring on her finger.

The year he'd turned fifteen had been the bleakest year of his life. It was the year he'd had every child's basest fear confirmed—that his father did not love him, did not love anyone or anything but himself. It was also the start of Sakis's hatred of the media, who'd not only exposed his worst fears but trumpeted it to the world.

Ari had withstood the invasion of their lives with his usual unflappable demeanour, although Sakis had a feeling his brother had been just as devastated, if not more so, than he had been. Theo, thirteen at that time, with fresh teenage hormones battering him, had gone off the rails. To this day, their mother had never found out how many times Theo had run away from home because Ari, seventeen going on seventy, had found him every single time and brought him back.

In all that chaos, Sakis had watched his mother deteriorate before his eyes, culminating in her seeking a solution so horrific, he still shuddered at the memory.

He pushed the events of decades past out of his mind and focused on the woman in front of him, who watched him with barely veiled curiosity.

Silently, he held her gaze until hers fell away. That he immediately wished it back made him suppress a frustrated growl.

'The journalists we hand-picked know this could be the opportunity of a lifetime for them as long as they play ball. I'll make sure they portray an open and honest account of what we're doing to remedy the situation, while infusing the appropriate rhetoric to protect the company's reputation.'

A smile tugged at his mouth. 'You should've been a diplomat, Moneypenny.'

Her shoulder lifted in a shrug that drew his attention to where it had no business being, specifically the pulse beating beneath her flawless skin.

'We all have something we desire more than anything. Wasting the opportunity when it presents itself is plain foolishness.'

The temptation to look inside the tin was too much to pass up. 'And what is it *you* want?'

Her startled gaze flew to his. 'Excuse me?'

'What do you want more than anything?'

She shook her head and looked away, a hint of desperation in the movement. He saw her relieved expression as his driver approached, her small carry-all in his hand.

Striding forward, she took the case from the surprised driver and stowed it in the boot. Then she opened the back door and got in.

Sakis took his time to walk to the other door. He ignored her nervous glance and waited until they were both buckled in and the jeep was moving along the dusty road running alongside the beach. The moment she relaxed, he pounced. 'Well?'

'Well what?'

'I'm waiting for an answer.'

'About what I want?' she asked.

Her stall tactics didn't go unnoticed. 'Yes,' he pressed.

'I...want the chance to prove that I can do a good job and be recognised for it.'

He exhaled impatiently. 'You already do an exemplary job, and you're highly paid and highly valued for it.'

He battled the disappointment rising inside. He'd wanted *personal*. From the assistant he'd warned against getting personal. So what? Finding out a little bit about what went on behind that professional façade didn't mean either of them risked losing their highly functional relationship. Besides, Moneypenny knew of his liaisons; she arranged the lunches, dinners and the odd, discreet parting gift.

The balance needed adjusting, just a little. 'Do you have a boyfriend?'

Her head whipped round, perfect eyebrows arching. 'I beg your pardon?'

'It's a very simple question, Moneypenny. One that demands a simple yes or no answer.'

'I know it is, but I fail to see how that's *relevant* within the realms of our working relationship.'

He noted the agitated cadence of her breathing and hid a

smile. 'I believe it's company policy to have a yearly appraisal. You've been working for me for almost eighteen months and you're yet to have your first appraisal.'

'HR gave me my appraisal six months ago. They sent you the results, I believe.'

'Probably, but I haven't read it yet.'

'So you want to do your own evaluation...*now*?'

He shrugged, a little irritated with himself now that he was pushing the subject. But, now the question was out there, it niggled and, yes, he wanted to know if Brianna Moneypenny had urges just like the rest of the human race. She wasn't a robot. She'd felt warm and most definitely feminine when her body had brushed against his on the boat. Her comment about restoring the beach for the local inhabitants had also uncovered a hitherto hidden soft side he hadn't expected.

Moneypenny was human. And compassionate. And he was curious about her.

He shifted to ease the sudden restless throb in his body. 'Call it a mini-appraisal. I just want to know if anything on your CV has changed since you joined me. You listed your marital status as single when I employed you. I merely want to know if that's changed in any significant way.'

'So you want to know, purely from a professional point of view, whether I'm sleeping with anyone or not?' Her tone dripped cynicism. 'Do you want to know which brand of underwear I prefer and what I like for breakfast as well?

Sakis felt no shame. *Redressing the balance.* Plus he needed something to take his mind off what had been a hellish day... if only for a moment. 'Yes to my first question; the other two are optional.'

Brianna's chin lifted. 'In that case, since it's for *purely professional* purposes, no, I don't have a lover, my underwear is my own business and I have an unhealthy weakness for pancakes. Are you satisfied?'

The thrill of gratification that arrowed through him made his pulse race dangerously. Disturbingly.

He glanced at the tight coil of golden hair that gleamed as they passed under bright streetlights, at her pert nose and generously wide and full mouth; the dimple that winked in her cheek when she pursed her lips in irritation, like she was doing now...

The thrill escalated, rushing through his blood.

Theos...

He rubbed at his tired eyes with the heels of his palms. What the hell was wrong with him? Strong coffee; that was what he needed. Or a stiff drink to knock everything back into perspective.

Because there was no way in hell he planned on following through with this insane attraction to Moneypenny. No damned way...

The streets were deserted as they approached the leafy centre of Pointe Noire. Their hotel was pleasant enough with a sweeping circular driveway that ended in front of the white three-storey, shutter-windowed pre-colonial building.

The manager waited in the foyer to greet them personally, although his gaze widened when it lit on Brianna.

'Welcome to the Noire, Monsieur Pantelides. Your suite is ready, although I was told you would be the sole occupant?'

'You were misinformed.'

'Ah, well, my apologies for the lack of more prestigious suites but the rooms were all booked up the moment the crash...er...the moment the unfortunate event happened.' He couldn't quite keep the gloating pride from his voice.

As the manager called the lift and they entered the small space, he sensed Brianna's tension mount. The moment they were let into the suite, he understood why.

The 'suite' label had clearly been a lofty idea in someone's deluded mind. The room was only marginally larger than a double room with the sleeping area separated from the double sofa by a TV and drinks unit.

He only half-listened as the manager expounded on the many features of the room. His attention was caught on Brianna, who stood staring at the bed as if it was her mortal enemy, her shoulders stiff and her face even stiffer. Had their whole reason for being here not so dire, he'd have been amused.

He dismissed the manager. He'd barely left when a knock came at the door.

Brianna jumped.

'Relax, it's only our bags,' he reassured her with a frown.

'Oh, yes, of course.'

The porters entered and Sakis made sure they left just as quickly.

Silence reigned, thick and heavy, permeating the air with a sexual atmosphere he recognised but was determined to ignore. It had no business here.

And yet, it refused to be stemmed.

He watched as she came towards him and reached for the bag the porter had left beside him.

'You take the shower first,' he said. The image that slammed into his mind sent a dark tremor through him but he forced himself to breathe through it.

She straightened and her gaze darted to the bathroom door in the so-called suite. 'If you're sure.'

'Yes, I'm sure.' Then, unable to stop himself, even while every sense screamed at him to step away, he reached out and rubbed the smudge on her cheek.

Her breath caught on a strangled gasp, sending another punch of heat through him. His senses screamed harder, but his fingers stayed put, stroking her soft, warm skin.

'You have an oil streak right there.' He rubbed again.

With a sharply drawn breath, she moved away, but her eyes stayed on him, and in their depths Sakis saw the clear evidence of lust...and another emotion he'd never seen in a woman's eyes when it came to him: fear.

What the hell?

Before he could question her, she swung away. 'I...I'll try not to take too long.'

With quick strides, she disappeared into the bathroom and slammed the door, leaving him standing there staring at the door with a growing erection and an ever-rising pulse rate that made him certain he risked serious health problems if he didn't get it under control.

Thee mou... Of all the times and places—and sheer idiocy, bearing in mind the recipient—it seemed his libido had taken this moment to run rampant and to focus its attention on the one person he should absolutely not focus on.

Crisis heightened the senses and made men and women succumb to inappropriate urges, leading to serious errors of judgment that later came back to bite them in the ass.

Whatever was happening here, he needed to kill it with a swift, merciless death. And he certainly needed not to think of Moneypenny behind that door, removing her clothes, stepping naked, beneath the warm shower...

Moving the drinks cabinet, he poured himself a shot of whiskey. As he downed it, his gaze strayed to the bathroom door.

Nothing was going to happen. He refused to let it.

As if hammering home the point, he heard the distinct sound of the lock sliding home.

And poured himself another drink.

Brianna sagged against the door, unable to catch her breath. The bag slid uselessly from her fingers and she didn't need to look down to see evidence of her body's reaction to Sakis Pantelides. She could feel every inch of her skin tightening, burning, reacting to his touch as if he was still rubbing her cheek.

No. No. No!

Anger lent her strength, enough to tug her boots off and fling them away with distressed disgust. Her oil-smudged cargo pants went the same way, followed by her once white T-shirt. About to reach for the bra clasp, she glanced up and caught the reflection of her tattoo in the wide bathroom mirror.

Sucking in a deep breath, she stepped forward, clutched the sink and struggled to regulate her breathing.

She stared hard at the tattoo on her shoulder. *I refuse to sink*. It was the mantra she'd recited second by second in her darkest days. And one she'd tapped from whenever she needed strength or self-belief…anything to get her through a tough day. It was a reminder of what she'd survived as a child and as an adult. A reminder that depending on anyone for her happiness or wellbeing was asking to be devastated. She'd made that mistake once and look where she'd ended up.

The tattoo was a reminder never to forget. To keep swimming. Never to sink.

And yet it was exactly what she was doing; sinking into Sakis's eyes, into the miasma of erotic sensations that had reduced her control to nothing. Sensation that had grown with each look, each careless touch, and was now threatening to choke all common sense out of her.

Her hand settled over her heart as if she could stem its chaotic beating. Then she slowly traced it down, past the scar on her hip to the top of her panties and the heat pooling just below.

The urge to touch herself was strong, almost supernatural. The urge to have stronger, more powerful hands touch her *there* was even more visceral.

Gritting her teeth, she traced her fingers back up to the scar.

Slowly, strength and purpose returned.

Between the tattoo and the scar, she had vivid reminders of why she could never let her guard down again, never trust another human being again. She intended to cling to them with everything she had. Because the purpose she'd seen in Sakis's eyes had scared her.

A determined Sakis was a formidable Sakis.

She would need all the strength she could muster. Because she had a feeling this crisis was far from over; that Sakis would demand more from her than he ever had.

She whirled from the sink and entered the shower. By the time she'd washed the grime off her body, a semblance of calm had returned.

She dried herself and dressed quickly in a T-shirt and the short leggings she used for the gym that—thank God—she'd had the forethought to pack. If she'd been alone, the T-shirt would've sufficed but there was no way she was going out there, sharing a room with Sakis Pantelides, with a thigh-skimming T-shirt and bare legs.

The fiery sensation she'd managed to bank threatened to rise again. Quickly, she brushed her teeth, pulled her hair into its no-nonsense bun and left the bathroom.

Sakis stood outside on the tiny balcony that served the room, a drink in his hand, staring out into the sultry, humid night. His other hand was braced on the iron railing.

She paused and stared as he turned his head. His commanding profile caught and held her attention. His full lower lip was now drawn in a tight line as he stared into the contents of his glass. A wave of bleakness passed over his face and she wondered if he was replaying the journalist's question about his father.

Sakis didn't often display emotion, but she'd seen the way he'd reacted to that personal question. And his answer had been a revelation in itself. He bore no loving memories of his father but he certainly bore scars from his father's legacy.

Unbidden, the earlier wave of protectiveness resurged.

He lifted his glass and swallowed half its contents. Mesmerised, she watched his throat as he swallowed, then her gaze moved to his well-defined chest as he heaved in a huge breath.

Move! But she couldn't heed the silent command pounding

in her brain. Her feet refused to move. She was still immobilised when he swung towards the room.

He stilled, dark-green eyes zeroing in on her in that fiercely focused, extremely unnerving way.

After several seconds, his gaze travelled over her, head to bare toes, and back again. Slowly, without taking his gaze off her, he downed the rest of his drink. His tongue glided out to lick a drop from his lower lip.

The inferno stormed through her, ravaging her senses with merciless force.

No. Hell, no! This could *not* be happening.

Her fingers tightened around her bag until pain shot up her arms. With brutal force, she wrenched her gaze away, walked towards the sofa and dropped her bag beside it.

'I'm done with the bathroom. It's all yours.' She cringed at the quiver in her voice, a telling barometer of her inner turmoil. Her tablet lay where she'd left it on the table. Itching for something to do with her dangerously restless hands, she grabbed it.

He came towards her and passed within touching distance to set his glass down on the cabinet. Brianna decided breathing could wait until he was out of scenting range.

'Thanks.' He grabbed his bag and walked to the door. 'And Moneypenny?'

The need to breathe became dangerously imperative but not yet; a few more seconds, until she didn't have to breathe the same air as him. 'Yes?' she managed.

'It's time to clock off.'

The tightness in her chest grew. 'I just wanted to—'

'Turn that tablet off and put it away. That's an order.'

It was either argue with him, or breathe. The need for oxygen won out. She placed the tablet back on the table and stuffed her hands under her thighs.

Satisfaction gleamed in his eyes as he opened the bathroom door. 'Good.' His gaze darted to the bed. 'You take the bed,

I'll take the sofa,' he said. Then he entered the bathroom and shut the door behind him.

Brianna sucked in a long, sustaining breath, trying desperately to ignore the traces of Sakis's scent that lingered in the air. She eyed the bed, then the sofa.

The logic was irrefutable. She pulled out and made up the sofa bed in record time. And she made damned sure she was in it and turned away from the bathroom door by the time she heard the shower go off.

The consequences of giving lust any room was much too great to contemplate. Because giving in to her emotions, trusting it would turn to more—perhaps even the love she'd been blindingly desperate for—was what had landed her in prison.

Being in prison had nearly killed her.

Brianna had no intention of failing. No intention of sinking again.

CHAPTER FOUR

SHE WOKE TO the smell of strong coffee and an empty room. Relief punched through her as she tossed the light sheet aside and rose from the sofa bed. A quick glance at the ruffled bed showed evidence of Sakis's presence but, apart from that, every last trace of him had been wiped from the room, including his bag.

Before she could investigate further, her tablet pinged with an incoming message.

Grasping it, she tried to get into the zone—business as usual. Just the way she wanted her life to run. Turning the tablet on, she went through the messages as she poured her coffee.

Two of them were from Sakis, who'd taken up residence in the conference room downstairs. Several of them were from people interested in joining the salvage process or blogging about it. But there was still no word about the missing crew.

After answering Sakis's message to join him downstairs as soon as she was ready, she tackled the most important emails, took a quick shower and dressed in a clean pair of khaki combat trousers and a cream T-shirt.

By the time she'd tied her hair into its usual French knot, the events of last night had been consigned a 'temporary aberration' status. Thankfully, she'd been asleep by the time he emerged from the bathroom and, even though she'd woken once and heard his light, even breathing, she'd managed to go back to sleep with no trouble.

Which meant she really didn't have to fear that the rhythm of their relationship had changed.

It hadn't. After this crisis was over, they would return to London and everything would go back to machine-smooth efficiency.

She shrugged on her dark-green jacket, grabbed her case and went downstairs to find Sakis on the phone in the conference room.

He indicated the extensive breakfast tray; she'd just bitten into a piece of honeyed toast when he hung up.

'The salvage crew have contained the leak in the last compartment and the transport tanker for the undamaged oil will arrive in the next few hours.'

'So the damaged tanker can be moved in the next few days?'

He nodded. 'After the International Maritime Investigation Board has completed its investigation it will be tugged back to the ship-building facility in Piraeus. And, now we have a full salvage team in place, there's no need for any remaining crew to stay. They can go home.'

Brianna nodded and brushed crumbs off her fingers. 'I'll arrange it.'

Even though she powered up her tablet ready to action his request, she felt the heat of his gaze on her face.

'You do my bidding without question when it comes to matters of the boardroom. And yet you blatantly disobeyed me last night,' he said in a low voice.

She paused mid-swallow and looked up. Arresting green eyes caught and locked onto hers. 'I'm sorry?'

He twirled a pen in his hand. 'I asked you to take the bed last night. You didn't.'

She forced herself to swallow and tried to look away. She really tried. But it seemed as if he'd charged the very air with a magnetic field that held her captive. 'I didn't think your jump-when-I-say edict extended beyond the boardroom to the bedroom, Mr Pantelides.'

Too late, she realised the indelicacy of her words. His eyes gleamed with lazy green fire. But she wasn't fooled for a second that it was harmless.

'It doesn't. When it comes to the bedroom, I like control, but I'm not averse to relinquishing it...on occasion.'

Noting that she was in serious danger of going up in flames at the torrid images that cascaded through her mind, she tried to move on. 'Logic dictated that since I'm smaller in stature the sofa would be more suited to me. I didn't see the need for chivalry to get in the way of a good night's sleep for either of us.'

One brow shot up. 'Chivalry? You think I did it out of *chivalry*?' His amusement was unmistakeable.

A damning tide of heat swept up her face. But she couldn't look away from those mesmerising eyes. 'Well, I'm sure you had your own reasons... But I thought...' She huffed. 'It doesn't really matter now, does it?'

'I suggested it because it wouldn't have been a hardship for me.'

'I'm sure it wouldn't, but you don't have a monopoly on pain and discomfort, Mr Pantelides.'

He stiffened. 'Excuse me?'

'I just meant...whatever the circumstances of your past, at least you had a mother who loved you, so it couldn't have been all bad.' She couldn't stem the vein of bitterness from bleeding into her voice, nor could she fail to realise she'd strayed dangerously far from an innocuous subject. But short of blurting out her own past this was the only way she could stop the slippery slope towards believing Sakis cared about her wellbeing.

She'd suffered a childhood hopelessly devoid of love and comfort, and the threat of a life of drugs had been an ever-present reality. Sleeping on a sofa bed was heaven in comparison.

His narrowed eyes speared into her. 'Don't mistake guilt for love, Moneypenny. I've learned over the years that this so-called love is a convenient blanket that's thrown over most feelings.'

She sucked in a breath. 'You don't think that your mother loves you?'

His jaw tightened. 'A weak love is worse than no love. When it crumbles under the weight of adversity it might as well not be present.'

Brianna's fingers tightened around her tablet as shock roiled through her. For the second time in two days, she was glimpsing a whole new facet of Sakis Pantelides.

This was a man who had hidden, painful depths that she'd barely glimpsed in all the time she'd worked for him.

'What adversity?'

He shrugged. 'My mother believed the man she *loved* could do no wrong. When the reality hit her, she chose to give up and leave her children to fend for themselves.' Casually, he flipped his pen in his hand. 'I've been taking care of myself for a very long time, Moneypenny.'

She believed him. She'd always known he possessed a hardened core of steel beneath that urbane façade, but now she knew how it'd been honed, she felt that wave of sympathy and connection again.

Ruthlessly, she tried to reel back the unravelling happening inside her.

'Thanks for sharing that with me. But the sofa was really no hardship for me either and, as long as we're both rested, that should be the end of the subject, surely?'

His eyes remained inscrutable. 'Indeed. I know when to pick my battles, Moneypenny, and I will let this one go.'

The notion that there would be other heated battles between them disturbed her in an altogether too excited way. Before she could respond, he carried on.

'You'll also be happy to know there won't be any need for me to crowd your personal space any longer. Another room has become available. I've taken it.'

Expecting strong relief, she floundered when all she felt was a hard bite of disappointment.

'Great. That's good to know.'

Her tablet pinged a message. Grateful beyond words, she jumped on it.

After breakfast they returned to the site, suited up, and joined the clean-up process. Towards mid-afternoon, she was working alongside Sakis when she felt him tense.

The pithy Greek curse he uttered didn't need translating. 'What the hell are they doing here?'

Her heart sank when she saw the TV crew. 'This is one wave we're just going to have to ride. Nothing I can do to send them away, but I may be able to get them to play nice. You just have to trust me.' The moment the words left her lips, she froze.

So did he. Trust was an issue they both had problems with. She had no business asking for his when she hid a past that could end their relationship in a heartbeat.

But slowly, the look in his eyes changed from hard-edged displeasure to appreciative gleaming. '*Efkharisto.* I have no idea what I'd do without you, Moneypenny,' he said in a low, rumbling voice.

Her heart lurched, then hammered with a force that made her fear for the integrity of her internal organs. 'That's good, because I've devised this cunning plan to make sure that you don't have to.'

A corner of his mouth rose and fell in a swift smile. His gaze dropped to her lips, then rose to recapture hers. 'When Ari threatened to poach you, I nearly knocked him out with my oar,' he said, his voice rumbling in that gravel-rough pitch that made the muscles in her stomach flutter and tighten.

'I wouldn't have gone.' Not in a million years. She loved working with Sakis, even if the last two days had sent her on a knuckle-rattling emotional rollercoaster.

'Good. You belong to me and I have no intention of letting you go. I'll personally annihilate anyone who tries to take you away from me.'

Her pulse raced faster. *Work. He's talking about your professional relationship. Not making a statement of personal intent.* Brianna forced that reminder on her erratic senses and tried to breathe normally. When her belly continued to roil, she sucked in air through her mouth.

Sakis made a small, hoarse sound in his throat. Heat arched between them, making her skin tingle and the flesh between her legs ache with desperate need.

Hastily she took a step back. 'I…I'll go and speak to the TV crew.'

She turned and fled. And with every step she prayed desperately for her equilibrium to return.

The TV crew refused to leave but agreed not to interview any member of the crew. For that she had to be content.

Sakis's meeting with the maritime disaster investigators went smoothly because he had already admitted liability and agreed to make reparations, and he barely blinked at the mind-bogglingly heavy fine they imposed on Pantelides Inc.

But his behaviour with her was anything but smooth. Throughout the meeting, Sakis would turn to her for her opinion, touch her arm to draw her attention to something he needed written down or shoot her a question. Fear coursed through her as she realised that the almost staid, rigidly professional team they'd been seventy-two hours ago had all but disappeared.

By the time the meeting concluded, she knew she was in trouble.

Sakis pushed a frustrated hand through his hair and paced the conference room, anger beating beneath his skin. The investigators had just confirmed the accident was human error.

Striding to his desk, he threw himself in the chair.

'Has Morgan Lowell's file arrived yet?' he asked Brianna.

She came towards him and he tried not to let his gaze drop to the sway of her hips. All damned day, he'd found himself checking her out. He'd even stopped asking himself what the hell was wrong with him because he knew.

Lust.

Untrammelled, bloody, lust. From the easily controlled attraction he'd felt when he'd first met her, it now threatened to drown him with every single breath he took in her presence.

She held out the information he'd asked for and he tried not to stare at the delicate bones of her wrist.

'What do we know about him?' he asked briskly.

'He's married; no children; his wife lives with his parents. As far as we can tell, he's the sole provider for his family. And he's been with the company the last four years. He came straight from the navy, where he was a commander.'

'I know all of that.' He flicked past the personal details to the work history and paused, a tingle of unease whispering down his spine. 'It says here he's refused to take leave in the last three years. And he's been married...just over three years. Why would a newly wedded man not want to be with his wife?'

'Perhaps he had something to prove, or something to hide,' came the stark, terse response.

Surprised, he glanced up. Unease slid through her blue eyes before she lowered them. He continued to stare, and right before his eyes his normally serenely professional PA became increasingly...flustered. The intrigue that had dogged him since seeing that damned tattoo on her ankle rose even higher.

He sat back in his chair. 'Interesting observation, Moneypenny. What makes you say that?'

She bit her lip and blood roared through his veins. 'I...didn't mean anything by it. Certainly nothing based on solid fact.'

'But you said it anyway. Instinctive or not, you suspect there's something else going on here, no?'

She shrugged. 'It was just a general comment, gleaned from observing natural human behaviour. Most people fall into one of those two categories. It could be that Captain Lowell falls into both.' She firmed her lips as if she wanted to prevent any more words from spilling out.

'What do you mean?' he asked. Impatience grew when she just shook her head. 'Come on, you have a theory. Let's hear it.'

'I just think the fact that both Lowell and his two deputies are missing is highly questionable. I can't think why all three would be away from the bridge and not respond when the alarm was raised.'

Ice slammed into his chest. 'The investigators think it was human error but you think it was deliberate?' Reactivating the tablet, he flicked through the rest of Morgan Lowell's work history but nothing in there threw up any red flags.

On paper, his missing captain was an extremely competent leader with solid credentials who'd piloted the Pantelides tanker efficiently for the last four years.

On paper.

Sakis knew first-hand that 'on paper' meant nothing when it came right down to it.

On paper Alexandrou Pantelides, his father, had been an honourable, hard-working and generous father to those who hadn't known better. Only Sakis, his brothers and mother had known it was a façade he presented to the world. It was only when a scorned lover had tipped off a hungry journalist who'd chosen to dig a little deeper that the truth had emerged. A truth that had unearthed a rotten trough full of discarded mistresses and shady business dealings that had overnight heaped humiliation and devastation on the innocent.

On paper Giselle had seemed an efficient, healthily ambitious executive assistant, until Sakis's rejection of her one late-night advance had unearthed a spiteful, cold-blooded, psychopathic nature that had threatened to destabilise his company's very foundation.

'On paper' meant nothing if he couldn't look into Lowell's eyes, ask what had happened and get a satisfactory answer.

'We need to find him, Moneypenny,' he bit out, bitterness replacing the ice in his chest. 'There's too much at stake here to leave this unresolved for much longer.' For one thing, the media would spin itself out of control if word of this got out. 'Contact the head of security. Tell them to dig deeper into Lowell's background.'

Sakis looked up in time to see Brianna pale a little. 'Is something wrong?' he asked.

Her mouth showed the tiniest hint of a twist. 'No.'

His gaze dropped to hands that would normally be flying over her tablet as she rushed to do his bidding. They were clasped together, unmoving. 'Something obviously is.'

Darkened eyes met his and he saw rebellion lurking in their depths. 'I don't think it's fair to dig into someone's life just because you have a hunch.'

Her words held brevity that made Sakis frown. 'Did you not suggest minutes ago that Lowell could be hiding something?'

She gave a reluctant nod.

'Then shouldn't we try and find out what that something *is*?'

'I suppose.'

'But?'

'I think he deserves for his life not to be turned inside out on a hunch. And I'm sorry if I gave you the impression that was what I wanted, because it's not.'

A tic throbbed in his temple. Restlessness made him shove away from the desk. His stride carried him to the window and back to the desk next to where she sat, unmoving fingers resting on her tablet.

'Sometimes we have to bear the consequences of unwanted scrutiny for the greater good.' As much as he'd detested the hideous fallout, having his father's true colours exposed had ultimately been to his benefit. He'd learned to look beneath the surface. Always.

She looked at him. 'You're advocating something that you hated having done to you. How did you feel when your family's secrets were exposed to the whole world?'

Shock slammed into him at her sheer audacity. Planting his hands on the desk, he lowered his head until his gaze was level with hers. '*Excuse me?* What the hell do you think you know about my family?' he rasped.

She drew back a touch but her gaze remained unflinching. 'I know what happened with your father when you were a teenager. The Internet makes information impossible to hide. And your reaction to the tabloid hack's question yesterday—'

'There was *no* reaction.'

'I was there. I saw how much you hated it.' Her voice was soft with sympathy.

The idea of being pitied made his fist tighten on the table.

'And you think this should make me bury my head in the sand about Lowell?'

'No, I'm just saying that turning his life inside out doesn't feel right. Since you've been in his shoes—'

'Since I don't know anything more than what his human resources file says, that's a lofty conclusion to draw. And, unlike what you think you know about me and my family, what I find out about Captain Lowell won't find its way to the tabloid press or any social media forum for the world at large to feast over and make caricatures out of. So I say no, there is *nothing* even remotely similar between the two situations.'

She drew in a slow, steady breath. 'If you say so.' Her gaze dropped and she pulled the tablet towards her.

Sakis stayed exactly where he was, the urge to invade her space further an almighty need that stomped through him. In the last twenty-four hours, his PA had acted out of character, challenged him in ways she'd never done before.

The incident with the tent and the sleeping on the sofa bed, he was willing to let go. This latest challenge—breaching the taboo subject of his father—should've made him fire her on the spot. But, as much as he hated to admit it, she was right. The journalist's question *had* shaken him and unearthed volcanic feelings he preferred masked.

In silence, he watched her compose a succinct email to his security chief, stating his exact wishes.

The electronic 'whoosh' of the outgoing email perforated the silence in the conference room. It was as if the very air was holding its breath.

Brianna raised her head after setting the tablet down. 'Is there anything else?'

His gaze traced over her. A tendril of hair had escaped its tight prison and caressed the wild pulse beating in her neck. His fingers tingled with the need to smooth it away and trace the pulse with his fingers; to keep tracing down the length of her sleek neck to the delicate collarbone hidden beneath her T-shirt.

'You disagree with what I'm doing?'

Her full pink lips firmed. That dimple winked again. His groin tightened unbearably.

'Privacy is a right and I detest those who breach it. I know you do too, so I'm struggling with this a little, but I also get why it needs to be done. I also apologise if I stepped out of line but…I trust you when you say you won't let it fall into unscrupulous hands.'

Her last words drilled down and touched a soft place inside him, soothed the ruffled edge of his nerves a little. 'You have my word that whatever we discover about Lowell will be held in strictest confidence.' The knowledge that he was reassuring her, was justifying his behaviour to his assistant, threw him a little, as did the knowledge that he *wanted* her to approve of what he was doing. He pushed the feeling away as she nodded.

The movement slid the silky hair against her nape. The

soft scent of her crushed-lilies shampoo hit his nostrils and his fingers renewed their mad tingling.

'And, Moneypenny?'

She glanced up. This close, her eyes were even more enthralling. His heart raced and his blood rushed south with a need so forceful, he sucked in a shocked breath.

'Yes?' Her lips were parted, the tip of her wet tongue peeking through even teeth.

Sakis struggled to remember what he'd meant to say. 'I don't trust easily but that doesn't mean I don't appreciate people who place their trust in me. In all the time you've worked for me, you've proved yourself trustworthy and someone I can rely on. Your help especially in the past two days has been priceless. Thank you.'

Her eyed widened. God, she was beautiful. How the hell had he never noticed that?

'Of…of course, Mr Pantelides.'

Curiously, she paled a little bit more. Sakis frowned then chalked it down to exhaustion. They'd both been driven by dire circumstances to the pinnacle of their endurance. He needed to let her go to her room instead of crouching over her like some dark lord about to demand a virgin sacrifice.

He grimaced and stepped back, slamming down the need to stay where he was. Tension stretched over every of inch of his skin until he felt taut and uncommonly sensitive. 'I think we find ourselves in a unique enough situation where it's okay for you to call me Sakis.'

She shook her head. 'No.'

His brow shot up. 'Just…*no*?'

'I'm sorry, but I can't.' Edging away from him, she sprang to her feet. 'If that's all you need tonight, I'll say goodnight.'

'Goodnight…Brianna.' Her name sounded like the sweetest temptation on his lips.

She hesitated. 'I would really prefer it if you kept calling me Moneypenny,' she said.

Immediate refusal rose to his lips. Until he remembered he was supposed to be her unimpeachable boss, not a demanding lover who was at this moment repeating her given name over and over in his mind. 'Very well. See you in the morning, Moneypenny.'

He straightened from the table and watched her walk away, her pert bottom tight and deliciously curvy beneath her khaki pants, causing blood to rush hot and fast southward.

He still sported a hard-on that wouldn't die when his phone rang in his suite an hour later. He stopped pacing his small balcony long enough to snag it from the coffee table where he'd dumped it.

'Pantelides.'

The short conversation that ensued made him curse long and fluently for several minutes after he hung up.

CHAPTER FIVE

THE FIRM HAMMERING on her door made Brianna's already racing heart threaten to knock itself into early retirement. Considering the way it'd been racing for the past hour—ever since her wits had deserted her in the conference room—it would've been merciful.

What the hell had she been *thinking*?

Hard knuckles gave the wooden door another impatient workout.

Consciously loosening her tense shoulders, she blew out a reassuring breath and forced composure back into her body. The hastily pulled together bland look was in place when she answered the door.

Sakis stood on the threshold, frowning down at his phone.

'What's wrong?' she asked before she could stop herself. The feeling that passed through her, she recognised as worry, a curiously recurring feeling over the past two days. *Not cool, Brianna*. In fact, a wincingly large percentage of her reactions today had been...off. From the moment he'd stared down at her and told her in that mesmerising voice, 'I don't know what I'd do without you,' her judgement had been skewed.

Watching him pace with mounting frustration all day, wishing there was something she could do, had rammed home the fact that her professional equanimity was still very much in jeopardy.

Now...now he looked as if he'd clawed frustrated fingers

through his hair several times. And the lines bracketing his mouth had deepened. She cleared her throat.

'I mean, is there something you need, Mr Pantelides?'

His gaze flicked over her then returned to her face. 'You haven't changed for bed yet. Good. The pilot is readying the chopper for take-off in fifteen minutes.'

'Take-off?'

His hand tightened around the phone as it signalled another incoming message. 'We're leaving for the airport. I've called an emergency meeting first thing in the morning back in London.'

'We're returning to London? But...why?'

His lips firmed. 'It seems more vultures are circling over our disaster.'

Stunned, she stared at him. The thought that anyone would want to challenge Sakis Pantelides at any time, let alone when he was at his most edgy and dangerous, made her doubt his opponent's sanity. 'Media or corporate?'

His smile was deadly. 'Corporate. I'm guessing the usual suspects who chest-thump every now and then will be feeling bolder in light of the slumping share price as a result of the tanker accident.'

She retrieved the bag she'd left at the foot of her bed. 'But the shares have started to recover again after the initial nosedive. Your statement and the very public admission of liability made it stabilise very quickly. Why would they...?'

'News of a takeover bid would make it plunge again and that's what they're counting on.' His phone pinged again and he growled. 'Especially if two of those companies are announcing their intended merger in the morning.'

He cursed in Greek, using a particular word that made heat rise to her cheeks as she dove into the bathroom for her toiletries bag.

'Which two companies?' she called out as she zipped up

her bag and checked the room to make sure she hadn't left anything important.

Exiting, she saw the lines of fatigue etched into his face and her heart lurched.

'Moorecroft Oil and Landers Petroleum.'

It was only because he'd turned away, his attention once more on this phone, that Sakis didn't see she'd stopped dead in her tracks; that the blood had drained from her face with a swiftness that made her dizzy for a moment.

It couldn't be. No. It had to be pure coincidence that the petroleum company shared the same name with Greg, her ex-boyfriend. Landers was a fairly common name...wasn't it? Besides, Greg's company when she'd been a part of it before he'd struck the deal that had doomed her, had been a gas-brokering company; a company that had since declared bankruptcy. And certainly not one large enough to take on the juggernaut that was Pantelides Shipping.

'I'd like to get out of here this side of— Brianna? What's wrong?'

For goodness' sake, pull yourself together!

Dry-mouthed and heart thumping, Brianna forced herself to breathe. 'Nothing; it's the heat, I think.'

Keen eyes scoured her face and gentled a fraction as he pocketed his phone. 'Not to mention the lack of sleep. My apologies for dragging you off like this. You can sleep on the plane.'

Stepping forward, he held out his hand for her bag. Their fingers touched, lingered. Heat shot through her and she hastily pulled back from the scorching contact. Swallowing, she followed him out and shut the door behind her. 'I'll be fine. And you'll need me to find out everything we can about the two companies.' Not to mention *she* needed to know whether Greg had anything to do with Landers Petroleum.

The thought that he might have started another company,

might be cultivating another patsy the same way he'd cultivated her, made her stomach lurch sickeningly.

Could she alert Sakis without drawing attention to herself? Out herself as the needy woman, so desperate for love she hadn't seen the trap set for her until it'd been too late?

Her belly churned with fear and anxiety as they left the hotel and rode the short helicopter journey to the private hangar at Agostinho Neto airport.

Dear God. She could lose everything.

The thought sent a shudder so strong, she stumbled over her own feet a few steps from the airplane.

Sakis caught her arm and steadied her. Then his fingers dropped to encircle her wrist, keeping a firm hold on her as he mounted the steps into the plane.

She swallowed down the wholly different trepidation that stemmed from having Sakis's hand on her. She tried to pull away, but he held on until they stood before the guest-cabin bedroom opposite the plane's master suite. He opened the door and set her bag down just inside it, then led her back to the seating area.

At Sakis's signal, the pilot shut the door.

'Buckle up. Right after we take off, we're going to bed.'

Her mouth dropped open as her pulse shot sky-high. '*I beg your pardon*?' she squeaked. Her whole body throbbed and she couldn't glance away from his disturbingly direct gaze.

His grim smile held a wealth of masculine arrogance as he shoved a frustrated hand through his hair. Taking his seat opposite her, he set his phone—which had thankfully stopped pinging—on a nearby table. 'A...poor choice of words, Moneypenny. What I mean is, it's the middle of the night in London. Not much we can do from here.'

'I can still pull up as much information as I can on the companies...'

He shook his head. 'I already have people working on that. You need to get some sleep. I need you sharp and—'

'You need to stop treating me like some fragile flower and let me do my job!'

Moss-green eyes narrowed. 'Excuse me?'

Anger lent her voice desperation and she leaned forward, hands planted on the table separating them. The fact that this close she could almost touch the stubble layering his hard, chiselled jaw and see the darker, mesmerising flecks in his irises sparked another tingle of awareness through her. But the remotest possibility that Greg could be lurking in the periphery of her life, ready to expose her, made her stand her ground.

She'd gone through too much, sacrificing everything she had to prevent her debilitating weakness from being exposed. She no longer needed love. She'd learned that she could live without it. What she couldn't live with was having her previous sins exposed to Sakis Pantelides.

'You seem to think I need a full night's sleep or a warm bed to function properly, but that couldn't be farther from the truth.' Warning bells rang in her head, telling her seriously to apply brakes on her runaway mouth. But she couldn't help herself. 'I've slept in places where I had to keep one eye open or risk losing more than just the clothes on my back. So please don't treat me like some pampered princess who needs her beauty sleep or she'll go to pieces.'

His eyes narrowed, followed almost instantly by a keen speculation that screamed what was coming next. 'When did you sleep rough?' His voice was low, husky, full of unabashed curiosity.

Alarm bells shrieked harder, in tandem with the jet engines powering for take-off. Sharp memories rose, images of drug dens and foul-smelling narcotics bringing nausea she fought to keep down. 'It doesn't matter.'

He leaned forward on his elbows and stared her down. 'Yes, it does. Answer me.'

'It was a very long time ago, Mr Pantelides.'

'Sakis,' he commanded in that low, deep tone that sent a shiver through her.

Again she shook her head. 'Let's just say my childhood wasn't as rosy as the average child's, but I pulled through.'

'You were an orphan?' he probed.

'No, I wasn't, but I might as well have been.' Because her junkie mother had been no use to herself, never mind the child she'd given birth to. The remembered pain bruised her insides and unshed tears burned the backs of her eyes. She blinked rapidly to stop them falling but a furtive glance showed Sakis had noticed the crack in her composure.

The plane lifted off the ground and shot into the starlit sky.

Sakis's gaze remained on her for long minutes. 'Do you want to talk about it?' he asked gently.

Brianna's heart hammered harder. 'No.' She'd already said too much, revealed far more than was wise. Deliberately unclenching her fists, she prayed he would let the matter rest.

The jet started to level out. Snatching his phone from the table, Sakis nodded and unbuckled his seatbelt. 'Regardless of your protests, you need to sleep.' He held out his hand to her. The look on his face told her nothing but her acquiescence would please him.

Immensely relieved that he wasn't probing into her past any longer, she thought it wise to stifle further protest. Unbuckling her seatbelt, she placed her hand in his and stood. 'If I do, then so do you.'

His smile was unexpected. And breath-stealing. Heat churned within her belly, sending an arrow of need straight between her thighs.

'We've dovetailed right back to the very point I was trying to make. I have every intention of getting some sleep. Even super-humans like me deserve some down time.'

A smile tugged at her lips. 'That's a relief. You were beginning to show us mere mortals up.'

His smile turned into an outright laugh, his face transforming into such a spectacular vision of gorgeousness that her breath caught. Then her whole body threatened to spontaneously combust when his hand settled at her waist. With a firm nudge, he guided her back down the aisle.

'No one in their right mind would call you a mere mortal, Moneypenny. You've proved beyond any doubt that you're the real thing—an exceptionally gifted individual with a core of integrity that most ambitious people lose by the time they reach your age.'

At the door to her cabin, she turned to face him, her heart hammering hard enough to make her head hurt a little. 'I think what you've done since the tanker crashed shows you're willing to go above and beyond what most people would do in the same circumstances. *That* is integrity.'

His gaze dropped to her lips, lingered there in a way that turned her body furnace hot. 'Hmm, is this the start of an exclusive mutual admiration society?'

The breath she'd never quite managed to recapture fractured even further. When his eyes dropped lower, her nipples tightened, stung into life by green fire that lurked in those depths. Reaching behind her, she grasped the doorknob, desperate for something to cling to.

'I'm just trying to point out that I'm nothing special, Mr Pantelides. I just try to be very good at my job.'

His gaze recaptured hers. 'I beg to differ. I think you're very special.' He stepped closer and his scent filled her nostrils. 'It's also obvious no one has told you that enough.' The hand that still rested at her waist slid away to cover the hand she'd gripped on the door. Using the pressure of hers, he turned the knob. 'When this is all over, I'll make a point to show you just how special you are.'

The door gave way behind her and she swayed backward, barely managing to catch herself before she stumbled. 'You... don't have to. Really, you don't.'

His smile was a touch strained and he braced his hands

on the doorjamb as if forcibly stopping himself from entering the room. 'You say you're not special and yet you refuse even the promise of a reward where most people would be making a list.'

'I work for one of the most forward-thinking men in one of the best organisations in the world. That's reward enough.'

'Careful, there; you're in danger of swelling my ego to unthinkable proportions.'

'Is that a bad thing?' She wasn't sure where the need for banter came from but her breath caught when his sensual lips curved in a dangerously sexy smile.

'At a time when everything around me seems to be falling apart, it could be a lethal thing.' His gaze shot to the bed and his smile slipped a fraction, in proportion to the escalating strain on his face. 'Time for you to hit the sack. *Kalispera*, Brianna,' he murmured softly before, stepping back abruptly, he strode to his own door.

At the click of his door shutting, Brianna stumbled forward and sagged onto the bed, her knees turned to water.

She glanced down at her shaking hands as reality hit her square in the face.

Sakis Pantelides found her attractive. She wasn't naïve enough to mistake the look in his eyes, nor was she going to waste time contemplating the *why*. It was there, like a ticking time bomb between them, one she needed to diffuse before the unthinkable happened.

Brianna could only hope that, once they were back on familiar ground, things would return to normal.

They had to. Because, frankly, she was terrified of what she would let happen if they didn't.

Sakis stood under the cold shower and cursed fluidly. *Theos*. I seemed as if he'd spent the last forty-eight hours cursing in one form or the other. Right now, he cursed the rigid erection that seemed determined to defy the frigid temperature.

He wanted to have sex with Brianna Moneypenny. Wanted to shut off the shower, stride next door, strip the clothes off her body and drive into her with a grinding force that defied rhyme or reason.

He slapped his palm against the soaked tile and cursed some more. Gritting his teeth, his hand dropped to grip his erection. A single stroke made him groan out loud. Another stroke, and his knees threatened to buckle.

With an angry grunt, he dropped his hand and turned the shower off. He was damned if he was going to fondle himself like an over-eager teenager. Things were fraught for sure. That and the fact that he hadn't had sex in months was messing with his mental faculties, making him contemplate paths he would never otherwise have done. For God's sake, sex had no place in his immediate to-do list.

What he needed to do was focus on getting the threat of a takeover annihilated and the situation at Pointe Noire brought under control.

Once they were back on familiar ground, things would return to normal.

He ruthlessly silenced the voice that mocked him not to be so sure...

Three hours later, Brianna sat wide awake in her luxurious cabin bed, staring through a porthole at the pitch-black night that rested on a bed of white clouds. She'd left her tablet in one of the two briefcases she'd seen the stewardess stow in Sakis's cabin. Short of knocking on his door and asking for it, she had nothing to do but sit here, her thoughts jumbling into a mass of anxiety at what awaited her in London.

She had no doubt Sakis would trounce the takeover bid into smithereens—he was too skilled a businessman not to have anticipated such a move. And he was too calculating not to have the answers at his fingertips.

All the same, Greg had proved, much to her shock and disbelief, that he was just as ruthless—and without a single ounce of integrity—and she shuddered at the chaos he could bring to Sakis should he be given the opportunity.

Her shoulder tingled as her tattoo burned. Raising her hand, she slid her fingers under her light T-shirt and touched the slightly raised words etched into her skin.

Greg had succeeded in taking away her livelihood once; had come terrifyingly close to destroying her soul.

There was no way she could rest until she made sure he wasn't a threat to Sakis and to her. Not that he had any reason to seek her out. No, she was the gullible scapegoat he'd led to the slaughter—then walked away from scot-free. The last thing he'd expect was for her to have risen from the ashes of the fire he'd thrown her in.

That was how she wanted things to stay. Once upon a time, she'd harboured feelings of revenge and retribution; how could she not, when she'd been stuck in an six-by-eight dark space, racked alternatively with fear and deep bitterness? But those feelings had burned themselves out.

Now she just wanted to be Brianna Moneypenny, executive assistant to Sakis Pantelides, the most dynamically sexy, astoundingly intelligent man she knew.

A man she'd come disastrously close to kissing more than once in the last forty-eight hours...

No. Her fingers pressed down harder over the tattoo, letting the pain of each word restore her equilibrium.

Nothing had changed.

Nothing *could* change.

The board members were gathered in the large, grey mosaic-tiled conference room on the fiftieth floor of Pantelides Towers, the iconic, futuristically designed building poised on the edge of the River Thames.

Sakis strode in at seven o'clock sharp. He nodded to the

men around the table and the three executives video-conferencing in on three wide screens.

Brianna's heart thumped as she followed him in. She had no idea if the information-gathering Sakis had implemented before they'd boarded the plane had yielded any results. He didn't know either—she'd asked him. Only the files currently placed in front of each executive held the answer as to whether Greg Landers was in part behind this hostile takeover bid.

Seeing a spare copy on the stationery table off to one side of the boardroom, Brianna moved towards it.

'I won't need you for this meeting. Return to the office. I'll come and find you when I'm done.'

Shock ricocheted through her. She barely managed to keep it from showing on her face. 'Are you sure? I can—'

His jaw tensed. 'I think we've already established that you're invaluable to me. Please don't overplay your hand, Moneypenny. Otherwise alarm bells will start ringing.'

The tight grit behind his words took her aback. It was the same tone he'd used since he'd emerged from his cabin an hour before they'd landed. His whole façade was icily aloof and the potent sexual charge that had surrounded them a few short hours before, the fire in his eyes as he'd looked at her outside her cabin on the plane, was nowhere in sight.

She held her breath for the relief that confirmed that things were back to normal, only to experience a painful pang of disconcerting disappointment, immediately followed by a more terrifying notion.

Did Sakis know? Had he somehow found out about her past? She stared at him but his expression gave nothing away, certainly nothing that indicated he knew her deepest, darkest secret.

He didn't know. She'd been much too careful in exorcising her past; had used every last penny she'd owned two years ago to ensure there would be no coming back from what she'd been before.

All the same, it took a huge effort to swallow the lump in her throat. 'I don't... I'm not sure I know what you're talking about. I'm only trying to do—'

'Your job. I know. But right now your job isn't here. I need you to take point on the situation on Point Noire. Make sure the media are kept in line and the investigators update us on developments. I don't want the ball dropped on this. Can you handle that?'

Her gaze slid to the file marked confidential lying so innocuously on the table, fear and trepidation eating away inside her. Then she forced her gaze to meet his. 'Of course.'

The hard glint in his eyes softened a touch. 'Good. I'll see you in a few hours. Or sooner, if anything needs my attention.'

He stepped into the room and the electronic door slid shut behind him. Brianna gasped at the bereft feeling that hollowed out her stomach.

He isn't shutting you out. It's just a delicate situation that needs careful handling.

Nevertheless, as she walked back towards her office and desk situated just outside Sakis's massive office suite, she couldn't help but feel like she'd lost a part of her functioning self.

Ridiculous.

For the next several hours, she threw herself into her work. At two o'clock on the button, her phone rang.

'I haven't had an update in four hours,' came Sakis's terse demand.

'That's because everything's in hand. You have enough on your plate without resorting to micro-management,' she snapped, then bit her lip. She was letting her anxiety get the better of her. 'What I mean is, you have the right people in place to deal with this. Let them do their jobs. It's what you pay them for, after all.'

'Duly noted.' A little bit of the terseness had leached from his voice but the strain still remained. She could barely hold back from asking the question burning on her lips: *is Greg Landers one of those challenging to take over Pantelides Shipping*? 'Update me anyway.'

'The tug boat is on site and preparing to move the tanker away. The salvage crew co-ordinator tells me our marine biologist is providing invaluable advice, so we scored big there.'

'*You* scored big.' His voice had dropped lower, grown more intimate. A fresh tingle washed over her.

'Um...I guess. The social media campaign has garnered almost a million followers and the feedback shows a high percentage support Pantelides Shipping's stance on the salvage and clean-up process. The blogger is doing a superb job, too.'

'Brianna?'

'Yes?'

'I'm glad I took your advice about the media campaign. It's averted a lot of the bad press we could've had with this crash.'

Her normal, professional, politically correct answer faded on her tongue. Heart hammering, she gripped the phone harder and spoke from the heart. 'I care about this company. I didn't want to see its reputation suffer.'

'Why? Why do you care?' His voice had dropped even lower.

'You...you gave me a chance when I thought I would have none. You could've chosen someone else from over a hundred applicants for this job. You chose me. I don't take that lightly.'

'Don't sell yourself short, Brianna. I didn't pick your name out of a box. I picked you because you're special. And you continue to prove to me every day what a valuable asset you are.'

She loved the way he said her name. The realisation sent a pulse of heat rushing through her.

'Thank you, Mr Pantelides.'

'Sakis,' came the rumbled response.

She shook her head in immediate refusal, even though he couldn't see her. 'N...no,' she finally managed.

'I *will* get you to call me Sakis before very long.' His voice held a rough texture that made her tremble.

Closing her eyes, she forced herself to breathe and focus. 'How are things going with the...the board meeting?'

'Most of the key players have been identified. I've fired the warning shot. They can heed it or they can choose to come at me again.' His words held a distinct relish that made her think he almost welcomed the challenge of his authority. Sakis was a man who needed an outlet for his passions, hence the rowing when he could, and the fully equipped gyms in his penthouse and homes all around the world.

He would be just as passionate in the bedroom. She hurriedly pushed the thought away.

'Have we heard anything else?' he asked, his voice turning brisk once more.

She knew he meant the missing crew. 'No, nothing. The search parameters have been widened.' And because she feared what would spill from her lips if she hung on, she said, 'I need to make a few more phone calls; rearrange your schedule...'

He went silent for several seconds, then he sighed. 'If Lowell's wife calls, put her straight through to me.'

'I will.' She hung up quickly before she could ask about what he'd found out. Unwilling even to think of it, she threw herself back to her work.

At six, the executive chef Sakis employed for his senior staff poked his head through her office door and asked if she wanted dinner.

She rolled her shoulders, registered the stiffness in her body and shook her head.

'I'm going to hit the gym first, Tom. Then I'll forage for myself, thanks.'

He nodded and left.

Picking up her phone and tablet, she quickly made her way via the turbo lift to the sixtieth floor, where Sakis's private multi-roomed penthouse suites were located. There were six suites in total, four separate and two inter-connected. Sakis used the largest suite which was linked by a set of double doors to her own suite when she stayed here. From this high, the view across London's night sky was stunning. The Opera House gleamed beneath the iconic London Eye, with the Oxo Tower's famous lights glittering over the South Bank.

She took the shortcut through Sakis's living room, her feet slowing as they usually did when confronted with the visually stunning architectural design of the penthouse.

One side was taken up by a rough sandstone wall dominated by a huge fireplace regulated by a computerised temperature monitor. Directly in front of the fireplace, large slate-coloured, square-shaped sofas were grouped around an enormous stark white rug, which was the only covering on the highly polished marble floors.

Beyond the seating area, on carefully selected pedestals and on the walls were displayed works of art ranging from an exquisite pair of katanas, said to have belonged to a notorious Samurai, to a post-impressionist painting by Rousseau that galleries around the world vied for the opportunity to exhibit.

Moving towards her own suite, her gaze was drawn outside to the gleaming infinity pool that stretched out beyond the gleaming windows. The first time she'd seen it, she'd gasped with awe and thanked her lucky stars that she didn't suffer from vertigo when Sakis had shown her around the large deck where the only protection from the elements was a steel and glass railing.

From this high up, the Thames was a dark ribbon interspersed by centuries-old bridges, and from where she stood she could almost make out the Tube station where she caught the train to her flat.

Her flat. Her sanctuary. The place she hadn't been for days. The place she could lose if Sakis ever found out who she really was.

Her spine straightened as she approached the large wooden swivel door that led to her suite.

As long as she had breath in her body she would fight for what she'd salvaged from the embers of her previous life. Greg wouldn't be allowed to win a second time.

Entering the bedroom where Sakis had insisted she kept a fully furnished wardrobe in case he needed to travel with her at short notice, she changed into her pair of three-quarter-length Lycra training shorts and a cropped T-shirt.

She pounded the treadmill for half an hour, until endorphins pumped through her system and sweat poured off her skin. Next she tackled the elliptical trainer.

She was in the middle of stretching before hitting the weights when Sakis walked in.

He stopped at the sight of her. His hair was severely ruffled, the result of running his hands through the short strands several times, and he'd loosened his tie, along with a few buttons. Between the gaping cotton, she saw silky hairs that bisected his deep, chiselled chest.

Their eyes clashed through the mirrors lining two sides of the room, before his gaze left her to slowly traverse over her body.

Brianna froze, very much aware her breath was caught somewhere in her solar plexus. And that her leg was caught behind her, mid-stretch. The hand braced against the mirror trembled as his gaze visibly darkened with a hunger that echoed the sensation spiking up through her pelvis.

'Don't let me interrupt you,' he drawled as he went to the cooler and plucked a bottle of water off the shelf. Leaning against the rung of bars holding the weights, he stared at her as he drank deeply straight from the bottle.

She tried not to let her eyes devour the sensual movement of his throat as he swallowed. With a deep breath that cost her every ounce of self-control she possessed, she lifted and grabbed her other foot behind her, extending her body into a taut stretch, while studiously avoiding his gaze.

She'd never been more aware of the tightness of her gym clothes or the sheen of sweat coating her skin. Thankfully, she'd secured her hair so tight it hadn't escaped its bun…yet.

Sinking low, she extended in a sideways stretch that made her inner thigh muscles scream. Her heartbeat was hammering so loudly in her ears, she was sure she'd imagined Sakis's sharp indrawn breath.

Silence grew around them until she couldn't bear being the sole focus of his gaze. Rising after her last stretch, she contemplated the wisdom of approaching where he stood, right in front of the weights she needed.

Contemplated and abandoned the idea. Instead, she mimicked him and went to the well-stocked fridge for a bottle of water. 'How did the rest of the board meeting go?' she asked to fill the heavy silence.

Sakis tossed the empty bottle in the recycle bin, pulled his tie free, rolled it up and stuffed it in his trouser pocket. 'I had no doubt we would find the relevant weak points. Everyone has skeletons in their closets, Moneypenny. Things they don't want anyone else to discover. Growing up as a Pantelides taught me that.' His voice was pure steel, but she caught the underlying thread of pain beneath it.

She wanted to offer comforting words but the mention of skeletons sliced her with apprehension, tightening her insides so she could barely breathe. 'What sort of skeletons?'

'The usual. In this case, less than stellar financial record-keeping; one or two shady dealings that deserve closer scrutiny.'

'Are…are we talking about Landers Petroleum?' She held her breath.

'No.' He dismissed them with a wave of his hand. 'They're small fry compared to Moorecroft Oil and were probably hitching their wagon to the big boys in hopes of a large payday. For now, I'm more interested in Moorecroft. They're the ones who started this, but they should've cleaned up their own backyard before attempting to sully mine. Tomorrow morning, their CEO, Richard Moorecroft, will be receiving a call from the Financial Conduct Authority. He'll need to answer a few hairy questions.'

She told herself it was too early to hope this was over but she allowed herself a tiny breath of relief. 'And...you think that's the end of it?'

His hand went to the next unopened button and slid it free. 'If they know what's good for them. If they don't and they keep sabre-rattling, things will just get decidedly...dirtier.'

'You mean you'll dig deeper,' she murmured, unable to take her gaze off the hands slowly revealing more and more of his mouth-watering torso. 'What are you doing?' she gasped, her fist tightening around the plastic bottle as another bolt of heat drilled through her belly. It cracked under the force of her fist, echoing loudly through the room.

'Taking a leaf out of your book.' He shrugged out of his shirt, balled it up and threw it into the corner.

'I... But...'

He paused, his hand on his belt. 'Does my body make you uncomfortable, Moneypenny?'

Her tongue threatened to not work. 'You've undressed in front of me many times.'

'That wasn't what I asked you.' The belt slid free.

Arousal roared to life, tightening her nipples into deliciously painful points, weakening her knees, shooting fiery sensation between her legs. 'W...what does it matter? I'm invisible, remember? You've never seen me in the past.'

He came forward, his long legs eating up the short distance between them until he stood in front of her.

'Only because I've trained myself not to look...not to betray the slightest interest. Not since...' He paused, lips pursed. Then, shaking off whatever thought he'd had, he shrugged.

'You're not invisible to me now. I see you. *All* of you.' His gaze slid down, paused and caressed the valley between her breasts, before reaching out to boldly stroke the hard, pointed crests. Her needy gasp made him caress her more intimately, rolling her nipple between his fingers until she had to bite her lip hard to keep from crying out. 'And just like I knew you would be like…a potent wine, promising intoxication even before the first sip.'

Reason tried to surge forth through the miasma of sensation shaking her very foundations. But her body had a mind of its own. It swayed towards him but she managed to stop herself from taking the fatal step.

'I wouldn't really know. I…I don't drink.' Another ruthless stance she'd taken since Greg. That last night before the police had crashed in and carted her away, he'd plied her with vintage champagne and caviar. She'd been so drunk she'd been barely coherent when her life had taken a nosedive into hell.

'My, what a virtuous life you lead, Moneypenny. Do you have any vices *at all*? Apart from your pancakes, that is?'

'None that I wish to divulge,' she responded before she managed to stop herself.

Sakis gave a low, rich laugh that soaked into her senses before fizzing pleasure along her nerve endings. 'I find that infinitely intriguing.' His gaze dropped to her mouth in a blatant, heated caress. His lips parted and a slow rush of breath hissed through them. Slowly, almost leisurely, he stepped closer, bringing his body heat within singeing distance.

Move, Brianna!

Her feet finally heeded the frenzied warning fired by her brain but she'd barely taken a step when Sakis reached out. He caught her around the waist and brought her flush against him.

The contact fired through her, so powerful and potent, she lost her footing. One strong hand cupped her chin and raised her head to his merciless gaze. In his eyes, she read dangerous intent that made her stomach hollow with anticipation and feverish need, even as the last functioning brain cells shrieked for her to fight against the dangerous sensations.

'I'm going to kiss you now, Moneypenny,' Sakis breathed. 'It's not wise and it probably won't be safe.'

'Then you shouldn't do it...' She half-pleaded but already wet heat oozed between her thighs.

He gave a half-pained groan. 'I can't seem to stop myself.'

'Mr Pantelides—'

'Sakis. Say it. Say my name.'

She shook her head.

His head dropped another fraction. 'You're doing it again.'

'D-doing what?'

'Refusing to obey me.'

'We're no longer in the office.'

'Which is all the more reason why we should drop formalities. Say my name, Brianna.'

The way he said her name, the soft stresses on the vowels, made her insides clench hard. She tried desperately to fight against the overwhelming sensation. 'No.'

He walked her back until he had her pinned between the gym wall and the solid column of his hot body. The hard muscles of his bare chest were torture against her heavy breasts but it was the firm, unmistakeable imprint of his erection against her belly that made her stop breathing.

'Luckily for you, the need to taste you overwhelms the need to command your obedience.' His lips brushed hers in the fleetest of caresses. 'But I *will* hear you say it before very long.'

Eyelids too heavy to sustain fluttered downwards. Drowsy with lust, she fought to answer him. 'Don't count on it. I have a few rules of my own. This is one of them.'

The very tip of his tongue traced her lower lip, again with the fleetest of touches, and the fiery blaze of need raged through her. 'What's another?'

'Not to get involved with the boss.'

'Hmm, that's one I agree with.'

'Then…what are you *doing*?' she asked plaintively.

'Proving that this isn't more than temporary insanity.' His voice reflected the dazed confusion she felt.

'Won't walking away prove the same thing? As you said, this might not be exactly wise.'

'Or this is nothing but a no-big-deal kiss. It'll only become a big deal if we aren't able to handle what happens afterwards.'

No big deal. Was it really? And would it hurt to experience just a kiss? They were both clothed…well, he was technically only half-clothed…but she could put the brakes on this any time she wanted…couldn't she?

'Afterwards?' she blurted.

'Yes, when we go back to what we are. You'll continue to be the aficionado who runs my business life and I'll be the boss who demands too much of you.'

'Or we could stop this right now. Pretend it never happened?'

A hard gleam entered his eyes. 'Pretence has never been my style. I leave that to people who wish to hide their true colours; who want the world to perceive them as something other than what they are. I detest people like that, Moneypenny.' His mouth dropped another centimetre closer, his hands tightening around her waist as his eyes darkened with hot promise. 'It's why I won't pretend that the thought of kissing you, of being inside you, hasn't been eating me alive these past few days. It's also why I know neither of us will misconstrue this. Because you're above pretence. You're exactly who you say you are. Which is why I appreciate you so much.'

He kissed her then, his mouth devouring hers with a hunger so wild, so ferocious, it melted every single thought from her head.

Which was fortunate. Because otherwise she wouldn't have been able to stop herself from showing her reaction to his stark words; from blurting out that she was not even remotely who he thought she was.

CHAPTER SIX

SAKIS FELT HER moan of desire shudder through her sexy body and groaned in return. *Theos*, he'd been so determined not to be seen by another woman in the work environment in the way that Giselle had portrayed him in court and in the media that he'd deliberately blinded himself to just how sexy, how utterly feminine and incredibly gorgeous, Brianna was. Now he let his reeling senses register her attributes—the hands' span soft but firm curve of her bare waist underneath his fingers; the saucy shape of her bottom and the way the supple globes felt in his hands.

And *Theos*, her mouth! Delicious and silky soft, it was pure torture just imagining it around the hard, stiff part of his anatomy. Sure enough, the image slammed into his brain, firing the mother lode of all sex bombs straight to his groin.

He wanted her with a depth that seriously disturbed him. He wanted her spread underneath him, naked and needy, in endless positions...

She gave a hitched cry as his tongue breached her sweet plump lips and mercilessly plunged in. He was being too rough. His brain fired at him to slow down but he couldn't pull back. He'd had a taste of her but somehow that first taste had demanded a second, a third...

He pressed down harder, demanding more of her. His hips ground into her lower body until he was fully cradled between her thighs but even that wasn't enough. His hands cupped her breasts and another shudder raked through her as his fingers tweaked her nipples. Blood roared through his ears at the thought of tasting them, of suckling them, tugging on them with his teeth.

When her hands finally rose to clutch his bare shoulders, when her nails dug into his skin, the rush of lust was so potent he feared he'd pass out there and then.

What the hell was happening here?

He'd never been this swept away by lust, even when he'd been in the clutches of his hormones as a young adult. Sex was great. He was a healthy, virile male who was rich and powerful enough to command the best female attention whether he wanted it or not. When he wanted it, he went all in for the enjoyment of it.

But never had he experienced this urgency, this slightly crazed need that threatened to take him out at the knees.

And they hadn't even left first base yet!

Brianna opened her mouth wider to accommodate his rough demand. One hand left his shoulder and plunged into his hair, scraping his scalp as her fingers tightened.

He welcomed the mild pain with a glee that seriously worried him.

He'd never gone for kinky but with every scrape of her fingers his erection grew harder, more painful. God, he was so turned on, he couldn't see straight.

Which was why it took a full minute to realise the fingers in his hair were pulling him back, not egging him on; that the hand on his shoulder was pushing him away with more than a little desperation.

'No!' The force of his kiss smothered the word but it finally penetrated his lust-engorged senses.

With a shocked groan, he lifted his head and staggered back.

Brianna stared up at him, her ragged breath rushing through lips swollen with the force of his kisses. But it was the expression in her turquoise eyes that froze his insides. Besides the shock mingled with arousal, the apprehension was back again.

Self-loathing ripped through him like a tornado. He might not have understood why she'd been terrified the first time, but this time he knew the blame lay squarely with him. He'd fallen on her like a horny barbarian.

He clenched his fists and took another step back. His chest rose and fell like a felon in the heat of pursuit and he dimly registered that he hadn't bothered to breathe since he'd first tasted her.

'I...think this has gone far enough,' she said, her eyes darkening as they fell to his chest and skittered away.

Sakis wanted to refute that, to growl that it hadn't gone far enough. But he would be speaking from the depths of whatever insanity gripped him.

Insanity...

Was that what he'd scornfully professed he wanted to test?

Well, now he knew. His gaze dropped to her mouth again and fresh need slammed into him.

Damn it...He *knew*, and yet he wanted more. Of course, 'more' was out of the question. Brianna held far more value to him as his assistant than she would as his lover.

Potential lovers were a dime a dozen. He only had to scroll through his diary...

The thought of doing just that for the sake of slaking the lust-monkey riding him made his mouth curl with distaste. He wasn't his father, taking and discarding women with barely a thought between incidents, not caring about who bore the brunt of his actions.

Sucking in another breath, he forced a nod.

'*Ne*, you're right.' He licked his lower lip, tasted her again and nearly groaned. He clawed a hand through his hair and fought to regain the control that had been all but non-existent since he walked into the gym, fully intent on a mind-clearing workout, only to find her contorted in a highly suggestive stretch that had fried his brain cells. 'Let's chalk it down to the pressure of the past seventy-two hours.'

A look passed through her eyes before her lids lowered. 'Is this how you normally deal with a crisis?'

He gave another tight smile, whirled away and came face to face with his image.

Theos, no wonder she was frightened.

He looked like a crazed animal, a monster with wild eyes burning with stark hunger and a raging hard-on. He kept his back to her then forced himself to answer evenly.

'No, I normally fly down to the lake and take a scull out on the water. Or I come here to the gym and use the rowing machine. Physical labour helps me work things through.' Unfortunately, the physical he had in mind now involved Brianna beneath him, her thighs spread out in response to his hard, demanding thrusts.

'Um…okay. I guess I was in your way, then. Shall I…let you get on with it?' The slight question in her tone demanded reassurance.

Sakis had none to give. He remained exactly where he was, his back to her as he willed his body under control.

'Mr Pantelides?'

He winced at the rigid formality in those two words. Gritting his teeth, he turned to face her. 'Don't worry, Moneypenny. Nothing's changed. You tasted sweet enough but this was nothing to lose my head over. Our little experiment is over. The board is reconvening at eight. I'll see you in the office at seven-thirty.'

A gym workout was now out of the question. Brianna's scent lingered in the air and threatened to mess with his mind.

'Okay. I'll see you in the morning, then. Goodnight, Mr—'

'*Kali nichta*, Moneypenny.' He cut her off before she could trot out his title again.

Sakis scooped up his shirt, thought about putting it back

on and discarded the idea. Since he couldn't stay here, a two-
— no, make that three-—mile swim in his pool was the next
best option.

He was still staring at his shirt when she walked past him
smelling of crushed lilies, rampant sex and sweat. God, what
a combination. Against his will, his gaze tracked her sleek
form. The taut, bare skin of her waist taunted him, as did the
tight curve of her ass as she swayed her way out. With each
sexy stride, the fire sweeping through his groin threatened to
rage out of control.

It took a full minute after she'd left to realise he was still
standing in the middle of the gym, clutching his shirt, gazing
at the space where she'd been. With his fist tightening around
the creased cotton, Sakis forced himself to admit that things
indeed were about to get way worse before they got better.

And not just with his company.

*'You tasted sweet enough but this was nothing to lose my head
over...'* Brianna forced herself to dwell on the relief rather than
the sharp hurt burrowing inside her. The dangerous theory
had been tested, the fire had been breached and they'd come
out unscathed.

Are you sure? Brianna kicked off her leotard with more
force than was necessary. 'Yes, I'm sure,' she said out loud.
'One-hundred per cent sure,' she added for good measure.

Her top followed and she strode into the lavish cream-and-
gold decorated bathroom. Turning on the shower, she stepped
beneath the spray. Hot rivulets coursed over her face, over the
mouth Sakis had devoured less than five minutes ago, and a
fresh wave of desire rushed over her.

'No!' Her hands shook as she reached for the shower gel
and spread it over her body. This wasn't happening. *But it
was... It had...*

She'd let Sakis kiss her, had fallen into his hands like a ripe peach at harvest. She'd chosen to test the waters and had almost drowned in the process.

Because that kiss had rocked her to the depths of her soul. He'd kissed her like she was the last tangible thing in his universe, like he wanted to devour her. Aside from the pleasure of it, she'd felt his need as keenly as the need she'd fought so hard to suppress.

She didn't want to *need*. For as long as she could remember, needing had only brought her disaster. As a child, her needs had come last for a mother who was only interested in her next drug fix. As a grown woman, she'd let her need for affection blind her into believing Greg's lies.

Nothing would make her return to that dark, *needful* place.

Her fingers drifted once again to her tattoo.

Whatever it was Sakis needed, he could find it elsewhere.

Sakis was already in the office when she arrived just before seven. He was on the phone but cool, green eyes skated over her as she entered. Replaying the pep talk she'd given herself before she'd come downstairs, she indicated his half-finished espresso cup and he nodded. The gaze that met hers as she stepped forward to pick up his cup was all ruthless business. There was no hint of the gritty, desire-ravaged man from the gym last night.

Sakis Pantelides, suave CEO and master of his world, was back in residence.

Brianna forced herself to emulate his expression as she walked out on decidedly shaky legs towards the state-of-the-art coffee machine in the little alcove just behind her office. Setting the cup beneath the stainless silver spouts, she pressed the button.

Last night's lurid dreams, which had kept her tossing and turning in heated agitation, needed to be swept under the carpet of professionalism where they belonged. It was obvious

Sakis had consigned the gym incident to 'done and forgotten'. She needed to do the same or risk—

'Is the machine delivering something other than coffee this morning? The daily horoscope, perhaps?' he drawled.

She whirled around. Sakis stood directly behind her, his powerful and overwhelming physique shrinking the space to even smaller proportions. 'I...sorry?'

His gaze flicked to the freshly made espresso and back to her face. 'The coffee is ready and yet you're staring at the machine as if you're expecting a crystal ball to materialise alongside the beverage.'

'Of course I wasn't. I was just...' She stopped, then with pursed lips picked up his cup and handed it to him. 'I wasn't that long, Mr Pantelides.'

His lips pursed at the use of his name but, now they were back in the work environment and back to being *professional*, he couldn't exactly object.

Expecting him to move, her heartbeat escalated when he stayed put, blocking her escape back to her office. 'Was there something else?'

His gaze dropped to her lips as he took a sip of his espresso. 'Did you sleep well?'

Unwanted flames licked at the muscles clenching in her belly. She wanted to tell him that how she slept was none of his business. But she figured answering him would make him get out of her way faster. 'I did. Thank you for asking.'

She waited. He didn't move. 'I didn't,' he rasped. 'Last night was the worst night's sleep I've had in a very long time.'

'Oh... Um...' She started to lick her lips, thought better of it and blew out a short breath instead. Seriously, she had to find a way to douse these supremely inconvenient flames that leapt inside her whenever he was near. 'It's been a stressful few days. It was bound to affect you in some way sooner or later.'

One corner of his mouth lifted. '*Ne*, I'm sure you're right.' Once again his gaze dragged over her mouth. The tingling of her lips almost made her rub her fingers over them, to do something to make it stop.

She clamped her hands round her middle instead. 'Was there something else you needed?'

He threw back the rest of the hot espresso and placed the cup on the counter. Several seconds passed in silence then he heaved a sigh. 'I'm…sorry if I frightened you last night. I didn't mean to get so carried away.'

Brianna's breath caught. 'I wasn't… You didn't…' She stopped speaking, her senses clamouring a warning as he stepped closer.

'Then why did you look so scared? Has someone hurt you in the past?'

She meant to say no, to diffuse the highly inquisitive gleam in his eyes before it got out of hand. But… 'Haven't we all been hurt at some point by someone we trusted? Someone we thought loved us?' Her stark answer hung in the air between them.

He paled a little, the lines bracketing his mouth deepening. 'I hope I didn't remind you of this person.'

'Not any more than I reminded you of your father.'

Her breath caught in her chest as anguish etched into his face. Until two days ago, she'd only known him to display the utmost control when it came to matters of business. Except this wasn't business. This was intensely private and intensely painful. Witnessing his raw pain made the ice surrounding her heart crack. Before she knew it, her hands were loosening and she was reaching for his arm. She stopped herself just in time. 'Sorry, I didn't mean to bring that up.'

His smile was grim as his fingers clawed through his hair. 'Unfortunately, memories once resurrected aren't easy to dismiss, no matter how inconvenient the timing.'

'Is there ever a convenient time to dredge up past hurt?' Pain ripped through her question.

He heard it and froze. Green eyes speared hers in a look

so intense her heart stuttered. 'Who hurt you, Brianna?' he asked again softly.

Feeling herself floundering, she sagged against the counter for support. 'I...this isn't really a topic for the office.'

'*Who*?' he insisted.

'You had problems with your father. Mine was with my mother.' Her voice sounded reedy, fraught with the anguish raking through her.

His smile held no mirth. 'Look at us: a pair of hopeless cases with mummy and daddy issues. Think what a field day psychologists would have with us.'

Not once in the past eighteen months had she believed she had anything in common with Sakis. But hearing his words brought a curious balm to her pain.

'Maybe we should ask for a group discount?' She attempted her own smile.

His eyes darkened then the pain slowly faded, to be replaced by another look, one she was becoming intimately familiar with. 'Was there a reason you came looking for me?' she asked a third time.

Sakis's jaw tightened. 'The investigators have confirmed there's a connection between the crash and the takeover.'

'Really?'

He nodded. 'It's highly suspect that a day after my tanker crashes Moorecroft Oil and Landers Petroleum make a bid for my company.' He turned and headed back into his office. 'Their timing was a little too precise for it to be opportunistic.'

She entered his office in time to see him snatch up his phone. 'Sheldon.' He addressed his head of security. 'I need you to dig deeper into Moorecroft Oil and Landers Petroleum.'

At the mention of Landers, Brianna froze. Thankfully, her ringing phone gave her the perfect excuse to return to her desk.

When Sakis emerged, she'd found some semblance of control, enough to accompany him into the board meeting without giving the state of her agitation away.

The conference call to Richard Moorecroft descended into chaos less than five minutes after Sakis had him on the line.

'How dare you accuse me of such a preposterous thing, Pantelides? You think I would stoop so low as to sabotage your vessel in order to achieve my ends?'

'You haven't achieved anything except draw attention to your own devious dealings.' A note of disdain coated Sakis's voice. 'Did you really think I'd roll over like a puppy because of one mishap?'

'You underestimate the might of Moorecroft. I'm a giant in the industry—'

'The fact that you feel the need to point that out impresses me even less.'

A huff of rage came over the conference line. 'This isn't over, Pantelides. You can count on it.'

'You're right, this isn't over. As we speak, I'm digging up any connection between what happened to my tanker and your company.'

'You won't find any!' The bravado in Moorecroft's voice was tinged with a shadowy nervousness that made Sakis's eyes gleam.

'Pray that I don't. Because, if I do, you can rest assured that I *will* come after you. And I won't be satisfied until I rip your precious company to little pieces and feed them to my pet piranhas.' The menace in his voice made ice crawl over Brianna's skin. 'And any accomplices will not be spared either.'

He stabbed the 'end' button and glanced around the other members of his board. 'I'll apprise you of any news if the investigation reaps any information.'

Sakis turned to where Brianna sat three seats to his left. He'd deliberately placed her out of his eyeline so she wouldn't prove a distraction. Not that he hadn't noticed her tapping away all during the conference. Now that he'd let himself experience the power of his attraction for her, he noticed everything about her. From the way her sleek, navy designer skirt hugged her bottom, to the arch of her feet when she walked into his presence.

At the most inappropriate times he'd caught himself wondering how long her hair was, whether it would feel soft and silky. Many times during his sleepless night, he'd pictured himself kissing her again, imagining the many ways he'd explore her lips again given another chance.

Only now, he noticed a little bit more. Like the vulnerability she tried to hide beneath the brusque exterior. Whatever her mother had done to her still had the power to wound her. His chest tightened with the need to go to her, brush his knuckles down her cheek and reassure her that he would take care of her...

Theos!

With gritted teeth, he tried to pull himself back under control. There would be no reassuring, just as there would be no repeat of last night's events. What happened in his gym last night couldn't be allowed to happen again.

Absolutely, without a shadow of a doubt.

So why was he walking towards her, letting his gaze devour the exposed line of her neck as she bent over her tablet? Why was he imagining himself lifting her up from that chair, sliding that tight skirt up—did she favour garter belts or thigh-high stockings?—and bending her over his boardroom table?

Stasi.

He was losing it and it wasn't even nine o'clock in the morning! With a curt command, he dismissed his board members.

He waited until the room cleared before he murmured her name.

She lifted her head and stared straight at him. Deep turquoise eyes met his and Sakis wasn't sure whether the interest it held was personal or professional. That he couldn't even read her properly any more, sent a fizz of annoyance through him.

'So, what happens now? I didn't think you'd let Moorecroft know we were investigating his connection with the tanker.'

Stopping a mere foot from her, he shrugged. 'I called his bluff and it paid off. I wasn't sure until I heard it in his voice. He's involved.'

'Then why not go after him?'

'He knows he's cornered. Between the FCA investigation and my own, he'll either come clean or he'll try to do whatever he can to cover his tracks. Either way, his time is fast running out. I'll give him a few hours to decide which way he wants to go.'

'And if he reveals a connection?'

Sakis heard the tremble in her voice and wondered at it.

'Then I'll make sure he pays to the fullest extent.' His father had got away with shady business deals for a long time before he'd been brought to justice. The same newspapers that had uncovered his treachery had uncovered the many families and employees his father had duped out of their rightful rewards.

Once his father had been put behind bars and Ari had been old enough to take over the reins of the company, the first thing he'd done was make sure the affected families were recompensed.

Letting anyone get away with fraud and duplicity would never happen.

He glanced down into the face of the woman whose body had invaded his dreams last night. She'd paled considerably, her eyes wide and haunted. His frown deepened.

'What's wrong?'

She surged to her feet and started gathering her things. 'Nothing.'

'Wait.' He placed a halting hand on her waist and immediately felt her tense. Another stream of irritation rushed upward.

'Y-yes?' Her voice wasn't quite steady and her head was bent, hiding her expression.

'Brianna, what's the hell is going on?'

'Why should there be anything wrong? I'm merely returning to my office to get on with the rest of the day.' Her words emerged in a rush.

Something was definitely wrong; something he'd said. He replayed his last words in his head, then his lips pursed.

'You think my views are too harsh?'

Her mouth tightened but she still avoided eye contact. 'What does it matter what I think?'

'Tell me, what would you do?' His hand curved firmly around her waist. When she moved, he felt the warm softness beneath his fingers. He wanted to pull her closer, glide his hand upward and cup her breast the way he had last night. It took every single ounce of willpower for him to hold himself still.

'I…I would listen to them, find out the motive behind their actions first, before I throw them to the wolves.'

'Greed is greed. Betrayal is betrayal. The reason for it ceases to matter once the act is done.'

Her soft lips pursed. Her nostrils flared and Sakis caught a sense of anger bubbling beneath her skin. 'If you truly believe that, then I don't see the point of you asking me.'

'Under what circumstances would you forgive such an action?'

She gave a small shrug. The movement drew his attention to her breast. Sakis swallowed and cursed the heat flaring through his groin. 'If the act was done to protect someone you cared about. Or perhaps it was done without the perpetrator knowing he was committing an act of betrayal.'

Sakis's lips twisted. 'My father's betrayal was an active undertaking. So is Moorecroft's.'

Her eyes clashed with his then she glanced away. 'You can't assign your father's sins to every situation in your life, Mr Pantelides.'

This was getting personal again. But he couldn't seem to stop himself from spilling the jagged pain in his chest. 'My father actively cheated and bribed his way through his business dealings for decades. He betrayed his family over and over, letting us think he was one thing when he was in fact another. Even after he was found out, he was remorseless. Even jail didn't change him. He went to his grave unrepentant.' He sucked in a breath and forcibly steered his thoughts away from the bitterness of his past. 'You're deluding yourself if you think there's such a thing as blind, harmless betrayal.'

A shaft of pain and sympathy flitted through her eyes, just like it had back at Point Noire. She even started to move towards him before she visibly stopped herself.

Sakis felt curiously bereft that she succeeded.

'I'm sorry for what happened to you. I…I have emails to catch up on so, if you don't mind, I'll get back to the office.'

'No.'

She stared at him in surprise. 'No?'

He glanced at his watch. 'You haven't had breakfast yet, have you?'

'No, but I was going to order some fruit and cereal from the kitchen.'

'Forget that. We're going out.'

'I don't see why—'

'I do. We've both been cooped up in here since yesterday. Some fresh air and a proper meal will do us some good. Come.' He started to walk out and felt a hint of satisfaction when after several seconds he heard her footsteps behind him.

Sakis took her to a café on a quiet street in Cheapside. The manager greeted him with a smile and offered them a red high-backed booth set back from the doorway. One look at the menu and her eyes flew to collide with Sakis's.

He was regarding her with a seriously sexy smile on his face.

'All they serve here are pancakes,' she blurted.

'I know, which is why I brought you here. Time to indulge that *weakness* of yours.' The way he stressed the word made a spike of heat shoot through her.

'But...why?' Frantically, she scrambled to gather her rapidly unravelling control. Far from being back on the professional footing she'd thought, the morning was turning into one huge, personal landmine. One she wasn't sure she would survive.

'Because it's perfect ammunition.' Again he smiled and her heart lurched.

'You see my weakness for pancakes as *ammunition*?' She felt her lips twitch and allowed herself a small smile. Just then, a waiter walked past with a steaming heap of blueberry pancakes dripping in honey. She barely managed to stifle her groan, but Sakis heard it.

A dark, hungry look entered his eyes that made her stomach muscles clench hard. 'I'm not so sure whether to be pleased or irritated that I've uncovered this piece of information about you, Brianna. On the one hand, it could be the perfect weapon to get you to do whatever I want.'

'I already do whatever you want.' The loaded answer made heat crawl up her neck. His keen gaze followed it then scoured her face before locking on hers.

'Do you? I distinctly recall a few times when you've refused to do my bidding.'

'I wouldn't have lasted two minutes if I'd pandered to you in any shape or form.'

'No, you wouldn't have. I told Ari you were my Rottweiler.'

She gave a shocked gasp. 'You compared me to a dog?'

He grimaced and had the grace to look uncomfortable. 'It was a metaphor but, in hindsight, I should've used a more... flattering description.' He beckoned the waiter who'd been hovering a booth away.

Her curiosity got the better of her. 'How would you describe me?'

He didn't answer immediately. Instead he gave the waiter their order—coffee and two helpings of blueberry pancakes.

Brianna stopped the waiter with a hand on his arm. 'Can I have a side-helping of blueberries, please? And a bowl of honey? Oh, and some icing sugar and fresh cream…and two wedges of lemon…and some butter…' She stopped when she saw Sakis's eyebrow quirk in deep amusement. She dropped her arm and this time was unable to stop her blush from suffusing her face as their waiter walked away. 'Sorry, I didn't mean to sound like a complete glutton.'

'Don't apologise for your desires. Indulging every now and then is completely human.'

'Until I have to pay for it with hours in the gym. Then I'll hate every single mouthful I'm about to take.'

Immediately her mind homed in on what had happened between them last night. From the way his green eyes darkened, he was remembering too. God, what was wrong with her? Or maybe that was the wrong question. She knew what was wrong. Despite cautioning herself against it, she was attracted to Sakis with a fierce compulsion that defied reason. She accepted that now. What she needed was a cure for this insanity before it raged out of control.

'If you regret the act before it's happened, you take away the enjoyment of it.'

'So you're saying I should just ignore what will come afterwards and just live in the moment?'

His gaze dropped to her lips, the heat of it almost a caress that made her want to moan. 'Exactly.' He breathed the word then said nothing else.

Silence grew between them, the only sound the distant clatter of plates and cutlery from other diners.

She could only stand it for a few minutes until she felt as if she'd combust from the sizzling tension in the air. Forcefully, she cleared her throat and searched for a neutral subject, one that would defuse the stressful atmosphere. 'You were going to tell me what your description of me would be.' *Oh, nice one, Brianna.*

He sat back in his seat, extended his arm along the back of

the booth. Her eyes fell on rippling muscle beneath his shirt and she barely managed to swallow.

'Perhaps now is not the time, or the place.'

Leave it, Brianna...leave it. 'Oh, is it that bad?'

'No, it's that *good*.'

She breathed deeply and opted for silence. When their food arrived, she pounced on it, feeding her culinary appetite the way she couldn't let herself feed on the dark, carnal promise in Sakis's eyes.

She looked up several minutes later to find him watching her with an expression of mingled shock and amusement.

'Sorry, it's your fault. Now you've unleashed my innermost craving, there's no stopping me.' She took another sinful bite and barely managed to stop her eyes rolling in pleasure.

'On the contrary, seeing you eat something other than a salad and with such...relish is a pleasurable experience in itself.'

'Don't worry; I'm not going to re-enact a *When Harry Met Sally* moment.'

A puzzled frown marred his forehead. 'A what?'

She laughed. 'You've never seen that clip where the actress simulates an orgasm in a restaurant?'

He swallowed. 'No, I haven't. But I prefer my orgasmic experiences not to be simulated. When it comes to orgasms, only the real thing will do. Do you not agree?'

Dear Lord, was she really having breakfast with her boss, discussing orgasms? 'I wasn't... This was...' She stopped, silently willing her racing pulse to quieten. 'I was merely making conversation. I don't have an opinion on orgasms one way or another.'

His low laugh caressed her senses like soft butterfly wings. '*Everyone* has an opinion on orgasms, Brianna. Some of us may have stronger opinions than others, but we all have them.'

She was not going to think about Sakis and orgasms together. *She was not*. 'Um…okay; point taken. But I'd rather not discuss it any longer, if that's okay with you?'

He finished the last of his pancakes and picked up his black coffee. 'Certainly. But some subjects have a habit of lingering until they're dealt with.'

'And other subjects deserve more attention than others. What was your other point?'

'Sorry?'

'Before the subject went…sideways you said "on the one hand". I was wondering what the other was.'

It was a purely diversionary tactic, but she wanted—no, needed—to get off the subject that was making desire dredge through her pelvis like a pervasive drug, threatening to fool her into thinking she could taste the forbidden and come out whole.

There would be no coming out whole once she gave in to the hunger that burned within her, that burned relentlessly in Sakis's eyes. Wanting—or, God forbid, *needing*—a man like Sakis would destroy her eventually. Their conversation in the boardroom had reiterated the fact that he was emotionally scarred from what his father had done to him. He would never allow himself to trust anyone, never mind reaching the point of *needing* another human being to the extent she suspected she would crave if she didn't control her feelings.

'On the other hand, I'm glad I know this weakness. Because I have a feeling you don't give yourself permission enough to enjoy the simple things in life.'

Her heart hammered with something suspiciously like elation. 'And you…you want to give me that?'

'I want to give you that. I want to indulge you like you've never been indulged before.'

Simple words. But oh, so dangerous to her current state of mind.

'Why?' she blurted before she could stop herself.

Her question seemed to surprise him. His lashes swept

down and veiled his eyes. 'For starters, I'm hoping to be rewarded with one of those rare smiles of yours.' He looked back up and his expression stopped her breath. There was a solemn kinship, a gentleness in their depths, that made her heart flip. 'And because I had my brothers while I dealt with my daddy issues. But you, as far as I know, are an only child, correct?'

Emotion clogged her throat. 'Correct,' she croaked, battling the threat of tears.

That weird connection tightened, latched and embedded deeply, frightening but soothing at the same time. 'Let's call this therapy, then.' He glanced down at her plate where one last square of honey-soaked pancake was poised on her fork. 'Are you finished?'

She hadn't but the thought of putting that last morsel in her mouth while he watched with those all-seeing eyes was too much to bear. 'Yes, I'm done. And thank you…for this, I mean. And for…' She stumbled to a halt, alien feelings rushing through her at dizzying speed.

He nodded, stood and held out his hand. 'It was my pleasure, *agapita*.'

By the time they returned to the office, Brianna knew something had fundamentally changed between them. She didn't even bother to figure out a way back to equanimity; she couldn't. Curiously, she didn't feel as devastated at losing that particular battle.

It helped that they were barely in the door when Sakis threw out a list of things he wanted her to do but, despite the breakneck speed of dealing with his demands, they were soon both plugged into events at Point Noire, especially the clean-up process and the still missing Pantelides Six crewmembers.

After speaking to Morgan Lowell's wife Perla for the fifth time at six o'clock, Sakis threw his pen on his desk and ran both hands over his stubbled jaw.

'Are you okay?'

Tired eyes trained on her with breath-stopping intensity.

'I need to get out of here,' he rasped as he strode to the door and shrugged into his designer overcoat.

She swallowed and nodded. 'Do you want me to book a restaurant table for you? Or call a friend to...um...' She stopped, purely because the thought of arranging a date for Sakis with one of the many women who graced his electronic diary stuck in her gut like a sharp knife.

'I'm not in the mood to listen to inane conversation about the latest Hollywood gossip or who is screwing whom in my circle of friends.'

His response pleased her way more than it should have. 'Okay, what can I do?'

His eyes gleamed for a moment, before he looked away and headed towards the door. 'Nothing.' He stopped with a hand on the door. 'I'm meeting Ari for a drink. And you're logging off for the night. Is that clear, Moneypenny?'

She nodded slowly and watched him walk out, hollowness in her stomach that made her hate herself. She wanted to be with him. She wanted to be the one who wiped away that look of weariness she'd seen in his eyes. And all through today, every time he'd called her 'Moneypenny', she'd wanted to beg him to call her 'Brianna'. Because she loved the way he said her name.

She glanced down at the fingers resting on her keyboard and wasn't surprised to see them trembling. Her whole being trembled with the depth of the feelings that had been coursing through her all day. Frankly, it scared the hell out of her.

Hurriedly, she shut down the computer and gathered her tablet, phone and handbag. She'd just slid her chair neatly into the space beneath her desk when the phone rang. Thinking it was Sakis—because who else would ring her at seven-thirty on a work night?—she pounced on the handset.

'Hello?'

'May I speak to Anna Simpson?'

A spear of ice pinned her in place as her lips parted on a soundless gasp. A full minute passed. Her lungs burned until she managed to force herself back from the brink of unconsciousness. 'Excuse me, I...I think you've got the wrong number.'

The ugly laugh at the end of the line shook her to the very soul. 'We both know I don't have the wrong number, don't we, sweetheart?

She didn't respond—couldn't—because the phone had fallen from her nerveless fingers.

Another full minute passed. 'Hello?' came the impatient echoing voice. 'Anna?'

Numbness spreading through her, she picked up the phone. 'I told you there...there's no one by that name working here.'

But it was too late. She recognised the taunting, reedy voice at the end of the line. It was a voice she'd been dreading hearing again since her return from Point Noire.

'I can play along if you prefer, Anna. Hell, I'll even call you by your new name, *Brianna Moneypenny*. But we both know to me you'll always be Anna, don't we?' mocked Greg Landers.

CHAPTER SEVEN

'What do you want, Greg?' Brianna snapped into her mobile phone as she threw her bag on the tiny sofa in her small living room.

'What? No hello, no pleasantries? Never mind. I'm glad you were sensible enough to return my call. Although, I don't get why you didn't want to speak to me at your office. I made sure Pantelides wasn't there before I called.'

Shock made her grip the edge of the seat. 'You're having him watched?'

'No, I'm having *you* watched. You're the one I'm interested in.'

'Me?'

'Yes. For now, at least. Tell me, why the name change?'

Bitterness rose in a sweltering tide, bringing a sickening haze that made the furnishings of her small flat blur. 'Why the hell do you think? You destroyed my life, Greg. After you lied and swore under oath in court that I embezzled funds from your company, when we both know that it was you who set up that Cayman Islands account in my name. Do you think after what you put me through anyone would've hired me once they knew I'd been to prison for embezzlement?'

'Tsk-tsk, let's not blow things out of proportion, shall we? You served well under half of the four-year prison term. If it's any consolation, I only expected you to get a slap on the wrist.'

'It's *not* a consolation!'

'Besides,' he continued as if she hadn't interrupted, 'I hear those prisons are just a step down from glorified holiday camps.'

The scar on her hip—the result of a shiv, courtesy of an inmate whose attention she wouldn't return—burned at the careless dismissal of what had been a horrific period of her life. 'It's a shame you decided not to try it out for yourself, then, instead of turning coward and letting someone else take the blame for your greed. Now, are you going to tell me what this call is about or shall I hang up?'

'Hang up and I'll make sure your salacious past is the first thing Pantelides reads about when he steps into that ivory tower of his tomorrow morning.'

Brianna's hand tightened around the phone at the ruthless tone. 'How did you find me, anyway?' Not that it mattered now. But she'd used every last penny to erase her past, to make sure every trace of Anna Simpson was wiped clean as soon as she'd attained her freedom.

'I didn't. *You* found *me*, through the wonderful medium of TV. Imagine my surprise when I tuned in, like every environmentally conscious individual out there who's horrified about the Pantelides oil spillage, to find you right behind the main man himself. It took me a few minutes to recognise you, though. I much prefer you blonde to the brunette you used to be. Which is the real thing?'

'I fail to see...' She stopped because the Greg she'd known, the man she'd once foolishly thought herself in love with, hadn't changed. He believed himself a witty and clever conversationalist and was never one to get to the point until he was ready. It was one of the things—many things, she realised now—that had irritated her about him. 'Blonde is my natural colour.'

Greg sighed. 'Such a shame you chose to wear that dull brown when I knew you. Maybe I'd have thought twice before taking the route I took.'

'No, you wouldn't have. Your slimy nature makes you interested in taking care of number one. Are you going to tell me what you want any time soon?'

'You're distressed so I'll let that insult slide. But be careful now or I'll forget my manners. Now, what do I want? It's very simple: I want Pantelides Shipping. And you're going to help me get it.'

You're out of your mind was the first of many outraged responses that rushed into her head. She managed to stop herself before they spilled out. Slowly, she sank onto her sofa, the only piece of furniture in her living room aside from a lone coffee table, as her mind raced.

'And why would I do that?'

'To protect your dirty little secret, of course.'

She licked her lips as fear threatened to swamp any semblance of clear thinking. 'What makes you think my boss doesn't already know?'

'Don't take me for a fool, Anna.'

'My name is Brianna.' The woman Greg thought he knew no longer existed.

'If you want to keep calling yourself that, you'll give me what I want. And don't bother telling me Pantelides knows about your past. He's scrupulous when it comes to any hint of scandal. You're the last person he'd employ if he knew your past was as shady as his father's.'

This time her gasp was audible. It echoed around the room in tones of pain, shock and anger. 'You know about his father?'

'I do my homework, sweetheart. And if he'd bothered to do his he'd have discovered who you really were. But I'm glad he didn't, because now you're in the perfect position to help me.'

The vice tightened harder around her chest. 'What exactly is it you want me to do?'

'I need information. As much as you can get your hands on. Specifically, which of the board members hold the largest shares, aside from Pantelides. And which of the other members will be amenable to selling what shares they have.'

'You know this will never work, don't you? Sakis—Mr Pantelides—will crush you if you come within a whisper of his company.'

'God, you haven't gone and done it again, have you, Anna?' came the soft taunt.

Brianna shivered. 'Done what?'

'Offered that foolish little heart of yours on a silver platter to another boss?' he murmured in a pitying voice.

'I don't know what you're talking about.' But deep down there was no hiding from the truth. Her feelings for Sakis had morphed from purely professional to something else. Something she was vehemently unwilling to examine right now, when she needed all her wits about her to defend herself against what her grimy ex was intent on pulling her into.

'You have four days, Anna. I'll be in touch and I expect you to have the information I need.'

Her mouth went dry. Her heart hammered with sick fear and loathing and the unmistakeable, sinking feeling of inevitability. 'And if I don't?'

'Then your boss will wake up to a most tantalising double-page spread of his treasured assistant in the tabloid press on Saturday morning. I'm pretty sure with very little effort I can get Pantelides Shipping to start trending again on all social media.'

Her belly quivered and she clenched her muscles hard. 'Why are you doing this? Haven't you done enough? Aren't the millions you squirrelled away enough?'

'Every Joe Bloggs knows how to make a million these days. No, sweetheart, my ambitions are set much higher than that. I'd hoped my association with Moorecroft would see me there but the fool folded at the first sign of adversity. Fortunately, I have you now.'

'I haven't agreed to anything.'

'But you will. You covet your position almost as much as I covet the prospect of acquiring Pantelides Shipping. Make no mistake, I will have it.'

'Greg—'

'I'll be in touch on Friday. Don't disappoint me, Anna.'

He hung up before she could appeal to his better nature. Who was she kidding? Greg had no better nature. He was a vulture who ruthlessly fed on the weak.

The discovery that he'd engineered her to take the fall for his failing company over three years ago had rocked her to the core. When he'd pleasantly asked her to act as his co-director, she'd thought nothing of it, especially when he'd brought in a legal expert to explain things to her. Of course, it'd turned out the so-called legal expert had been in on the scheme to bleed his company dry before declaring bankruptcy and leaving her to take the fall.

She'd had time to dwell on her stupidity and gullibility in the maximum-security prison the judge had sentenced her to, to set an example.

Brianna staggered up from the sofa, swaying on shaky legs as her mind spun with the impossibility of her situation.

The very idea of betraying Sakis made her stomach turn over in revulsion.

He would never forgive her if she brought his company under unpalatable scrutiny so soon after his tanker's crash and having the memory of his father resurrected.

She could resign with immediate effect. But what would stop Greg from spewing his vitriol purely out of spite?

Telling Sakis the truth was out of the question.

Betrayal is betrayal. The reason for it ceases to matter once the act is done.

Casting her gaze around the almost empty room, another shiver raked through her.

Run!

The stark reality of her harsh childhood had made it impossible for her to fully imbed herself in any one place, even this place she called her sanctuary. At least, if she had to run, she could be out of here in less than half an hour.

She pressed her lips together as a spike of rebellion clayed her feet. Why should she run? She'd done nothing wrong. Her only folly had been to delude herself into thinking Greg cared for her. But she'd paid the price for it.

No more. *No more!*

Throwing down the mobile phone, she went into her equally sparsely furnished bedroom. The bed lay on wooden slats on the floor. Aside from a super-sized *papier-mâché* cat she'd bought at a Sunday market months ago, only a tall, broad-leafed ficus plant graced the room. Her only indulgence was the luxury cashmere throw and the fluffy pillows on the bed. Even the built-in wardrobe held only the collection of designer suits Sakis had insisted she used her expense account for when she'd joined Pantelides Shipping. Her own clothes consisted of a few pairs of jeans and tops, one set of jogging bottoms and jumper and two pairs of trainers.

Those would be easy to pack.

No; she refused to think like a fugitive. She had nothing to be ashamed of.

With shaky fingers, she undressed and entered the *en suite* bathroom, suddenly eager to wash away the grime of her conversation with Greg. But his threat lingered in the air, in the water. No matter how much she scrubbed, she felt tainted by the thought that she had even contemplated betrayal to save her own skin.

The pounding at her door finally registered over the hammering of her heart and the rush of the shower. Twisting the tap shut, she heard the faint sound of her mobile just before another round of hammering made her lunge for her dressing down. With a quick sluice of a towel over her body, she went to her door and peered through the peephole.

The massive frame of Sakis looming through the distorted

glass quickly eroded the relief that Greg hadn't found his way to her flat.

It seemed the two people responsible for the angst in her life were determined to breach her sanctuary at all costs today.

Pulse skittering out of control, Brianna cracked open the door. 'I...I didn't know you knew where I lived.' She looked into his clenched-jawed face and her words died on her lips. 'Why are you here?'

'I came here because...' He stopped, then clawed a hand through his hair. 'Hell, I'm not exactly sure why I came here. But I know I didn't want to be at the penthouse by myself.' He raked his hand through his hair again. The weariness she'd glimpsed on his face earlier seemed amplified a hundred-fold. The soft place inside her chest that had been expanding since their pancake episode this morning widened even further and she found herself stepping back.

'I... Would you like to come in?'

Lips pursed, he nodded. Standing to one side in the narrow hallway, she held her breath as he entered her sanctuary.

Immediately, he dwarfed the space. She shut the door and entered the living room to find him pacing the space in short, jerky strides.

'Can I get you a drink?' She hadn't touched the bottle of scotch that had come with her Christmas hamper last year. Now she was grateful for it as she produced the bottle and Sakis nodded.

She took out a glass, poured a healthy measure and passed it to him.

'Aren't you having one?' Despite his question, his gaze was focused on the amber liquid in his hand.

'I don't really...' She stopped. After what she'd been through already tonight, what she sensed was coming, perhaps a small drink wouldn't hurt. She poured a single shot for herself, took a sip and nearly choked as the liquid burned a fiery path through her chest.

With a grim smile, Sakis tossed his own drink back in one unflinching gulp. He set his glass down on the coffee table and faced her.

'Why did you leave?'

The reason for returning home blazed at the back of her mind. Although she'd done nothing wrong, guilt clawed through her nevertheless. She licked her lips then froze when his eyes darkened. 'I haven't been home in a while. I just wanted to touch base.'

'And touching base precluded you from answering your phone?'

She glanced at the phone she'd abandoned on the sofa after her call with Greg. Picking it up, she activated it and saw twelve missed calls on the screen.

'Sorry, I was in the shower.'

His agitated pacing brought him closer. He stopped a couple of feet from her. But the distance meant nothing because she could feel the heat of his body reaching out, caressing her, claiming her. Tendrils of damp hair that had escaped the knot clung to her nape, sending tiny rivulets of water down her back. Supremely conscious that she was naked beneath her gown, she tried to take a step back but her feet were frozen on the carpet.

His gaze traced over her and stopped at the rapid rise and fall of her chest. She watched his fists clench and release as stark hunger transformed his face into a mesmerising mask.

'I'm sorry to have disturbed you,' he rasped, but nothing in his tone or his face showed contrition. Instead, his stare intensified, whipping the air around her until a helpless moan escaped her lips.

Abandoning reason, Brianna stepped closer, bringing her body flush against his. Knowing she risked betraying her very soul, but unable to stop herself, she cupped his jaw. 'You ordered me to stop working. I didn't think you'd need me tonight.'

Her breath caught as his gaze moved hungrily over her lips.

'No, Brianna. Far from it. I need you. More now than I've ever needed you before. You're the only one who makes the world make sense to me.'

'I...I am?'

'*Ne*. I didn't like it when I couldn't reach you.' His head dropped a fraction until his forehead touched hers. 'I can't function without you by my side.'

'I'm here now,' she whispered, her throat clogged with emotions she couldn't give name to. No, scratch that: it was desire, passion and compassion all rolled into one needful and relentless ache. That visceral need to connect with Sakis that she'd never felt with anyone else, not even her own mother. 'Whatever you need, I'm here.'

One hand fisted her damp, precariously knotted hair, pulling it back almost roughly so her face was tilted up and exposed to his. 'Are you?' he enquired roughly.

She gave a shaky nod. 'Yes.'

'Be very sure, *glikia mou*. Because this time I won't be able to stop. If you don't want me to go any further, tell me now.' His eyes searched her urgently, his need clearly displayed in the harsh whistle of breath that escaped his parted lips.

The hard body plastered to hers made thinking near impossible but Brianna knew one thing—this could be her one chance to be with Sakis. After Friday, she'd be out of a job— one she would be sacked from or have to resign from.

From a purely selfish point of view, this could be her last chance to experience the fervid promise of bliss she'd felt in the gym last night—to be bold enough to reach for something she'd once dared to crave.

'Brianna?' His fierce tone held a hint of vulnerability that struck deep.

Sakis needed her. And she...she needed to blank out the heartache the future held.

'Yes, I want you...'

He swallowed the words with the savage demand of his kiss. The hand at her waist lowered to grasp her bottom and he pulled her into stinging contact with his groin, giving a low groan as the force of his erection probed her belly.

For an endless age, he devoured her mouth with a hunger born of desperation. Brianna gave as much as she got, her hunger just as maddeningly urgent. When his tongue curled around hers, she opened her mouth wider to feel even more of it.

Sakis groaned again and walked her back until the back of her legs touched her small sofa. He'd barely pushed her down before he covered her with his immense body. Searing heat engulfed her as they lay plastered from chest to thigh. Raising his head, his gaze scoured her face as if imprinting her features on his memory. When it touched her lips, the urge to lick them overcame her. She passed her tongue over them and watched in secret delight as his eyes darkened dramatically.

'I suspected that underneath those severe business suits you were a seductress, Moneypenny.'

'I'm sure I have no idea what you mean.' She licked her lips again.

His growl was her first warning but she was too far gone to heed it.

Brianna quickly pulled his head down and brushed his lips with hers. She kissed him again and felt her heart leap with joy when he deepened it.

When he suddenly surged off her and stood, Brianna fought not to cry out in disappointment. But he merely shrugged out of his jacket and tie before plucking her off the seat. 'I'm so lucky to have you. But my gratitude does not extend to making love to you on a sofa made for elves.'

'Oh. I guess it is a little on the small side, isn't it?'

'Perhaps not, if you're trying to be inventive. We'll leave it for another time.'

The thrill that went through her escalated when he caught

her up in his arms and took her lips in another searing kiss. 'Which way to the bedroom?'

Brianna pointed and he immediately steered her in that direction. At the door, she hesitated. What would he think when he saw how sparsely decorated her room was? She was scrambling to think of excuses when he pulled her hips into his groin.

'I don't mind doing it standing up if that's what you'd prefer, *glikia mou*. Just say the word,' he breathed against her neck, one hand sneaking up to cup her bare breast where her gown had fallen open. With another groan, he squeezed before teasing the nub between his fingers. 'But say it quickly before I combust from neglect.'

'The...the bedroom is fine.' She opened the door and held her breath. But Sakis was only interested in the bed, not the state of the near-empty room. He propelled her firmly towards it, shucking off his shoes, socks and shirt without letting go completely. With a firm hand he pushed her onto the bed and fell onto his knees behind her.

Pulling her back, he ground his hips into her. 'You have no idea how many times I've imagined you in this position before me.' Urgent hands slid up her dressing gown and he growled with ragged need as he bared her naked bottom to his heated gaze. '*Theos*, no knickers. This is even better than I imagined.' Roughly, he reached for the sleeves of the gown and jerked it off her completely.

Brianna was thankful she wasn't facing him so that she didn't have to explain her tattoo to him just yet, especially since, with the depth of her need, she wasn't sure she wouldn't blurt out the truth behind it. The other thing was her scar. She couldn't hide it for ever but she was grateful she didn't have to explain it right this minute.

Because the sensation of Sakis touching her naked bottom, caressing and decadently moulding it, made her senses melt.

'*Theos*, I love your ass,' he growled with dirty reverence.

Pure feminine delight fizzed through her. 'I can tell,' she responded breathily.

His laugh was low and deep, doing nothing to disguise his hunger. She jerked with surprise and delight when she felt his mouth touch each globe in an open-mouthed kiss before biting lightly on her flesh.

He continued to knead her with his large hands, massaging down to her hips before returning to fondle her with both hands. The eroticism of the act made her breath catch. But it was when he pushed her forward and spread apart her thighs that she stopped breathing.

Sakis blew a hot breath on her parted folds, making her thighs quiver in anticipation of what was to come. When it came, when the tip of his tongue flicked over her most sensitive place, Brianna couldn't stop the cry of pleasure that spilled from her throat. Hands shaking in a monumental effort to keep her from collapsing onto the bed, she clamped her eyes shut and held her breath for another burn of sensation.

Another flick, then several more, then Sakis opened her wider, baring her to his gaze. He muttered something in Greek before he placed the most shocking, open-mouthed kiss on her. He devoured her as if she was his favourite meal. Sensation built upon sensation until Brianna wasn't sure which move pleased her more—his teeth grazing her clitoris or his relentlessly probing tongue inside her.

All she knew was that the majestic peak that promised both exquisite torture and intense pleasure loomed closer. Fire burned behind her closed lids. Her fingers spasmed into a death grip on her sheets. With one long, merciless pull of his mouth on her clitoris, he sent her over the edge.

He gave a long, satisfied groan as he drank her in. For endless minutes, he lapped her with his tongue until her convulsions ceased. Vaguely, she heard him leave the bed and shuck off his trousers. Limp and breathless, she started to sag.

One hand caught her around the waist. 'Stay right there; I'm not finished with you yet.'

Brianna clawed back reason enough to demand huskily, 'Um...condom?'

'Taken care of.' His hand caressed up her stomach to cup one breast before teasing her nipple. She felt the other fumble for the loose knot in her hair. 'You know I've never seen your hair down?'

'Hmm...yes.'

He pulled her up and released the knot, then groaned as his fingers weaved through the heavy blonde tresses that went all the way down her back. '*Theos*, it's a travesty to keep this gorgeous hair tied up day after day. You deserve punishment for that, Moneypenny.'

The sharp tap on her rump sent excitement sizzling along her nerves. She bit her lip when she felt the thick evidence of his desire lying between the crease of her bottom, a relentless reminder that there was another experience to be celebrated.

'You don't think you've tortured me enough?' she asked.

His thumbs flicked over her nipples. 'Not nearly enough, *pethi mou*. Open your legs wider.'

She obeyed because she wanted this more than she wanted her next breath. At the first probe of his erection, she held her breath. He used one hand to hold her still and fed another inch inside her.

Stars burst across her vision. 'Sa—' How could it be that she was bared to him in the most intimate of ways and yet the taste of his name on her lips felt a touch too far?

'Say it,' he commanded.

'I can't...'

He started to withdraw. Her body clenched in fierce denial. 'No!'

'Say my name, Brianna.'

'Sa...Sakis,' she gasped. He pushed back in with a deep groan. 'Oh God.'

'*Again!*'

'S...Sakis!'

'Good girl.' He plunged in until he was fully embedded, then held still. 'Now, tell me how you want this to go. Fast or slow. Either way will be torture for me but I want to please you.'

Brianna wanted to tell him he'd already pleased her, a thousand times more than she'd ever imagined possible.

'Now, *glikia mou*, while my brain still functions...' Pushing her forward, he covered her with his body and trapped her splayed hands under his on the bed.

The first signs of her climax clawed at her. 'Fast, Sakis. I want it fast. And hard.'

'*Theos!*' His response through clenched teeth was a hot breath in her ear. 'Your wish is my command.' With a loud groan, he pulled out and surged back in, then proceeded to set a blistering pace that made her die a little each time her orgasm drew closer.

When he rocked back on his knees, Brianna's chest collapsed onto the bed, her feeble arms unable to sustain the barrage of sensations that rippled through her. Taking one last, gasping breath, she screamed as blissful convulsions seized her. Dimly, she heard Sakis's long, drawn-out growl as his pleasure overtook him. Deep within her, she felt his thickness pump his pleasure over and over until he was spent.

He collapsed sideways onto the bed and took her with him. In the dark room, he tucked her back against his chest, their harsh breaths gradually slowing until only the occasional spasm raked through them.

CHAPTER EIGHT

What felt like hours later, Sakis pulled her closer and brushed back her hair from her face.

The kiss he planted on her temple was gentle but possessive. 'That was sensational, *glikia mou*.'

'What does that mean?'

He gave a low laugh. 'You have an intelligent mind, Moneypenny. Find out.'

'You like to say my surname quite a lot. In fact, you don't go more than a minute or two when we're talking before going "Moneypenny this" or "Moneypenny that".'

She felt his grin against her neck. 'And this surprises you? I find your surname very intriguing, sexy.'

She fought not to tense at the interest in his tone and responded with forced lightness. 'Sexy?'

He shrugged. 'Before I met you, I'd only ever heard that name in a spy movie.'

'And you think she's sexy?'

'Extremely, and also hugely underestimated.'

'I agree with you there. But she was often overlooked in favour of sexier, in-your-face female leads; she was also the one who never got her guy.'

Sakis drew closer and traced his lips along the line of her shoulder. 'Well, I think we've remedied that tonight. Plus, she had astonishing staying power. Just like you. No one in their right mind would overlook you, Moneypenny, even though you try to hide it with that hypnotic swan-glide.'

She laughed. 'Swan glide?'

'Outwardly, you're serene, so damned efficient, and yet below you're paddling madly. Watching you juggle virtual balls is damned sexy.'

'Damn; and there I thought no one could see the mad paddling underneath.'

'Sometimes, there's just a little ruffle. Like when I misbehave and you itch to put me in my place.'

'So you know you're misbehaving? Acceptance is the first step, I suppose.'

She shivered as he rocked his hips forward in a blatantly masculine move that had her moaning. But then he pulled out of her a second later and flipped her to face him. 'Like all men in my position, I live to push the boundaries. But I get that I need an anchor sometimes. You're my anchor, Brianna.' He spoke with a low but fierce intensity that made tears prickle behind her eyes.

'Sakis...I...'

He kissed her, a slow, luxurious exploration that soon became something else, something more. She wanted to protest when he lifted his head. 'Hold that thought; I need to change condoms. Bathroom?'

She pointed and watched him head towards her tiny bathroom, her eyes glued to his toned, chiselled physique. The thought that she was about to make love with this virile, sexy man again made her tremble so hard, she clutched the pillow.

But, alone, dread began to creep in. She'd gone beyond *what the hell am I doing?* Now she had to deal with *what the hell am I going to do?*

Sakis might not have meant to but tonight he'd revealed just how much he treasured and respected her. How ironic that, just when she could've felt secure in the knowledge that her job was safe, that she didn't need to prove herself as the invaluable asset in Sakis's life, she would have to walk away.

Because there really was no choice. She would never betray Sakis the way he'd been betrayed before. As for Greg, he deserved to burn in hell.

She toyed with confessing but brushed it away. Now she understood just what he'd been through with his father, she couldn't bear for him to look at her and see another fraud, someone who'd failed to reveal the whole truth about her past.

Her only option would be to resign and find herself another job somewhere far away, perhaps in another country even, where neither Greg's vile threats or Sakis's condemnation would touch her.

A deep pool of sadness welled up inside her, bringing with it a sharp pain that made her groan and bury her face in the pillow.

She jumped when a warm hand caressed her back.

'Should I be offended that you were so far away you'd forgotten I exist?'

Composing herself, she turned to face him. *God, he was gorgeous*, even with the shadows of the past few days' stress lurking in his eyes. Perhaps that was what made him even more breath-taking—the fact that, despite being the ruthless entrepreneur feared by most competitors, he still had a caring heart.

Unable to stop herself, she reached for him and glided her hand over his warm, sculpted chest to draw him closer. 'I hadn't forgotten. I always know when you're near, Sakis. Always.'

His eyes darkened as he stretched out beside her and took her mouth in a long, deep kiss. 'I can't believe I waited this long to make you mine.'

The stamp of possessiveness in his voice made her heart jump in thrilling delight even though deep down she knew it was a futile reaction. She would never be truly his because this wouldn't last beyond the week. She pushed the disturbing thoughts away.

'Even though I was sweet enough, but nothing to lose your head over?' She quoted his words back at him and watched a shamefaced look cross his features.

He cursed under his breath. 'I think we both know that was a blatant lie.'

'What was the truth then?'

His lips drifted lazily over hers but she wasn't fooled that it was a casual caress. Against her thigh his re-energised erection pulsed with urgent demand, eliciting an electrifying reaction inside her body.

'The truth was that I wanted nothing more than to throw you on the nearest gym mat and take you until you couldn't speak. What would you have done if I'd said that, instead of the lame excuse I came up with?'

She leaned up and caught his earlobe in a saucy bite. 'I'd have said *bring it on.*'

The tremor that went through him preceded a guttural curse as he surged over her and proceeded to claim her in the most elemental way possible.

Within seconds, he had her on the knife-edge of need, a need so visceral she didn't know whether to beg for mercy or to beg him never to stop.

'S...Sakis...please,' she begged as he roughly tongued one nipple.

'I love the sound of my name on your lips. Say it again,' he murmured against her skin, his gaze rising to capture hers.

She shook her head in silent denial. A fiercely determined light entered his eyes and her heart sank.

He tugged on her engorged nub. 'Say my name, Brianna.'

'Why?' she asked defiantly.

'Because there's something potent and infinitely sexy about you crying out my name in the heat of passion.'

'But it sounds... It feels...'

'Too intimate?' He continued the erotic path between her breasts, his gaze never leaving hers as she nodded. 'It makes it all the more intense, no?'

Firm hands parted her thighs and one thumb lazily stroked her.

'Yes.' She sucked in a jagged breath as arousal spiked her blood with drugging pleasure. Her lids grew heavy and her back arched off the bed as the pressure escalated.

'That's it; lose yourself in it, Brianna…'

The lazy, continental drawl of her name had the right effect. Liquid heat oozed through her, making her limbs grow heavy and weak. *'Oh God.'*

'Wrong deity,' he said on a low laugh. The sound grazed over her, adding another dimension to the emotions bombarding her. Teeth bit her inner thigh; his warm tongue immediately soothed the bite, then proceeded to draw in ever closer circles to where his thumb wrecked mindless chaos.

Pleasure roared through her, eliciting the exact response she knew he wanted.

Sakis. The name echoed through her, over and over, seeking release. *Sakis*.

Her skin tightened as her climax grew closer. His tongue lapped her once, twice.

At the outer reaches of her mind, she heard a tearing sound.

Sakis.

His thumb left her clitoris and was replaced immediately by his tongue. Brianna shut her eyes on a long, keening moan that was ripped from the depths of her soul.

Dear Lord, she was going to come like she never had before. She reached out, intending to grip the sheets, and instead encountered hot, muscled flesh.

Her eyes flew open just as he reared above her and plunged, hot, stiff and deep inside her.

'Sakis!'

'Yes! *Theos*, you look so hot like that.'

She repeated his name in a strangled litany as the most forceful orgasm she'd ever had laid her to waste. Through it all he kept up the rhythm, his groans of pleasure prolonging hers, so she milked him with her muscles.

'Brianna, *eros mou*.' He fell onto his elbows and plunged his fingers into her hair, holding her down as he plundered her mouth with his. 'You're incredible,' he breathed against her lips as he surged deeper inside her. 'I can't get enough of you.'

His fingers tightened in her hair as his mouth drifted over her jaw to her neck. His breath grew harsh, his body momentarily losing its steady rhythm as waves of pleasure washed over them.

Gritting his teeth, Sakis forced back control into his body, if only temporarily, because he knew he was fighting a losing battle. But it was a battle he was perfectly willing to surrender.

The warm, sexy body undulating beneath him blew his mind. While half of him declared himself insane for waiting this long to give in to the spellbinding attraction, the other half rejoiced at waiting. It was clear Brianna wouldn't have given in under normal circumstances.

Something had happened today at the café. He didn't know what and couldn't pinpoint it but the simple meal had taken an unexpected turn, had shaken him in a way that had left him reeling.

She'd felt it too; he knew it. Whether it was the reason she'd ended up here, he didn't know, but he intended to grasp this golden opportunity with both hands.

Her inner muscles tightened again and he nearly lost it. The swollen temptation of her roughly kissed mouth parted on a breath and he groaned. Sweet heaven, everything about her blew his mind, but never in a thousand years had he dreamed the sex with her would be this great, this intense.

She breathed his name again, as if now she'd given herself permission to use it she couldn't say it enough. That was okay with him...more than okay. The sound of his name on her lips was a potent aphrodisiac all by itself.

He was leaning down to take those impossibly delectable lips again when he saw it. Buried beneath the cascade of her hair was an elegant scroll across her left collarbone.

She surged blindly up at that moment, impatient for his kiss, and her hair fell away.

'I refuse to sink', the tattoo read. And beside it was a tiny etching of a soaring phoenix.

He already knew she was brave beyond words. The glimpse of her life she'd shared with him had alerted him to a not-so-rosy past, perhaps a harsh childhood. Sakis was struck again by how little he really knew of her. Nevertheless, he knew he didn't need to dig to find out she had a core of integrity that had remained unblemished, despite whatever adversities she'd faced.

The knowledge jolted something deep and alien inside him. Shockingly, he desired her even more. He bucked into her and revelled in her hitched breathing. But he wanted more; felt an unrelenting need to touch her in the way she'd touched him tonight.

'Open your eyes, *pethi mou*,' he demanded hoarsely.

Slowly her lids parted, displaying exquisite turquoise eyes drenched in desire. 'What?'

'I want you to see me, Brianna. Feel what you do to me and know that I appreciate you more than you know.'

Her mouth dropped open in wordless wonder. Unable to help himself, he kissed her again. Then all too soon the climax that had been building inexorably surged with brutal force. He spread her thighs wider and pumped hard and fast inside her.

Her cry of ecstasy echoed his own minutes later as he came in a torrent of dizzying pleasure.

He waited until their breaths had returned to normal before he brushed aside her hair and looked closely at the tattoo. Slowly, he let his finger drift over it, telling himself he'd imagined it, when she stiffened.

'This is interesting...'

The invitation to confess was blatant.

But Brianna couldn't open that can of worms. Not after she'd already opened so much of herself that she was sure Sakis could see straight through her by now. God, how had she imagined that she could just live in this moment, satisfy the clawing need then walk away?

With just a handful of words, Sakis had split her heart wide open.

I want you to see me... You're my anchor, Brianna... I appreciate you more than you know.

'Brianna?' The demand was more powerful.

She scrambled to find a reasonable explanation. 'I got it after I left my...my last job...' She stopped, her heart hammering as she realised that she was highly emotional from their love-making and really shouldn't be talking.

'Most people take a holiday between jobs. But you got a tattoo?' Scarily, his curiosity had deepened. 'And a symbolic one, at that. Did you feel as if you were sinking?' His fingers drifted over the words again, and despite her roiling emotions she shivered with fresh need.

She forced a laugh. 'I guess I'm not most people.' *Stop talking now. Stop. Stop. Stop!* 'And yes, I felt like I was sinking. For a while I lost my way.' God, no...

His fingers touched the phoenix then he brushed it with his mouth. 'But then you triumphed.'

She let out a shaky breath. 'Y-yes.'

'Hmm, we're agreed on one thing—you're not most people. You're exquisitely unique.' His hand drifted down, paused over her breast then trailed lower to touch the scar on her hip. 'And this?'

Her breath caught anew. How had she thought he wouldn't notice? He'd spent an inordinate amount of time exploring every inch of her body, much to her shameless delight. Of course Sakis's astute gaze would've caught the slightly puckered flesh where the sharp, white-hot lance of the inmate's blade had stabbed deep and ruptured her spleen.

'I...I was attacked. It was a mugging.' That at least was the truth. What she couldn't confess was where she'd been when it had happened.

His fingers stilled then he swore hard. 'When?'

'Two years ago.'

He cupped her jaw. 'Was your attacker caught?'

Brianna shut her eyes against the probing of his. 'Yes, they were caught. And there was even some semblance of justice.' If you could call six months' solitary confinement for a prisoner already serving life 'justice'.

That seemed to satisfy Sakis. When she risked a glance at him, the harshness she'd heard in his voice was not evident in his face. 'Good,' he breathed as his fingers resumed its bone-melting caress. 'I'm glad.'

Before she could draw another breath, his head dropped and his lips touched the puckered scar. Her skin heated then burned as his lips, then his tongue moved over her flesh.

She expected him to ask about her ankle tattoo, the one she'd caught him eyeing on the plane. But he seemed to have regained his zealous exploration of her body.

Her breath hitched as his mouth wreaked blissful havoc. Within seconds, her brain ceased to function.

Brianna woke to the sound of movement in her bedroom. Struggling up from an exquisitely saucy dream featuring Sakis, she opened her eyes to find him standing at the foot of her bed, his gaze on her as he secured his cufflinks.

The look on his face immediately gripped her attention. Gone was the lover who'd whispered ardent words of pleasure and worship against her skin last night. In its place was Sakis, billionaire shipping magnate. But, as she watched, she saw the mask slip to reveal the stress he hadn't completely banished.

'I have to go,' he said. 'There's been a development.'

Brianna sat up and pushed her hair from her face. 'What?'

His fingers stilled on his cuff. 'The bodies of two crew-members have been found.'

Shock and grief rocked through her in equal measures. 'When did you find out?'

'Ten minutes ago. They were found two miles away where converging tides had hidden the bodies. The investigators think they drowned.'

She started to throw the covers off, experienced a fierce wave of self-consciousness and talked herself out of it. This wasn't the time. 'Give me ten minutes to shower and I'll come with you. I… We need to see about getting them home.'

He rounded the bed and stopped in front of her. One hand caressed her cheek. 'It's been taken care of. I woke my head of HR. Those men died on my company's watch so they're my responsibility. He's arranging everything, but I'm meeting the families this morning to express my condolences…' He stopped and breathed in deep.

A wave of sadness washed over her. 'It wasn't the outcome any of us wanted. Which two were found?'

'The deputy captain and the first officer.'

'So there's still no sign of Morgan Lowell?'

'No.'

Which meant they still had no answer to what had happened to the tanker. 'I'll do my best to keep it out of the press but there are no guarantees.' She strove for a semblance of professionalism—professionalism which became precarious as his arms banded around her waist and pulled her closer. Desire's inferno raged through her body.

'It's all been handled. Foyle assures me there's a procedure to dealing with this. We can't do anything more.'

'So for now I'm redundant?'

'Never,' he breathed. 'You will never be redundant to me.'

The intensity of his answer sent alarm skittering over her skin. She was in danger of fooling herself again. In danger of believing that Sakis was beginning to want her, to need her the way she'd once dreamed of being needed.

Forcing a laugh, she pulled out of his arms. 'Never say never. Shower time; I'll be out in ten.' She backed away, all the while noting he remained where he stood, his intense eyes on her. 'Um, there's coffee in the kitchen if you want some. I'm afraid I don't have much in the way of food as I wasn't expecting to stop here last night.'

Finally, he nodded. 'Coffee will suffice.'

Brianna held her breath until he left her room, then flew into the bathroom.

Eight minutes later she was slipping on high-heeled designer leopard-print shoes as she pinned her hair up in its usual chignon. With one last look to check her appearance, she tugged the sleeves of her black Prada suit, picked up her large handbag containing her tablet and left the room.

Sakis stood at her tiny living-room window gazing down at the street below. He turned at her entrance and handed her the second cup in his hand just before his phone buzzed. As she sipped her coffee, Brianna couldn't stop staring at the magnificent man who paced her living room.

A man who'd not only taken her body but had found his way into parts of her heart she'd imagined had withered and died.

The thought of walking away from this man for ever gouged her with pain that left her breathless. When he speared her with those mesmerising eyes, she fought hard to stop her feelings from showing.

She would have time to deal with the heartache later. Because, of course, there would be heartache. Her feelings for Sakis had gone way beyond the professional. She'd known that before she'd slept with him last night. This morning, watching him struggle with fresh adversity made those feelings more intense.

So intense she set her coffee cup down before her trembling hands gave her away. 'Do you need anything else before we leave?'

'Yes. Come here.'

She went willingly, unable to resist him. He looked around the room then set the coffee mug on the window sill. 'You'll enlighten me as to why this apartment has barely any furniture in it later, but for now I have a greater need.'

'What?'

He pulled her closer and cupped her face in his large hands. 'I haven't said good morning properly. I may not get the chance once we leave here.' He sealed his mouth over hers in a long, exploratory kiss. When he finally lifted his head, his eyes were the dark green she associated with extreme emotion. 'Good morning, *pethi mou*,' he murmured.

'G-good morning,' she responded in a voice husky with fresh need.

Reluctantly he dropped his hand and stepped back. 'Let's get out of here now or we'll never leave.'

The journey to the office was completed in near silence. Sakis seemed lost in thought, his answers monosyllabic as she tried to slip back into professional mode.

As they entered the underground car park at Pantelides Towers, she couldn't bear it any more. Turning to him, she waited until he faced her. 'If you're wondering how to play this, you need not worry. No one needs to know about what happened last night. I know what happened with Giselle—'

'Is ancient history. What's going on between us is different.'

Her heart lurched then hammered. 'You mean you don't mind if anyone finds out?'

He stiffened. 'I didn't say that.'

The hurt that scythed through her was as unbearable as it was irrational.

When the car stopped she scrambled to get out. Sakis grabbed her arm to stay her and waved the driver away when he approached.

'Wait, that didn't come out right. What I meant was that the last thing I want is for you to be caught in the crosshairs because of my past. It's very easy for the wrong person to put two and two together and come up with fifteen. You don't deserve to suffer for my father's sins.'

She sagged backwards. 'Was he... He wasn't always that bad, was he?' It was unthinkable that they both could've suffered such outwardly different, but inwardly similar and painful upbringings. At least, she hoped not, because her heart ached for the pain in his voice every time he spoke about his father.

She had come to terms, somewhat, with her non-relationship with her mother.

He sucked in a long breath. 'Yes, he was. He was a philanderer and an extortionist who was corrupt to the core and very clever at hiding his true colours. When his deeds were finally uncovered, our lives were turned inside out. Our every word and deed was scrutinised. Several times, our house staff discovered tabloid journalists digging through our garbage in the middle of the night, looking for more dirt.'

Distress for him scythed through her. 'That's horrible.'

'As horrible as that was, I mistakenly thought that was the worst of it.'

She was almost afraid to ask. 'What else did you find?'

'It turned out my father had mistresses stashed all over the globe, not just the secretary who'd grown tired of his philandering ways and empty promises—she was the one who blew the whistle that started the ball rolling, by the way. Once the first mistress crawled out of the woodwork, they were unstoppable. And you know why they all came forward, every single one of them?'

She shook her head despite the dread crawling through her stomach.

'*Money*. With my father's arrest and all our assets frozen, they knew the money that funded their lavish lifestyles would dry up. They had to sell their stories quickly and to the highest bidder before they became yesterday's news—regardless of the fact that their actions would push my mother into attempting to take her own life.'

She gasped. '*God*, I'm so sorry, Sakis.'

Pain was etched deep on his face but he slid his fingers through hers and brought her hand up to his mouth. But, although his touch was gentle, the gleam in his was anything but. 'So you see why I find it hard to trust the motives of others?'

Dry-mouthed, she nodded. 'I do, but it doesn't hurt to occasionally give the benefit of the doubt.' The knowledge that she was silently pleading for herself sent a wave of shame through her.

His gaze raked her face, his own features a harsh stamp of implacability. Then slowly, as she watched, his face relaxed. He reached across and cupped her face, pulled her close and kissed her.

'For you, Brianna, I'm willing to suspend my penchant for expecting the worst, to let go of my bias and cynicism—because, believe me, in this instance I relish the chance to be proved wrong.'

But he wasn't proved wrong.

At three o'clock that afternoon, Richard Moorecroft rang with a full confession for his part in the tanker crash.

CHAPTER NINE

AN HOUR LATER, Sakis was pacing his office when he heard his head of security enter and exchange greetings with Brianna.

'Get in here, both of you!' he bellowed, the anger he was fighting to contain roiling just beneath his skin.

He turned from his desk as they entered. He tried to concentrate on his security chief. But, as if it acted independent of his control, his gaze strayed to Brianna.

She was as contained and self-assured as he'd always known her to be. There was no trace of the woman who'd writhed beneath him last night, screaming her pleasure as he'd taken her to the heights of ecstasy, or the gentle soul who'd listened to him spill his guts about his father in the car, her eyes haunted with pain for him.

He wanted to hate her for her poise and calm but he realised that he admired her for it—something *else* he admired about her. *Theos*, his list of things he admired about Brianna Moneypenny grew by the day. Anyone would think she meant more to him than—

His mind screeched to a halt but his legs were weakening with the force of the unknown emotion that smashed through him. Folding his arms, he gritted his teeth and perched on the edge of his desk.

'What do you have for me?' he demanded from Sheldon.

'As you requested, we dug a little deeper into the financials of First Mate Isaacs and Deputy Captain Green. A deposit of one hundred thousand euros was made into each of their accounts seven days ago.'

Sakis's hands tightened around his biceps as bitterness tightened like a vice around his chest. 'Have we traced the source of the funds?' Even now when he had the evidence, he didn't want to believe his employees were guilty.

Only this morning, he would've believed the worst. But Brianna's caution to give them the benefit of the doubt had settled deep within him. When he'd given her words further thought he'd realised how much he'd let cynicism rule his life. Letting go even a little had felt…liberating. He'd breathed easier for the first time in a very long time.

But now the hard ache was back full force along with memories he couldn't seem to bury easily.

'Moorecroft used about half a dozen shell companies to obfuscate his activities. Without his confession it'd have taken a few more days but knowing where to look helped. It also helped that the crew members did nothing to hide the money they received,' Sheldon said.

'Because they thought they were home free,' Sakis rasped. The confirmation from Moorecroft that he'd paid his crew to deliberately crash his tanker to spark a hostile takeover made a tide of rage rise within him. Sakis could forgive the damage to his vessel—it was insured and he would be more than compensated for it once the investigation was over. But it was the senseless loss of lives he couldn't stomach, along with the fact that the rest of his crew had been put at severe risk.

After his phone call with Moorecroft, with the pain-racked faces of his dead employees' families fresh in his mind, he hadn't hesitated to let his broken adversary know to expect full criminal charges against him.

He'd experienced a twinge when he'd looked up from the phone call and caught Brianna's expression but he'd pushed the feeling away.

Greed had driven another man to put others' lives at risk. There was no way he could forgive that.

'What about Lowell's account?'

'We're trying to access it but it's a bit more complicated.'

Sakis frowned. 'How complicated?'

'His salary was wired to a routing account that went to a Swiss bank account. Those are a little tougher to crack.'

Surprise shot him upright. He turned to Brianna. 'Did we flag that up in his HR details?'

She bit her lip. Heat flared in his groin, followed closely by another guilty twinge for his harsh tone. 'No,' she answered.

Sakis sucked in a deep breath. 'That will be all, Sheldon. Let me know as soon as you have anything new.'

Sheldon nodded and left.

Silence reigned for several minutes. Then Brianna walked forward. 'I'm expecting an "I told you so".'

He settled his attention fully on her in a way he'd been reluctant to do with another person in the room. Even now he feared his features would betray the extent of the alien emotions roaring through him.

Theos, he needed a drink. *Why the hell not?*

'There's no point. It is what it is.'

'Then why are you pouring yourself a drink in the middle of a work day?'

'It's not the middle of the day, it's almost five o'clock.'

'It's five o'clock for most people but for you it's not, since you work till midnight most nights.'

Sakis barely glanced at the fifty-year-old single malt as he lifted it to his lips and drained it. 'If you must know, I'm trying to understand what drives anyone to depths of betrayal such as this with little regard for how it'll hurt their family and people who care about them.'

She started to come towards him and his senses leapt, but at the last moment she veered away and started straightening the papers on his desk. Sakis barely stopped himself from growling his frustration.

'And are you getting any answers from the bottom of your glass?'

He slammed the glass down and strode to where she stood. 'Are you trying to rile me? Because, trust me, you're succeeding.'

'I'm just trying to make you see that you can't blame yourself for the choices other people make. You can either forgive them or...'

'Or?'

For a single moment, her face creased with something similar to the bitterness and despair clawing through him. 'Or you can cut them out of your life, I suppose.'

He frowned. 'Who cut you out of their life, Brianna?'

Stark pain washed over her features before she tried to mask it. 'This isn't about me.'

He took her by the arms. 'It most definitely is. What did she do to you?'

She made a sound that caught and tightened around his heart. The sort of sound a wounded animal made when they were frightened.

'She...she chose drugs over me.' She stopped and sucked in a gulping breath. 'I don't really want to talk about this.'

'You encouraged me to bare my soul to you this morning. I think it's only fair that you do the same.'

'More therapy?' She tried pull away but he held fast.

'Tell me about her. Where is she? Is she still alive?'

A sad little shiver went through her. 'Yes, she's alive. But we're not in touch. We haven't been for a while.'

'Why not?'

She cast a desperate glance around, anywhere but at him. 'Sakis, this isn't right. I'm your... You're my boss.'

'We went way beyond that last night. Answer my question, unless you wish me to demonstrate our revised positions?'

Her lips parted on a tiny gasp that made him want to plunge his tongue between them but he restrained himself. For once, the need to see beneath the surface of Brianna Moneypenny trumped everything else.

'I...I've already told you I didn't grow up in the best of circumstances. Because of her drug habit we...lived on the street from when I was about four until I was ten. Sometimes I went for days without a proper meal.'

Shock slammed through Sakis. For several moments he was unable to reconcile the woman who stood before him, poised and breathtakingly stunning, with the bedraggled, haunted image she portrayed.

'How... Why?' he demanded, cursing silently when he saw her pale face.

Bruised eyes finally met his. 'She couldn't hold down a job for longer than a couple of weeks but she was cunning enough to evade the authorities for the better part of six years. But finally her luck—if you can call it that—ran out. Social Services took me away from her when I was ten. I found her when I turned eighteen.'

Another bolt of shock went through him. 'You *found* her? After what she did to you, you went to look for her?'

Her eyes darkened with pain. When his hands slid down her arms to hers, she gripped him tight. But he knew her mind was firmly in the past.

'She was my mother. Don't get me wrong, I hated her for a long time, but I had to eventually accept the fact that she was also a human being caught in the grip of an addiction that almost ruined her life,' she said.

Sakis saw her raw pain, clenched his jaw and silently cursed the woman who'd done this to her. More than anything, he wanted to obliterate her pain.

Theos, what the hell was happening to him?

Wait... 'Almost?'

She gave a jerky nod. 'She got it together in the end. In the eight years we were apart, she beat her addiction and got her act together. I...can't help but think I was the one who was holding her back.'

His growled curse made her jump. Leaning down, he kissed her hard and fast.

'She never made an effort to kick her habit when I was around. And she would get this look in her eyes whenever she looked at me—like she hated me.'

Sakis wanted to swear again, but he bit his tongue. 'No child should ever be blamed for being born. She had a duty to look after you. She failed. So she got herself better, then what?'

'She remarried and had another child.'

'So, it was a happy ending for her?' He couldn't stop a hint of bitterness from spilling out. He and his brothers hadn't been granted a happy ending. And his mother continued to live a hollow existence, a shadow of the vibrant woman she'd been for the first decade of his life. 'But she cut you from her life?'

'Yes; I suppose she didn't want the reminder,' she answered lightly; a little too breezily.

Sakis knew she was glossing over her pain. Wasn't it the same way he'd glossed over his for years? But something else struck him, made him reel all over again.

She'd had a mother who had done her wrong in the most fundamental of ways—she'd failed to look after her daughter when she was young and helpless and needed her most. And yet, Brianna had gone out of her way to find her after she was grown and on her own two feet.

The depth of compassion behind such forgiveness rocked him to his soul. 'I never forgave my father for what he did to us, and especially what he did to my mother. Hell, sometimes I think he purposefully died of a heart attack in her arms just to twist the knife in further, because she sure as hell almost died mourning him.'

She touched his cheek with fingers that trembled. 'Don't

be too hard on her. She had her heart broken the same way yours was.'

But then he'd had his brothers and the myriad cousins, aunts and uncles who'd rallied round when the going had got tough. Even in his darkest days, there'd always been someone around and, although he'd never been one to reach out, deep down he'd known there was someone around.

Whereas, Brianna had had nobody.

His insides clenched with the same emotion he'd experienced earlier. Like a magnet drawn to her irresistible presence, he pulled her closer.

'You're amazing, do you know that?' he murmured against her hair, satisfied for the moment to just hold her close like this.

'I am?' Her delicate eyelids fluttered as she looked up at him.

'Yes. You have a unique way of holding up a mirror to some of my deeply held beliefs that make me question them.'

She gave a shaky laugh. 'And that's a good thing?'

'Forcing me to examine them is a good thing. Learning to forgive is another...' He felt her stiffen but she felt too good in his arms for him to question her reaction. 'But perhaps I can try to understand the reason why people act the way they do.'

When she tried to pull away, he reluctantly let her place several inches between them.

'I should get back to work.'

Sakis frowned. He didn't want distance. He didn't like the threat of tears in her eyes. But already he could feel her withdrawing.

Belatedly, he remembered where they were.

But so what? They were alone in his inner sanctum. No one would dare breach it without incurring his wrath. Besides, both his door and hers were shut. And all he wanted was a quick kiss. Well...he gave an inner grimace...he wanted way more than that but...

He focused to find her halfway to the door. What the hell…?

In swift strides he reached the door and slammed his hand against the heavy polished steel-and-timber frame, the feeling that he was missing something fundamental eating away at him. She jumped, her wide-eyed gaze swinging to his.

'What's the matter?' he demanded.

'Nothing. I'm just going back to my desk, Mr—'

'Don't you even dare think about calling me that!'

'Okay.' She licked her plump lower lip. 'Sakis…can I go back to my desk?'

His ire grew along with his hard-on. He grasped her waist. 'After what just happened? No way.'

She eyed the closed door with a longing he wanted transferred to him, preferably with single-minded devotion to the granite-hard part of his anatomy. 'Please…'

He tracked back over their conversation and sighed. 'I can't change who I am overnight, Brianna. Forgiveness comes easily to you, but I'm going to need time.'

Her eyes widened even further with alarm. 'I don't want you to change…not unless you want to. I mean, I'm not invested in anything here…with you. Certainly not enough to warrant you going out of your way to make those sorts of reassurances.'

Those words spilling from her lips sent him into the stratosphere. With a snarl born of frustration, anxiety and piercing arousal, he locked the door, caught her around the waist and swung her up in his arms.

'*Sakis!*'

'Let's just see how invested you are, shall we?'

'Put me down!'

Ignoring her demand, he carried her to the desk she'd straightened so efficiently minutes ago. Setting her on the edge, he slashed one hand across the polished surface, sending the papers flying.

'I seriously hope you don't expect me to clean that up!'

Her colour was hectic, her breath coming out in pants as she glared at him.

Yes, this was what he wanted: her fire, her spirit. He hated the sad, frightened, achingly lonely Brianna. He hated cool, calm and distant Brianna even more, especially after last night. Not after seeing the generous heart and fiery passion that resided beneath the prim exterior.

'If that's what I desire, then you shall do it, no?'

Her chin rose and his senses roared. 'In your dreams. My job description doesn't include cleaning up after you. I'm not your chambermaid.'

He caught her hands and planted them on his chest. 'As of last night, your job description includes doing whatever pleases me in the bedroom.'

Despite her protests, her fingers curled into his chest. He nearly shouted with triumph and relief. 'We're not in the bedroom. Besides, what about what I want?'

His hand fisted in her hair, sought and found the hidden clasp and tugged. Vibrant golden hair spilled over his arm. Using it, he pulled her close until his jaw grazed her soft cheek. 'Call this mutually beneficial therapy. Besides, I'm a quick study, *glikia mou*. I know *exactly* what you want.'

Her breath caught, making him laugh. He pushed her back, using her slight imbalance to swiftly undo the single button of her jacket. It was off before she could take another surprised breath.

'Sakis, for goodness' sake! We're in your office.'

'My *locked* office. And it's the end of the day for everyone else except us.'

'I still think...'

He kissed her, the temptation too much to resist. That it effectively shut her up was a great bonus, as was her fractured moan that vibrated through him.

He made easy work of the zipper of her dress and slid it off with minimal protest. He didn't notice what she wore beneath until he spread her backwards across his desk. A strangled choke made its way up his throat as he froze.

'*Theos*, tell me you haven't been wearing lingerie like these since you started working for me?'

A provocative smile dispelled the nervous apprehension on her face. 'Fine. I won't.'

She stretched under his gaze, arching her back in a sinuous move that made him think of a sleek cat. Over the top of the bustier bra that connected the garter to the top of her sheer stockings, the plump slopes of her breasts taunted him. His mouth watered and his fingers itched to touch with a need so strong he staggered forward. Roughly he pulled one cup down and circled a rosy nipple with his tongue.

Her ragged cry of delight was music to his ears, because the knowledge that he wasn't in this insane feeling alone soothed a stunned and confused part of him.

He rolled the nub in his mouth and tugged with his teeth while he frantically undressed. Naked, he straightened and glanced down at her, spread across his desk like a decadent offering. Struck dumb, he just stared at her stunning perfection.

'You're about to tell me you've imagined me spread out like this across your desk, aren't you?' she asked huskily.

Surprisingly, this particular scenario had never once crossed his mind. 'No, and it's a good thing too. I don't think I'd ever have got any work done if I had a picture such as this in my mind,' he rasped, his voice thick and alien. 'I've imagined you elsewhere though—in my shower, across the back seat of my car, in my lift…'

A shiver went through her. 'Your lift?'

'*Ne*. In my mind, my private lift has seen a lot of action featuring you in very many compromising ways. But *this* beats even my most fevered imaginings.'

He continued to stare at the vision before him. He must have stared for too long because she started to squirm. With one hand he held her down. With the other, he pulled down the skimpiest thong ever created and slid his hands between her thighs. Her wet heat coated his fingers and in that moment Sakis believed he'd never been so turned on. The next moment, he realised he was wrong.

Brianna laid her hand on his thigh and that simple action sent his heart rate soaring out of control. Then her hand moved upward...and her searching fingers boldly settled over his hard length.

'Theos!'

'Wrong deity,' she responded saucily.

His laugh scraped his throat as she gripped him hard. From root to tip, she caressed him, over and over, until he was sure he'd lost his hold on reality. His altered state was why he didn't read her intention when she moistened her lip and wriggled down his desk. Before he could admonish her for not staying put, she boldly took him in her perfect mouth.

'Brianna!' He slammed a hand on the desk to steady himself against the deep shudder powering through him. The sight of him in her mouth nearly unmanned him. His breath hissed out as he fought not to gush his climax like a hormonal teenager right then and there. He groaned deep and long as her tongue swirled over him and her hand pumped, teased, threatened to blow his mind to smithereens. *'Yes!* Just like that!'

He suffered the sweet torture until the tell-tale tightening forced him to pull back. When she clung and made a sound of protest, Sakis seriously considered giving in, but no...

The chance to take her again, stamp his possession on her, was paramount. He needed to obliterate that distance he'd sensed her trying to put between them. The reason for it was irrelevant. The need was too strong to question.

He trailed hot kisses down her body, making her squirm anew for him. The seconds it took to locate and put on the condom felt like decades. But at last he parted her thighs and positioned himself at her entrance. She lifted her head and looked at him, her expression one of rapt hunger that almost equalled his own.

'Are you invested in this?' he rasped.

A glimmer of alarm skittered through her eyes. 'Sakis...'

'Are you? Because I am, Brianna.'

Her mouth parted on a shocked exhalation. 'Please, Sakis, don't say that.'

'Why not?'

'Because you don't mean it.'

'Yes, I do. I fought it for as long as I could, but in the end it was no use. I want you. I want this. Do you want it too?'

Her breath shivered out of her. 'Y-yes. I want this.'

He plunged into her, perhaps a little more roughly than he'd intended, but his need was too great. Watching her breasts bounce with each thrust, Sakis wondered if a heart had ever burst from too much excitement, too much need.

Because, even as he took her to the brink, he realised it wasn't enough. He'd never get enough of Brianna. But this... *Theos*, this was a brilliant start. Later he would pause to examine his feelings a little bit more, reassure himself exactly what he was dealing with and how best to handle the strange feelings inside him. Because something *was* happening to him. Something he couldn't define.

As his brain melted from pleasure overload, he let his hands drift upward in a slow caress. His fingers grazed her scar and a feeling of primitive rage rose through him at the person who'd done this to her. If he hadn't received Brianna's reassurance that justice had been done, he'd have hunted the culprit down and torn him apart with his bare hands.

Overwhelming protectiveness—another alien feeling he had to grapple with. Gripping her nape, he forced her up to receive his kiss as he surged one last time inside her, felt her spasm around him and let go.

The rush was the best yet. With a groan that stemmed from

his soul, he shut his eyes and gave in to it. It was a long time before reality descended on him again.

Brianna's arms tightened around Sakis as their breaths returned to normal, fear clutching her heart.

She'd spilled her guts to him about her mother. He'd been outraged on her behalf. He'd shown her sympathy that had touched her soul and made her realise that, while she'd forgiven her mother for an addiction she hadn't been able to conquer, it was the pain of her abandonment when she was clean that hurt the most.

But Sakis had readily admitted forgiveness was a rare commodity to *him*.

She tried to tell herself it didn't matter. Come Friday, when her time ran out, she would be out of here. Greg had taken to sending her hourly reminders of her deadline. To stop Sakis from getting suspicious, she'd put her phone on silent and zipped it out of sight in her jacket pocket.

But her imminent departure wasn't the reason she'd given Sakis a glimpse into her past.

It was because she'd desperately wanted him to see her—not the ruthlessly efficient personal assistant but *her*, Brianna Moneypenny, the person who'd started life as Anna Simpson, daughter of a crackhead, and then had taken her grandmother's maiden name and forged a new identity for herself.

She'd bared herself to Sakis, and now she felt more vulnerable than ever.

His stance on betrayal remained rigid. If he ever found out about her past, he would never forgive her for bringing her soiled reputation to his company.

'I can hear you thinking,' he said, his voice a husky muffle against her neck.

'I've just had sex with you on your desk. That merits a little bit of thinking time, don't you think?'

'Perhaps. But, since it's going to be a familiar feature in our relationship, I suggest you get used to it.'

He heard her sudden intake of breath. Rearing up, he rested on his elbows and speared her with a probing look. One she couldn't meet for long before she settled her gaze on the pulse beating in his neck. 'The word "relationship" frightens you?'

She willed her pulse to slow, forcing the hope that had no business fluttering in her chest to die a swift death. There could be no future between them. None.

'Not the word, no, but I think this is going a little too…fast. We only started sleeping together last night.'

'After eighteen months of holding back. I think asking for restraint right now is asking for the impossible. I'll need several weeks at least to take the edge off.'

She looked into intense green eyes. 'You warned me at my interview, conducted across this very desk, not to even dream of getting involved with you.'

He had the grace to look shamefaced, but even that look held a lethal charm that doomed her. 'It was so soon after Giselle; I was still angry. Everyone I'd interviewed reminded me of her. You were the first one who didn't. When I found myself getting attracted to you, I fought it with everything I had because I didn't want that nasty business repeating itself.'

Unable to resist, she slid her fingers through his thick hair. 'She really did a number on you, didn't she?'

His smile was wry. 'I'm not beyond admitting I was blinded to her true nature until it was much too late.'

'Wow, I'm not sure whether to be pleased or disappointed that you're fallible.'

He straightened and picked her up from his desk as if she weighed nothing. 'I never claimed to be perfect, except when it comes to winning rowing championships. Then I'm unequalled,' he boasted as he started to stride across the office.

'Modesty is such a rare and beautiful thing, Sakis.'

His deep, unfettered laugh made her heart swell with pleasure. 'Yes, so is the ability to state things as they are.'

'No one will accuse you of being a wallflower. Wait, where are you taking me?'

'Upstairs, to get you therapeutically wet and soapy in my shower.'

'I think you're taking this therapy thing a bit far. Sakis, put me down. Our clothes!' She wriggled until he let her slide down his body to stand upright.

'Leave them.' He keyed in the code for his turbo lift.

'Absolutely not. No way am I letting the cleaner find my knickers and stuff all over your office floor!' She ran back and started gathering them. 'And don't just stand there, pick up your own damn clothes.'

With a husky laugh, Sakis followed and picked up his discarded clothes. Then, because she really couldn't stand to leave them, she gathered the strewn papers and placed them back on the desk. When his mocking laugh deepened, she rounded on him.

'Next time, you pick them up yourself.'

He caught her to him and smacked her lightly on the bottom. When she yelped, he kissed her. 'That's for disobeying me again. But I like that you admit there'll be a next time.'

She looked up and her gaze caught his. For the first time, she glimpsed a vulnerability she'd never seen before in his eyes. As if he hadn't been sure she would let anything like what had happened occur between them again.

Desolation caught at her heart. She would pay a steep price for letting this thing continue but the need to be with him in every way until she left was too strong. Going closer, she raised herself on tiptoe and kissed along his jaw.

'There'll be a next time only if I get to go on top.'

Sakis jerked awake to the sound of a phone buzzing. Beside him Brianna was out cold, worn out from the relentless demands he'd made of her body. The same lethargy swirled through him, making him toy with the idea of ignoring the phone.

The buzzing increased.

Rubbing the sleep from his eyes, he started to reach for his phone, but realised the ringing was from Brianna's.

Getting off the bed, he hunted through their discarded clothes until he located the phone in her jacket pocket.

Palming it, Sakis hesitated again. Relief coursed through him when it stopped ringing. But, almost immediately, it started to buzz again. With an impatient sigh, he pressed the button.

'Anna?' A man's impatient voice, one he didn't recognise. Not that he had first-hand knowledge of the men who called Brianna, of course... A spike of intense dislike filled him at the thought of anyone who'd been given the permission to call her...*Anna*?

Sakis frowned. 'You've got the wrong number. This is *Brianna's* phone. Who is this?'

And why the hell are you calling at three a.m.?

Silence greeted his demand. A moment later, the line went dead.

Sakis pulled the phone away and searched for the number. It was blocked.

Dropping her jacket, he went back to bed and set the phone down on the bedside table. He tucked his arms beneath his head, unable to stem the unease that spiralled through his gut.

He had no grounds to suspect anything other than a wrongly dialled number. It could be pure coincidence that another man had called his lover demanding to speak to *Anna*.

And yet, Sakis was still awake two hours later, unable to shake the mild dread. When the phone pinged with an incoming message, he snatched it up before it could wake her.

With a sinking feeling in the pit of his stomach, he slid his thumb across the interactive surface. Again the number was blocked but the words on the screen iced his spine:

Just a friendly reminder that you have three days to get me what I need. G.

CHAPTER TEN

IT'S NOTHING. YOU'RE blowing things out of proportion.

Sakis repeated the words over and over as he pulled the handles of the rowing machine in his gym just after six o'clock. Right this moment he'd have loved to be doing the real thing but this wasn't the time to jump in his car and drive to his rowing club, no matter how powerful the temptation.

He smothered the voice that suggested he was running away from the truth.

What truth?

He didn't know what the text on Brianna's phone meant. Sure, the easiest thing would've been to wake her up and demand an answer. Instead, he'd got up, returned the phone to her jacket pocket and high-tailed it to the gym.

He yanked on the row bars and welcomed the burn of pain between his shoulders and the sweat that poured off his skin. He tried to ignore the question hammering through his brain but the truth of his actions was as clear as the scowl he could see in his reflection in the gym's mirrors.

Are you invested in this? When he'd blurted those words out last night, he'd been stunned by the need to hear her answer in the affirmative. Because in that moment he'd realised just how truly invested he was in having Brianna in his life and not just as his personal assistant. Even now, with suspicion warring with his new-found intentions to trust more and judge less, the thought of not having her around made a red haze cloud his senses.

You have three days to get me what I need...

Was it a professional request? Who would be making such a demand of her professionally?

If it was a personal one...

He emitted the deep growl that had been growing in his chest as jealousy spiked through his gut.

At that moment, Brianna walked into the gym and froze. In the mirror, their eyes meshed. The look on his face was fierce and unwelcoming—he knew that. He wasn't surprised when her eyes widened and she hesitated.

'I can come back later if I'm disturbing you.'

With one last, vicious yank on the row bar, he let it go, watched it clatter against the spinning wheel and stood and advanced towards her.

The sight of her in skin-clinging, midriff-baring Lycra made adrenaline and arousal spike higher. The thought of making another of his myriad sexual fantasies come true pounded through his blood and groin with a ferocity that made him grit his teeth. He barely managed to catch himself from lunging for her, and veered towards the row of treadmills.

'Disturb me. I was in danger of letting my imagination get the better of me.' He gave a smile he knew fell far short of the mark and busied himself with programming the treadmill next to his. When he was done, he waved her over.

'Thirty minutes okay?' he asked.

He caught the look of wariness on her face as she nodded and approached the machine.

About to set his own programme, he glanced over and was pretty sure he burst a blood vessel when she bent over to stretch.

'*Theos!*' His hiss brought her head up and she slowly straightened.

Her gaze travelled down his chest and dropped to the loose

shorts that did nothing to hide the power of her effect of him. When her mouth dropped open, he let out a strained laugh. 'Now you see the power you have over me.'

She stepped onto the treadmill and pressed start. 'You don't sound too happy about it.'

'I like being in control, *agapita*. And you're detonating mine with that tight body of yours.'

He watched the blush creep up from her neck to stain her cheeks. 'It's not exactly a walk in the park for me either, if that helps you?'

Sakis fought to reconcile the blushing, sexually innocent woman in front of him with one who could be capable of duplicity.

Don't judge before you know the facts...

Brianna's words flashed through his churning mind. With a deep breath, he started his own machine and began jogging alongside her.

One minute, one full minute, was how long he lasted before he gave in to the urge to glance over at her. The sight of her breasts bouncing beneath her clinging tank top made him groan. Only his ingrained discipline from his professional rowing days stopped him from losing his footing.

But he didn't glance away. He stared his fill. And then he stared some more as his body moved to the spinning treadmill entirely independent of his frenzied thoughts.

She tried to ignore him. But after stumbling a fourth time, she used the handlebars to raise herself and planted her feet on the stationary part of the machine.

'Sakis, please stop doing that. I can't concentrate.'

He blew out a breath and slammed his hand on the stop button. 'Then let's both end this before one of us does themselves an injury.' He reached over and did the same to her machine. 'If you want a workout, I can think of a much better one.'

'Sakis!'

'I can't think why I let you call me Mr Pantelides for the

last eighteen months, when the sound of my name on your lips makes me harder than I've ever been in my life.'

The gurgling sound she made was somewhere between outrage and reproach as he swung her into his arms, but her arms curved around his neck all the same.

'Should I even ask where you're taking me?'

'I'd love nothing better than to bend you over the handlebars of that treadmill, but I don't have a condom down here, and I can't risk one of my executives walking in on us. My steam room will have to suffice this time.'

He made short work of getting her into his shower to sluice off their sweat before he pushed her into the smoky interior of his private steam room.

He ruthlessly ignored the mocking voice that suggested he was hiding behind sex instead of confronting her about the text.

But, as he pulled her astride him and plunged deep inside her, Sakis knew he would have to confront her sooner rather than later. He refused to allow suspicion to eat away at him. He'd found a precious peace of mind in her arms this past couple of days and he refused to let distrust and shadows of the past erode it.

Her arms tightened round him as her climax gathered.

'Oh God, Sakis. It feels so good,' she sobbed against his neck.

His own control cracked wider. 'Yes, *agapita*. It would be a shame if something came along and ruined it.' His hand slid into her hair and brought her head up so he could look into her eyes. 'Wouldn't it?' He pushed higher insider her, possessing her completely.

Her lips parted in a pre-climactic gasp as her muscles gripped him tight. 'Yes.'

'Good. Then let's keep that from happening, yes?'

The touch of confusion that clouded her eyes was washed

away a second later with the onset of ecstatic wonder that transformed her face from stunning to exquisitely beautiful.

He groaned deep as her convulsions triggered his own release, making him loosen his possessive hold on her. Her head fell back onto his shoulder and it was all he could do to hang on as he was plunged into the longest climax of his life.

He walked them back into the shower as spasms continued to seize her frame.

In silence, he washed her, then himself, all the while aware of the puzzled glances she sent his way.

They made it as far as his bedroom before she rounded on him.

'Is this tense silent treatment part of your morning-after ritual or is there something going on here I should know about?'

He damned his suspicious nature and his inability to shake his gut's warning. His gaze swung past the temptation of her wet, towel-clad body to the bedside table and he tensed further when he saw her phone.

She'd seen the message.

'Sakis?'

He met her troubled blue gaze. 'I start negotiations on the China oil deal this morning and they're not the best customers to deal with at the best of times. In light of what's happened, I want nothing to impede this deal.'

Her brow cleared. 'Oh. Well, I don't see anything that will hinder your negotiations.'

His chest lightened at the reassurance then immediately tightened at the thought that the message had been personal, from a man who viewed himself in a position to make demands from the woman Sakis had claimed as his lover. It struck home again just how little he really knew Brianna Moneypenny. Or was it *Anna*?

Sucking in a deep breath, he went to his drawer and pulled out a pair of boxers. 'Are you sure? The last thing we need are skeletons popping out of closets right now. I think my company's had enough of those to last a millennium.'

Her pause lasted a few seconds, but it felt like years to him. 'I'm sure.'

He turned. 'Good.'

When he saw her catch her lower lip between her teeth, his pulse spiked. *Theos*, how could he crave her again after the many times he'd taken her last night and the intense orgasm he'd experienced with her barely fifteen minutes ago? He mentally shook his head, turned away and carried on dressing. If he gave in to his need, they'd never leave this room.

He heard the towel slide from her body and his fingers clenched around his socks.

'So...this is about the Chinese deal and has nothing to do with...with what's happened between us?'

He shoved his leg into his trousers with more force than was necessary. 'I made my feeling clear on that score, *agapita*. You haven't forgotten already, have you?'

'No, I haven't.'

Was that a tremble in her voice? Every instinct screamed at him to ask her about the text.

Private or not, if Brianna was hiding something should he not confront her about it now rather than later?

Heartbeat accelerating wildly, he shrugged on his shirt and faced her.

'Great. Then do you mind telling me what that text on your phone is all about?'

He knows!

It took every single ounce of control Brianna could summon not to let out the cry of anguish that ripped through her chest.

'The text?' She hated the breathless prevarication but she needed to buy herself more time.

'Your phone rang in the middle of the night. Someone asked for Anna then hung up. Then the text came. Care to explain?'

No, no, no, she wasn't ready. She'd woken up this morning and had lain in the bed knowing without a shadow of a doubt that she'd fallen for Sakis. And also that she needed to come clean and throw herself at his mercy. But she hadn't planned to do it now. Not when Sakis had so much on his plate. She'd planned to type up her resignation then hand it to him with a confession about her past in the hope that he would choose forgiveness over condemnation for her lie about who she really was.

'Brianna?' Sakis's voice was as cold as his expression.

Despair washed over her. 'It's a friend... He wants a favour from me.'

He frowned. 'A *favour*. And he calls you at three in the morning? What sort of favour?'

'Help with his...his work.'

His frown intensified. 'So it wasn't a personal call?'

That she could answer without flinching at the half-truth. 'No.'

Her breath caught as he stalked to where she stood. The sight of him, standing so close with his shirt loose and his ridged chest within touchable distance, made heat spike through her.

'He's not from a competitor, is he? He's not trying to poach you?'

'He's not trying to poach me, no.'

His hand tugged her chin up until her face was exposed to his scrutiny. Whatever he saw there must have satisfied him because after a minute he nodded. Tugging her to him, he grabbed the towel she barely held together and whisked it from her body. He sealed her mouth with his and then proceeded to explore her exposed body with demanding hands. Just when she thought she would expire from need, he set her free.

'That's good to know because otherwise I'd have hunted this man down and torn him limb to limb, as I promised. Now, go and get dressed. And wear one of those no-nonsense suits.

It'll kill me to imagine what's underneath it but at least outwardly it'll keep me from jumping you every time you walk into my office.'

A ragged gasp left her at the reprieve she'd been granted and the cowardly way she'd grasped it. In a way, it was a testament to just how pressured Sakis was that he hadn't probed deeper.

Or it could be that he's beginning to trust you?

Anguish made her feet slow as she collected her clothes from last night and went into her suite. She'd been granted a reprieve, yes, but had she rendered her eventual confession worthless by not admitting the truth now? Because surely, once she told Sakis just who'd texted her, he'd damn her for ever?

She loved him. Everything about Sakis made her heart beat faster and her soul ache with regret that they hadn't met in another time...a time before she'd been forced to hide her past and unknowingly compromise her future.

Her phone buzzed as she stepped into the grey-and-black platform heels that matched her grey Versace suit.

She knew who it was before she pressed 'answer'.

'I need more time,' she blurted before he'd finished speaking.

Silence. 'You haven't been found out, have you?' Greg demanded.

Brianna sank down onto the hard seat of the dressing stool in her suite's walk-in closet. 'No, but you calling and texting me at three a.m. doesn't help.'

'If you haven't been found out then what's the problem?' he fired back.

'I just... There's a lot of attention on me right now. I need to make sure I do things properly or this will end badly... for both of us.' Her skin burned with each lie. And any minute she suspected the heavens to crack open and lightning to strike her down.

He gave an irritated sigh. 'I have to go out of town unexpectedly. I could be a few days, maybe a week. You have until I get back to get me the information I need. If you don't have it on my return, it's game over.' His tone vibrated with dark menace. 'Word of warning—don't test me, Anna.'

The name scoured across her senses, making her flinch. She was no longer Anna Simpson. Deciding to change her name had been a step in reinventing herself but it wasn't until she'd seen herself through Sakis's eyes that she'd felt truly reborn.

He'd called her amazing yesterday. And throughout the night he'd shown her a powerful ecstasy beyond the physical, made more wonderful because of her feelings for him.

The thought of living without him, of walking away, sent a poker-hot lance of pain through her heart. She was still silently mourning losing Sakis when she walked into the dining room.

The sight of the assorted platters of pancakes, waffles, chocolate and strawberry syrup and endless more condiments made tears prickle her eyes.

Sakis sauntered towards her, one eyebrow raised. 'We made love long and hard last night, and not once did you cry. I'm trying very hard not to let my ego be dented by the fact that it's the sight of pancakes for breakfast that makes you cry and not our lovemaking.'

'I... It's not... No one's ever done anything like this for me,' she finally blurted.

His expression morphed from teasing to compassionate in a heartbeat. 'It's the least of what you deserve, *glikia mou*.' Cupping her face, he sealed his mouth over hers.

Tell him. Tell him now.

But how could she tell him about Greg without it all coming out wrong? And how could she confess her love without it sounding like a tool with which to beg his forgiveness?

She'd been gifted extra time with him. And she selfishly,

desperately, wanted that time. Maybe she could use it to show him how much he meant to her.

Action, not words.

Clutching his nape, she deepened the kiss until he groaned and reluctantly pulled away.

'For kisses like that, you can have pancakes every day. And, before you mention calories, I assure you the workout you'll get in my bed will ensure calories are never an issue.'

He laughed at the flames creeping into her face, helped her into her seat and forked blueberry pancakes onto her plate.

Sunlight slanted through the windows on a bright London morning, throwing his stunning looks into sharp relief.

His grin as he watched her eat made her heart lift and tighten at the same time. When the look turned smouldering, her belly clenched hard with need.

His buzzing phone ripped through the sensual atmosphere. Sighing, he answered and let the world intrude. Taking the lift down—after a strategic pause, when he kissed her senseless and threatened to take her where she stood if she didn't stop casting him glances from under her lashes—their day swung into full flow.

When at six o'clock he bellowed her name, she entered his office, tablet fired up and ready. His tense expression made her freeze.

'We've tracked him down to Thailand.'

'Captain Lowell?'

He nodded.

'So he's alive?'

'As of yesterday, yes. Although the authorities think there may be someone else besides my security people after him.' His face settled into grimmer lines.

It couldn't be Greg...could it? Nervously, she licked her lips. 'What do you need me to do?' she asked.

'Nothing for the moment. I'm waiting for the lawyers to apprise me of the full situation, then I'll take it from there.'

'What about the party you wanted me to organise for the crew? Do you want me to cancel it?' She'd been liaising with event organisers all day for the company party Sakis intended to host in Greece.

'No. The party goes ahead. The crew and the volunteers deserve it for the hard work they've put in. I'm not prepared to let one man derail the well-being of my other employees.'

'What about Lowell's wife? Are you going to tell her you've found him?'

A look of distress crossed his face and she knew he was remembering his own mother's situation when the press and gossip-mongers had torn her life apart. 'I don't like keeping her in the dark, but I don't want to cause her pain by revealing half-facts. I'll contact her when we know the full details.'

She nodded and started to return to her desk. 'I'll carry on with arrangements to fly the crew to Greece, then.'

'Wait,' he commanded. He strode to where she stood and kissed her, quick and hard. 'When this is all over, I'm taking you to my Swiss chalet. We'll lock the door behind us and gorge on each other for a week. If one week proves unsatisfactory, we'll take another, and another, until we're too sated to move. Then and only then will we let the world back in. Agreed?'

Her heart skipped several beats. By the time this was over, she'd be gone. But she nodded anyway and hurried back to her desk.

Sinking into her chair, she clenched her shaking hands into fists and fought to stop the unrelenting waves of pain and despair that threatened to drown her.

Eventually, she managed to place a thin veil over her emotions, enough to function for the rest of the day.

The news that Lowell had been arrested and was refusing to cooperate threw the rest of the night into disarray. At one a.m., Sakis stopped pacing long enough to pull her up from the seat on the other side of the sofa where she was busy putting together the itinerary for the next day.

'Go to bed, *agapita*.'

Unable to stop herself, she swayed towards his hard warmth. 'Alone?'

His lips trailed over her cheek to the corner of her mouth. 'I'll join you as soon as I have the latest update from the lawyers.'

By the time he joined her an hour later, Brianna was almost delirious with need. As he took her on another sheet-burning journey of bliss, she knew without a doubt that, no matter where she went, her heart would always belong to Sakis Pantelides.

CHAPTER ELEVEN

SAKIS'S PRIVATE GREEK home was a sun-baked slice of bliss that rose from stunning turquoise waters west of the Ionian Islands. Traditionally built and whitewashed in true Greek style, the large villa nevertheless boasted extensive modern designs: the swimming pool had been designed around the villa and traversed under the indoor-to-outdoor living room, reflecting Sakis's love of water.

On her first night here two days ago, Brianna had walked out of her bedroom to find herself faced with an immense mobile hot-tub on her terrace, in which had resided a smug, gloriously naked Sakis with two crystal glasses and vintage champagne chilling on ice next to his elbow. But, if there was one thing she loved about Sakis's island retreat, it was the peace and tranquillity.

Although on this particular Sunday, with teeming bodies enjoying the unfettered generosity of their host, the island paradise was more island rave.

Brianna stood away from the crowd, absently keeping an eye on a couple of employees who were bent on getting hammered as quickly as possible.

Her phone buzzed in her hand and her heart contracted.

Need update, pronto. G.

Greg's texts had got increasingly frequent and terse in the

last day. Although she'd managed to fob him off with non-answers, she was fast running out of time. From experience, she knew his patience would only hold out for so long.

She fired back an inadequate *'Soon'*, a cold shiver coursing through her veins despite the fierce summer sun.

She'd greedily grasped the chance to spend some more time with Sakis. But, like sand through an hourglass, it had inevitably run out.

Looking over to where the man who'd taken over one-hundred per cent of her waking thoughts stood with his two brothers, her insides twisted.

The three brothers were gorgeous in their own rights. But, to her, Sakis stood head and shoulders above Ari and Theo.

It had nothing to do with the way his lips curved when he smiled, or the way a lock of hair fell over his forehead when he nodded to something Theo was saying to him...

No, there was a presence about him, an aura of strength and self-containment, that struck a deep place inside her. And the fierce protectiveness he'd displayed towards those loyal to him made her heart ache.

How would it have felt to be loved and cherished by a man such as him? Tears prickled her eyes at the thought that she'd never find out; never know how it would feel to be loved just once by somebody worth giving her own love to.

Her phone buzzed again.

How soon?????? Answer me now!

In a fit of anger and torment, she turned it off and dashed blindly towards the steps that led to the beach. Tears blurred her vision but she forged ahead, cursing fate for handing her what she most wanted with one hand and ruthlessly taking it away with the other.

Of course, the beach was occupied with more Pantelides Inc. employees. She plastered on a smile and answered greetings, but continued to walk until the sound of partying and music was far behind her.

Locating a rough, flat rock, she sank down and let the tears she'd held back flow. By the time she was wrung dry, her decision had solidified in her chest.

'So, how's your wonder woman doing?'

Sakis barely managed to stop his teeth from gnashing loudly at Ari's dry query.

'If you don't want me to put a dent in that already messed up face of yours, I suggest you watch your mouth.' He cursed the rough intensity of his tone the moment he spoke.

Sure enough, both Ari's and Theo's eyebrows shot up. A second later, Theo chuckled and nudged their oldest brother. 'The last time he reacted so violently about a girl was when I suggested I bring a lollipop to Iyana when we were kids. I barely managed to avoid being flattened when he tried to run me down with his bike. You better watch out, Ari.'

'Shut the hell up, Theo.' Sakis's mood darkened further as his brothers laughed some more at his expense.

He downed more champagne and raised his head in time to catch Ari's narrow-eyed stare. Staring back defiantly, he watched Ari's mouth drop open.

'Damn it, you've done it, haven't you? You've slept with her. *Theos*, don't you have any brains in that head of yours?'

Theo let out another rich chuckle. 'Depends on which head you're talking about, bro.'

Sakis released the growl that'd been lurking in his chest for what felt like days. 'I'm warning you both, stay the hell out of my personal life.'

'Or what?' Theo countered. 'I recall you taking delight in causing havoc in mine more than a few times. You sent flowers to that crazy woman you knew I was trying as hard as hell to cut out of my life. And remember that time you stole my phone and used it to sex-text the wrestler brother of that model I was dating? I couldn't return to my apartment for a week because he'd camped outside my building. Payback's a bitch, bro, and I'm only getting started.'

He swallowed the searing response because he knew that what was eating at him wasn't his brothers' ribbing.

It was Brianna. And the secret text messages she was still receiving.

She believed he didn't notice her apprehension every time her phone pinged.

Hell, she'd left his bed at five a.m. this morning. When he'd demanded she come back to bed, she'd waved him away with some excuse about making sure everything was in hand for the party.

Five a.m.! Yeah, shocking. Wasn't that the same time you interviewed her for her job?

He smothered the mocking voice and stared into the golden bubbles. This had gone on long enough. He'd swallowed her explanation without probing too deeply. Tonight, after the party, he'd find out what the hell was making her so jumpy. And then he'd fix it. He wanted her undivided attention on him and he sure as hell didn't want her leaving him in bed at the crack of dawn to go do…whatever the hell…

'You're giving us the silent treatment? Really? Wow, you must have it bad!' Theo mocked.

'Sweet mother of— So what if I have a thing for her, hmm?' he demanded wildly.

'Some of us would wonder how many times you had to be burned before you learned your lesson,' Ari said, his gaze and his words holding a steady warning that made Sakis's heart slide to his toes.

'She's not like that, Ari. I…trust her.' It was true. Somehow she'd wormed her way in and embedded herself deep in a place he'd thought dead after his father's betrayal. And, *Theos*, it felt…right. It felt good. He didn't feel so desolate, so bitter any more. And he planned to hang on to it.

'Are you sure?' Ari probed.

Righteous anger rose on Brianna's behalf but he stopped himself from venting it. His brothers were only looking out for him.

He wanted to tell them they didn't need to. But a tiny niggling stopped him. What if they did...?

Brushing the thought away, he turned towards Theo, readying himself for more ribbing.

But his brother's face had turned serious. 'Are the investigators close to wrapping up the Lowell issue?' Theo asked.

The other source of his frustration made his nape tighten. 'Not yet. They think there's a third party at play. Lowell may have been double-dealing both Moorecroft and someone else, someone who's keeping him from talking. They've found a paper trail. They should have a name for me in the next twenty-four hours.'

He heard a drunken shout and looked over to see one of his junior executives falling over a pretty blonde. Realising he hadn't spotted Brianna for a while, he frowned. This was the sort of function where she excelled with her organisational skills.

And yet she was nowhere in sight.

'She went that way, towards the beach,' Ari supplied softly.

Sakis looked at his brother and Ari shrugged, an almost resigned understanding in his eyes.

Were his feelings really so obvious? Who cared? Brianna had breached every single barrier he'd put in place around his heart. He craved her when she wasn't around, and he couldn't have enough of her when she was.

Some might call what he was feeling *love*; he preferred to call it... He searched for a suitable description and came up empty. Whatever it was, he'd decided to risk embracing it, see where it took him.

But before that he needed to get to the bottom of what was bothering her.

The junior executive let out another drunken guffaw. The pretty blonde looked ready to burst into tears. Just then a crash came from the other side of the tent.

'Ari, you go take care of Mr Smooth over there. I'll go check out the other thing?' Theo offered.

Nodding gratefully, Sakis discarded his champagne glass and headed towards his other guests. His heart sank when Ari fell into step beside him.

'Are you sure about what you're doing?' he asked.

'I've never been surer.' His answer held a steady certainty that shifted some hitherto unknown weight from his chest. He wanted Brianna in his life.

Permanently.

'Then I wish you well, brother.' Deep emotion and gratitude shifted through him when Ari clasped his shoulder. Before he could swallow the lump in his throat and respond, Ari was moving towards the crowd. Within seconds, the junior executive had been banished to the water fountain to sober up and the blonde was blushing under Ari's dry-witted charm.

Sakis looked towards the beach just as Brianna reappeared at the top of the steps.

The sight of her made his breath catch. It was the first time he'd seen her in such an outfit. Her dress was made of light cotton in a red-and-gold material and stopped just above her knees. The sleeveless, cinched-in waist and flared design moved with her seductive sway as she re-entered the crowd and smiled at a greeting.

He was striding towards her before he could stop himself, not that he wanted to stop.

Her head swung towards him and Sakis's jaw clenched when he saw the momentary wariness that clouded her eyes before she blinked it away. By the time he reached her, she had her game face on.

'It's almost time for your speech,' she said.

'I wish to hell I hadn't agreed to make one.' He wanted to

take her face in his hands and kiss away whatever was bothering her, office gossip be damned. But she wouldn't welcome that, so he kept his hands to himself.

Soon, he promised himself.

'But you have to. They're expecting it.'

'Right…fine.'

He started to turn away.

'Wait.' She stopped him with a hand on his arm, which she dropped quickly, much to his escalating frustration. 'I…I need to talk to you. Tonight, after the party.'

Real trepidation had darkened her eyes. The unease he'd banked but which had never left him since he'd seen that first text roared to life.

He forced a nod and went to give his speech, then for the next hour he mingled with his employees, the volunteers and salvage crew. But he made sure Brianna was glued to his side. Whatever it was that needed to be aired, he wouldn't let it get in the way of what they had.

He breathed a sigh of relief once the boats arrived to ferry his guests to Argostoli, where the chartered flight waited to take them back to London.

Once the last guest had boarded the boat, he headed towards where Brianna was dismissing the catering staff.

Finally…

The need to touch her made his fingers tingle as he came within a few feet of her. She looked up and her desolate expression made his insides clench hard.

'Brianna? What the hell is it?'

She shook her head and looked around. 'Not here. Can we…can we go inside?'

Breaching the gap between them, he caught her hand and kissed the back of it as he steered her towards the villa. 'Sure, but whatever this is let's make it quick. I've been waiting since the crack of dawn to make love to you again. I'm not sure how much longer I can last.'

Her sideways glance was ragged and pain-filled, and he felt his heart stutter then triple its beat as trepidation ramped up higher.

He passed Theo and Ari in the hallway and barely noticed their exchanged glances.

Entering his study, he shut the door and turned to her. 'What's on your mind?'

For several seconds, she didn't speak. She looked lost, miserable, like the bottom had gone out of her world. His heart swelled with the need to take away her pain.

'Brianna, *pethi mou*, whatever the hell it is, I can't fix it until I know what it is.'

That got her attention. She slowly shook her head. 'That's just it. I don't think you can fix this, Sakis.'

His palms grew cold. Clenching his fists tight, he waited.

'A few years ago, I worked for Greg Landers.'

The name popped like a firework in his brain. 'Landers? The guy who was working with Moorecroft?'

'Yes. But back then he owned a gas brokerage firm.'

'And?' he demanded, because his gut told him there was more. Much, much more. 'He's the one who's been texting you. He's *G*.' He didn't try to frame it as a question. He knew.

She licked her lips and, despite the fear and desperation clawing through his belly, he couldn't stop his body's sexual reaction. 'Yes.'

Sakis breathed in deep, but the control kept unravelling. It took every ounce of strength he had to remain standing. 'Is he your lover?'

She gasped. 'No!' A look very much like shame crossed her face. 'But he was,' she whispered.

He'd never understood jealousy up until now. Never got why it compelled strong emotion in others. In that moment, he understood. All Sakis could see in that moment was *red*, fiery red anger, and white-hot pain. 'Why does he call you "Anna"?'

'Because that's my name. My real name is Anna Simpson. I changed it to Brianna Moneypenny after...after...'

'After what?'

'After I served just under two years in jail for embezzlement and fraud.'

Ice, sharp and deadly, clenched hard around his chest. 'You went to *jail*? For *fraud*?'

Tears brimmed in her eyes as she nodded.

Sakis couldn't breathe. His whole body had gone numb. He'd been betrayed *again*. And this time by a woman he loved. And, yes, he could finally admit that the feeling was love because nothing else came close to describing his emotions.

He tried to move towards her and absently noted that his feet were carrying him in the other direction. Numbness spread until his whole body felt frozen to the core.

'You lied to me,' he rasped around the pain gripping his throat.

Slowly, she nodded. Then she cleared her throat. 'Yes.'

'You colluded with a criminal to defraud and then you wormed your way into my company and my bed to do it all over again. You were helping him to topple my company, risking the livelihood of thousands of people.' His voice shook, his insides raw with agony.

'No! Please listen—I didn't. I'd never do that to you.'

'How long have you and Landers been involved in your little scheme?' he snarled, his senses reeling.

Her arms stretched out towards him, palms open wide in false supplication. 'There's no scheme, Sakis. Please believe me.'

His frozen heart twisted painfully. '*Believe you?* That's a joke, right? How long, Brianna?'

Guilt, raw and glaring, slashed across her whitened features. In that moment, Sakis felt as if he'd been turned to stone then smashed into a million pieces.

'I...I've known about it since that last night at Point Noire.'

'And this abrupt confession? You knew it was only a matter of time before the investigators sniffed you both out, didn't you?'

Brianna couldn't stop the distressed cry that ripped from her throat. 'I wanted to tell you. But I...I didn't want to lose you.'

His devilish laugh sliced through her chest, shredding her already bleeding heart. 'You didn't want to lose me, so you thought you'd do the one thing guaranteed to make that happen? For a woman whose intelligence I once valued, that's shockingly stupid.'

She flinched.

He barely blinked at her pain. 'So, what was the plan? I want to hear it. In detail.'

'Greg wanted information to help him in a new takeover bid: shareholding percentages, personal information about board members to give him an edge.'

His grip on the corner of his desk tightened until his knuckles whitened. 'And you fed him this information? Come clean now because I *will* find out.'

'No! I wouldn't... I'd never...' She stopped and swallowed down the sob that threatened to choke her. 'I know it's too late for me to make you believe me but—'

'What did you expect to receive in return?' he ground out chillingly.

'Nothing! I wanted no part of it. Greg was blackmailing me. He found out I'd changed my name and threatened to expose me.'

'Right; next you'll be telling me you were framed the first time round too.'

'I was!'

'You mean a jury didn't find you guilty and a judge didn't sentence you?' Sakis's numbness was receding and pure rage was taking its place. He welcomed the painful sting in his legs and arms, welcomed the surge of power it brought.

'They did, but Greg had engineered it and made sure I took the fall.'

'How?'

Her tongue darted out to lick her lips. Sakis felt the lash of desire and crushed it dead. 'I signed some papers he asked me to and—'

'Did he force you to?'

'What?'

'You say you signed papers, which I assume implicated you. Did he force you to sign them? Did he stand over you with a gun or threaten you in any way?'

'Um…no, he didn't. He tricked me.'

His disbelieving snort stopped the flow of her words. 'You expect me to believe that the ruthlessly efficient executive assistant who's been in my employ these last eighteen months was the same person who would sign papers without first checking them in triplicate? I assume you were so in love with him, you believed every saintly word that fell from his lips?'

She flinched but remained silent and her hands dropped.

Sakis was glad his rage had ravaged every other emotion otherwise he'd have felt the drowning desolation of that silent confirmation. The woman he loved…loved someone else.

Jerking to his feet, he rounded his desk and called his head of security. Once he'd hung up, he stared down at the papers on his desk, willing his frozen mind to focus. 'Give me your phone.'

She frowned. 'What?'

'Your phone. I know you've got it in your pocket. Hand it over.'

Almost in a daze, she did as he asked. 'What are you going to do with it?'

He threw it in his desk drawer, locked it and pocketed the key. 'As of right now, it's evidence of your duplicity. I'll hand it over to the police when the time is right.'

She sucked in a frightened breath. 'No! Please, Sakis. I can't...I can't go back to prison.'

Despite thinking he was too numb to feel, the torment and horror in her eyes sent a shaft of pain through him.

His gaze dropped to her hip, to the place where her scar resided. 'That's where you sustained that injury, wasn't it? In jail?' he asked, feeling another shot of scalding pain.

'Yes. I was attacked.'

Theos! He turned to face the window so she wouldn't see his eyes clamp shut or the steadying breath he took.

When he heard the knock on his door, relief flooded him. Sheldon entered and Sakis shoved unsteady hands deeper into his pocket and turned around.

'Escort Miss *Moneypenny* off my property. Put her on the same plane returning the other company employees. I want her under twenty-four-hour guard until you hear from me. If she tries to run, you have my permission to physically restrain her and call the police. Is that understood?'

A stunned Sheldon nodded. 'Yes, sir.'

'Sakis, I know you don't believe me, but please be careful. Greg's a slippery bastard.'

He didn't turn around.

'Sakis!' Her desperate plea made him flinch but her betrayal cut too deep.

Nevertheless, he allowed himself one last look. Her face was devoid of colour and her lips trembled uncontrollably. But her eyes, even though they pleaded with him, held a condemnation that made his fists curl in his pockets.

Sakis wasn't sure how long he stood there. It might have been minutes, it might have been hours.

When his door was thrust open, he turned slowly, his body feeling alien and frozen.

'Is everything okay?' Ari asked as he sauntered in, Theo

close behind. There was an almost pitying note in his voice that made Sakis's belly clench hard.

'No, everything is *not* okay.'

'Ah, that's too bad, brother. Because all hell's broken loose.'

CHAPTER TWELVE

Brianna dragged herself out of bed and walked to her window, hoping for a miracle but knowing hope was useless.

Sure enough, Sakis's guard dog was in place in the dark SUV, just like he'd been for the last three days. She didn't bother looking out of her kitchen window because she knew there would be another SUV stationed in the back alley behind her building, should she get the notion of flinging herself out of her second-floor apartment window and making a run for it.

Forcing herself to enter her kitchen and turn on the kettle, she sagged against the counter and tried to breathe through the waves of pain that had become her endless reality since she'd been marched from Sakis's Greek office.

She clamped her eyes shut to block out the look on his face after her confession.

You lied to me.

Such simple words, yet with those words her world had fallen apart. Because there was no going back. Sakis would always see her as the woman who'd worked her way into his bed only to betray him, especially when she'd known just how much betrayal and lies had ruined his childhood.

The kettle whistled. About to grab a mug from the cupboard, she heard the heavy slam of a car door, followed almost immediately by another. When several followed, she set the mug down and moved closer to the window.

The sight of a paparazzo clinging to the side of a cherry

picker as it rose to her window was so comical, she almost laughed. When he raised his camera and aimed it towards her, Brianna dived for her kitchen floor. Through the window she'd opened to let in the non-existent summer breeze, she heard him shout her name.

'Do you have a comment on the allegations against you, Miss Simpson?'

Crawling on her belly, she made her way to her hallway just as someone leaned on her doorbell.

The realisation that Sakis had truly thrown her to the wolves sent a lance of pain through her, holding her immobile for a full minute, until her pride kicked in.

She refused to hide away like a criminal. And she refused to be trapped in her own home.

If nothing else, she had a right to defend herself. Gritting her teeth for strength, and ignoring the incessant, maddening trill of her doorbell, she dashed into her room.

Grabbing the first set of clothes that came to hand, she pulled them on. Unfortunately, trainers and her suit didn't go, so she forced her feet into four-inch heels, grabbed her bag and pulled a brush through her hair.

She opened the door and shot past Sakis's shocked guards before they had a chance to stop her.

'Miss Moneypenny, wait!'

She rounded on them as they caught up with her at the top of the stairs. 'Lay a finger on me, and *I'll* be the one calling the police. I'll hit you with assault charges so fast, you'll wonder what century it is.' She felt a bolt of satisfaction when they gingerly stepped back.

She hurried down the stairs, noting that they gave hot pursuit but didn't attempt to restrain her.

The glare of morning sunlight coupled with what seemed like a thousand camera flashes momentarily blinded her.

Questions similar to what the first cherry-picker-riding

pap had flung at her came her way, but she'd been doing her job long enough to know never to answer tabloid questions.

With her sight adjusted, she plunged through the crowd and headed for the high street two hundred yards away. When she heard the soft whirr of an engine beside her, she didn't turn around.

'What the hell do you think you're doing, making yourself paparazzi bait?' came the rough demand as rougher hands grasped her arms.

Brianna's heart lurched. The sight of him, right there in front of her, fried her brain cells with pleasure and pain so strong she couldn't breathe for a few precious seconds.

She'd missed him. *God, she'd missed him.*

Then memories of their last meeting smashed through. Sucking in a painful breath, she pulled herself away. 'Nothing that concerns you any longer, Sakis.'

He caught her elbow. 'Brianna, wait.'

'No. Let me go!' She managed to pry her hand away and walk a few steps before he caught up with her again.

'Didn't my security people warn you about the press headed your way?'

'Why should they have? Wasn't that what you planned?'

The hand he reached out to her shook. Or at least she *thought* she saw it tremble. She was feeling very shaky herself and could've imagined it. 'No, it wasn't. I had nothing to do with this. Brianna, please come with me. We need to talk,' he said urgently.

'Not in this lifetime. You made your feelings about me *abundantly* clear—' She gave a yelp of shock as Sakis pulled her in the limo. 'What the hell—?'

'The paparazzi are increasing by the second. My security won't be able to hold them back for much longer. And I really need to talk to you. *Please*,' he tagged on in a ragged voice.

The mouth she'd opened to blast him with clamped shut again. Glancing closer at him, she noticed the shadows in his eyes and the pinched skin bracketing his lips. Against her better judgement, her heart lurched but she still pulled away until her back was braced against the door. He saw her retreat and his lips firmed.

'You have two minutes, then I'm getting out of this car.'

Before she'd finished speaking, the car was rolling forward. Half a minute later, they were in a school yard three streets away parked in front of a familiar aircraft.

'You landed your helicopter on a school compound in the middle of London?' she asked as he helped her out of the car.

'Technically, this isn't the middle of London, and the school is shut for the holidays. I'll pay whatever fine is levied and, if I have to go jail, well, it'll be worth it.'

'*What* will be worth it?'

He didn't respond, only held the door to the chopper open. With the paparazzi within sniffing distance, it would be only a matter of time before they pounced again.

She got in. Sakis followed her. When he reached over to help her buckle her seatbelt, she shook her head. Having him this close was already shredding her insides. His touch would completely annihilate her.

The journey to Pantelides Towers was conducted in silence. So was the journey in the lift that took them to his penthouse.

'What am I doing here, Sakis?'

He closed his eyes for a second and Brianna remembered how he'd said the sound of his name on her lips made him feel. But that had all been an illusion. Because his unforgiving heart had cast her away from him with the precision of a surgeon wielding a scalpel.

'Where were you going when you left her your apartment?'

'None of your damned business. You can't push me around any more, Sakis. My life is my own—but go ahead, do your worst. I'll fight whatever charges you bring against me. If I lose, so be it. But from here on in, *I* control my destiny.'

She ground to a halt, her breath rushing in and out. Sakis glanced from her face to the phone he'd taken from his pocket.

Belatedly, she realised it was her phone. 'What are you still doing with that? I thought you were going to turn it over to the authorities.' Her voice trembled but she raised her chin and glared at him.

'Not after I saw what was on it.'

'What…what did you see?'

He walked slowly towards her, contrition and desperation in his eyes as he held the screen in front of her face.

'I saw this.' The shaken reverence in his voice sent an electrified current through her. Almost fearing to, she glanced down.

You can go rot in hell, Greg. You once tricked me into taking the fall for something you did. And now you want me to betray the man I love? No chance.

She looked up from the screen, her heart hammering against her ribs. 'So what? You shouldn't believe everything you read. For all you know, I could've sent that text just to throw you off the scent.'

He glanced down at the screen again and stared at the words as if imprinting them on his brain for all time. 'Then why did you warn me about him?'

She shrugged.

'Brianna, Greg confessed that he coerced you into signing the papers he used to divert funds into his offshore account.'

Shock ricocheted through her body. 'He came clean? Why?'

'He's facing charges in three countries for bribing Lowell to crash the tanker. I told him I would delay the Greek charges if he gave me any useful information. He gave up the dates, figures and codes to his Cayman Islands accounts and confessed he tricked you into helping him siphon off the money.'

The handbag she clutched slipped from her fingers. 'So… you believe me?'

Pain washed over his face. 'Wasting time feeling sorry for myself gave Landers time to spill your real identity to the tabloids. But I shouldn't have doubted you in the first place.'

'I don't really care that everyone knows who I was. And, given the overwhelming evidence, you would've been a saint not to doubt me.'

He flung the phone away and stalked to where she stood. He started to reach for her then clasped both hands behind his nape. 'Then I should damn well have applied for sainthood. What he did to you…what *I* did…*Theos*, I'm even surprised you agreed to come here with me.'

'I was heading here anyway,' she confessed.

Surprise flared in his eyes, along with hope. 'You were?'

'Don't flatter yourself, Sakis. I wasn't on my way to beg you for my life back, if that's what you think. I was coming to clear my desk, or ask security to clear it for me if I was still barred from entering these hallowed grounds.'

'You're not barred. You'll *never* be barred, Brianna.'

'You don't have to call me that. You know who I am now.'

The hard shake of his head made a lock of hair fall over his eyes. 'You'll always be Brianna to me. She was the woman I fell in love with. The woman who possesses more strength and integrity in her little finger than anyone else I know. The woman I stupidly discarded before I got the chance to tell her how much I love her and treasure her.'

Her legs finally gave way beneath her. Sakis caught her before she crumpled onto the sofa. They fell back together. His gaze dropped to her mouth that had fallen open with wordless wonder, and he groaned. 'I know what I did was unforgivable but I want to try all the same to make it up—'

'You love me.'

'To you. Name your price. Anything you want, I'll give

it. I've already put steps in place to have your conviction revoked—'

'You love me?'

He paused and gave a solemn nod but it was the adoration in his eyes that struck pure, healing happiness into her heart. 'I love you more than I desire my next breath. I need you in my life. I'll do anything, *anything,* to have you back, *agapita.*'

'What does that mean?'

'What does what…? Oh—*agapita*? It means "beloved".'

She pulled back. 'But you started calling me that even before we slept together. It was that day when you took me for pancakes.'

He seemed startled by the remark. Then a smile warmed his stricken face. 'I think my subconscious was telling me how I felt about you.'

She caressed a hand down his rough jaw. 'When did the rest of you catch up?'

'In Greece, after I withstood Ari and Theo's ribbing and I admitted that I didn't want to live without you. I intended to tell you after the party.'

'Tell me again now.'

He repeated it, then pulled back after kissing her senseless, his gaze dark with a vulnerability she'd never seen. 'Can you ever forgive me for what I did?'

His cheeks were warm and vibrant beneath her hands. 'You took steps to find out the truth about what happened to me. You could've walked away and condemned me, but you came back for me. I told you about my past, about my mother, and you didn't judge me or make me feel worthless. I loved you for that. More than I already did before I sent Greg that text.'

The shock on his face made her smile. It was the shock that made her get away with kissing him thoroughly before the alpha male in him took over. When he pulled away from her, she gave a groan of protest.

'Do you have one of those go bags ready for a trip? If you don't, we'll manage, but we need to leave now.'

'I do, but—?'

He was up and striding towards her suite before she could finish the question. He returned, two bags in one hand and the other stretched out to her.

'Where are we going?' Hurriedly, she straightened her clothes and hair.

'I've blocked off my calendar for a month. I believe there's a Swiss chalet waiting for us.'

'You think a month is going to be enough?' Happiness made her saucy, she discovered.

Pulling her close, he kissed her until they were both breathless. 'No chance. But it's a damned good start.'

The fire roared away in the enormous stone hearth as Sakis pulled the luxury throw closer around them and fed her oysters from the shell. Brianna wrinkled her nose at the peculiar taste.

'Don't worry, *agapita*. You get used to it after a while.'

'I don't think I'll ever get used to it; I'm not afraid to admit this is one lost cause to me.'

His eyes darkened. 'I'm glad you didn't condemn me as a lost cause.'

'How could I, when you tell me you fought your own board for me? How hellish was it to keep them from crucifying me?'

'I almost resigned at one point but, when I pointed out that *you* deserved all the credit because you saved the company from another stock market slide, they came round to my way of thinking.'

Her eyes widened. 'I did?'

He nodded. 'Telling me about Greg saved the investigators a lot of time. Once we knew who we were looking for, finding him hiding away in Thailand with Lowell was easy. Didn't you see the arrests on the news?'

'Sakis, I could barely get out of bed to feed myself. Watching the news and risking seeing you was too much.'

He froze and jagged pain slashed his features. '*Theos*, I'm so sorry.'

She kissed him then watched him pile more food on her plate. 'You have enough there to feed two armies. I can't possibly eat all of that.'

'Try. I don't like hearing that you didn't eat because of me. I watched my mother wither away from not eating after what my father did to her.'

Pain for him scoured her heart. 'Oh, Sakis…'

He shook his head. 'Eat, *agapita*, and tell me you forgive me.'

'I'll forgive you anything if you keep calling me that.'

After she ate more than was good for her, he stretched her out on the rug and pulled the sheepskin throw off her. Kissing his way down her body, he repeated the endearment over and over again, until she sobbed with need for him.

In the aftermath of their love-making, he brushed the tears from her eyes and kissed her lids.

'I've made you cry with happiness and there're no pancakes in sight. That, *agapita*, is what I call a result.'

* * * * *

A MARRIAGE FIT FOR A SINNER

CHAPTER ONE

'ONE PLATINUM CHRONOGRAPH WATCH. A pair of diamond-studded cufflinks. Gold signet ring. Six hundred and twenty-five pounds cash, and...Obsidian Privilege Card. Right, I think that's everything, sir. Sign here to confirm return of your property.'

Zaccheo Giordano didn't react to the warden's sneer as he scrawled on the barely legible form. Nor did he react to the resentful envy in the man's eyes when his gaze drifted to where the sleek silver limousine waited beyond three sets of barbed wire.

Romeo Brunetti, Zaccheo's second-in-command and the only person he would consider draping the term *friend* upon, stood beside the car, brooding and unsmiling, totally unruffled by the armed guard at the gate or the bleak South East England surroundings.

Had Zaccheo been in an accommodating mood, he'd have cracked a smile.

But he wasn't in an accommodating mood. He hadn't been for a very long time. Fourteen months, two weeks, four days and nine hours to be exact. Zaccheo was positive he could count down to the last second if required.

No one would require it of him, of course. He'd served his time. With three and a half months knocked off his eighteen-month sentence *for good behaviour*.

The rage fused into his DNA bubbled beneath his skin. He showed no outward sign of it as he pocketed his belongings. The three-piece Savile Row suit he'd entered prison in stank of decay and misery, but Zaccheo didn't care.

He'd never been a slave to material comforts. His need for validation went far deeper. The need to elevate himself into a better place had been a soul-deep pursuit from the moment he was old enough to recognise the reality of the life he'd been born into. A life that had been a never-ending whirlpool of humiliation, violence and greed. A life that had seen his father debased and dead at thirty-five.

Memories tumbled like dominoes as he walked down the harshly lit corridor to freedom. He willed the overwhelming sense of injustice that had festered for long, harrowing months not to explode from his pores.

The doors clanged shut behind him.

Zaccheo froze, then took his first lungful of free air with fists clenched and eyes shut. He absorbed the sound of birds chirping in the late-winter morning sun, listened to the distant rumble of the motorway as he'd done many nights from his prison cell.

Opening his eyes, he headed towards the fifteen-foot gate. A minute later, he was outside.

'Zaccheo, it's good to see you again,' Romeo said gravely, his eyes narrowing as he took him in.

Zaccheo knew he looked a sight. He hadn't bothered with a razor blade or a barber's clippers in the last three months and he'd barely eaten once he'd unearthed the truth behind his incarceration. But he'd spent a lot of time in the prison gym. It'd been that or go mad with the clawing hunger for retribution.

He shrugged off his friend's concern and moved to the open door.

'Did you bring what I asked for?' he asked.

Romeo nodded. '*Sì*. All three files are on the laptop.'

Zaccheo slid onto the plush leather seat. Romeo slid in next to him and poured them two glasses of Italian-made cognac.

'*Salute,*' Romeo muttered.

Zaccheo took the drink without responding, threw back the amber liquid and allowed the scent of power and affluence—the tools he'd need for his plan to succeed—to wash over him.

As the low hum of the luxury engine whisked him away from the place he'd been forced to call home for over a year, Zaccheo reached for the laptop.

Icy rage trembled through his fingers as the Giordano Worldwide Inc. logo flickered to life. His life's work, almost decimated through another's greed and lust for power. It was only with Romeo's help that GWI hadn't gone under in the months after Zaccheo had been sent to prison for a crime he didn't commit. He drew quiet satisfaction that not only had GWI survived—thanks to Romeo—it had thrived.

But his personal reputation had not.

He was out now. Free to bring those culpable to justice. He didn't plan on resting until every last person responsible for attempting to destroy his life paid with the destruction of theirs.

Shaking out his hand to rid it of its tremble, he hit the Open key.

The information was thorough although Zaccheo knew most of its contents. For three months he'd checked and double-checked his sources, made sure every detail was nailed down tight.

He exhaled at the first picture that filled his screen.

Oscar Pennington III. Distant relative to the royal family. Etonian. Old, if spent, money. Very much part of the establishment. Greedy. Indiscriminate. His waning property portfolio had received a much-needed injection of capital exactly fourteen months and two weeks ago when he'd become sole owner of London's most talked about building—The Spire.

Zaccheo swallowed the savage growl that rumbled from his soul. Icily calm, he flicked through pages of Pennington celebrating his revived success with galas, lavish dinner parties and polo tournaments thrown about like confetti. One picture showed him laughing with one of his two children.

Sophie Pennington. Private education all the way to finishing school. Classically beautiful. Ball-breaker. She'd proven beyond a doubt that she had every intention of becoming Oscar's carbon copy.

Grimly, he closed her file and moved to the last one.

Eva Pennington.

This time the growl couldn't be contained. Nor could he stem the renewed shaking in his hand as he clicked her file.

Caramel-blonde hair tumbled down her shoulders in thick, wild waves. Dark eyebrows and lashes framed moss-green eyes, accentuated dramatically with black eyeliner. Those eyes had gripped his attention with more force than he'd been comfortable with the first time he'd looked into them. As had the full, bow-shaped lips currently curved in a smouldering smile. His screen displayed a head-and-shoulders shot, but the rest of Eva Pennington's body was imprinted indelibly on Zaccheo's mind. He didn't struggle to recall the petite, curvy shape, or that she forced herself to wear heels even though she hated them, in order to make herself taller.

He certainly didn't struggle to recall her individual atrocity. He'd lain in his prison bed condemning himself for being astounded by her singular betrayal, when the failings of both his parents and his dealings with the *establishment* should've taught him better. He'd prided himself on reading between the lines to spot schemers and gold-diggers ten miles away. Yet he'd been fooled.

The time he'd wasted on useless bitterness was the most excruciating of all; time he would gladly claw back if he could.

Firming his lips, he clicked through the pages, running through her life for the past year and a half. At the final page, he froze.

'How new is this last information?'

'I added that to the file yesterday. I thought you'd want to know,' Romeo replied.

Zaccheo stared at the newspaper clipping, shock waves rolling through him. *'Sì, grazie...'*

'Do you wish to return to the Esher estate or the penthouse?' Romeo asked.

Zaccheo read the announcement again, taking in pertinent details. Pennington Manor. Eight o'clock. Three hundred guests. Followed by an intimate family dinner on Sunday at The Spire.

*The Spire...*the building that should've been Zaccheo's greatest achievement.

'The estate,' he replied. It was closer.

He closed the file as Romeo instructed the driver.

Relaxing against the headrest, Zaccheo tried to let the hum of the engine soothe him. But it was no use. He was far from calm.

He'd have to alter his plan. Not that it mattered too much in the long run.

A chain is only as strong as its weakest link. While all three Penningtons had colluded in his incarceration, this new information demanded he use a different tactic, one he'd first contemplated and abandoned. Either way, Zaccheo didn't plan to rest until all of them were stripped of what they cherished most—their wealth and affluence.

He'd intended to wait a day or two to ensure he had Oscar Pennington where he wanted him before he struck. That plan was no longer viable.

Bringing down the family who'd framed him for criminal negligence couldn't wait till Monday.

His first order of business would be tackled *tonight*.

Starting with the youngest member of the family—Eva Pennington.

His ex-fiancée.

Eva Pennington stared at the dress in her sister's hand. 'Seriously? There's no way I'm wearing that. Why didn't you tell me the clothes I left behind had been given away?'

'Because you said you didn't want them when you moved out. Besides, they were old and out of fashion. I had *this* couriered from New York this morning. It's the latest couture and on loan to us for twenty-four hours,' Sophie replied.

Eva pursed her lips. 'I don't care if it was woven by ten thousand silk worms. I'm not wearing a dress that makes me look like a gold-digger *and* a slut. And considering the state of our finances, I'd have thought you'd be more careful what you splashed money on.' She couldn't stem her bewilderment as to why Sophie and her father blithely ignored the fact that money was extremely tight.

Sophie huffed. 'This is a one-of-a-kind dress, and, unless I'm mistaken, it's the kind of dress your future husband likes his women to wear. Anyway, you'll be out of it in less than four hours, once the right photographs have been taken, and the party's over.'

Eva gritted her teeth. 'Stop trying to manage me, Sophie. You're forgetting who pulled this bailout together. If I hadn't come to an agreement with Harry, we'd have been sunk come next week. As to what he likes his women to wear, if you'd bothered to speak to me first I'd have saved you the trouble of going to unnecessary expense. I dress for myself and no one else.'

'Speak to you first? When you and Father neglected to afford me the same courtesy before you hatched this plan behind my back?' Sophie griped.

Eva's heart twisted at the blatant jealousy in her sister's voice.

As if it weren't enough that the decision she'd spent the past two weeks agonising over still made her insides clench in horror. It didn't matter that the man she'd agreed to marry was her friend and she was helping him as much as he was helping her. Marriage was a step she'd rather not have taken.

It was clear, however, her sister didn't see it that way. Sophie's escalating discontentment at any relationship Eva tried to forge with their father was part of the reason Eva had moved out of Pennington Manor. Not that their father was an easy man to live with.

For as long as she could remember, Sophie had been possessive of their father's attention. While their mother had been alive, it'd been bearable and easier to accept that Sophie was their father's preferred child, while Eva was her mother's, despite wanting to be loved equally by both parents.

After their mother's death, every interaction Eva had tried to have with their father had been met with bristling confrontation from Sophie, and indifference from their father.

But, irrational as it was, it didn't stop Eva from trying to reason with the sister she'd once looked up to.

'We didn't go behind your back. You were away on a business trip—'

'Trying to use the business degree that doesn't seem to mean anything any more. Not when *you* can swoop in after three years of performing tired ballads in seedy pubs to save the day,' Sophie interjected harshly.

Eva hung on to her temper by a thread, but pain stung deep at the blithe dismissal of her passion. 'You know I resigned from Penningtons because Father only hired me so I could attract a suitable husband. And just because my dreams don't coincide with yours—'

'That's just it. You're twenty-four and still *dreaming*. The rest of us don't have that luxury. And we certainly don't land on our feet by clicking our fingers and having a millionaire solve all our problems.'

'Harry is saving *all of us*. And you really think I've *landed on my feet* by getting engaged for the second time in two years?' Eva asked.

Sophie dropped the offensive dress on Eva's bed. 'To everyone who matters, this is your first engagement. The other one barely lasted five minutes. Hardly anyone knows it happened.'

Hurt-laced anger swirled through her veins. '*I* know it happened.'

'If my opinion matters around here any more, then I suggest you don't broadcast it. It's a subject best left in the past, just like the man it involved.'

Pain stung deeper. 'I can't pretend it didn't happen because of what occurred afterwards.'

'The last thing we need right now is any hint of scandal. And I don't know why you're blaming Father for what happened when you should be thanking him for extricating you from that man before it was too late,' Sophie defended heatedly.

That man.

Zaccheo Giordano.

Eva wasn't sure whether the ache lodged beneath her ribs came from thinking about him or from the reminder of how gullible she'd been to think he was any different from every other man who'd crossed her path.

She relaxed her fists when they balled again.

This was why she preferred her life away from their family home deep in the heart of Surrey.

It was why her waitress colleagues knew her as Eva Penn, a hostess at Siren, the London nightclub where she also sang part-time, instead of Lady Eva Pennington, daughter of Lord Pennington.

Her relationship with her father had always been difficult, but she'd never thought she'd lose her sister so completely, too.

She cleared her throat. 'Sophie, this agreement with Harry wasn't supposed to undermine anything you were doing with Father to save Penningtons. There's no need to be upset or jealous. I'm not trying to take your place—'

'Jealous! Don't be ridiculous,' Sophie sneered, although the trace of panic in her voice made Eva's heart break. 'And you could never take my place. I'm Father's right hand, whereas you…you're nothing but—' She stopped herself and, after a few seconds, stuck her nose in the air. 'Our guests are arriving shortly. Please don't be late to your own engagement party.'

Eva swallowed down her sorrow. 'I've no intention of being late. But neither do I have any intention of wearing a dress that has less material than thread holding it together.'

She strode to the giant George III armoire opposite the bed, even though her earlier inspection had shown less than a fraction of the items she'd left behind when she'd moved out on her twenty-first birthday.

These days she was content with her hostess's uniform when she was working or lounging in jeans and sweaters while she wrote her music on her days off. Haute couture, spa days and primping herself beautiful in order to please anyone were part of a past she'd happily left behind.

Unfortunately this time there'd been no escaping. Not when she alone had been able to find the solution to saving her family.

She tried in vain to squash the rising memories being back at Pennington Manor threatened to resurrect.

Zaccheo was in her past, a mistake that should never have happened. A reminder that ignoring a lesson learned only led to further heartache.

She sighed in relief when her hand closed on a silk wrap. The red dress would be far too revealing, a true spectacle for the three hundred guests her father had invited to gawp at. But at least the wrap would provide a little much-needed cover.

Glancing at the dress again, she shuddered.

She'd rather be anywhere but here, participating in this sham. But then hadn't her whole life been a sham? From parents who'd been publicly hailed as the couple to envy, but who'd fought bitterly in private until tragedy had struck in the form of her mother's cancer, to the lavish parties and expensive holidays that her father had secretly been borrowing money for, the Penningtons had been one giant sham for as long as Eva could remember.

Zaccheo's entry into their lives had only escalated her father's behaviour.

No, she refused to think about Zaccheo. He belonged to a chapter of her life that was firmly sealed. Tonight was about Harry Fairfield, her family's saviour, and her soon-to-be fiancé.

It was also about her father's health.

For that reason alone, she tried again with Sophie.

'For Father's sake, I want tonight to go smoothly, so can we try to get along?'

Sophie stiffened. 'If you're talking about Father's hospitalisation two weeks ago, I haven't forgotten.'

Watching her father struggle to breathe with what the doctors had termed a cardiac event had terrified Eva. It'd been the catalyst that had forced her to accept Harry's proposition.

'He's okay today, isn't he?' Despite her bitterness at her family's treatment of her, she couldn't help her concern for her remaining parent. Nor could she erase the secret yearning that the different version of the father she'd connected with very briefly after her mother's death, the one who wasn't an excess-loving megalomaniac who treated her as if she was an irritating inconvenience, hadn't been a figment of her imagination.

'He will be, once we get rid of the creditors threatening us with bankruptcy.'

Eva exhaled. There was no backing out; no secretly hoping that some other solution would present itself and save her from the sacrifice she was making.

All avenues had been thoroughly explored—Eva had demanded to see the Pennington books herself and spent a day with the company's accountants to verify that they were indeed in dire straits. Her father's rash acquisition of The Spire had stretched the company to breaking point. Harry Fairfield was their last hope.

She unzipped the red dress, resisting the urge to crush it into a wrinkled pulp.

'Do you need help?' Sophie asked, although Eva sensed the offer wasn't altruistic.

'No, I can manage.'

The same way she'd managed after her mother's death; through her father's rejection and Sophie's increasingly unreasonable behaviour; through the heartbreak of finding out about Zaccheo's betrayal.

Sophie nodded briskly. 'I'll see you downstairs, then.'

Eva slipped on the dress, avoiding another look in the mirror when the first glimpse showed what she'd feared most. Her every curve was accentuated, with large swathes of flesh exposed. With shaky fingers she applied her lipstick and slipped her feet into matching platform heels.

Slipping the gold and red wrap around her shoulders, she finally glanced at her image.

Chin up, girl. It's show time.

Eva wished the manageress of Siren were uttering the words, as she did every time before Eva stepped onto the stage.

Unfortunately, she wasn't at Siren. She'd promised to marry a man she didn't love, for the sake of saving her precious family name.

No amount of pep talk could stem the roaring agitation flooding her veins.

CHAPTER TWO

THE EVENT PLANNERS had outdone themselves. Potted palms, decorative screens and subdued lighting had been strategically placed around the main halls of Pennington Manor to hide the peeling plaster, chipped wood panelling and torn Aubusson rugs that funds could no longer stretch to rectify.

Eva sipped the champagne she'd been nursing for the last two hours and willed time to move faster. Technically she couldn't throw any guest out, but *Eight to Midnight* was the time the costly invitations had stated the party would last. She needed something to focus on or risk sliding into madness.

Gritting her teeth, she smiled as yet another guest demanded to see her engagement ring. The monstrous pink diamond's sole purpose was to demonstrate the Fairfields' wealth. Its alien weight dragged her hand down, hammering home the irrefutable point that she'd sold herself for her pedigree.

Her father's booming voice interrupted her maudlin thoughts. Surrounded by a group of influential politicians who hung onto his every word, Oscar Pennington was in his element.

Thickset but tall enough to hide the excess weight he carried, her father cut a commanding figure despite his recent spell in hospital. His stint in the army three decades ago had lent him a ruthless edge, cleverly counteracted by his natural charm. The combination made him enigmatic enough to attract attention when he walked into a room.

But not even that charisma had saved him from economic devastation four years ago.

With that coming close on the heels of her mother's illness, their social and economic circles had dwindled to nothing almost overnight, with her father desperately scrambling to hold things together.

End result—his association with Zaccheo Giordano.

Eva frowned, bewildered that her thoughts had circled back to the man she'd pushed to the dark recesses of her mind. A man she'd last seen being led away in handcuffs—

'There you are. I've been looking for you everywhere.'

Eva started, then berated herself for feeling guilty. Guilt belonged to those who'd committed crimes, who lied about their true motives.

Enough!

She smiled at Harry.

Her old university friend—a brilliant tech genius—had gone off the rails when he'd achieved fame and wealth straight out of university. Now a multimillionaire with enough money to bail out Penningtons, he represented her family's last hope.

'Well, you found me,' she said.

He was a few inches taller than her five feet four; she didn't have to look up too far to meet his twinkling soft brown eyes.

'Indeed. Are you okay?' he asked, his gaze reflecting concern.

'I'm fine,' she responded breezily.

He looked unconvinced. Harry was one of the few people who knew about her broken engagement to Zaccheo. He'd seen beneath her false smiles and assurances that she could handle a marriage of convenience and asked her point-blank if her past with Zaccheo Giordano would be a problem. Her swift *no* seemed to have satisfied him.

Now he looked unsure.

'Harry, don't fret. I can do this,' she insisted, despite the hollowness in her stomach.

He studied her solemnly, then called over a waiter and exchanged his empty champagne glass for a full one. 'If you say so, but I need advanced warning if this gets too weird for you, okay? My parents will have a fit if they read about me in the papers this side of Christmas.'

She nodded gratefully, then frowned. 'I thought you were going to take it easy tonight?' She indicated his glass.

'Gosh, you already sound like a wife.' He sniggered. 'Leave off, sweetness, the parents have already given me an earful.'

Having met his parents a week ago, Eva could imagine the exchange.

'Remember why *you're* doing this. Do you want to derail the PR campaign to clean up your image before it's even begun?'

While Harry couldn't care less about his social standing, his parents were voracious in their hunger for prestige and a pedigree to hang their name on. Only the threat to Harry's business dealings had finally forced him to address his reckless playboy image.

He took her arm and tilted his sand-coloured head affably towards hers. 'I promise to be on my best behaviour. Now that the tedious toasts have been made and we're officially engaged, it's time for the best part of the evening. The fireworks!'

Eva set her champagne glass down and stepped out of the dining-room alcove that had been her sanctuary throughout her childhood. 'Isn't that supposed to be a surprise?'

Harry winked. 'It is, but, since we've fooled everyone into thinking we're *madly* in love, faking our surprise should be easy.'

She smiled. 'I won't tell if you don't.'

Harry laid a hand across his heart. 'Thank you, my fair Lady Pennington.'

The reminder of why this whole sham engagement was happening slid like a knife between her ribs. Numbing herself to the pain, she walked out onto the terrace that overlooked the manor's multi-acre garden.

The gardens had once held large koi ponds, a giant summer house and an elaborate maze, but the prohibitive cost of the grounds' upkeep had led to the landscape being levelled and replaced with rolling carpet grass.

A smattering of applause greeted their arrival and Eva's gaze drifted over the guests to where Sophie, her father and Harry's parents stood watching them.

She caught her father's eye, and her stomach knotted.

While part of her was pleased that she'd found a solution to their family problems, she couldn't help but feel that nothing she did would ever bring her closer to her sister or father.

Her father might have accepted her help with the bailout from Harry, but his displeasure at her chosen profession was yet another bone of contention between them. One she'd made clear she wouldn't back down on.

Turning away, she fixed her smile in place and exclaimed appropriately when the first elaborate firework display burst into the sky.

'So...my parents want us to live together,' Harry whispered in her ear.

'What?'

He laughed. 'Don't worry, I convinced them you hate my bachelor pad so we need to find a place that's *ours* rather than mine.'

Relief poured through her. 'Thank you.'

He brushed a hand down her cheek. 'You're welcome. But I deserve a reward for my sacrifice,' he said with a smile. 'How about dinner on Monday?'

'As long as it's not a paparazzi-stalked spectacle of a restaurant, you're on.'

'Great. It's a date.' He kissed her knuckles, much to the delight of the guests, who thought they were witnessing a true love match.

Eva allowed herself to relax. She might find what they were doing distasteful, but she was grateful that Harry's visit to Siren three weeks ago had ended up with him bailing her out, and not a calculating stranger.

'That dress is a knockout on you, by the way.'

She grimaced. 'It wasn't my first choice, but thank you.'

The next series of firework displays should've quieted the guests, yet murmurs around her grew.

'*Omigod*, whoever it is must have a death wish!' someone exclaimed.

Harry's eyes narrowed. 'I think we may have a last-minute guest.'

Eva looked around and saw puzzled gazes fixed at a point in the sky as the faint *thwopping* sound grew louder. Another set of fireworks went off, illuminating the looming object.

She frowned. 'Is that…?'

'A helicopter heading straight for the middle of the fireworks display? Yep. I guess the organisers decided to add another surprise to the party.'

'I don't think that's part of the entertainment,' Eva shouted to be heard over the descending aircraft.

Her heart slammed into her throat as a particularly elaborate firework erupted precariously close to the black-and-red chopper.

'Hell, if this is a stunt, I take my hat off to the pilot. It takes iron balls to fly into danger like that.' Harry chuckled.

The helicopter drew closer. Mesmerised, Eva watched it settle in the middle of the garden, her attention riveted to its single occupant.

The garden lights had been turned off to showcase the fireworks to maximum effect so she couldn't see who their unexpected guest was. Nevertheless, an ominous shiver chased up her spine.

She heard urgent shouts for the pyrotechnician to halt the display, but another rocket fizzed past the rotating blades.

A hush fell over the crowd as the helicopter door opened. A figure stepped out, clad from head to toe in black. As another blaze of colour filled the sky his body was thrown into relief.

Eva tensed as if she'd been shot with a stun gun.

It couldn't be...

He was behind bars, atoning for his ruthless greed. Eva squashed the sting of guilt that accompanied the thought.

Zaccheo Giordano and men of his ilk arrogantly believed they were above the law. They didn't deserve her sympathy, or the disloyal thought that he alone had paid the price when, by association, her father should've borne some of the blame. Justice ensured they went to jail and stayed there for the duration of their term. They weren't released early.

They certainly didn't land in the middle of a firework display at a private party as if they owned the land they walked on.

The spectacle unfolding before her stated differently.

Lights flickered on. Eva tracked the figure striding imperiously across the grass and up the wide steps.

Reaching the terrace, he paused and buttoned his single-breasted tuxedo.

'Oh, God,' she whispered.

'Wait...you know this bloke?' Harry asked, his tone for once serious.

Eva wanted to deny the man who now stood, easily head and shoulders above the nearest guests, his fierce, unwavering gaze pinned on her.

She didn't know whether to attribute the crackling electricity to his appearance or the look in his eyes. Both were viscerally menacing to the point of brutality.

The Zaccheo Giordano she'd had the misfortune of briefly tangling with before his incarceration had kept his hair trimmed short and his face clean-shaven.

This man had a full beard and his hair flowed over his shoulders in an unruly sea of thick jet waves. Eva swallowed at the pronounced difference in him. The sleek, almost gaunt man she'd known was gone. In his place breathed a Neanderthal with broader shoulders, thicker arms and a denser chest moulded by his black silk shirt. Equally dark trousers hugged lean hips and sturdy thighs to fall in a precise inch above expensive handmade shoes. But nothing of his attire disguised the aura he emanated.

Uncivilised. Explosively masculine. Lethal.

Danger vibrated from him like striations on baking asphalt. It flowed over the guests, who jostled each other for a better look at the impromptu visitor.

'Eva?' Harry's puzzled query echoed through her dazed consciousness.

Zaccheo released her from his deadly stare. His eyes flicked to the arm tucked into Harry's before he turned away. The breath exploded from her lungs. Sensing Harry about to ask another question, she nodded.

'Yes. That's Zaccheo.'

Her eyes followed Zaccheo as he turned towards her family.

Oscar's look of anger was laced with a heavy dose of apprehension. Sophie looked plain stunned.

Eva watched the man she'd hoped to never see again cup his hands behind his back and stroll towards her father. Anyone would've been foolish to think that stance indicated supplication. If anything, its severe mockery made Eva want to do the unthinkable and burst out laughing.

She would've, had she not been mired in deep dread at what Zaccheo's presence meant.

'Your ex?' Harry pressed.

She nodded numbly.

'Then we should say hello.'

Harry tugged on her arm and she realised too late what he meant.

'No. Wait!' she whispered fiercely.

But he was either too drunk or genuinely oblivious to the vortex of danger he was headed for to pay attention. The tension surrounding the group swallowed Eva as they approached. Heart pounding, she watched her father's and Zaccheo's gazes lock.

'I don't know what the hell you think you're doing here, Giordano, but I suggest you get back in that monstrosity and leave before I have you arrested for trespass.'

A shock wave went through the crowd.

Zaccheo didn't bat an eyelid.

'By all means do that if you wish, but you know exactly why I'm here, Pennington. We can play coy if you prefer. You'll be made painfully aware when I tire of it.' The words were barely above a murmur, but their venom raised the hairs on Eva's arms, triggering a gasp when she saw Sophie's face.

Her usually unflappable sister was severely agitated, her face distressingly pale.

'*Ciao*, Eva,' Zaccheo drawled without turning around. That deep, resonant voice, reminiscent of a tenor in a soulful opera, washed over her, its powerfully mesmerising quality reminding her how she'd once longed to hear him speak just for the hell of it. 'It's good of you to join us.'

'This is my engagement party. It's my duty to interact with my guests, even unwelcome ones who will be asked to leave immediately.'

'Don't worry, *cara*, I won't be staying long.'

The relief that surged up her spine disappeared when his gaze finally swung her way, then dropped to her left hand. With almost cavalier laziness, he caught her wrist and raised it to the light. He examined the ring for exactly three seconds. 'How predictable.'

He released her with the same carelessness he'd captured her.

Eva clenched her fist to stop the sizzling electricity firing up her arm at the brief contact.

'What's that supposed to mean?' Harry demanded.

Zaccheo levelled steely grey eyes on him, then his parents. 'This is a private discussion. Leave us.'

Peter Fairfield's laugh held incredulity, the last inch of

champagne in his glass sloshing wildly as he raised his arm. 'I think you've got the wrong end of the stick there, mate. You're the one who needs to take a walk.'

Eva caught Harry's pained look at his father's response, but could do nothing but watch, heart in her throat, as Zaccheo faced Peter Fairfield.

Again she was struck by how much his body had changed; how the sleek, layered muscle lent a deeper sense of danger. Whereas before it'd been like walking close to the edge of a cliff, looking into his eyes now was like staring into a deep, bottomless abyss.

'Would you care to repeat that, *il mio amico*?' The almost conversational tone belied the savage tension beneath the words.

'Oscar, who *is* this?' Peter Fairfield demanded of her father, who seemed to have lost the ability to speak after Zaccheo's succinct taunt.

Eva inserted herself between the two men before the situation got out of hand. Behind her, heat from Zaccheo's body burned every exposed inch of skin. Ignoring the sensation, she cleared her throat.

'Mr and Mrs Fairfield, Harry, we'll only be a few minutes. We're just catching up with Mr Giordano.' She glanced at her father. A vein throbbed in his temple and he'd gone a worrying shade of puce. Fear climbed into her heart. 'Father?'

He roused himself and glanced around. A charming smile slid into place, but it was off by a light year. The trickle of ice that had drifted down her spine at Zaccheo's unexpected arrival turned into a steady drip.

'We'll take this in my study. Don't hesitate to let the staff know if you need anything.' He strode away, followed by a disturbingly quiet Sophie.

Zaccheo's gaze swung to Harry, who defiantly withstood the laser gaze for a few seconds before he glanced at her.

'Are you sure?' Harry asked, that touching concern again in his eyes.

Her instinct screamed a terrible foreboding, but she nodded. 'Yes.'

'Okay. Hurry back, sweetness.' Before she could move, he dropped a kiss on her mouth.

A barely audible lethal growl charged through the air.

Eva flinched.

She wanted to face Zaccheo. Demand that he crawl back behind the bars that should've been holding him. But that glimpse of fear in her father's eyes stopped her. She tugged the wrap closer around her.

Something wasn't right here. She was willing to bet the dilapidated ancestral pile beneath her feet that something was seriously, *dangerously* wrong—

'Move, Eva.'

The cool command spoken against her ear sent shivers coursing through her.

She moved, only because the quicker she got to the bottom of why he was here, the quicker he would leave. But with each step his dark gaze probed her back, making the walk to her father's study on the other side of the manor the longest in her life.

Zaccheo shut the door behind him. Her father turned from where he'd been gazing into the unlit fireplace. Again Eva spotted apprehension in his eyes before he masked it.

'Whatever grievance you think you have the right to air, I suggest you rethink it, son. Even if this were the right time or place—'

'I am *not* your son, Pennington.' Zaccheo's response held lethal bite, the first sign of his fury breaking through. 'As for why I'm here, I have five thousand three hundred and twenty-two pieces of documentation that proves you colluded with various other individuals to pin a crime on me that I didn't commit.'

'What?' Eva gasped, then the absurdity of the statement made her shake her head. 'We don't believe you.'

Zaccheo's eyes remained on her father. 'You may not, but your father does.'

Oscar Pennington laughed, but the sound lacked its usual boom and zest. When sweat broke out over his forehead, fear gripped Eva's insides.

She steeled her spine. 'Our lawyers will rip whatever evidence you think you have to shreds, I'm sure. If you're here to seek some sort of closure, you picked the wrong time to do it. Perhaps we can arrange to meet you at some other time?'

Zaccheo didn't move. Didn't blink. Hands once again tucked behind his back, he simply watched her father, his body a coiled predator waiting to strike a fatal blow.

Silence stretched, throbbed with unbearable menace. Eva looked from her father to Sophie and back again, her dread escalating. 'What's going on?' she demanded.

Her father gripped the mantel until his knuckles shone white. 'You chose the wrong enemy. You're sorely mistaken if you think I'll let you blackmail me in my own home.'

Sophie stepped forward. 'Father, don't—'

'Good, you haven't lost your hubris.' Zaccheo's voice slashed across her sister's. 'I was counting on that. Here's what I'm going to do. In ten minutes I'm going to leave here with Eva, right in front of all your guests. You won't lift a finger to stop me. You'll tell them exactly who I am. Then you'll make a formal announcement that I'm the man your daughter will marry two weeks from today and that I have your blessing. I don't want to trust something so important to phone cameras and social media, although your guests will probably do a pretty good job. I noticed a few members of the press out there, so that part of your task should be easy. If the articles are written to my satisfaction, I'll be in touch on Monday to lay out how you can begin to make reparations to me. However, if by the time Eva and I wake up tomorrow morning the news of our engagement isn't in the press, then all bets are off.'

Oscar Pennington's breathing altered alarmingly. His

mouth opened but no words emerged. In the arctic silence that greeted Zaccheo's deadly words, Eva gaped at him.

'You're clearly not in touch with all of your faculties if you think those ridiculous demands are going to be met.' When silence greeted her response, she turned sharply to her father. 'Father? Why aren't you saying something?' she demanded, although the trepidation beating in her chest spelled its own doom.

'Because he can't, Eva. Because he's about to do exactly as I say.'

She rounded on him, and was once again rocked to the core by Zaccheo's visually powerful, utterly captivating transformation. So much so, she couldn't speak for several seconds. 'You're out of your mind!' she finally blurted.

Zaccheo's gaze didn't stray from its laser focus on her father. 'Believe me, *cara mia*, I haven't been saner than I am in this moment.'

CHAPTER THREE

ZACCHEO WATCHED EVA'S head swivel to her father, confusion warring with anger.

'Go on, Oscar. She's waiting for you to tell me to go to hell. Why don't you?'

Pennington staggered towards his desk, his face ashen and his breathing growing increasingly laboured.

'Father!' Eva rushed to his side—ignoring the poisonous look her sister sent her—as he collapsed into his leather armchair.

Zaccheo wanted to rip her away, let her watch her father suffer as his sins came home to roost. Instead he allowed the drama to play out. The outcome would be inevitable and would only go one way.

His way.

He wanted to look into Pennington's eyes and see the defeat and helplessness the other man had expected to see in his eyes the day Zaccheo had been sentenced.

Both sisters now fussed over their father and a swell of satisfaction rose at the fear in their eyes. Eva glanced his way and he experienced a different punch altogether. One he'd thought himself immune to, but had realised otherwise the moment he'd stepped off his helicopter and singled her out in the crowd.

That unsettling feeling, as if he were suffering from vertigo despite standing on terra firma, had intrigued and annoyed him in equal measures from the very first time he'd seen her, her voice silkily hypnotic as she crooned into a mic on a golden-lit stage, her fingers caressing the black microphone stand as if she were touching a lover.

Even knowing exactly who she was, what she represented,

he hadn't been able to walk away. In the weeks after their first meeting, he'd fooled himself into believing she was different, that she wasn't tainted with the same greed to further her pedigree by whatever means necessary; that she wasn't willing to do whatever it took to secure her family's standing, even while secretly scorning his upbringing.

Her very public denouncement of any association between them on the day of his sentencing had been the final blow. Not that Zaccheo hadn't had the scales viciously ripped from his eyes by then.

No, by that fateful day fourteen months ago, he'd known just how thoroughly he'd been suckered.

'What the hell do you think you're doing?' she muttered fiercely, her moss-green eyes firing lasers at him.

Zaccheo forced himself not to smile. The time for gloating would come later. 'Exacting the wages of sin, *dolcezza*. What else?'

'I don't know what you're talking about, but I don't think my father is in a position to have a discussion with you right now, Mr Giordano.'

Her prim and proper tones bit savagely into Zaccheo, wiping away any trace of twisted mirth. That tone said he ought to *know his place*, that he ought to stand there like a good little servant and wait to be addressed instead of upsetting the lord of the manor with his petty concerns.

Rage bubbled beneath his skin, threatening to erupt. Blunt nails bit into his wrist, but the pain wasn't enough to calm his fury. He clenched his jaw for a long moment before he trusted himself to speak.

'I gave you ten minutes, Pennington. You now have five. I suggest you practise whatever sly words you'll be using to address your guests.' Zaccheo shrugged. 'Or not. Either way, things *will* go my way.'

Eva rushed at him, her striking face and flawless skin flushed with a burst of angry colour as she stopped a few feet away.

Out on the terrace, he'd compelled himself not to stare too long at her in case he betrayed his feelings. In case his gaze devoured her as he'd wanted to do since her presence snaked like a live wire inside him.

Now, he took in that wild gypsy-like caramel-blonde hair so out of place in this polished stratosphere her family chose to inhabit. The striking contrast between her bright hair, black eyebrows and dark-rimmed eyes had always fascinated him. But no more than her cupid-bow lips, soft, dark red and sinfully sensual. Or the rest of her body.

'You assume I have no say in whatever despicable spectacle you're planning. That I intend to meekly stand by while you humiliate my family? Well, think again!'

'Eva...' her father started.

'No! I don't know what exactly is going on here, but I intend to play no part in it.'

'You'll play your part, and you'll play it well,' Zaccheo interjected, finally driving his gaze up from the mouth he wanted to feast on more than he wanted his next breath. *That'll come soon enough*, he promised himself.

'Or what? You'll carry through with your empty threats?'

His fury eased a touch and twisted amusement slid back into place. It never ceased to amaze him how the titled rich felt they were above the tenets that governed ordinary human beings. His own stepfather had been the same. He'd believed, foolishly, that his pedigree and connections would insulate him from his reckless business practices, that the Old Boys' Club would provide a safety net despite his poor judgement.

Zaccheo had taken great pleasure in watching his mother's husband squirm before him, cap in hand, when Zaccheo had bought his family business right from underneath his pompous nose. But even then, the older man had continued to treat him like a third-class citizen...

Just as Oscar Pennington had done. Just as Eva Pennington was doing now.

'You think my threats empty?' he enquired softly. 'Then do nothing. It's after all your privilege and your right.'

Something of the lethal edge that rode him must have transmitted itself to her. Apprehension chased across her face before she firmed those impossibly sumptuous lips.

'Do nothing, and watch me bury your family in the deepest, darkest, most demeaning pit you can dream of. Do nothing and watch me unleash a scandal the scale of which you can only imagine on your precious family name.' He bared his teeth in a mirthless smile and her eyes widened in stunned disbelief. 'It would be *my* privilege and pleasure to do so.'

Oscar Pennington inhaled sharply and Zaccheo's gaze zeroed in on his enemy. The older man rose from the chair. Though he looked frail, his eyes reflected icy disdain. But Zaccheo also glimpsed the fear of a cornered man weighing all the options to see how to escape the noose dangling ever closer.

Zaccheo smiled inwardly. He had no intention of letting Pennington escape. Not now, not ever.

The flames of retribution intensifying within him, he unclasped his hands. It was time to bring this meeting to an end.

'Your time's up, Pennington.'

Eva answered instead of her father. 'How do we know you're not bluffing? You say you have something over us, prove it,' she said defiantly.

He could've walked out and let them twist in the wind of uncertainty. Pennington would find out soon enough the length of Zaccheo's ruthless reach. But the thought of leaving Eva here when he departed was suddenly unthinkable. So far he'd allowed himself a brief glimpse of her body wrapped in that obscenely revealing red dress. But that one glimpse had been enough. Quite apart from the rage boiling his blood, the steady hammer of his pulse proved that he still wanted her with a fever that spiked higher with each passing second.

He would take what he'd foolishly and piously denied

himself two years ago. He would *take* and *use*, just as they'd done to him. Only when he'd achieved every goal he'd set himself would he feel avenged.

'You can't, can you?' Oscar taunted with a sly smile, bringing Zaccheo back to the room and the three aristocratic faces staring at him with varying degrees of disdain and fear.

He smiled, almost amused by the older man's growing confidence. 'Harry Fairfield is providing you with a bridging loan of fifteen million pounds because the combined running costs of the Pennington Hotels and The Spire have you stretched so thin the banks won't touch you. While you desperately drum up an adequate advertising budget to rent out all those overpriced but empty floors in The Spire, the interest owed to the Chinese consortium who own seventy-five per cent of the building is escalating. You have a meeting with them on Monday to request more time to pay the interest. In return for Fairfield's investment, you're handing him your daughter.'

Eva glared at him. 'So you've asked a few questions about Penningtons' business practices. That doesn't empower you to make demands of any of us.'

Zaccheo took a moment to admire her newfound grit. During their initial association, she'd been a little more timid, and in her father's shadow, but it looked as if the kitten had grown a few claws. He curbed the thrill at what was to come and answered.

'Yes, it does. Would you be interested to know the Chinese consortium sold their seventy-five per cent of The Spire to me three days ago? So by my calculation you're in excess of three months late on interest payments, correct?'

A rough sound, a cross between a cough and a wheeze, escaped Pennington's throat. There was no class or grace in the way he gaped at Zaccheo. He dropped back into his chair, his face a mask of hatred.

'I knew you were a worthless bet the moment I set eyes on you. I should've listened to my instincts.'

The red haze he'd been trying to hold back surged higher. 'No, what you wanted was a spineless scapegoat, a *capro espiatorio*, who would make you rich and fat and content and even give up his life without question!'

'Mr Giordano, surely we can discuss this like sensible business-minded individuals,' Sophie Pennington advanced, her hands outstretched in benign sensibility. Zaccheo looked from the hands she willed not to tremble to the veiled disdain in her eyes. Then he looked past her to Eva, who'd returned to her father's side, her face pale but her eyes shooting her displeasure at him.

Unexpectedly and very much unwelcome, a tiny hint of compassion tugged at him.

Basta!

He turned abruptly and reached for the door handle. 'You have until I ready my chopper for take-off to come to me, Eva.' He didn't need to expand on that edict. The *or else* hung in the air like the deadly poison he intended it to be.

He walked out and headed for the terrace, despite every nerve in his body straining to return to the room and forcibly drag Eva out.

True, he hadn't bargained for the visceral reaction to seeing her again. And yes, he hadn't quite been able to control his reaction to seeing another man's ring on her finger, that vulgar symbol of ownership hollowing out his stomach. The knowledge that she'd most likely shared that hapless drunk's bed, given the body he'd once believed to be his to another, ate through his blood like acid on metal. But he couldn't afford to let his emotions show.

Every strategic move in this game of deadly retribution hinged on him maintaining his control; on not letting them see how affected he was by all this.

He stepped onto the terrace and all conversation ceased. Curious faces gaped and one or two bolder guests even tried to intercept him. Zaccheo cut through the crowd, his gaze on the chopper a few dozen yards away.

She would come to him. As an outcome of his first salvo, nothing else would be acceptable.

His pulse thudded loud and insistent in his ears as he strolled down the steps towards the aircraft. The fireworks amid which he'd landed had long since gone quiet, but the scent of sulphur lingered in the air, reminding him of the volatility that lingered beneath his own skin, ready to erupt at the smallest trigger.

He wouldn't let it erupt. Not yet.

A murmur rose behind him, the fevered excitement that came with the anticipation of a spectacle. A *scandal*.

Zaccheo compelled himself to keep walking.

He ducked beneath the powerful rotors of his aircraft and reached for the door.

'Wait!'

He stopped. Turned.

Three hundred pairs of eyes watched with unabashed interest as Eva paused several feet from him.

Behind her, her father and sister stood on the steps, wearing similar expressions of dread. Zaccheo wanted them to stew for a while longer, but he found his attention drawn to the woman striding towards him. Her face reflected more defiance than dread. It also held pride and not a small measure of bruised disdain. Zaccheo vowed in that moment to make her regret that latter look, make her take back every single moment she'd thought herself above him.

Swallowing, he looked down at her body.

She held the flimsy wrap around her like armour. As if that would protect her from him. With one ruthless tug, he pulled it away. It fluttered to the ground, revealing her luscious, heart-stopping figure to his gaze. Unable to stem the frantic need crashing through him, he stepped forward and speared his fingers into the wild tumble of her hair.

Another step and she was in his arms.

Where she belonged.

* * *

The small pocket of air Eva had been able to retain in her lungs during her desperate flight after Zaccheo evaporated when he yanked her against him. Her body went from shivering in the crisp January air to furnace-hot within seconds. The fingers in her hair tightened, his other arm sliding around her waist.

Eva wanted to remain unaffected, slam her hands against his chest and remove herself from that dangerous wall of masculinity. But she couldn't move. So she fought with her words.

'You may think you've won, that you own me, but you don't,' she snapped. 'You never will!'

His eyes gleamed. 'Such fire. Such determination. You've changed, *cara mia*, I'll give you that. And yet here you are, barely one minute after I walked out of your father's study. Mere hours after you promised yourself to another man, here you are, Eva Pennington, ready to promise yourself to me. Ready to become whatever I want you to be.'

Her snigger made his eyes narrow, but she didn't care. 'Keep telling yourself that. I look forward to your shock when I prove you wrong.'

That deadly smile she'd first seen in her father's study reappeared, curling fear through her. It reeked with far too much gratification to kill that unshakeable sensation that she was standing on the edge of a precipice, and that, should she fall, there would be no saving her.

She realised the reason for the smile when he lifted her now bare fingers to his eye level. 'You've proved me right already.'

'Are you completely sure about that?' The question was a bold but empty taunt.

The lack of fuss with which Harry had taken back his ring a few minutes ago had been a relief.

She might not have an immediate solution to her family's

problems, but Eva was glad she no longer had to pretend she was half of a sham couple.

Zaccheo brought her fingers to his mouth and kissed her ring finger, stunning her back to reality. Flashes erupted as his actions were recorded, no doubt to be streamed across the fastest mediums available.

Recalling the conversation she'd just had with her father, she tried to pull away. 'This pound-of-flesh taking isn't going to last very long, so I suggest you enjoy it while it lasts. I intend to return to my life before midnight—'

Her words dried up when his face closed in a mask of icy fury, and his hands sealed her body even closer to his.

'Your first lesson is to stop speaking to me as if I'm the hired help. Refraining from doing so will put me in a much calmer frame of mind to deal with you than otherwise,' he said with unmistakeable warning.

Eva doubted that anyone had dared to speak to Zaccheo Giordano in the way he referred, but she wasn't about to debate that point with him with three hundred pairs of eyes watching. She was struggling enough to keep upright what with all the turbulent sensations firing through her at his touch. 'Why, Zaccheo, you sound as if you've a great many lessons you intend to dole out...' She tried to sound bored, but her voice emerged a little too breathless for her liking.

'Patience, *cara mia*. You'll be instructed as and when necessary.' His gaze dropped to her mouth and her breath lodged in her sternum. 'For now, I wish the talking to cease.'

He closed the final inch between them and slanted his mouth over hers. The world tilted and shook beneath her feet. Expertly sensual and demanding, he kissed her as if he owned her mouth, as if he owned her whole body. In all her adult years, Eva had never imagined the brush of a beard would infuse her with such spine-tingling sensations. Yet she shivered with fiery delight as Zaccheo's silky facial hair caressed the corners of her mouth.

She groaned at the forceful breach of his tongue. Her arms drifted over his taut biceps as she became lost in the potent magic of his kiss. At the first touch of his tongue against hers, she shuddered. He made a rough sound and his sharp inhalation vibrated against her. His fingers convulsed in her hair and his other hand drifted to her bottom, moulding her as he stepped back against the aircraft and widened his stance to bring her closer.

Eva wasn't sure how long she stood there, adrift in a swirl of sensation as he ravaged her mouth. It wasn't until her lungs screamed and her heart jackhammered against her ribs did she recall where she was...what was happening.

And still she wanted to continue.

So much so she almost moaned in protest when firm hands set her back and she found herself staring into molten eyes dark with savage hunger.

'I think we've given our audience enough to feed on. Get in.'

The calm words, spoken in direct counteraction to the frenzied look in his eyes, doused Eva with cold reality. That she'd made even more of a spectacle of herself hit home as wolf whistles ripped through the air.

'This was all for *show*?' she whispered numbly, shivering in the frigid air.

One sleek eyebrow lifted. 'Of course. Did you think I wanted to kiss you because I was so desperate for you I just couldn't help myself? You'll find that I have more self-restraint than that. Get in,' he repeated, holding the steel and glass door to the aircraft open.

Eva brushed cold hands over her arms, unable to move. She stared at him, perhaps hoping to find some humanity in the suddenly grim-faced block of stone in front of her. Or did she want a hint of the man who'd once framed her face in his hands and called her the most beautiful thing in his life?

Of course, that had been a lie. Everything about Zaccheo

had been a lie. Still she probed for some softness beneath that formidable exterior.

His implacable stare told her she was grasping at straws, as she had from the very beginning, when she'd woven stupid dreams around him.

A gust of icy wind blew across the grass, straight into her exposed back. A flash of red caught her eye and she blindly stumbled towards the terrace. She'd barely taken two steps when he seized her arm.

'What the hell do you think you're doing?' Zaccheo enquired frostily.

'I'm cold,' she replied through chattering teeth. 'My wrap...' She pointed to where the material had drifted.

'Leave it. This will keep you warm.' With one smooth move, he unbuttoned, shrugged off his tuxedo and draped it around her shoulders. The sudden infusion of warmth was overwhelming. Eva didn't want to drown in the distinctively heady scent of the man who was wrecking her world, didn't welcome her body's traitorous urge to burrow into the warm silk lining. And most of all, she didn't want to be beholden to him in any way, or accept any hint of kindness from him.

Zaccheo Giordano had demonstrated a ruthless thirst to annihilate those he deemed enemies in her father's study.

But she was no longer the naive and trusting girl she'd been a year and a half ago. Zaccheo's betrayal and her continued fraught relationship with her father and sister had hardened her heart. The pain was still there—would probably always be there—but so were the new fortifications against further hurt. She had no intention of laying her heart and soul bare to further damage from the people she'd once blithely believed would return the same love and devotion she offered freely.

She started to shrug off the jacket. 'No, thanks. I'd prefer not to be stamped as your possession.'

He stopped her by placing both hands on her arms.

Dark grey eyes pinned her to the spot, the sharper, icier

burst of wind whipping around them casting him in a deadlier, more dangerous light.

'You're already my possession. You became mine the moment you made the choice to follow me out here, Eva. You can kid yourself all you want, but this is your reality from here on in.'

CHAPTER FOUR

@Ladystclare OMG! Bragging rights=mine! Beheld fireworks w/in fireworks @P/Manor last night when LadyP eloped w/convict lover! #amazeballs

@Aristokitten Bet it was all a publicity stunt, but boy that kiss? Sign me up! #Ineedlatinlovelikethat

@Countrypile That wasn't love. That was an obscene and shameless money-grabbing gambit at its worst! #Donotencouragerancidbehaviour

EVA FLINCHED, her stomach churning at each new message that flooded her social-media stream.

The hours had passed in a haze after Zaccheo flew them from Pennington Manor. In solid command of the helicopter, he'd soared over the City of London and landed on the vertiginous rooftop of The Spire.

The stunning split-level penthouse's interior had barely registered in the early hours when Zaccheo's enigmatic aide, Romeo, had directed the butler to show her to her room.

Zaccheo had stalked away without a word, leaving her in the middle of his marble-tiled hallway, clutching his jacket.

Sleep had been non-existent in the bleak hours that had followed. At five a.m., she'd given up and taken a quick shower before putting on that skin-baring dress again.

Wishing she'd asked for a blanket to cover the acres of flesh on display, she cringed as another salacious offering popped into her inbox displayed on Zaccheo's tablet.

Like a spectator frozen on the fringes of an unfolding train wreck, she read the latest post.

@Uberwoman Hey ConvictLover, that flighty poor little rich girl is wasted on you. Real women exist. Let ME rock your world!

Eva curled her fist, refusing to entertain the image of any woman rocking Zaccheo's world. She didn't care one way or the other. If she had a choice, she would be ten thousand miles away from this place.

'If you're thinking of responding to any of that, consider yourself warned against doing so.'

She jumped at the deep voice a whisper from her ear. She'd thought she would be alone in the living room for at least another couple of hours before dealing with Zaccheo. Now she wished she'd stayed in her room.

She stood and faced him, the long black suede sofa between them no barrier to Zaccheo's towering presence.

'I've no intention of responding. And you really shouldn't sneak up on people like that,' she tagged on when the leisurely drift of those incisive eyes over her body made her feel like a specimen under a microscope.

'I don't sneak. Had you been less self-absorbed in your notoriety, you would've heard me enter the room.'

Anger welled up. 'You accuse *me* of being notorious? All this is happening because *you* insisted on gatecrashing a private event and turning it into a public spectacle.'

'And, of course, you were so eager to find out whether you're trending that you woke up at dawn to follow the news.'

She wanted to ask how he'd known what time she'd left her room, but Eva suspected she wouldn't like the answer. 'You assume I slept at all when sleep was the last thing on my mind, having been blackmailed into coming here. And, FYI, I don't read the gutter press. Not unless I want the worst kind of indigestion.'

He rounded the sofa and stopped within arm's length. She stood her ground, but she couldn't help herself ogling the breathtaking body filling her vision.

It was barely six o'clock and yet he looked as vitally masculine as if he'd been up and ready for hours. A film of sweat covered the hair-dusted arms beneath the pulled-up sleeves, and his damp white T-shirt moulded his chiselled torso. His black drawstring sweatpants did nothing to hide thick thighs and Eva struggled to avert her gaze from the virile outline of his manhood against the soft material. Dragging her gaze up, she stared in fascination at the hands and fingers wrapped in stained boxing gauze.

'Do you intend to spend the rest of the morning ogling me, Eva?' he asked mockingly.

She looked into his eyes and that potent, electric tug yanked hard at her. Reminding herself that she was immune from whatever spell he'd once cast on her, she raised her chin.

'I intend to attempt a reasonable conversation with you in the cold light of day regarding last night's events.'

'That suggests you believe our previous interactions have been unreasonable?'

'I did a quick search online. You were released yesterday morning. It stands to reason that you're still a little affected by your incarceration—'

His harsh, embittered laugh bounced like bullets around the room. Eva folded her arms, refusing to cower at the sound.

He stepped towards her, the tension in his body barely leashed. 'You think I'm a *"little affected"* by my incarceration? Tell me, *bella*,' he invited softly, 'do you know what it feels like to be locked in a six-by-ten, damp and rancid cage for over a year?'

A brief wave of torment overcame his features, and a different tug, one of sympathy, pulled at her. Then she reminded herself just who she was dealing with. 'Of course not. I just don't want you to do anything that you'll regret.'

'Your touching concern for my welfare is duly noted. But I suggest you save it for yourself. Last night was merely you and your family being herded into the eye of the storm. The real devastation is just getting started.'

As nightmarish promises went, Zaccheo's chilled her to the bone. Before she could reply, several pings blared from the tablet. She glanced down and saw more lurid posts about what *real women* wanted to do to Zaccheo.

She shut the tablet and straightened to find him slowly unwinding the gauze from his right hand, his gaze pinned on her. Silence stretched as he freed both hands and tossed the balled cloth onto the glass-topped coffee table.

'So, do I get any sort of itinerary for this impending apocalypse?' she asked when it became clear he was content to let the silence linger.

One corner of his mouth lifted. 'We'll have breakfast in half an hour. After that, we'll see whether your father has done what I demanded of him. If he has, we'll take it from there.'

Recalling her father's overly belligerent denial once Zaccheo had left the study last night, anxiety skewered her. 'And if he hasn't?'

'Then his annihilation will come sooner rather than later.'

Half an hour later, Eva struggled to swallow a mouthful of buttered toast and quickly chased it down with a sip of tea before she choked.

A few minutes ago, a brooding Romeo had entered with the butler who'd delivered a stack of broadsheets. The other man had conversed in Italian with a freshly showered and even more visually devastating Zaccheo.

Zaccheo's smile after the short exchange had incited her first panic-induced emotion. He'd said nothing after Romeo left. Instead he'd devoured a hearty plate of scrambled eggs, grilled mushrooms and smoked pancetta served on Italian bread with unsettling gusto.

But as the silence spread thick and cloying across the room she finally set her cup down and glanced to where he stood now at the end of the cherrywood dining table, his hands braced on his hips, an inscrutable expression on his face.

Again, Eva was struck by the change in him. Even now he was dressed more formally in dark grey trousers and a navy shirt with the sleeves rolled up, her eyes were drawn to the gladiator-like ruggedness of his physique.

'Eva.' Her name was a deep command. One she desperately wanted to ignore. It held a quiet triumph she didn't want to acknowledge. The implications were more than she could stomach. She wasn't one for burying her head in the sand, but if her father had done what Zaccheo had demanded, then—

'Eva,' he repeated. Sharper. Controlled but demanding.

Heart hammering, she glanced at him. 'What?'

He stared back without blinking, his body deathly still. 'Come here.'

Refusing to show how rattled she was, she stood, teetered on the heels she'd had no choice but to wear again, and strode towards him.

He tracked her with chilling precision, his eyes dropping to her hips for a charged second before he looked back up. Eva hated her body for reacting to that look, even as her breasts tingled and a blaze lit between her thighs.

Silently she cursed herself. She had no business reacting to that look, or to any man on any plane of emotion whatsoever. She had proof that path only ended in eviscerating heartache.

She stopped a few feet from him, made sure to place a dining chair between them. But the solid wood couldn't stop her senses from reacting to his scent, or her nipples from furling into tight, needy buds when her gaze fell on the golden gleam of his throat revealed by the gap in his shirt. Quickly crossing her arms, she looked down at the newspapers.

That they'd made headlines was unmistakeable. Bold black letters and exclamation marks proclaimed Zaccheo's antics. And as for *that* picture of them locked together...

'I can't believe you landed a helicopter in the middle of a fireworks display,' she threw out, simply because it was easier than acknowledging the other words written on the page binding her to Zaccheo, insinuating they were something they would never be.

He looked from her face to the front-page picture showing him landing his helicopter during a particularly violent explosion. 'Were you concerned for me?' he mocked.

'Of course not. You obviously don't care about your own safety so why should I?'

A simmering silence followed, then he stalked closer. 'I hope you intend to act a little more concerned towards my well-being once we're married.'

Any intention of avoiding looking at him fled her mind. '*Married?* Don't you think you've taken this far enough?' she snapped.

'Excuse me?'

'You wanted to humiliate my father. Congratulations, you've made headlines in every single newspaper. Don't you think it's time to drop this?'

His eyes turned into pools of ice. 'You think this is some sort of game?' he enquired silkily.

'What else can it be? If you really had the evidence you claim to have, why haven't you handed it over to the police?'

'You believe I'm bluffing?' His voice was a sharp blade slicing through the air.

'I believe you feel aggrieved.'

'Really? And what else did you *believe*?'

Eva refused to quail beneath the look that threatened to cut her into pieces. 'It's clear you want to make some sort of statement about how you were treated by my father. You've done that now. Let it go.'

'So your father did all this—' he indicated the papers '—just to stop me throwing a childish tantrum? And what about you? Did you throw yourself at my feet to buy your family time to see how long my bluff would last?'

She flung her arms out in exasperation. 'Come on, Zaccheo—'

They both stilled at her use of his name. Eva had no time to recover from the unwitting slip. Merciless fingers speared into her hair, much as they had last night, holding her captive as his thumb tilted her chin.

'How far are you willing to go to get me to be *reasonable*? Or perhaps I should guess? After all, just last night you'd dropped to an all-time low of whoring yourself to a drunken boy in order to save your family.' The thick condemnation feathered across her skin.

Rage flared in her belly, gave her the strength to remain upright. He stood close. Far too close. She stepped back, but only managed to wedge herself between the table and Zaccheo's towering body. 'As opposed to what? Whoring myself to a middle-aged criminal?'

He leaned down, crowding her further against the polished wood. 'You know exactly how old I am. In fact, I recall precisely where we both were when the clock struck midnight on my thirtieth birthday. Or perhaps you need me to refresh your memory?' His smooth, faintly accented voice trailed amused contempt.

'Don't bother—'

'I'll do it anyway, it's no hardship,' he offered, as if her sharp denial hadn't been uttered. 'We were newly engaged, and you were on your knees in front of my penthouse window, uncaring that anyone with a pair of decent binoculars would see us. All you cared about was getting your busy, greedy little hands on my belt, eager to rid me of my trousers so you could wish me a happy birthday in a way most men fantasise about.'

Her skin flushed with a wave of heat so strong, she feared spontaneous combustion. 'That wasn't my idea.'

One brow quirked. 'Was it not?'

'No, you dared me to do it.'

His mouth twitched. 'Are you saying I forced you?'

Those clever fingers were drifting along her scalp, lazily caressing, lulling her into showing her vulnerability.

Eva sucked in a deep breath. 'I'm saying I don't want to talk about the past. I prefer to stick to the present.'

She didn't want to remember how gullible she'd been back then, how stupidly eager to please, how excited she'd been that this god of a man, who could have any woman he wanted with a lazy crook of his finger, had pursued *her*, chosen *her*.

Even after learning the hard way that men in positions of power would do anything to stay in that power, that her two previous relationships had only been a means to an end for the men involved, she'd still allowed herself to believe Zaccheo wanted her for herself. Finding out that he was no better, that he only wanted her to secure a *business deal*, had delivered a blow she'd spent the better part of a year burying in a deep hole.

At first his demands had been subtle: a business dinner here, a charity event there—occasions she'd been proud and honoured to accompany him on. Until that fateful night when she'd overheard a handful of words that had had the power to sting like nothing else.

She's the means to an end. Nothing more...

The conversation that had followed remained seared into her brain. Zaccheo, impatiently shutting her down, then brazenly admitting he'd said those words. That he'd used her.

Most especially, she recalled the savage pain in knowing she had got him so wrong, had almost given herself to a man who held such careless regard for her, and only cared about her pedigree.

And yet his shock when she'd returned his ring had made her wonder whether she'd done the right thing.

His arrest days later for criminal negligence had confirmed what sort of man she'd foolishly woven her dreams around.

She met his gaze now. 'You got what you wanted—your name next to mine on the front page. The whole world knows I left with you last night, that I'm no longer engaged to Harry.'

His hand slipped to her nape, worked over tense muscles. 'And how did Fairfield take being so unceremoniously dumped?' he asked.

'Harry cares about me, so he was a complete gentleman about it. Shame I can't say the same about you.'

Dark grey eyes gleamed dangerously. 'You mean he wasn't torn up at the thought of never having access to this body again?' he mocked.

She lifted a brow. 'Never say never.'

Tension coiled his body. 'If you think I'll tolerate any further interaction between you and Fairfield, you're severely mistaken,' he warned with a dark rumble.

'Why, Zaccheo, you sound almost jealous.'

Heat scoured his cheekbones and a tiny part of her quailed at her daring. 'You'd be wise to stop testing me, *dolcezza*.'

'If you want this to stop, tell me why you're doing this.'

'I'm only going to say it one more time, so let it sink in. I don't intend to stop until your father's reputation is in the gutter and everything he took from me is returned, plus interest.'

'Can I see the proof of what you accuse my father of?'

'Would you believe even if you saw it? Or will you cling to the belief that I'm the big, bad ogre who's just throwing his weight about?' he taunted.

Eva looked down at the papers on the table, every last one containing everything Zaccheo had demanded. Would her father have done it if Zaccheo's threats were empty?

'Last night, when you said you and I…' She stopped, unable to process the reality.

'Would be married in two weeks? *Sì*, I meant that, too. And to get that ball rolling, we're going shopping for an engagement ring in exactly ten minutes, after which we have a full day ahead, so if you require further sustenance I suggest you finish your breakfast.'

He dropped his fingers from her nape and stepped back. With a last look filled with steely determination, he picked up the closest paper and walked out of the room.

CHAPTER FIVE

THEIR FIRST STOP was an exclusive coat boutique in Bond Street. Zaccheo told himself it was because he didn't want to waste time. The truth mocked him in the form of needing to cover Eva Pennington's body before he lost any more brain cells to the lust blazing through his bloodstream.

In the dark cover of her family terrace and the subsequent helicopter journey home, he'd found relief from the blatant temptation of her body.

In the clear light of day, the red dress seemed to cling tighter, caress her body so much more intimately that he'd had to fight the urge to lunge for her each time she took a breath.

He watched her now, seated across from him in his limo as they drove the short twenty-minute distance to Threadneedle Street where his bankers had flown in the diamond collection he'd requested from Switzerland.

Her fingers plucked at the lapel of the new white cashmere coat, then dropped to cinch the belt tighter at her tiny waist.

'You didn't need to buy me a coat,' she grumbled. 'I have a perfectly good one back at my flat.'

He reined in his fascination with her fingers. 'Your flat is on the other side of town. I have more important things to do than waste an hour and a half sitting in traffic.'

Her plump lips pursed. 'Of course, extracting your pound of flesh is an all-consuming business, isn't it?'

'I don't intend to stop at a mere pound, Eva. I intend to take the whole body.'

One eyebrow spiked. 'You seem so confident I'm going to hand myself to you on a silver platter. Isn't that a tad foolish?'

There was that tone again, the one that said she didn't believe him.

'I guess we'll find out one way or the other when the sordid details are laid out for you on Monday. All you need to concern yourself about today is picking out an engagement ring that makes the right statement.'

Her striking green eyes clashed with his and that lightning bolt struck again. 'And what statement would that be?' she challenged.

He let loose a chilling half-smile that made his enemies quake. 'Why, that you belong to me, of course.'

'I told you, I've no intention of being your possession. A ring won't change that.'

'How glibly you lie to yourself.'

She gasped and he was once again drawn to her mouth. A mouth whose sweet taste he recalled vividly, much to his annoyance. 'Excuse me?'

'We both know you'll be exactly who and what I want you to be when I demand it. Your family has too much at stake for you to risk doing otherwise.'

'Don't mistake my inclination to go along with this farce to be anything but my need to get to the bottom of why you're doing this. It's what families *do* for each other. Of course, since you don't even speak about yours, I assume you don't know what I'm talking about.'

Zaccheo called himself ten kinds of fool for letting the taunt bite deep. He'd lost respect for his father long before he'd died in shame and humiliation. And watching his mother whore herself for prestige had left a bitter taste in his mouth. As families went, he'd been dealt a bad hand, but he'd learned long ago that to wish for anything you couldn't create with your own hard-working hands was utter folly. He'd stopped making wishes by the time he hit puberty. Recalling the very last wish he'd prayed night and day for as a child, he clenched his fists. Even then he'd known fate would laugh at his wish for a brother or sister. He'd known that wish, despite his mother being pregnant, would not come true. He'd *known*.

He'd programmed himself not to care after that harrowing time in his life.

So why the hell did it grate so much for him to be reminded that he was the last Giordano?

'I don't talk about my family because I have none. But that's a situation I intend to rectify soon.'

She glanced at him warily. 'What's that supposed to mean?'

'It means I had a lot of time in prison to re-examine my life, thanks to your family.' He heard the naked emotion in his voice and hardened his tone. 'I intend to make some changes.'

'What sort of changes?'

'The type that means you'll no longer have to whore out your integrity for the sake of the great Pennington legacy. You should thank me, since you seem to be the one doing most of the heavy lifting for your family.'

Zaccheo watched her face pale.

'I'm not a whore!'

He lunged forward before he could stop himself. 'Then what the hell were you doing dressed like a tart, agreeing to marry a drunken playboy, if not for cold, hard cash for your family?' The reminder of what she wore beneath the coat blazed across his mind. His temperature hiked, along with the increased throbbing in his groin.

'I didn't do it for money!' She flushed, and bit down on her lower lip again. 'Okay, yes, that was part of the reason, but I also did it because—'

'Please spare me any declarations of *true love*.' He wasn't sure why he abhorred the idea of her mentioning the word love. Or why the idea of her mentioning Fairfield's name filled him with rage.

Zaccheo knew about her friendship with Fairfield. And while he knew their engagement had been a farce, he hadn't missed the camaraderie between them, or the pathetic infatuation in the other man's eyes.

Sì, he was jealous—Eva would be his and no one else's. But he also pitied Fairfield.

Because love, in all forms, was a false emotion. Nothing but a manipulative tool. Mothers declared their love for their children, then happily abandoned them the moment they ceased to be a convenient accessory. Fathers professed to have their children's interest at heart because of *love*, but when it came right down to it they put themselves above all else. And sometimes even forgot that their children *existed*.

As for Eva Pennington, she'd shown how faithless she was when she'd dropped him and distanced herself mere days before his arrest.

'I wasn't going to say that. Trust me, I've learned not to toss the word *love* about freely—'

'Did you know?' he sliced at her before he could stop himself.

Fine brows knitted together. 'Did I know what?'

'Did you know of your father's plans?' The question had been eating at him far more than he wanted to admit.

'His plans to do what?' she asked innocently. And yet he could see the caginess on her face. As if she didn't want him to probe deeper.

Acrid disappointment bit through him. He was a fool for thinking, perhaps *wishing*, despite all the signs saying otherwise, that she'd been oblivious to Oscar Pennington's plans to make him the ultimate scapegoat.

'We're here, sir.' His driver's voice came through the intercom.

Zaccheo watched her dive for the door. He would've laughed at her eagerness to get away from the conversation that brought back too many volatile memories, had he not felt disconcerting relief that his question had gone unanswered.

He'd been a fool to pursue it in the first place. He didn't need more lies. He had cold, hard facts proving the Penningtons' guilt. Dwelling on the whys and wherefores of Eva's actions was a fool's errand.

He stepped out into the winter sunshine and nodded at the bank director.

'Mr Giordano, welcome.' The older man's expression vacillated between obsequiousness and condescension.

'You received my further instructions?' Zaccheo took Eva's arm, ignoring her slight stiffening as he walked her through the doors of the bank.

'Yes, sir. We've adhered to your wishes.' Again he caught the man's assessing gaze.

'I'm pleased to hear it. Otherwise I'm sure there would be other banks who would welcome GWI's business.'

The banker paled. 'That won't be necessary, Mr Giordano. If you'll come with me, the jewellers have everything laid out for you.'

It should've given him great satisfaction that he'd breached the hallowed walls of the centuries-old establishment, that he'd finally succeeded where his own father had tried so hard and failed, giving his life in pursuit of recognition.

But all Zaccheo could hear, could *feel*, was Eva's presence, a reminder of why his satisfaction felt hollow. She was proof that, despite all he'd achieved, he was still regarded as the lowest of the low. A nobody. An expendable patsy who would take any treatment his betters doled out without protest.

We shall see.

They walked down several hallways. After a few minutes, Eva cleared her throat. 'What instructions did you give him?' she asked.

He stared down at her. 'I told him to remove all pink diamonds from the collection and instruct my jewellers that I do not wish to deal with diamonds of that colour in the future.'

'Really? I thought pink diamonds were all the rage these days?'

He shrugged. 'Not for me. Let's call it a personal preference.'

The penny dropped and she tried to pull away from his hold. He refused to let go. 'Are you really that petty?' she asked as they approached a heavy set of oak doors. 'Just because Harry gave me a pink diamond...' Her eyes widened when he caught her shoulders and pinned her against the wall. When she started to struggle, he stepped closer, caging her in with his body.

'You'll refrain from mentioning his name in my presence ever again. Is that understood?' Zaccheo felt his control slipping as her scent tangled with his senses and her curvy figure moved against him.

'Let me go and you'll need never hear his name again,' she snapped back.

'Not going to happen.' He released her. 'After you.'

She huffed a breath and entered the room. He followed and crossed to the window, struggling to get himself under control as the director walked in with three assistants bearing large velvet trays. They set them on the polished conference table and stepped back.

'We'll give you some privacy,' the director said before exiting with his minions.

Zaccheo walked to the first tray and pulled away the protective cloth. He stared at the display of diamonds in all cuts and sizes, wondering for a moment how his father would've reacted to this display of obscene wealth. Paolo Giordano had never managed to achieve even a fraction of his goals despite sacrificing everything, including the people he should've held dear. Would he have been proud, or would he have bowed and scraped as the bank director had a few moments ago, eager to be deemed worthy of merely touching them?

'Perhaps we should get on with choosing a stone. Or are we going to stare at them all day?' Eva asked.

Eva watched his face harden and bit her tongue. She wasn't sure why she couldn't stop goading him. Did part of her want to get under his skin as he so effortlessly got under hers?

Annoyed with herself for letting the whole absurd situation get to her, she stepped forward and stared down at the dazzling array of gems. Large. Sparkling. Flawless. Each worth more than she would earn in half her lifetime.

None of them appealed to her.

She didn't want to pick out another cold stone to replace the one she'd handed back to Harry before running after Zaccheo last night.

She didn't want to be trapped into yet another consequence of being a Pennington. She wanted to be free of the guilty resentment lurking in her heart at the thought that nothing she did would ever be enough for her family. Or the sadness that came with the insurmountable knowledge that her sister would continue to block any attempt to forge a relationship with her father.

She especially didn't want to be trapped in any way with Zaccheo Giordano. That display of his displeasure a few moments ago had reminded her she wanted nothing to do with him. And it was not about his temper but what she'd felt when her body had been thrust against his. She'd wanted to be held there...indefinitely.

Touching him.

Soothing his angry brow and those brief flashes of pain she saw in his eyes when he thought she wasn't looking.

God, even a part of her wanted to coax out that heart-stopping smile she'd glimpsed so very rarely when he was pursuing her!

What was wrong with her?

'Is that the one you wish for?'

She jumped and stared down at the stone that had somehow found its way into her palm. She blinked in shock.

The diamond was the largest on the tray and twice as obscene as the one that had graced her finger last night. No wonder Zaccheo sounded so disparaging.

'No!' She hastily dropped it back into its slot. 'I'd never wear anything so gratuitous.'

His coldly mocking gaze made her cringe. 'Really?'

Irritation skated over her skin. 'For your information, I didn't choose that ring.'

'But you accepted it in the spirit it was given—as the cost of buying your body in exchange for shares in Penningtons?'

Icy rage replaced her irritation. 'Your continuous insults make me wonder why you want to put up with my presence. Surely revenge can't be as sweet as you wish it if the object of your punishment enrages you this much?'

'Perhaps I enjoy tormenting you.'

'So I'm to be your punching bag for the foreseeable future?'

'Is this your way of trying to find out how long your sentence is to be?'

'A sentence implies I've done something wrong. I *know* I'm innocent in whatever you believe I've done.'

His smile could've turned a volcano into a polar ice cap. 'I've found that proclamations of innocence don't count for a thing, not when the right palm is greased.'

She inhaled at the fury and bitterness behind his words. 'Zaccheo...'

Whatever feeble reply she'd wanted to make died when his eyes hardened.

'Choose the diamond you prefer or I'll choose it for you.'

Eva turned blindly towards the table and pointed to the smallest stone. 'That one.'

'No.'

She gritted her teeth. 'Why not?'

'Because it's pink.'

'No, it's not...' She leaned closer, caught the faint pink glow, and frowned. 'Oh. I thought—'

A mirthless smile touched his lips. 'So did I. Perhaps I'll change bankers after all.' He lifted the cover of the second tray and Eva stared dispassionately at the endless rows of sparkling jewels. None of them spoke to her. Her heart hammered as it finally dawned on her why.

'Is there any reason why you want to buy me a new ring?'

He frowned. *'Scusi?'*

'When you proposed the first time, you gave me a different ring. I'm wondering why you're buying me a different one. Did you lose it?' Despite the circumstances surrounding his proposal and her subsequent rejection of him, she'd loved that simple but exquisite diamond and sapphire ring.

'No, I didn't lose it.' His tone was clipped to the point of brusqueness.

'Then why?'

'Because I do not wish you to have it.'

Her heart did an achy little dance as she waited for further elaboration. When she realised none would be forthcoming, she pulled her gaze from his merciless regard and back to the display.

He didn't want her to have it. Why? Because the ring held special meaning? Or because she was no longer worthy of it?

Berating herself for feeling hurt, she plucked a stone from the middle of the tray. According to the size chart it sat in mid-range, a flawless two carat, square-cut that felt light in her palm. 'This one.' She turned and found him staring at her, his gaze intense yet inscrutable.

Wordlessly, he held out his hand.

Her fingers brushed his palm as she dropped the stone and she bit back a gasp as that infernal electricity zinged up her arm.

His eyes held hers for a long moment before he turned and headed for the door. The next few minutes passed in a blur as Zaccheo issued clipped instructions about mountings, scrolls and settings to the jeweller.

Before she could catch her breath, Eva was back outside. Flashes went off as a group of paparazzi lunged towards them. Zaccheo handed her into the car before joining her. With a curt instruction to the driver, the car lurched into traffic.

'If I've achieved my publicity quota for the day, I'd like to be dropped at my flat, please.'

Zaccheo focused those incisive eyes on her. 'Why would I do that?'

'Aren't we done? I'd catch a bus home, but I left my handbag and phone at Pennington Manor—'

'Your belongings have been brought to my penthouse,' he replied.

'Okay, thanks. As soon as I collect them, I'll be out of your hair.' She needed to get out of this dress, shower and practise the six songs she would be performing at the club tonight. Saturday nights were the busiest of the week, and she couldn't be late. The music producer who'd been frequenting the club for the last few weeks might make another appearance tonight.

A little bubble of excitement built and she squashed it down as that half-smile that chilled her to the bone appeared on Zaccheo's face.

'You misunderstand. When I mentioned your belongings, I didn't mean your handbag and your phone. I meant everything you own in your bedsit has been removed. While we were picking your engagement ring, your belongings were relocated. Your rent has been paid off with interest and your landlady is busy renting the property to someone else.'

'What on earth are you talking about?' she finally asked when she'd picked up her jaw from the floor and sifted through his words. 'Of course I still live there. Mrs Hammond wouldn't just let you into my flat. And she certainly wouldn't arbitrarily end my lease without speaking to me first.'

Zaccheo just stared back at her.

'How dare you? Did you threaten her?'

'No, Eva. I used a much more effective tool.'

Her mouth twisted. 'You mean you threw so much money at her she buckled under your wishes?'

He shrugged rugged, broad shoulders. 'You of all people

should know how money sways even the most veracious hearts. Mrs Hammond was thrilled at the prospect of receiving her new hip replacement next week instead of at the end of the year. But it also helps that she's a hopeless romantic. The picture of us in the paper swayed any lingering doubts she had.'

Eva's breath shuddered out. Her landlady had lamented the long waiting list over shared cups of tea and Eva had offered a sympathetic ear. While she was happy that Mrs Hammond would receive her treatment earlier than anticipated and finally be out of pain, a huge part of her couldn't see beyond the fact that Zaccheo had ripped her safe harbour away without so much as a by your leave.

'You had absolutely no right to do that,' she blazed at him.

'Did I not?' he asked laconically.

'No, you didn't. This is nothing but a crude demonstration of your power. Well, guess what, I'm unimpressed. Go ahead and do your worst! Whatever crimes you think we've committed, maybe going to prison is a better option than this...this kidnapping!'

'Believe me, prison isn't an option you want to joke with.'

His lacerated tone made her heart lurch. She looked into his face and saw the agony. Her eyes widened, stunned that he was letting her witness that naked emotion.

'You think you know what it feels like to be robbed of your freedom for months on end? Pray you never get to find out, Eva. Because you may not survive it.'

'Zaccheo... I...' She stuttered to a halt, unsure of what to make of that raw statement.

His hand slashed through the air and his mask slid back into place. 'I wanted you relocated as swiftly as possible with a minimum of fuss,' he said.

A new wave of apprehension washed over her. 'Why? What's the rush?'

'I thought that would be obvious, Eva. I have deep-seated trust issues.'

Sadly, she'd reaped the rewards of betrayed trust, but the fierce loyalty to her family that continued to burn within her made her challenge him. 'How is that my family's fault?'

His nostrils flared. 'I trusted your father. He repaid that trust with a betrayal that sent me to prison! And you were right there next to him.'

Again she heard the ragged anguish in his voice. A hysterical part of her mind wondered whether this was the equivalent of a captor revealing his face to his prisoner. Was she doomed now that she'd caught a glimpse of what Zaccheo's imprisonment had done to him?

'So you keeping me against my will is meant to be part of *my* punishment?'

He smiled. 'You don't have to stay. You have many options available to you. You can call the police, tell them I'm holding you against your will, although that would be hard to prove since three hundred people saw you chase after me last night. Or you can insist I return your things and reinstate your lease. If you choose to walk away, no one will lift a finger to stop you.'

'But that's not quite true, is it? What real choice do I have when you're holding a threat over my father's head?'

'Leave him to flounder on his own if you truly believe you're guilt-free in all of this. You want to make a run for it? Here's your chance.'

His pointed gaze went to the door and Eva realised they'd completed the short journey from the bank to the iconic building that had brought Zaccheo into her life and turned it upside down.

She glanced up at the building *Architectural Digest* had called 'innovative beyond its years' and 'a heartbreakingly beautiful masterpiece'.

Where most modern buildings boasted elaborate glass edifices, The Spire was a study in polished, tensile steel. Thin sheets of steel had been twisted and manipulated around the towering spear-like structure, making the tallest building in

London a testament to its architect's skill and innovation. Its crowning glory was its diamond-shaped, vertiginous platform, within which was housed a Michelin-starred restaurant surrounded by a clear twenty-foot waterfall.

One floor beneath the restaurant was Zaccheo's penthouse. Her new home. Her prison.

The sound of him exiting the car drew her attention. When he held out his hand to her, she hesitated, unable to accept that this was her fate.

A muscle ticced in his jaw as he waited.

'You'd love that, wouldn't you? Me helping you bury my father?'

'He's going down either way. It's up to you whether he gets back up or not.'

Eva wanted to call his bluff. To shut the door and return everything to the way it was this time yesterday.

The memory of her father in that hospital bed, strung up to a beeping machine, stopped her. She'd already lost one parent. No matter how difficult things were between them, she couldn't bear to lose another. She would certainly have no hope of saving her relationship with her sister if she walked away.

Because one thing was certain. Zaccheo meant to have his way.

With or without her co-operation.

CHAPTER SIX

EVA BLEW HER fringe out of her eyes and glanced around her. The guest suite, a different one from the one she'd slept in last night, was almost three times the size of her former bedsit. And every surface was covered with designer gowns and accessories. Countless bottles of exclusive perfumes and luxury grooming products were spread on the dresser, and a team of six stylists each held an item of clothing, ready to pounce on her the moment she took off the dress she was currently trying on.

She tried hard to see the bright side of finally being out of the red dress. Unfortunately, any hint of brightness had vanished the moment she'd stepped out of the car and re-entered Zaccheo's penthouse.

'How many more before we're done?' She tried to keep her voice even, but she knew she'd missed amiability by a mile when two assistants exchanged wary glances.

'We've done your home and evening-wear package. We just need to do your vacation package and we'll be done with wardrobe. Then we can move on to hair and make-up,' Vivian, the chief stylist, said with a megawatt smile.

Eva tried not to groan. She needed to be done so she could find her phone and call her father. There was no way she was twiddling her thumbs until Monday to get a proper answer.

Being made into Zaccheo's revenge punchbag...his *married* revenge punchbag...wasn't a role she intended to be placed in. When she'd thought there was a glimmer of doubt as to Zaccheo's threat being real, she'd gone along with this farce. But with each hour that passed with silence from her father, Eva was forced to believe Zaccheo's threats weren't empty.

Would he go to such lengths to have her choose precious gems, remove her from her flat, and hire a team of stylists to turn her into the sort of woman he preferred to date, if this was just some sort of twisted game?

Her hand clenched as her thoughts took a different path. What exactly was Zaccheo trying to turn her into? Obviously he wasn't just satisfied with attaining her pedigree for whatever his nefarious purposes were. He wanted her to look like a well-dressed mannequin while he was at it.

'Careful with that, Mrs Giordano. That lace is delicate.'

She dropped the dress, her heart hammering far too fast for her liking. 'Don't call me that. I'm not Mrs Giordano—'

'Not yet, at least, right, *bellissima*?'

Eva heard the collective breaths of the women in the room catch. She turned as Zaccheo strode in. His eyes were fixed on her, flashing a warning that made her nape tingle. Before she could respond, he lifted her hands to kiss her knuckles, one after the other. Her breathing altered precariously as the silky hairs of his beard and the warm caress of his mouth threw her thoughts into chaos.

'It's only a few short days until we're husband and wife, *sì*?' he murmured intimately, but loud enough so every ear in the room caught the unmistakeable statement of possession.

She struggled to think, to *speak*, as sharp grey eyes locked with hers.

'No...I mean, yes...but let's not tempt fate. Who knows what could happen in a *few short days*?' She fully intended to have placed this nightmare far behind her.

His thumbs caressed the backs of her hands in false intimacy. 'I've moved mountains to make you mine, *il mio prezioso*. Nothing will stand in my way.' His accent was slightly more pronounced, his tone deep and captivating.

Envious sighs echoed around the room, but Eva shivered at the icy intent behind his words. She snatched her hands from his. Or she attempted to.

'In that case, I think you ought to stop distracting me so I can get on with making myself beautiful for you.' She hoped her smile looked as brittle as it felt. That her intention to end this was clear for him to see. 'Or was there something in particular you wanted?'

His eyes held hers for another electrifying second before he released her. 'I came to inform you that your belongings have been unpacked.' He surveyed the room, his gaze taking in the organised chaos. 'And to enquire whether you wish to have lunch with me or whether you want lunch brought to you so you can push through?' He turned back to her, his gaze mockingly stating that he knew her choice before she responded.

She lifted her chin. 'Seeing as this makeover was a complete *surprise* that I'd have to *make* time for, we'll take lunch in here, please.'

He ignored her censorious tone and nodded. 'Your wish is my command, *dolcezza*. But I insist you be done by dinnertime. I detest eating alone.'

She bit her tongue against a sharp retort. The cheek of him, making demands on her time when *he'd* been the one to call in the stylists in the first place! She satisfied herself with glaring at his back as he walked out, his tall, imposing figure owning every square inch of space he prowled.

The women left three excruciating hours later. The weak sun was setting in grey skies by the time Eva dragged her weary body across the vast hallway towards the suite she'd occupied last night. Her newly washed and styled hair bounced in silky waves down her back and her face tingled pleasantly from the facial she'd received before the barely there makeup had been applied.

The cashmere-soft, scooped-neck grey dress caressed her hips and thighs as she approached her door. She'd worn it only because Vivian had insisted. Eva hadn't had the heart to tell her she intended to leave every single item untouched. But Eva couldn't deny that the off-shoulder, floor-length dress felt elegant and wonderful and exactly what she'd have chosen to wear for dinner. Even if it was a dinner she wasn't looking forward to.

Her new four-inch heels clicked on the marble floor as she opened the double doors and stopped. Her hands flew to cover her mouth as she surveyed the room. Surprise was followed a few seconds later by a tingle of awareness that told her she was no longer alone.

Even then, she couldn't look away from the sight before her.

'Is something wrong?' Zaccheo's enquiry made her finally turn.

He was leaning against the door frame, his hands tucked into the pockets of his black tailored trousers. The white V-necked sweater caressed his muscular arms and shoulders and made his grey eyes appear lighter, almost eerily silver. His slightly damp hair gleamed a polished black against his shoulders and his beard lent him a rakish look that was absolutely riveting.

His gaze caught and held hers for several seconds before conducting a detailed appraisal over her face, hair and down her body that made the tingling increase. When his eyes returned to hers, she glimpsed a dark hunger that made her insides quake.

Swallowing against the pulse of undeniable attraction, she turned back to survey the room.

'I can't believe everything's been arranged so precisely,' she murmured.

'You would've preferred that they fling your things around without thought or care?'

'That's not what I mean and you know it. You've reproduced my room almost exactly how it was before.'

He frowned. 'I fail to see how that causes you distress.'

She strolled to the white oak antique dresser that had belonged to her mother. It'd been her mother's favourite piece of furniture and one of the few things Eva had taken when she'd left Pennington Manor.

Her fingers drifted over the hairbrush she'd used only yesterday morning. It had been placed in the little stand just as she normally did. 'I'm not distressed. I'm a little disconcerted that my things are almost exactly as I left them at my flat yesterday morning.' When he continued to stare, she pursed her lips. 'To reproduce this the movers would've needed photographic memories.'

'Or a few cameras shots as per my instructions.'

She sucked in a startled breath. 'Why would you do that?'

His lashes swept down for a moment. Then he shrugged. 'It was the most efficient course of action.'

'Oh.' Eva wasn't sure why she experienced that bolt of disappointment. Was she stupid enough to believe he'd done that because he *cared*? That he'd wanted her to be comfortable?

She silently scoffed at herself.

Lending silly daydreams to Zaccheo's actions had led to bitter disappointment once before. She wasn't about to make the same mistake again.

She spotted her handbag on the bed and dug out her phone. The battery was almost depleted, but she could make a quick call to her father before it died. She started to press dial and realised Zaccheo hadn't moved.

'Did you need something?'

The corner of his mouth quirked, but the bleakness in his eyes didn't dissipate. 'I've been in jail for over a year, *dolcezza*. I have innumerable needs.' The soft words held a note of deadly intent as his gaze moved from her to the bed. Her heart jumped to her throat and the air seemed to evaporate from the room. 'But my most immediate need is sustenance. I've ordered dinner to be brought from upstairs. It'll be here in fifteen minutes.'

She managed to reply despite the light-headedness that assailed her. 'Okay. I'll be there.'

With a curt nod, he left.

Eva sagged sideways onto the bed, her grip on the phone tightening until her bones protested. In the brief weeks she'd dated Zaccheo a year and half ago, she'd seen the way women responded to his unmistakeable animal magnetism. He only needed to walk into the room for every female eye to zero in on him. She'd also witnessed his reaction. Sometimes he responded with charm, other times with arrogant aloofness. But always with an innate sexuality that spoke of a deep appreciation for women. She'd confirmed that appreciation by a quick internet search in a weak moment, which had unearthed the long list of gorgeous women he'd had shockingly brief liaisons with in the past. A young, virile, wealthy bachelor, he'd been at the top of every woman's 'want to bed' list. And he'd had no qualms about helping himself to their amorous attentions.

To be deprived of that for almost a year and a half...

Eva shivered despite the room's ambient temperature. No, she was the last woman Zaccheo would *choose* to bed.

But then, he'd kissed her last night as if he'd wanted to devour her. And the way he'd looked at her just now?

She shook her head.

She was here purely as an instrument of his vengeance. The quicker she got to the bottom of *that*, the better.

Her call went straight to voicemail. Gritting her teeth, she left a message for her father to call her back. Sophie's phone rang for almost a minute before Eva hung up. Whether her sister was deliberately avoiding her calls or not, Eva intended to get some answers before Monday.

Resolving to try again after dinner, Eva plugged in her phone to charge and left her room. She met two waiters wheeling out a trolley as she entered the dining room. A few seconds later, the front door shut and Eva fought the momentary panic at being alone with Zaccheo.

She avoided looking at his imposing body as he lifted the silver domes from several serving platters.

'You always were impeccably punctual,' he said without turning around.

'I suppose that's a plus in my favour.'

'Hmm...' came his non-committal reply.

She reached her seat and froze at the romantic setting of the table. Expensive silverware and crystal-cut glasses gleamed beneath soft lighting. And already set out in a bed of ice was a small silver tub of caviar. A bottle of champagne chilled in an ice stand next to Zaccheo's chair.

'Do you intend to eat standing up?'

She jumped when his warm breath brushed her ear. When had he moved so close?

'Of course not. I just wasn't expecting such an elaborate meal.' She urged her feet to move to where he held out her chair, and sat down. 'One would almost be forgiven for thinking you were celebrating something.'

'Being released from prison isn't reason enough to enjoy something better than grey slop?'

Mortified, she cursed her tactlessness. 'I...of course. I'm sorry, that was... I'd forgotten...' *Oh, God, just shut up, Eva.*

'Of course you had.'

She tensed. 'What's that supposed to mean?'

'You're very good at putting things behind you, aren't you? Or have you forgotten how quickly you walked away from me the last time, too?'

She glanced down at her plate, resolutely picked up her spoon and helped herself to a bite of caviar. The unique taste exploded on her tongue, but it wasn't enough to quell the anxiety churning her stomach. 'You know why I walked away last time.'

'Do I?'

'Yes, you do!' She struggled to keep her composure. 'Can we talk about something else, please?'

'Why, because your actions make you uncomfortable? Or does it make your skin crawl to be sharing a meal with an ex-convict?'

Telling herself not to rise to the bait, she took another bite of food. 'No, because you snarl and your voice turns arctic, and also because I think we have different definitions of what really happened.'

He helped himself to a portion of his caviar before he responded. 'Really? Enlighten me, *per favore*.'

She pressed her lips together. 'We've already been through this, remember? You admitted that you proposed to me simply to get yourself into the Old Boys' Club. Are you going to bother denying it now?'

He froze for several heartbeats. Then he ate another mouthful. 'Of course not. But I believed we had an agreement. That you knew the part you had to play.'

'I'm sorry, I must have misplaced my copy of the Zaccheo Giordano Relationship Guide.' She couldn't stem the sarcasm or the bitterness that laced her voice.

'You surprise me.'

'How so?' she snapped, her poise shredding by the second.

'You're determined to deny that you know exactly how this game is played. That you aristocrats haven't practised the *something-for-something-more* tenet for generations.'

'You seem to be morbidly fascinated with the inner workings of the peer class. If we disgust you so much, why do you insist on soiling your life with our presence? Isn't it a bit convenient to hold us all responsible for every ill in your life?'

A muscle ticced in his jaw and Eva was certain she'd struck a nerve. 'You think having my freedom taken away is a subject I should treat lightly?'

The trembling in her belly spread out to engulf her whole body. 'The *evidence* led to your imprisonment, Zaccheo. Now we can change the subject or we can continue to fight to see who gives whom indigestion first.'

He remained silent for several moments, his eyes boring into hers. Eva stared back boldly, because backing down would see her swallowed whole by the deadly volcanic fury lurking in his eyes. She breathed a tiny sigh of relief when that mocking half-smile made an appearance.

'As you wish.' He resumed eating and didn't speak again until their first course was done. 'Let's play a game. We'll call it *What If*,' he said into the silence.

Tension knotted her nape, the certainty that she was toying with danger rising higher. 'I thought you didn't like games?'

'I'll make an exception this time.'

She took a deep breath. 'Okay. If you insist.'

'What if I wasn't the man you think I am? What if I happened to be a stranger who was innocent of everything he's been accused of? What if that stranger told you that every day he'd spent in prison felt like a little bit of himself was being chipped away for ever? What would you say to him?' His voice held that pain-laced edge she'd first heard in the car.

She looked at his face but his eyes were downcast, his white-knuckled hand wrapped around his wine glass.

This was no game.

The tension that gripped her vibrated from him, engulfing them in a volatile little bubble.

'I'd tell you how sorry I was that justice wasn't served properly on your behalf.' Her voice shook but she held firm. 'Then I'd ask you if there was anything I could do to help you put the past behind you.'

Arctic grey eyes met hers. 'What if I didn't want to put it behind me? What if everything I believe in tells me the only way to achieve satisfaction is to make those responsible pay?'

'I'd tell you it may seem like a good course of action, but doing that won't get back what you've lost. I'd also ask why you thought that was the only way.'

His eyes darkened, partly in anger, partly with anguish. She half expected him to snarl at her for daring to dissuade him from his path of retribution.

Instead, he rose and went to dish out their second course. 'Perhaps I don't know another recourse besides crime and punishment?' he intoned, disturbingly calm.

Sorrow seared her chest. 'How can that be?'

He returned with their plates and set down her second course—a lobster thermidor—before taking his seat. His movements were jerky, lacking his usual innate grace.

'Let's say hypothetically that I've never been exposed to much else.'

'But you know better or you wouldn't be so devastated at the hand you've been dealt. You're angry, yes, but you're also wounded by your ordeal. Believe me, yours isn't a unique story, Zaccheo.'

He frowned at the naked bitterness that leaked through her voice. 'Isn't it? Enlighten me. How have *you* been wounded?'

She cursed herself for leaving the door open, but, while she couldn't backtrack, she didn't want to provide him with more ammunition against her. 'My family...we're united where it counts, but I've always had to earn whatever regard I receive, especially from my father. And it hasn't always been easy, especially when walls are thrown up and alliances built where there should be none.'

He saw through her vagueness immediately. 'Your father and your sister against your mother and you? There's no need to deny it. It's easy to see your sister is fashioning herself in the image of her father,' he said less than gently.

Eva affected an easy shrug. 'Father started grooming her when we were young, and I didn't mind. I just didn't understand why that meant being left out in the cold, especially...' She stopped, realising just how much she was divulging.

'Especially...?' he pressed.

She gripped her fork tighter. 'After my mother died. I thought things would be different. I was wrong.'

His mouth twisted. 'Death is supposed to be a profound leveller. But it rarely changes people.'

She looked at him. 'Your parents—'

'Were the individuals who brought me into the world. They weren't good for much else. Take from that what you will. We're also straying away from the subject. *What if* this stranger can't see his way to forgive and forget?' That ruthless edge was back in his voice.

Eva's hand shook as she picked up her glass of Chianti. 'Then he needs to ask himself if he's prepared to live with the consequences of his actions.'

His eyebrows locked together in a dark frown, before his lashes swept down and he gave a brisk nod. 'Asked and answered.'

'Then there's no further point to this game, is there?'

One corner of his mouth lifted. 'On the contrary, you've shown a soft-heartedness that some would see as a flaw.'

Eva released a slow, unsteady breath. Had he always been like this? She was ashamed to admit she'd been so dazzled with Zaccheo from the moment he'd walked into Siren two years ago, right until the day he'd shown her his true colours, that she hadn't bothered to look any deeper. He'd kissed her on their third date, after which, fearing she'd disappoint him, she'd stumblingly informed him she was a virgin.

His reaction had been something of a fairy tale for her. She'd made him out as her Prince Charming, had adored the way he'd treated her like a treasured princess, showering her with small, thoughtful gifts, but, most of all, his undivided time whenever they were together. He'd made her feel precious, adored. He'd proposed on their sixth date, which had coincided with his thirtieth birthday, and told her he wanted to spend the rest of his life with her.

And it had all been a lie. The man sitting in front of her had no softness, only that ruthless edge and deadly charm.

'Don't be so sure, Zaccheo. I've learnt a few lessons since our unfortunate association.'

'Like what?'

'I'm no longer gullible. And my family may not be perfect, but I'm still fiercely protective of those I care about. Don't forget that.'

He helped himself to his wine. 'Duly noted.' His almost

bored tone didn't fool her into thinking this subject had stopped being anything but volatile.

They finished their meal in tense silence.

Eva almost wilted in relief when the doorbell rang and Zaccheo walked away to answer it.

Catching sight of the time, she jumped up from the dining table and was crossing the living room when Zaccheo's hand closed over her wrist.

'Where do you think you're going?' he demanded.

'Dinner's over. Can you let me go, please? I need to get going or I'll be late.'

His brows furrowed, giving him a look of a dark predator. 'Late for what?'

'Late for work. I've already taken two days off without pay. I don't want to be late on top of everything else.'

'You still work at Siren?' His tone held a note of disbelief.

'I have to make a living, Zaccheo.'

'You still sing?' His voice had grown deeper, his eyes darkening to a molten grey as he stared down at her. Although Zaccheo's expression could be hard to decipher most of the time, the mercurial changes in his eyes often spelled his altered mood.

This molten grey was one she was familiar with. And even though she didn't want to be reminded of it, a pulse of decadent sensation licked through her belly as she recalled the first night she'd seen him.

He'd walked into Siren an hour before closing, when she'd been halfway through a sultry, soulful ballad—a song about forbidden love, stolen nights and throwing caution to the wind. He'd paused to order a drink at the bar, then made his way to the table directly in front of the stage. He'd sipped his whisky, not once taking his eyes off her. Every lyric in the three songs that had followed had felt as if it had been written for the man in front of her and the woman she'd wanted to be for him.

She'd been beyond mesmerised when he'd helped her off

the stage after her session. She'd said yes immediately when he'd asked her out the next night.

But she'd been wrong, so very wrong to believe fate had brought Zaccheo to the club. He'd hunted her down with single-minded intent for his own selfish ends.

God, how he must have laughed when she'd fallen so easily into his arms!

She yanked her arm free. 'Yes, I still sing. And I'd be careful before you start making any threats on my professional life, too. I've indulged you with the engagement-ring picking and the makeover and the homecoming dinner. Now I intend to get back to *my* reality.'

She hurried away, determined not to look over her shoulder to see whether he was following. She made it to her room and quickly changed into her going-to-work attire of jeans, sweater, coat and a thick scarf to ward off the winter chill. Scooping up her bag, she checked her phone.

No calls.

The unease in her belly ballooned as she left her suite.

Zaccheo was seated on the sofa in the living room, examining a small black velvet box. His eyes tracked her, inducing that feeling of being helpless prey before a ruthless marauder. She opened her mouth to say something to dispel the sensation, but no words emerged. She watched, almost paralysingly daunted as he shut the box and placed it on the coffee table next to him.

'Would it be too *indulgent* to demand a kiss before you leave for work, *dolcezza*?' he enquired mockingly.

'Indulgent, no. Completely out of the question, most definitely,' she retorted. Then silently cursed her mouth's sudden tingling.

He shook his head, his magnificent mane gleaming under the chandelier. 'You wound me, Eva, but I'm willing to wait until the time when you will kiss me freely without me needing to ask.'

'Then you'll be waiting an eternity.'

CHAPTER SEVEN

Zaccheo paced the living room and contemplated leaving another voicemail message.

He'd already left five, none of which Eva had bothered to answer. It was nearly two a.m. and she hadn't returned. In his gloomy mood, he'd indulged in one too many nightcaps to consider driving to the club where she worked.

His temperament had been darkening steadily for the last four hours, once he'd found out what Eva's father was up to. Pennington was scrambling—futilely of course, because Zaccheo had closed every possible avenue—to find financial backing. That was enough to anger Zaccheo, but what fuelled his rage was that Pennington, getting more desperate by the hour, was offering more and more pieces of The Spire, the building that he would no longer own come Monday, as collateral. The blatant fraud Pennington was willing to perpetrate to fund his lifestyle made Zaccheo's fists clench as he stalked to the window.

The view from The Spire captured the string of bridges from east to west London. The moment he'd brought his vision of the building to life with the help of his experienced architects had been one of the proudest moments of his life. More than the properties he owned across the world and the empire he'd built from the first run-down warehouse he'd bought and converted to luxury accommodation at the age of twenty, this had been the one he'd treasured most. The building that should've been his crowning glory.

Instead it'd become the symbol of his downfall.

Ironically, the court where he'd been sentenced was right across the street. He looked down at the courthouse, jaw clenched.

He intended it to be the same place where his name was cleared. He would not be broken and humiliated as his father had been by the time he'd died. He would not be whispered about behind his back and mocked to his face and called a parasite. Earlier this evening, Eva had demanded to know why he'd been so fascinated with her kind.

For a moment, he'd wondered whether his burning desire to prove they were not better than him was a weakness. One he should *put behind him*, as Eva had suggested, before he lost a lot more of himself than he already had.

As much as he'd tried he hadn't been able to dismiss her words. Because he'd lied. He knew how to forgive. He'd forgiven his father each time he'd remembered that Zaccheo existed and bothered to take an interest in him. He'd forgiven his mother the first few times she'd let his stepfather treat him like a piece of garbage.

What Zaccheo hadn't told Eva was that he'd eventually learned that forgiveness wasn't effective when the recipient didn't have any use for it.

A weakening emotion like forgiveness would be wasted on Oscar Pennington.

A keycard clicked and he turned as the entry code released the front door.

Sensation very close to relief gut-punched him.

'Where the hell have you been?' He didn't bother to obviate his snarl. Nor could he stop checking her over from head to toe, to ascertain for himself that she wasn't hurt or hadn't been a victim of an accident or a mugging. When he was sure she was unharmed, he snapped his gaze to her face, to be confronted with a quizzical look.

Dio, was she *smirking* at him?

He watched her slide her fingers through her heavy, silky hair and ignored the weariness in the gesture.

'Is it Groundhog Day or something? Because I could've sworn we had a conversation about where I was going earlier this evening.'

He seethed. 'You finished work an hour and a half ago. Where have you been since then?'

She tossed a glare his way before she shrugged off her coat. The sight of the jeans and sweater she'd chosen to wear instead of the roomful of clothes he'd provided further stoked his dark mood.

'How do you know when I finished work?'

'Answer the question, Eva.'

She tugged her handbag from her shoulder and dropped it on the coffee table. Then she kicked off her shoes and pushed up on the balls of her feet in a smooth, practised stretch reminiscent of a ballet dancer.

'I took the night bus. It's cheaper than a cab, but it took forty-five minutes to arrive.'

'*Mi scusi?* You took the *night bus*?' His brain crawled with scenarios that made his blood curdle. He didn't need a spell in prison to be aware of what dangerous elements lurked at night. The thought that Eva had exposed herself, *willingly*, to—

'Careful there, Zaccheo, you almost sound like one of those snobs you detest so much.'

She pushed up again, her feet arching and flattening in a graceful rise and fall.

Despite his blood boiling, he stared, mesmerised, as she completed the stretches. Then he let his gaze drift up her body, knowing he shouldn't, yet unable to stop himself. The sweater, decorated with a D-minor scale motif, hugged her slim torso, emphasising her full, heavy breasts and tiny waist before ending a half-inch above her jeans.

That half-inch of flesh taunted him, calling to mind the smooth warmth of her skin. The simmering awareness that had always existed between them, like a fuse just waiting to be lit, throbbed deep inside. He'd tried to deny it earlier this evening in the hallway, when he'd discovered she still sang at Siren.

He'd tried to erase the sound of her sultry voice, the evocative way Eva Pennington performed on stage. He'd cursed himself when his body had reacted the way it had the very first time he'd heard her sing. That part of his black mood also stemmed from being viscerally opposed to any other man experiencing the same reaction he did from hearing her captivating voice, the way he had been two years ago, was a subject he wasn't willing to acknowledge, never mind tackle.

He pulled his gaze from the alluringly feminine curve of her hips and shapely legs and focused on the question that had been burning through him all night.

'Explain to me how you have two million pounds in your bank account, but take the bus to and from work.'

Her mouth gaped for several seconds before she regained herself. 'How the hell do you know how much money I have in my bank account?' she demanded.

'With the right people with the right skills, very easily. I'm waiting for an answer.'

'You're not going to get one. What I do with my money and how I choose to travel is *my* business.'

'You're wrong, *cara*. As of last night, your welfare is very much my business. And if you think I'm willing to allow you to risk your safety at times when drunken yobs and muggers crawl out of the woodwork, you're very much mistaken.'

'*Allow* me? Next you'll be telling me I need your permission to breathe!'

He spiked his fingers through his hair, wondering if she'd ever been this difficult and he'd somehow missed it. The Eva he remembered, before his eyes had been truly opened to her character, had possessed a quiet passion, not this defiant, wild child before him.

But no, there'd never been anything *child*like about Eva.

She was all woman. His libido had thrilled to it right from the first.

Understandably this acute reaction was because he'd been without a woman for over a year. Now was not the time to let it out of control. The time would arrive soon enough.

She tossed her head in irritation, and the hardening in his groin threatened to prove him wrong.

'Since I need you alive for the foreseeable future, no, you don't require my permission to breathe.'

She had the nerve to roll her eyes. 'Thank you very much!'

'From now on you'll be driven to and from work.'

'No, thanks.'

He gritted his teeth. 'You prefer to spend hours freezing at a bus stop than accept my offer?'

'Yes, because the *offer* comes at a price. I may not know what it is yet, but I've no intention of paying it.'

'Why do you insist on fighting me when we both know you don't have a choice? I'm willing to bet your father didn't return a single one of your phone calls last night.'

Wide, startled eyes met his for a second before she looked away. 'I'm sure he has his reasons.'

It spoke volumes that she didn't deny trying to reach Oscar. 'Reasons more important than answering the phone to his daughter? Do you want to know what he's been up to?'

'I'm sure you're about to apprise me whether I want to hear it or not.'

'He's been calling in every single favour he thinks he's owed. Unfortunately, a man as greedy as your father cashed in most of his favours a long time ago. He's also pleading and begging his way across the country in a bid to save himself from the hole he knows I'm about to bury him in. He didn't take your calls, but he took mine. I recorded it if you wish me to play it back to you?'

Her fists clenched. 'Go to hell, Zaccheo,' she threw at him, but he glimpsed the pain in her eyes.

He almost felt sorry for her. Then he remembered her part in all this.

'Come here, Eva,' he murmured.

She eyed him suspiciously. 'Why?'

'Because I have something for you.'

Her gaze dropped to his empty hands before snapping

back to his face. 'There's nothing you have that I could possibly want.'

'If you make me come over there, I'll take that kiss you owe me from last night.' *Dio*, why had he said that? Now it was all he could think about.

Heat flushed her cheeks. 'I don't owe you a thing. And I certainly don't owe you any kisses.'

The women he'd dated in the past would've fallen over themselves to receive any gift he chose to bestow on them, especially the one he'd tucked into his back pocket.

Slowly, he walked towards her. He made sure his intent was clear. The moment she realised, her hands shot out. 'Stop! Didn't your mother teach you about the honey versus vinegar technique?'

Bitterness drenched him. 'No. My mother was too busy climbing the social ladder after my father died to bother with me. When he was alive, she wasn't much use either.'

She sucked in a shocked breath and concern furrowed her brow. 'I'm sorry.'

Zaccheo rejected the concern and let the sound of her husky voice, scratchy from the vocal strain that came with singing, wash over him instead. He didn't want her concern. But the sex he could deal with.

The need he'd been trying to keep under tight control threatened to snap. He took another step.

'Okay! I'm coming.' She walked barefooted to him. 'I've done as you asked. Give me whatever it is you want to give me.'

'It's in my back pocket.'

She inhaled sharply. 'Is this another of your games, Zaccheo?'

'It'll only take a minute to find out. Are you brave enough, *dolcezza*?' he asked.

Her gaze dropped and he immediately tilted her chin up with one finger. 'Look at me. I want to see your face.'

She blinked, then gathered herself in that way he'd always found fascinating. Slowly, she reached an arm around him. Her fingers probed until she found the pocket opening.

They slipped inside and he suppressed a groan as her fingers caressed him through his trousers. His blood rushed faster south as she searched futilely.

'It's empty,' she stated with a suspicious glare.

'Try the other one.'

She muttered a dirty word that rumbled right through him. Her colour deepened when he lifted his eyebrow.

'Let's get this over with.' She searched his right pocket and stilled when she encountered the box.

'Take it out,' he commanded, then stifled another groan when her fingers dug into his flesh to remove the velvet box. It took all the control he could muster not to kiss her when her lips parted and he glimpsed the tip of her tongue.

During his endless months in prison, he'd wondered whether he'd overrated the chemistry that existed between Eva and him. The proof that it was as potent as ever triggered an incandescent hunger that flooded his loins.

Sì, this part of his revenge that involved Eva in his bed, being inside her and implanting her with his seed, would be easy enough and pleasurable enough to achieve.

'I cannot wait to take you on our wedding night. Despite you no longer being a virgin, I'll thoroughly enjoy making you mine in every imaginable way possible. By the time I'm done with you, you'll forget every other man that you dared to replace me with.'

Her eyelids fluttered and she shivered. But the new, assertive Eva came back with fire. 'A bold assertion. But one, sadly, we'll both see unproven since there'll be no wedding *or* wedding night. And in case I haven't mentioned it, you're the last man I'd ever welcome in my bed.'

Zaccheo chose not to point out that she still had her hand in his pocket, or that her fingers were digging more firmly into his buttock.

Instead, he slid his phone from his front pocket, activated the recording app and hit the replay button.

Despite her earlier assertion that she'd grown a thicker skin, shadows of disbelief and hurt criss-crossed her face as she listened to the short conversation summoning her father to a meeting first thing on Monday. Unlike the night before where Pennington had blustered his way through Zaccheo's accusations, he'd listened in tense silence as Zaccheo had told him he knew what he was up to.

Zaccheo had given him a taster of the contents of the documents proving his innocence and the older man had finally agreed to the meeting. Zaccheo had known he'd won when Pennington had declined to bring his lawyers to verify the documents.

Thick silence filled the room after the recording ended.

'Do you believe me now, Eva? Do you believe that your family has wronged me in the most heinous way and that I intend to exact equal retribution?'

Her nostrils flared and her mouth trembled before she wrenched back control. But despite her composure, a sheen of tears appeared in her eyes, announcing her tumultuous emotion. 'Yes.'

'Take the box out of my pocket.'

She withdrew it. His instructions on the mount and setting had been followed to the letter.

'I intended to give it to you after dinner last night. Not on bended knee, of course. I'm sure you'll agree that once was enough?'

Her eyes darkened, as if he'd hurt her somehow. But of course, that was nonsense. She'd returned his first ring and walked away from him after a brief argument he barely recalled, stating that she didn't wish to be married to *a man like him*.

At the time, Zaccheo had been reeling at his lawyers' news that he was about to be charged with criminal negligence. He hadn't been able to absorb the full impact of Eva's betrayal until weeks later, when he'd already been in prison. His trial had been swift, the result of a young, overeager judge desperate to make a name for himself.

But he'd had over a year to replay the last time he'd seen Eva. In court, sitting next to her father, her face devoid of emotion until Zaccheo's sentence had been read out.

In that moment, he'd fooled himself into thinking she'd experienced a moment of agony on his behalf. He'd murmured her name. She'd looked at him. It was then that he'd seen the contempt.

That single memory cleared his mind of any extraneous feelings. 'Open the box and put on the ring,' he said tersely.

His tone must have conveyed his capricious emotional state. She cracked open the small case and slid on the ring without complaint.

He caught her hand in his and raised it, much as he had on Friday night. But this time, the acute need to rip off the evidence of another man's ownership was replaced by a well of satisfaction. 'You're mine, Eva. Until I decide another fate for you, you'll remain mine. Be sure not to forget that.'

Turning on his heel, he walked away.

Eva woke on Monday morning with a heavy heart and a stone in her gut that announced that her life was about to change for ever. It had started to change the moment she'd heard Zaccheo's recorded conversation with her father, but she'd been too shocked afterwards to decipher what her father's guilt meant for her.

Tired and wrung out, she'd stumbled to bed and fallen into a dreamless sleep, then woken and stumbled her way back to work.

Reality had arrived when she'd exited Siren after her shift to find Zaccheo's driver waiting to bring her back to the penthouse. She'd felt it when Zaccheo had told her to be ready to attend his offices in the morning. She'd felt it when she'd walked into her suite and found every item of clothing she'd tried on Saturday neatly stacked in the floor-to-ceiling shelves in her dressing room.

She felt it now when she lifted her hand to adjust her collar and caught the flash of the diamond ring on her finger. The flawless gem she'd chosen so carelessly had been mounted on a bezel setting, with further diamonds in decreasing sizes set in a platinum ring that fitted her perfectly.

You're mine, Eva. Until I decide another fate for you, you'll remain mine.

She was marrying Zaccheo in less than a week. He'd brought forward the initial two-week deadline by a whole week. She would marry him or her father would be reported to the authorities. He'd delivered that little bombshell last night after dinner. No amount of tossing and turning had altered that reality.

When she'd agreed to marry Harry, she'd known it would be purely a business deal, with zero risk to her emotions.

The idea of attaching herself to Zaccheo, knowing the depth of his contempt for her and his hunger for revenge, was bad enough. That undeniably dangerous chemistry that hovered on the point of exploding in her face when she so much as looked at him...*that* terrified her on an unspeakable level. And not because she was afraid he'd use that against her.

What she'd spent the early hours agonising over was her own helplessness against that inescapable pull.

The only way round it was to keep reminding herself why Zaccheo was doing this. Ultimate retribution and humiliation was his goal. He didn't want anything more from her.

An hour later, she sat across from her father and sister and watched in growing horror as Zaccheo's lawyers listed her father's sins.

Oscar Pennington sat hunched over, his pallor grey and his forehead covered in light sweat. Despite having heard Zaccheo's recording last night, she couldn't believe her father would sink so low.

'How could you do this?' she finally blurted when it got

too much to bear. 'And how the hell did you think you'd get away with it?'

Her father glared at her. 'This isn't the time for histrionics, Eva.'

'And you, Sophie? Did you know about this?' Eva asked her sister.

Sophie glanced at the lawyers before she replied, 'Let's not lose focus on why we're here.'

Anger shot through Eva. 'You mean let's pretend that this isn't really happening? That we're not here because Father *bribed* the builders to take shortcuts and blamed someone else for it? And you accuse me of not living in the real world?'

Sophie's lips pursed, but not before a guilty flush rushed into her face. 'Can we not do this now, please?' Her agitated gaze darted to where Zaccheo sat in lethal silence.

Eva stared at her sister, a mixture of anger and sadness seething within her. She was beginning to think they would never get past whatever was broken between them. And maybe she needed to be more like Zaccheo, and divorce herself from her feelings.

Eva glanced at him and the oxygen leached from her lungs.

God!

On Friday night, his all-black attire had lent him an air of suave but icy deadliness reminiscent of a lead in a mafia movie. Since then his casual attires, although equally formidable in announcing his breathtaking physique, had lulled her into a lesser sense of danger.

This morning, in a dark grey pinstripe suit, teamed with a navy shirt, and precisely knotted silver and blue tie, and his hair and beard newly trimmed, Zaccheo was a magnificent vision to behold.

The bespoke clothes flowed over his sleekly honed muscles and olive skin, each movement drawing attention to his powerfully arresting figure.

It was why more than one female employee had stared in

blatant interest as they'd walked into GWI's headquarters in the City this morning. It was why she'd avoided looking at him since they'd sat down.

But she'd made the mistake of looking now. And as he started to turn his head she *knew* she wouldn't be able to look away.

His gaze locked on her and she read the ruthless, possessive statement of ownership in his eyes even before he opened his mouth to speak. 'Eva has already given me what I want—her word that she's willing to do whatever it takes to make reparations.' His gaze dropped to the ring on her finger before he faced her father. 'Now it's your turn.'

CHAPTER EIGHT

'HERE'S A LIST of businesses who withdrew their contracts because of my incarceration.' Zaccheo nodded to one of his lawyers, who passed a sheet across the desk to her father.

Eva caught a glimpse of the names on the list and flinched. While the list was only half a page, she noticed more than one global conglomerate on there.

'You'll contact the CEO of each of those companies and tell them your side of the story.'

Fear flashed across her father's face. 'What's to stop them from spilling the beans?'

Zaccheo gave that chilling half-smile. 'I have a team of lawyers who'll ensure their silence if they ever want to do business with me again.'

'You're sure they'll still want your business?' Her father's voice held a newly subdued note.

'I have it on good authority their withdrawal was merely a stance. Some to gain better leverage on certain transactions and others for appearances' sake. Once they know the truth, they'll be back on board. But even if they don't come back to GWI, the purpose of your phone call would've been achieved.'

'Is this really necessary? Your company has thrived, probably beyond your wildest dreams, even while you were locked up. And this morning's stock-market reports show your stock at an all-time high.' Eva could hear the panic in her father's voice. 'Do I really need to genuflect in front of these people to make you happy?' he added bitterly.

'Yes. You do.'

Her father's face reddened. 'Look here. Judging by that rock I see on Eva's finger, you're about to marry my daughter. We're about to be *family*. Is this really how you wish to start our familial relationship?'

Bitterness pushed aside her compassion when she realised her father was once again using her as leverage for his own ends.

'You don't think this is the least you can do, Father?' she asked.

'You're taking his side?' her father demanded.

Eva sighed. 'I'm taking the side of doing the right thing. Surely you can see that?'

Her father huffed, and Zaccheo's lips thinned into a formidable line. 'I have no interest in building a relationship with you personally. You can drop dead for all I care. Right after you carry out my instructions, of course.'

'Young man, be reasonable,' her father pleaded, realising that for once he'd come up against an immoveable object that neither his charm nor his blustering would shift.

Zaccheo stared back dispassionately. No one in the room could harbour the misguided idea that he would soften in any way.

'I don't think you have a choice in the matter, Father,' Sophie muttered into the tense silence.

Eva glanced at her sister, searching for that warmth they'd once shared. But Sophie kept her face firmly turned away.

Eva jumped as her father pushed back his chair. 'Fine, you win.'

Zaccheo brushed off imaginary lint from his sleeve. 'Excellent. And please be sure to give a convincing performance. My people will contact each CEO on that list by Friday. Make sure you get it done by then.'

Her father's barrel chest rose and fell as he tried to control his temper. 'It'll be done. Sophie, we're leaving.'

Eva started to rise, too, only to find a hand clamped on her hip. The electricity that shot through her body at the bold contact had her swaying on her feet.

'What are you doing?' she demanded.

Zaccheo ignored her, but his thumb moved lazily over her hip bone as he addressed her father. 'You and Sophie may leave. I still have things to discuss with my fiancée. My secretary will contact you with details of the wedding in the next day or two.'

Her father looked from her face to Zaccheo's. Then he stormed out of the door.

Eva turned to Zaccheo. 'What more could we possibly have to discuss? You've made everything crystal clear.'

'Not quite everything. Sit down.' He waited until she complied before he removed his hand.

Eva wasn't sure whether it was relief that burst through her chest or outrage. Relief, most definitely, she decided. Lacing her fingers, she waited as he dismissed all except one lawyer.

At Zaccheo's nod, the man produced a thick binder and placed it in front of Zaccheo, after which he also left.

She could feel Zaccheo's powerful gaze on her, but she'd already unsettled herself by looking at him once. And she was reeling from everything that had taken place here in the last hour.

When the minutes continued to tick by in silence, she raised her head. 'You want my father to help rebuild the damage he caused to your reputation, but what about your criminal record? I would've thought that would be more important to you.'

'You may marry a man with a criminal record come Saturday, but I won't remain that way for long. My lawyers are working on it.'

Her heart lurched at the reminder that in a few short days she would be his wife, but she forced herself to ask the question on her mind. 'How can they do that without implicating my father? Isn't withholding evidence a crime?'

'Nothing will be withheld. How the authorities choose to apply the rule of law is up to them.'

Recalling the state of her father's health, she tightened

her fists in anxiety. 'So you're saying Father can still go to prison? Despite letting him believe he won't?'

The kick in his stare struck deep in her soul. 'I'm the one who was wronged. I have some leeway in speaking on his behalf, should I choose to.'

The implied threat didn't escape her notice. They would either toe his line or suffer the consequences.

She swallowed. 'What did you want to discuss with me?'

He placed a single sheet of paper in front of her.

'These are the engagements we'll be attending this week. Make sure you put them in your diary.'

She pursed her lips, denying that the deep pang in her chest was hurt. 'At least you're laying your cards on the table this time round.'

'What cards would those be?'

She shrugged. 'The ones that state your desire to conquer the upper class, of course. Wasn't that your aim all along? To walk in the hallowed halls of the Old Boys' Club and show them all your contempt for them?'

His eyes narrowed, but she caught a shadow in the grey depths. 'How well you think you know me.'

She cautioned herself against probing the sleeping lion, but found herself asking anyway, 'Why, Zaccheo? Why is it so important that you bring us all down a peg or two?'

He shifted in his seat. If she hadn't known that he didn't possess an ounce of humility, she'd have thought he was uneasy. 'I don't detest the whole echelon. Just those who think they have a right to lord it over others simply because of their pedigree. And, of course, those who think they can get around the laws that ordinary people have to live by.'

'What about me? Surely you can't hate me simply because our relationship didn't work out?'

'Was that what we had—a *relationship*?' he sneered. 'I thought it was a means for you to facilitate your father's plans.'

'*What?* You think I had something to do with my father scapegoating you?'

'Perhaps you weren't privy to his whole plan like your sister was. But the timing of it all was a little too convenient, don't you think? You walked away *three days* before I was charged, with a flimsy excuse after an even flimsier row. What was it? Oh, yes, you didn't want to marry *a man like me*?'

She surged to her feet, her insides going cold. 'You think I staged the whole thing? Need I remind you that you were the one who initiated our first meeting? That you were the one to ask me out?'

'An event carefully orchestrated by your father, of course. Do you know why I was at Siren that night?'

'Will you believe me if I said no?'

'I was supposed to meet your father and two of his investors there. Except none of them showed.'

She frowned. 'That's not possible. My father hates that I sing. He hates it even more that I work in a nightclub. I don't think he even knows where Siren is.'

'And yet he suggested it. Highly recommended it, in fact.'

The idea that her father had engineered their first meeting coated her mouth with bitterness. He'd used her strong loyalty to their family to manipulate her long before she'd taken a stand and moved out of Pennington Manor. But this further evidence showed a meticulousness that made her blood run cold.

'Were you even a virgin back then?' Zaccheo sliced at her.

The question brought her back to earth. 'Excuse me?'

'Or was it a ploy to sweeten the deal?'

'I didn't know you existed until you parked yourself in front of the stage that night!'

'Maybe not. But you must've known who I was soon after. Isn't that what women do these days? A quick internet search while they're putting on their make-up to go on the first date?'

Eva couldn't stop her guilty flush because it was exactly what she'd done. But not with the reprehensible intentions he'd implied. Zaccheo's all-consuming interest in her had seemed too good to be true. She'd wanted to know more about the compelling man who'd zeroed in on her with such unnerving interest.

What she'd found was a long list of conquests ranging from supermodels to famous sports stars. She'd been so intimidated, she'd carefully kept her inexperience under wraps. It was that desperately embarrassing need to prove her sophistication that had led to her boldly accepting his dare to perform oral sex on him on his thirtieth birthday. She'd been so anxious, she'd bungled it even before she'd unfastened his belt. In the face of his wry amusement, she'd blurted her inexperience.

The inexperience he was now denouncing as a ploy.

'I don't care what you think. All I care about is that I know what I'm letting myself in for now. I know exactly the type of man you are.' One whose ruthless ambition was all he cared about.

He regarded her for several tense seconds. 'Then this won't surprise you too much.' He slid a thick burgundy folder across to her. 'It's a prenuptial agreement. On the first page you'll find a list of independent lawyers who can guide you through the legalese should you require it. The terms are non-negotiable. You have twenty-four hours to read and sign it.'

She glanced from him to the folder, her mouth dropping open in shock. 'Why would I need a prenup? I've agreed to your demands. Isn't this overkill?'

'My lawyers go spare if I don't get everything in writing. Besides, there are a few items in there we haven't discussed yet.'

Something in his voice made her skin prickle. Her belly quaked as she turned the first page of the thick document. The first few clauses were about general schedules and routines, making herself available for his engagements within reason, how many homes he owned and her duty to oversee the running of them, and his expectation of her availability to travel with him on his business trips should he require it.

'If you think I'm going to turn myself into a pet you can pick up and hop on a plane with whenever it suits you, you're in for a shock.'

He merely quirked an eyebrow at her. She bristled but carried on reading.

She paused at the sixth clause. 'We can't be apart for more than five days in the first year of marriage?'

The half-smile twitched. 'We don't want tongues wagging too soon, do we?'

'You mean after the first year I can lock myself in a nunnery for a year if I choose to?'

For the first time since Zaccheo had exploded back into her life, she glimpsed a genuine smile. It was gone before it registered fully, but the effect was no less earth-shattering. 'No nunnery would accept you once you've spent a year in my bed.'

Her face flamed and the look in his eyes made her hurriedly turn the page.

The ninth made her almost swallow her tongue. 'I don't want your money! And I certainly don't need that much money *every* month.' The sum stated was more than she earned in a year.

He shrugged. 'Then donate it to your favourite charity.'

Since she wasn't going to win that one, she moved on to the tenth and last clause.

Eva jerked to her feet, her heart pounding as she reread the words, hoping against hope that she'd got it wrong the first time. But the words remained clear and stark and *frightening*. 'You want…*children*?' she rasped through a throat gone bone dry with dread.

'*Sì*,' he replied softly. 'Two. An heir and a spare, I believe you disparagingly refer to that number in your circles. More if we're lucky—stop shaking your head, Eva.'

Eva realised that was exactly what she was doing as he rose and stalked her. She took a step back, then another, until her backside bumped the sleek black cabinet running the length of the central wall.

He stopped in front of her, leaned his tall, imposing frame over hers. 'Of all the clauses in the agreement, this is non-negotiable.'

'You said they were all non-negotiable.'

'They are, but some are more non-negotiable than others.'

A silent scream built inside her. 'If this one is the most important why did you put it last?'

'Because you would be signing directly below it. I wanted you to feel its import so there would be no doubt in your mind what you were agreeing to.'

She started to shake her head again but froze when he angled himself even closer, until their lips were an inch apart. Their breaths mingling, he stared her down. Eva's heart climbed into her throat as she struggled to sift through the emotions those words on the page had evoked.

Zaccheo was asking the impossible.

Children were the reasons why her last two relationships before him had failed before they'd even begun.

Children were the reason she'd painfully resigned herself to remaining single. To spurning any interest that came her way because she hadn't been able to bear the thought of baring her soul again only to have her emotions trampled on.

She wouldn't cry. She wouldn't break down in front of Zaccheo. Not today. *Not ever.* He'd caused her enough turmoil to last a lifetime.

But he was asking the impossible. 'I can't.'

His face hardened but he didn't move a muscle. 'You can. You *will*. Three days ago you were agreeing to marry another man. You expect me to believe the possibility of children weren't on the cards with Fairfield?'

She shook her head. 'My agreement with Harry was different. Besides, he...' She stopped, unwilling to add to the flammable tension.

'He what?' Zaccheo enquired silkily.

'He didn't *hate* me!'

He seemed almost surprised at her accusation. Surprise slowly gave way to a frown. 'I don't hate you, Eva. In fact, given time and a little work, we might even find common ground.'

She cursed her heart for leaping at his words. 'I can't—'

'You have twenty-four hours. I suggest you take the time and review your answer before saying another word.'

Her stomach clenched. 'And if my answer remains the same?'

His expression was one of pure, insufferable arrogance. 'It won't. You make feeble attempts to kick at the demands of your ancestry and title, but inevitably you choose blood over freedom. You'll do anything to save your precious family name—'

'You really think so? After the meeting we just had? Are you really that blind, or did you not see the way my sister and my father treat me? We are not a close family, Zaccheo. No matter how much I wish it...' Her voice shook, but she firmed it. 'Have you stopped to think that you pushing me this way may be the catalyst I need to completely break away from a family that's already broken?'

Her terse words made his eyes narrow. But his expression cleared almost immediately. 'No, you're loyal. You'll give me what I want.'

'No—'

'Yes,' he breathed.

He closed the gap between them slowly, as if taunting her with the knowledge that she couldn't escape the inevitability of his possession.

His mouth claimed hers—hot, demanding, powerfully erotic. Eva moaned as her emotions went into free fall. He feasted on her as if he had all the time in the world, taking turns licking his way into her mouth before sliding his tongue against hers in an expert dance that had her desperately clutching his waist.

Wild, decadent heat swirled through her body as he lifted her onto the cabinet, tugged up the hem of her dress and planted himself between her thighs. Her shoulders met the wall and she gasped as one hand gripped her thigh.

Push him away. You need to push him away!

Her hands climbed from his waist to his chest, albeit far slower and in a far more exploratory fashion than her screeching brain was comfortable with. But she made an effort once she reached his broad shoulders.

She pushed.

And found her hands captured in a firm one-handed hold above her head. His other hand found her breast and palmed it, squeezing before flicking his thumb over her hardened nipple.

Sensation pounded through her blood. Her legs curled around his thickly muscled thighs and she found herself pulled closer to the edge of the cabinet, until the powerful evidence of his erection pushed at her core.

Zaccheo gave a deep groan and freed her hands to bury his in her hair. Angling her head for a deeper invasion, he devoured her until the need for air drove them apart.

Chests heaving, they stared at each other for several seconds before Eva scrambled to untangle her legs from around him. Every skin cell on fire, she struggled to stand up. He stopped her with a hand on her belly, his eyes compelling hers so effortlessly, she couldn't look away.

The other hand moved to her cheek, then his fingers drifted over her throbbing mouth.

'As much as I'd like to take you right here on my boardroom cabinet, I have a dozen meetings to chair. It seems everyone wants a powwow with the newly emancipated CEO. We'll pick this up again at dinner. I'll be home by seven.'

She diverted enough brainpower from the erotic images it was creating to reply. 'I won't be there. I'm working tonight.'

A tic throbbed at his temple as he straightened his tie. 'I see that I need to put aligning our schedules at the top of my agenda.'

She pushed him away and stood. 'Don't strain yourself too much on my account,' she responded waspishly. She was projecting her anger at her weakness onto him, but she couldn't help herself. She tugged her dress down, painfully aware of the sensitivity between her unsteady legs as she moved away from him and picked up her handbag and the folder containing the prenup. 'I'll see you when I see you.'

He took her hand and walked her to the door. 'I guarantee you it'll be much sooner than that.' He rode the lift down with her to the ground floor, barely acknowledging the keen interest his presence provoked.

Romeo was entering the building as they exited. The two men exchanged a short conversation in Italian before Zaccheo opened the door to the limo.

When she went to slide in, he stopped her. 'Wait.'

'What is it?' she demanded.

His lips firmed and he seemed in two minds as to his response. 'For a moment during the meeting, you took my side against your father. I'll factor that favourably into our dealings from now on.'

Eva's heart lifted for a moment, then plunged back to her toes. 'You don't get it, do you?'

He frowned. 'Get what?'

'Zaccheo, for as long as I can remember, all I've wished was for there to be *no sides*. For there not to be a *them* against *us*. Maybe that makes me a fool. Or maybe I'll need to give up that dream.'

His eyes turned a shade darker with puzzlement, then he shrugged. '*Sì, bellissima*, perhaps you might have to.'

And right in front of the early lunch crowd, Zaccheo announced his ownership of her with a long, deep kiss.

* * *

Eva could barely hear herself think above the excited buzz in Siren's VIP lounge as she cued the next song.

She was sure the unusually large Monday night crowd had nothing to with Ziggy Preston, the famous record producer who'd been coming to watch her perform on and off for the past month, and everything to do with the pictures that had appeared in the early-evening paper of her kissing Zaccheo outside his office this afternoon. Avoiding the news had been difficult, seeing as that kiss and a large-scale picture of her engagement ring had made front-page news.

One picture had held the caption *'Three Ring Circus'*— with photos of her three engagement rings and a pointed question as to her motives.

It'd been a relief to leave Zaccheo's penthouse, switch off her phone and immerse herself in work. Not least because blanking her mind stopped her from thinking about the last clause in the prenup, and the reawakened agony she'd kept buried since her doctor had delivered the harrowing news six years ago. News she'd only revealed twice, with devastating consequences.

She almost wished she could blurt it out to Zaccheo and let the revelation achieve what it had in the past—a swift about-face from keen interest to cold dismissal, with one recipient informing her, in the most callous terms, that he could never accept her as a full woman.

Pain flared wider, threatening the foundations she'd built to protect herself from that stark truth. Foundations Zaccheo threatened.

She clutched the mic and forced back the black chasm that swirled with desolation. Her accompanying pianist nodded and she cleared her throat, ready to sing the ballad that ironically exhorted her to be brave.

She was halfway through the song when he walked in. As usual, the sight of him sent a tidal wave of awareness through her body and she managed to stop herself from stumbling by the skin of her teeth. Heads turned and the buzz in the room grew louder.

Zaccheo's eyes raked her from head to toe before settling on her face. A table miraculously emptied in front of the stage. Someone took his overcoat and Eva watched him release the single button to his dinner jacket before pulling out a chair and seating himself at the roped-off table before her.

The sense of déjà vu was so overwhelming, she wanted to abandon the song and flee from the stage. She finished, she smiled and accepted the applause, then made her way to where he pointedly held out a chair for her.

'What are you doing here?' she whispered fiercely.

He took his time to answer, choosing instead to pull her close and place a kiss on each cheek before drawing back to stare at her.

'You couldn't make dinner, so I brought dinner to you.'

'You really shouldn't have,' she replied, fighting the urge to rub her cheeks where his lips had been. 'Besides, I can't. My break is only twenty minutes.'

'Tonight your break is an hour, as it will be every night I choose to dine with you here instead of at our home. Now sit down and smile, *mio piccolo uccello che canta*, and pretend to our avid audience that you're ecstatically happy to see your fiancé,' he said with a tone edged in steel.

CHAPTER NINE

Zaccheo watched myriad expressions chase across her face. Rebellion. Irritation. Sexual awareness. A touch of embarrassment when someone shouted their appreciation of her singing from across the room. One glance from Zaccheo silenced that inebriated guest.

But it was the shadows that lurked in her eyes that made his jaw clench. All day, through the heady challenge of getting back into the swing of business life, that look in her eyes when she'd seen his last clause in the prenuptial agreement had played on his mind. Not enough to disrupt his day, but enough for him to keep replaying the scene. Her reaction had been extreme and almost...distressed.

Yes, it bothered him that she saw making a family with him abhorrent, even though he'd known going in that, had she been given a choice, Eva would've chosen someone else, someone more *worthy* to father her children. Nevertheless, her reaction had struck hard in a place he'd thought was no longer capable of feeling hurt.

The feeling had festered, like a burr under his skin, eating away at him as the day had progressed. Until he'd abruptly ended a videoconference and walked out of his office.

He'd intended to return home and help himself to fine whisky in a toast to striking the first blow in ending Oscar Pennington's existence. Instead he'd found himself swapping his business suit for a dinner jacket and striding back out of his penthouse.

The woman who'd occupied far too much of his thoughts today swayed to her seat and sat down. The pounding in his blood that had never quite subsided after that kiss in his boardroom, and increased the moment he'd entered the

VIP room and heard her singing, accelerated when his gaze dropped to her scarlet-painted lips.

Before he'd met Eva Pennington, Zaccheo had never labelled himself a possessive guy. Although he enjoyed the thrill of the chase and inevitable capture, he'd been equally thrilled to see the back of the women he'd dated, especially when the clinginess had begun.

With Eva, he'd experienced an unprecedented and very caveman-like urge to claim her, to make sure every man within striking distance knew she belonged to him. And only him. That feeling was as unsettling as it was hard to eradicate. It wasn't helped when she toyed with her champagne glass and avoided eye contact.

'I don't appreciate you messing with my schedule behind my back, Zaccheo,' she said.

He wasn't sure why the sound of his name on her lips further spiked his libido, but he wanted to hear it again. He wanted to hear it fall from her lips in the throes of passion, as he took her to the heights of ecstasy.

Dio, he was losing it. Losing sight of his objective. Which was to make sure she understood that he intended to give no quarter in making her his.

He took a bracing sip of champagne and nodded to the hovering waiters ready to serve the meal he'd ordered.

'It was dinner here or summoning you back to the penthouse. You should be thanking me for bending like this.'

She glared. 'You really are a great loss to the Dark Ages, you know that?'

'In time you'll learn that I always get my way, Eva. *Always*.'

Her eyes met his and that intense, inexplicable connection that had throbbed between them right from the very start pulled, tightened.

'Did it even occur to you that I may have said yes if you'd asked me to have dinner with you?'

Surprise flared through him, and he found himself asking, 'Would you?'

She shrugged. 'I guess you'll never know. We need to discuss the prenup,' she said.

He knew instinctively that she was about to refuse him again. A different sort of heat bloomed in his chest. 'This isn't the time or place.'

'I don't...' She paused when the waiters arrived at the table with their first course. As if recalling where they were, she glanced round, took a deep breath, and leaned forward. 'I won't sign it.'

Won't, not *can't*, as she'd said before.

Bitterness surged through his veins. 'Because the thought of my seed growing inside you fills you with horror?'

Her fingers convulsed around her knife, but, true to her breeding, she directed it to her plate with understated elegance to cut her steak.

'Why would you want me as the mother of your children, anyway? I would've thought you'd want to spare yourself such a vivid reminder of what you've been through.'

'Perhaps I'm the one to give the Pennington name the integrity it's been so sorely lacking thus far.'

She paled, and he cursed himself for pursuing a subject that was better off discussed in private. Although he'd made sure their table was roped off and their conversation couldn't be overheard, there was still more than enough interest in them for each expression flitting across Eva's face to be captured and assessed.

'So we're your personal crusade?' she asked, a brittle smile appearing on her face as she acknowledged someone over his shoulder.

'Let's call it more of an experiment.'

Her colour rose with the passionate fury that intrigued him. 'You'd father children based on an *experiment*? After what you've been through...what we've both been through, you think that's fair to the children you intend to have to be used solely as a means for you to prove a point?' Her voice was ragged and he tensed.

'Eva—'

'No, I won't be a part of it!' Her whisper was fierce. 'My mother may have loved me in her own way, but I was still the tool she used against my father when it suited her. If my grades happened to be better than Sophie's, she would imply my father was lacking in some way. And believe me, my father didn't pull his punches when the situation was reversed.' She swallowed and raised bruised eyes to his. 'Even if I cou—wanted to why would I knowingly subject another child to what I went through? Why would I give you a child simply to use to *prove a point*?'

'You mistake my meaning. I don't intend to fail my children or use them as pawns. I intend to be there for them through thick and thin, unlike my parents were for me.' He stopped when her eyes widened. 'Does that surprise you?'

'I... Yes.'

He shrugged, even though it occurred to him that he'd let his guard down more with her than he ever had with anyone. But she had no power to hurt him. She'd already rejected him once. This time he knew the lay of the land going in. So it didn't matter if she knew his parental ambitions for the children they'd have.

'My children will be my priority, although I'll be interested to see how your family fares with being shown that things can be done differently. The *right* way.'

He watched her digest his response, watched the shadows he was beginning to detest mount in her eyes. He decided against probing further. There'd been enough turbulent emotions today. He suspected there would be further fireworks when she found out the new business negotiations he'd commenced this afternoon.

That a part of him was looking forward to it made him shift in his seat.

Since when had he craved verbal conflict with a woman?

Never. And yet he couldn't seem to help himself when it came to Eva.

He was debating this turn of events as their plates were removed when a throat cleared next to them.

The man was around his age, with floppy brown hair and a cocky smile that immediately rubbed Zaccheo the wrong way.

'Can I join you for a few minutes?' he asked.

The *no* that growled up Zaccheo's chest never made it. Eva was smiling—her first genuine smile since he'd walked in—and nodding. 'Mr Preston, of course!'

'Thanks. And call me Ziggy, please. Mr Preston is my headmaster grandfather.'

'What can we do for you, *Ziggy*?' Zaccheo raised an eyebrow at the furious look Eva shot him.

The other man, who was staring at Eva with an avidness that made Zaccheo's fist clench, finally looked in his direction. 'I came to pay my compliments to your girlfriend. She has an amazing voice.'

Eva blushed at his words.

Zaccheo's eyes narrowed when he noticed she wasn't wearing her engagement ring. 'Eva's my fiancée, not my girlfriend. And I'm very much aware of her exceptional talent,' he said, the harsh edge to his voice getting through to the man, who looked from him to Eva before his smile dimmed.

'Ah, congratulations are in order, then?'

'*Grazie,*' Zaccheo replied. 'Was there something else you wanted?'

'Zaccheo!' Eva glared harder, and turned to Ziggy. 'Pardon my *fiancé*. He's feeling a little testy because—'

'I want her all to myself but find other *things* standing in my way. And because you're not wearing your engagement ring, *dolcezza*.'

She covered her bare fingers with her hand, as if that would remove the evidence of the absence of his ring. 'Oh,

I didn't want to risk losing it. I'm still getting used to it.' The glance she sent him held a mixture of defiance and entreaty.

Ziggy cleared his throat again. 'I don't want to play the *Do-you-know-who-I-am?* card, but—'

'Of course I know who you are,' Eva replied with a charming laugh.

Ziggy smiled and produced a business card. 'In that case, would you like to come to my studio next week? See if we can make music together?'

Eva's pleased gasp further darkened Zaccheo's mood. 'Of course I can—'

'Aren't you forgetting something, *luce mio*?' he asked in a quietly lethal tone.

'What?' she asked, so innocently he wanted to grab her from the chair, spread her across the table and make her see nothing, no one, but him. Make her recall that she had given her word to be his and only his.

'You won't be available next week.' He didn't care that he hadn't yet apprised her of the details. He cared that she was smiling at another man as if *he* didn't exist. 'We'll be on our honeymoon on my private island off the coast of Brazil where we'll be staying for the next two weeks.'

Her eyes rounded, but she recovered quickly and took the business card. 'I'll *make* time to see you before I go. Surely you don't want to deny me this opportunity, *darling*?' Her gaze swung to him, daring him to respond in the negative.

Despite his irritation, Zaccheo curbed a smile. 'Of course. Anything for you, *dolcezza*.'

Ziggy beamed. 'Great! I look forward to it.'

The moment he was out of earshot, she turned to Zaccheo. 'How dare you try and sabotage me like that?'

'Watching you smile at another man like that fills me with insane jealousy. It also brings out the jerk in me. My apologies,' he growled. Her mouth dropped open. 'Close your mouth, Eva.'

She shook her head as if reeling from a body blow.

Welcome to my world.

'Where's your ring?' He stared at her, his control on a knife-edge.

Perhaps sensing the dangerously shifting currents, she pulled up the gold chain that hung between her pert, full breasts. His ring dangled from it.

'Put it on. Now,' he said, struggling to keep his voice even.

Undoing the clasp, she took the ring off the chain and slid it back on her finger. 'There. Can I return to work now or are you going to harangue me about something else?'

He told himself he did it because he needed to put his rampaging emotions *somewhere*. That it was her fault for pushing him to his limit. But when he plucked her from her seat, placed her in his lap and kissed her insanely tempting mouth, Zaccheo knew it was because he couldn't help himself. She *got* to him in a way no one else did.

By the time he pulled away, they were both breathing hard. Her high colour filled him with immense satisfaction, helping him ignore his own hopeless loss of control.

'Don't take the ring off again, Eva. You underestimate the lengths I'm prepared to go to in making sure you stick to your word, but for your sake I hope you start taking me seriously.'

In contrast to the vividness of Zaccheo's presence, the rest of the night passed in a dull blur after he left. By the time Eva collapsed into bed in the early hours, her head throbbed with the need to do something severely uncharacteristic. Like scream. Beat her fists against the nearest wall. Shout her anger and confusion to the black skies above.

She did nothing of the sort. More than anything, she craved a little peace and quiet.

After that kiss in the club, even more eyes had followed her wherever she went. Hushed whispers had trailed her to the bathroom. By the time her shift had ended three hours later, she'd been ready to walk out and never return.

She wouldn't, of course. Working at Siren gave her the free time to write her songs while earning enough to live on. Despite Zaccheo's heavy-handedness, she could never see a time when she'd be dependent on anyone other than herself.

'You underestimate the lengths I'm prepared to go to...'

The forceful statement had lingered long after he'd left, anchored by the heavy presence of the prenuptial agreement in her handbag.

He'd said he wouldn't negotiate. Eva didn't see that he had a choice in this matter. Refusing to marry him might well spell the end for her father, but withholding the truth and marrying him knowing she could never fulfil her part of the bargain would be much worse.

Turning in bed, she punched her pillow, dreading the long, restless night ahead. Only to wake with sunshine streaming through the window and her clock announcing it was ten o'clock.

Rushing out of bed, she showered quickly and entered the dining room just as Romeo was exiting, having finished his own breakfast. The table was set for one and Eva cursed herself for the strange dip in her belly that felt very much like disappointment.

'Good morning. Shall I get the chef to make you a cooked breakfast?' The man whose role she was beginning to suspect went deeper than a simple second-in-command asked.

'Just some toast and tea, please, thank you.'

He nodded and started to leave.

'Is Zaccheo around or has he left for the office?'

'Neither. He left this morning for Oman. An unexpected hiccup in the construction of his building there.'

Eva was unprepared for the bereft feeling that swept through her. She should be celebrating her temporary reprieve. Finding a way to see if she could work around that impossible clause. 'When will he be back?'

'In a day or two. Latest by the end of the week to be ready in time for the wedding,' Romeo said in that deep, modulated voice of his. 'This is for you.' He handed her a folded note and left.

The bold scrawl was unmistakeably Zaccheo's.

Eva,

Treat my absence as you wish, but never as an excuse to be complacent.

My PA will be in touch with details of your wedding dress fitting this morning and your amended schedule for the week.

You have my permission to miss me.

Z

Ugh! She grimaced at the arrogance oozing from the paper. Balling the note, she flung it across the table. Then quickly jumped up and retrieved it before Romeo returned. The last thing she wanted was for him to report her loss of temper to Zaccheo.

Her traitorous body had a hard enough time controlling itself when Zaccheo was around. She didn't want him to know he affected her just as badly when he was absent.

By the time breakfast was delivered, she'd regained her composure. Which was just as well, because close on the chef's heel was a tall, striking brunette dressed in a grey pencil skirt and matching jacket.

'Good morning, my name is Anyetta, Mr Giordano's PA. He said you were expecting me?'

'I was expecting a phone call, not a personal visit.'

Anyetta delivered a cool smile. 'Mr Giordano wanted his wishes attended to personally.'

Eva's appetite fled. 'I bet he did,' she muttered.

She poured herself a cup of tea as Anyetta proceeded to fill up her every spare hour between now and Saturday morning.

Eva listened until her temper began to flare, then tuned

out until she heard the word *makeover*. 'I've already had one makeover. I don't need another one.'

Anyetta's eyes drifted over Eva's hair, which she admitted was a little wild since she hadn't brushed it properly before she'd rushed out to speak to Zaccheo. 'Not even for your wedding day?'

Since there wasn't likely to be a wedding day once she told Zaccheo she had no intention of signing the agreement, she replied, 'It'll be taken care of.'

Anyetta ticked off a few more items, verified that Eva's passport was up to date, then stood as the doorbell rang. 'That'll be Margaret with your wedding dress.'

The feeling of being on a runaway train intensified as Eva trailed Anyetta out of the dining room. She drew to a stunned halt when she saw the middle-aged woman coming towards her with a single garment bag and a round veil and shoebox.

'Please tell me you don't have a team of assistants lurking outside ready to jump on me?' she asked after Anyetta left.

Margaret laughed. 'It's just me, Lady Pennington. Your fiancé was very specific about his wishes, and, meeting you now, I see why he chose this dress. He did say I was to work with you, of course. So if you don't like it, we can explore other options.'

Eva reminded herself that this situation hadn't arisen out of a normal courtship, that Zaccheo choosing her wedding dress for her shouldn't upset her so much. Besides, the likelihood of this farce ever seeing the light of day was very low so she was better off just going along with it.

But despite telling herself not to care, Eva couldn't suppress her anxiety and excitement.

She gasped as the dress was revealed.

The design itself was simple and clean, but utterly breathtaking. Eva stared at the fitted white satin gown overlaid with lace and beaded with countless tiny crystals. Delicate capped sleeves extended from the sweetheart neckline and the tiniest train flared out in a beautiful arc. At the back, more crystals had been embedded in mother-of-pearl buttons that went from nape to waist. Unable to resist, Eva reached out to touch the dress, then pulled herself back.

There was no point falling in love with a dress she'd never wear. No point getting butterflies about a marriage that would never happen once she confessed her flaw to Zaccheo. Her hands fisted and she fought the desolation threatening to break free inside her.

For six years, she'd successfully not dwelt on what she could never have—a husband who cared for her and a family of her own. She'd made music her life and had found fulfilment in it. She wasn't about to let a heartbreakingly gorgeous dress dredge up agonies she'd sealed in a box marked *strictly out of bounds*.

'Are you ready to try it on?' Margaret asked.

Eva swallowed. 'Might as well.'

If the other woman found her response curious, she didn't let on. Eva avoided her gaze in the mirror as the dress was slipped over her shoulders and the delicate chiffon and lace veil was fitted into place. She mumbled her thanks as Margaret helped her into matching-coloured heels.

'Oh, I'm pleased to see we don't need to alter it in any way, Lady Pennington. It fits perfectly. Looks like your fiancé was very accurate with your measurements. You'd be surprised how many men get it wrong...'

She kept her gaze down, frightened to look at herself, as Margaret tweaked and tugged until she was happy.

Eva dared not look up in case she began to *hope* and *wish*. She murmured appropriate responses and turned this way and that when asked and breathed a sigh of relief when the ordeal was over. The moment Margaret zipped up the bag and left, Eva escaped to her suite. Putting her headphones on, she activated the music app on her tablet and proceeded to drown out her thoughts the best way she knew how.

But this time no amount of doing what she loved best could obliterate the thoughts tumbling through her head.

At seventeen when her periods had got heavier and more painful with each passing month, she'd attributed it to life's natural cycle. But when stronger painkillers had barely alleviated the pain, she'd begun to suspect something major was wrong.

Collapsing during a university lecture had finally prompted her to seek medical intervention.

The doctor's diagnosis had left her reeling.

Even then, she'd convinced herself it wasn't the end of the world, that compared to her mother's fight against cancer, a fight she'd eventually lost a year later, Eva's problem was inconsequential. Women dealt with challenging problems like hers every day. When the time came, the man she chose to spend the rest of her life with would understand and support her.

Eva scoffed at her naiveté. Scott, the first man she'd dated in the last year of university, had visibly recoiled from her when she'd mentioned her condition. She'd been so shocked by his reaction, she'd avoided him for the rest of her time at uni.

Burnt, she'd sworn off dating until she'd met George Tremayne, her fellow business intern during her brief stint at Penningtons. Flattered by his attentiveness, she'd let down her guard and gone on a few dates before he'd begun to pressure her to take things further. Her gentle rejection and confession of her condition had resulted in a scathing volley of insults, during which she'd found out exactly why her father had been pressing her to work at Penningtons after graduation.

Oscar Pennington, already secure in his conscript of Sophie as his heir, was eager to offload his remaining daughter and had lined up a list of suitable men, George Tremayne, the son of a viscount, being on the top of that list. George's near-identical reaction to Scott's had hurt twice as much, and convinced Eva once and for all that her secret was best kept to herself.

Finding out she was yet another means to an end for Zaccheo had rocked her to the core, but she'd taken consolation in the fact the secret she'd planned on revealing to him shortly after their engagement was safe.

That secret was about to be ripped open.

As she turned up the volume of her music Eva knew disclosing it to Zaccheo would be the most difficult thing she would ever do.

CHAPTER TEN

Zaccheo scrolled through the missed calls from Eva on his phone as he was driven away from the private hangar. Romeo had relayed her increasingly frantic requests to reach him. Zaccheo had deliberately forbidden his number from being given to her until this morning, once he'd confirmed his return to London.

His jaw flexed as he rolled tight shoulders. The number of fires he'd put out in Oman would've wiped out a lesser man. But Zaccheo's name and ruthless nature weren't renowned for nothing, and although it'd taken three days to get the construction schedule back on track, his business partners were in no doubt that he would bring them to their knees if they strayed so much as one millimetre from the outcome he desired.

It was the same warning he'd given Oscar Pennington when he'd called yesterday and attempted an ego-stroking exercise to get Zaccheo to relent on his threats. Zaccheo had coldly reminded him of the days he'd spent in prison and invited Pennington to ask for clemency when hell froze over.

No doubt Eva's eagerness to contact him was born of the same desire as her father's. But unlike her father, the thought of speaking to Eva sent a pleasurable kick of anticipation through his blood, despite the fact that with time and distance he'd looked back on their conversations since his release with something close to dismay.

Had he really revealed all those things about his time in prison and his childhood to her?

What was even more puzzling was her reaction. She hadn't looked down her nose at him in those moments. Had in fact exhibited nothing but empathy and compassion. Pushing the bewildering thought away, he dialled her number, gratified when she picked up on the first ring.

'*Ciao*, Eva. I understand you're experiencing pre-wedding jitters.'

'You understand wrong. This wedding isn't going to happen. Not once you hear what I have to say.'

His tension increased until the knots in his shoulders felt like immoveable rocks. He breathed through the red haze blurring his vision. 'I take it you didn't miss me, then?' he taunted.

She made a sound, a cross between a huff and a sigh. 'We really need to talk, Zaccheo.'

'Nothing you say will alter my intention to make you mine tomorrow,' he warned.

She hesitated. Then, 'Zaccheo, it's important. I won't take up too much of your time. But I need to speak to you.'

He rested his head against the seat. 'You have less than twenty-four hours left as a single woman. I won't permit anything like male strippers anywhere near you, of course, but I won't be a total bore and deny you a hen party if you wish—'

'I don't want a damn hen party! What I want is five minutes of your time.'

'Are you dying of some life-threatening disease?'

'*What?* Of course not!'

'Are you afraid I won't be a good husband?' he asked, noting the raw edge to his voice, but realising how much her answer meant to him.

'Zaccheo, this is about me, not you.'

He let her non-answer slide. 'You'll be a good wife. And despite your less than auspicious upbringing, you'll be a good mother.'

He heard her soft gasp. 'How do you know that?'

'Because you're passionate when you care. You just need to channel that passion from your undeserving family to the one we will create.'

'I can't just switch my feelings towards my family off.

Everyone deserves someone who cares about them, no matter what.'

His heart kicked hard and his grip tightened around the phone as bitterness washed through him. 'Not everyone gets it, though.'

Silence thrummed. 'I'm sorry about your parents. Is… your mother still alive?' Her voice bled the compassion he'd begun to associate with her.

It warmed a place inside him even as he answered. 'That depends on who you ask. Since she relocated to the other side of the world to get away from me, I presume she won't mind if I think her dead to me.'

'But she's alive, Zaccheo. Which means there's hope. Do you really want to waste that?' Her pain-filled voice drew him up short, reminding him that she'd lost her mother.

When had this conversation turned messy and emotional?

'You were close to your mother?' he asked.

'When she wasn't busy playing up to being a Pennington, or using me to get back at my father, she was a brilliant mother. I wish… I wish she'd been a mother to both Sophie *and* me.' She laughed without humour. 'Hell, I used to wish I'd been born into another family, that my last name wasn't Pennington—' She stopped and a tense silence reigned.

Zaccheo frowned. Things weren't adding up with Eva. He'd believed her surname was one she would do just about anything for, including help cover up fraud. But in his boardroom on Monday, she'd seemed genuinely shocked and hurt by the extent of her father's duplicity. And there was also the matter of her chosen profession and the untouched money in her bank account.

A less cynical man would believe she was the exception to the abhorrent aristocratic rule…

'At least you had one parent who cared for you. You were lucky,' he said, his mind whirling with the possibility that he could be wrong.

'But that parent is gone, and I feel as if I have no one now,' she replied quietly.

The need to tell her she had him flared through his mind. He barely managed to stay silent. After a few seconds, she cleared her throat. Her next words made him wish he'd hung up.

'I haven't signed the prenup,' she blurted out. 'I'm not going to.'

Because of the last clause.

For a brief moment, Zaccheo wanted to tell her why he wanted children. That the bleak loneliness that had dogged him through his childhood and almost drowned him in prison had nearly broken him. That he'd fallen into a pit of despair when he'd realised no one would miss him should the worst happen.

His mother had emigrated to Australia with her husband rather than stay in the same city as him once Zaccheo had fully established himself in London. That had cut deeper than any rejection he'd suffered from her in the past. And although the news of his trial and sentencing had been worldwide news, Zaccheo had never once heard from the woman who'd given him life.

He could've died in prison for all his mother cared. That thought had haunted him day and night until he'd decided to do something about it.

Until he'd vowed to alter his reality, ensure he had someone who would be proud to bear his name. Someone to whom he could pass on his legacy.

He hadn't planned for that person to be Eva Pennington until he'd read about her engagement in the file. But once he had, the decision had become iron cast.

Although this course was very much a sweeter, more lasting experience, Zaccheo couldn't help but wonder if it was all worth the ground shifting so much beneath his feet.

Eva was getting beneath his skin. And badly.

Dio mio. Why were the feelings he'd bottled up for over two decades choosing *now* to bubble up? He exhaled harshly.

Rough and ruthless was his motto. It was what had made him the man he was today. 'You'll be in your wedding dress at noon tomorrow, ready to walk down the aisle where our six hundred guests will be—'

'*Six hundred?* You've invited six *hundred* people to the wedding?' Her husky disbelief made his teeth grind.

'You thought I intended to have a hole-in-the-wall ceremony?' A fresh wave of bitterness rolled over him. 'Or did you think my PA was spouting gibberish when she informed you of all this on Tuesday?'

'Sorry, I must've tuned out because, contrary to what you think, I don't like my life arranged for me,' she retorted. 'That doesn't change anything. I *can't* do this…'

Zaccheo frowned at the naked distress in her voice.

Eva was genuinely torn up about the prospect of giving herself to him, a common man only worthy of a few kisses but nothing as substantial as the permanent state of matrimony.

Something very much like pain gripped his chest. 'Is that your final decision? Are you backing out of our agreement?'

She remained silent for so long, he thought the line was dead. 'Unless you're willing to change the last clause, yes.'

Zaccheo detested the sudden clenching of his stomach, as if the blow he'd convinced himself would never come had been landed. The voice taunting him for feeling more than a little stunned was ruthlessly smashed away.

He assured himself he had another way to claim the justice he sought. 'Very well. *Ciao.*'

He ended the phone call. And fought the urge to hurl his phone out of the window.

Eva dropped the phone onto the coffee-shop table. She'd arrived at work only to discover she'd been taken off the roster due to her impending wedding. Since she had holiday due to her anyway, Eva hadn't fought too hard at suddenly finding herself with free time.

Her session with Ziggy yesterday had gone well, despite her head being all over the place. If nothing else came of it, she could add that to her CV.

Curbing a hysterical snort, she stared at her phone.

She'd done the right thing and ended this farce before it went too far. Before the longings she'd harboured in the last three days got any more out of control.

Deep in her heart, she knew Zaccheo would react the same way to her secret as Scott and George had. He wouldn't want to marry half a woman, especially when he'd stated his expectations in black and white in a formal agreement drafted by a team of lawyers, and then confounded her with his genuine desire to become a father.

So why hadn't she just told him over the phone?

Because she was a glutton for punishment?

Because some part of her had hoped telling him face-to-face would help her gauge whether there was a chance he would accept her the way she was?

Fat chance.

It was better this way. Clean. Painless.

She jumped as her phone pinged. Heart lurching, she accessed the message, but it was only the manageress from Siren, wishing her a lovely wedding and sinfully blissful honeymoon.

Eva curled her hand around her fast-cooling mug. Once the news got out that she'd broken her third engagement in two years, her chances of marrying anyone, let alone a man who would accept her just as she was, would shrink from nil to no chance in hell.

Pain spiked again at the reminder of her condition. Exhaling, she wrenched her mind to more tangible things.

Like finding a place to live.

She weighed her options, despair clutching her insides

when, two hours later, she faced the only avenue open to her. Going back home to Pennington Manor.

Reluctantly, she picked up her phone, then nearly dropped it when it blared to life. The name of the caller made her frown.

'Sophie?'

'Eva, what's going on?' The fear in her voice shredded Eva's heart.

'What do you mean?'

'I've just had to call the doctor because Father's had another episode!'

Eva jerked to her feet, sending her coffee cup bouncing across the table. 'What?'

'We got a call from Zaccheo Giordano an hour ago to say the wedding was off. Father's been frantic. He was about to call you when he collapsed. The doctor says if he's subjected to any more stress he could have a heart attack or a stroke. Is it true? Did you call off the wedding?' The strain in her sister's voice was unmistakeable.

'Yes,' Eva replied. She grabbed her bag and hurried out of the coffee shop when she began to attract peculiar looks. Outside, she shrugged into her coat and pulled up her hoodie to avoid the light drizzle.

'Oh, God. Why?' her sister demanded.

'Zaccheo wanted me to sign a prenuptial agreement.'

'So? Everyone does that these days.'

'One of the terms...he wants *children*.'

Her sister sighed. 'So he backed out when you told him?'

'No, he doesn't know.'

'But... I'm confused,' Sophie replied.

'I tried to tell him but he wouldn't listen.'

'You tried. Isn't that enough?'

Eva ducked into a quiet alley and leaned against a wall. 'No, it's *not* enough. We've caused enough harm where he's concerned. I won't go into this based on a lie.'

'Father's terrified, Eva.'

'Can I talk to him?'

'He's sleeping now. I'll let him know you called when he wakes up.' Sophie paused. 'Eva, I've been thinking...what you said on Saturday, about you not being out to replace me... I shouldn't have bitten your head off. It's just... Father isn't an easy man to please. He was relying on me to see us through this rough patch...'

'I didn't mean to step on your toes, Sophie.'

Her sister inhaled deeply. 'I know. But everything seems so effortless for you, Eva. It always has. I envied you because Mother chose you—'

'Parents shouldn't choose which child to love and which to keep at arm's length!'

'But that was our reality. He wanted a son. And I was determined to be that son. After Mother died, I was scared Father would think I wasn't worth his attention.'

'You were. You still are.'

'Only because I've gone along with whatever he's asked of me without complaint, even when I knew I shouldn't. This thing with Zaccheo... Father's not proud of it. Nor am I. I don't know where we go from here, but once we're through this, can we get together?' Sophie asked, her voice husky with the plea.

Eva didn't realise her legs had given way until her bottom touched the cold, hard ground.

'Yes, if you want,' she murmured. Her hands shook as she hung up.

The last time she'd seen Sophie's rigid composure crumble had been in the few weeks after they'd buried their mother. For a while she'd had her sister back. They'd been united in their grief, supporting each other when their loss overwhelmed them.

As much as Eva missed *that* Sophie, she couldn't stomach having her back under similar circumstances. Nor could she bear the danger that her father faced.

She wasn't sure how long she sat there.

Cold seeped into her clothes. Into her bones. Into her heart.

Feeling numb, she dug into her bag and extracted the prenup and read through it one more time.

She couldn't honour Zaccheo's last clause, but that didn't mean she couldn't use it to buy herself, and her father, time until they met and she explained. Despite his own past, he wanted a family. Maybe he would understand why she was trying to salvage hers.

Slowly, she dialled. After endless rings, the line clicked through.

'Eva.' His voice was pure cold steel.

'I...' She attempted to say the words but her teeth still chattered. Squeezing her eyes shut, she tried again. 'I'll sign the agreement. I'll marry you tomorrow.'

Silence.

'Zaccheo? Are you there?'

'Where are you?'

She shivered at his impersonal tone. 'I'm...' She looked up at the street sign in the alley and told him.

'Romeo will be there in fifteen minutes. He'll witness the agreement and bring it to me. You'll return to the penthouse and resume preparations for the wedding.' He paused, as if waiting for her to disagree.

'Will I see you today?' She hated how weak her voice sounded.

'No.'

Eva exhaled. 'Okay, I'll wait for Romeo.'

'Bene.' The line went dead.

The grey mizzle outside aptly reflected Eva's mood as she sat, hands clasped in her lap, as the hairdresser finished putting up her hair. Behind her, Sophie smiled nervously.

Eva smiled back, knowing her sister's nervousness stemmed from the fear that Eva would change her mind again.

But this time there was no going back. She meant to come clean to Zaccheo at the first opportunity and open herself up to whatever consequences he sought.

Just how she would manage that was a puzzle she hadn't untangled yet, but since Zaccheo was hell-bent on this marriage, and she was giving him what he wanted, technically she was fulfilling her side of the bargain.

God, when had she resorted to seeing things in shades of grey instead of black and white, truth and lie? Was Zaccheo right? Did her Pennington blood mean she was destined to do whatever it took, even if it meant compromising her integrity, for the sake of her family and pedigree?

No. She wouldn't care if she woke up tomorrow as ordinary Eva Penn instead of Lady Pennington. And she *would* come clean to Zaccheo, no matter what.

Except that was looking less likely to happen *before* the wedding. Zaccheo hadn't returned to the penthouse last night. She hadn't deluded herself that he was observing the quaint marriage custom. If anything, he was probably making another billion, or actively sowing his last wild oats. She jerked at the jagged pain that shot through her.

Sophie stood up. 'What's wrong?'

'Nothing. How's Father?'

Sophie's face clouded. 'He insists he's well enough to walk you down the aisle.' Her sister's eyes darted to the hairdresser who had finished and was walking out to get Margaret. 'He's desperate that everything goes according to plan today.'

Eva managed to stop her smile from slipping. 'It will.'

Sophie met her gaze in the mirror. 'Do you think I should talk to Zaccheo…explain?'

Eva thought about the conversation she'd had with Zaccheo yesterday, the merciless tone, the ruthless man on a mission who'd been released from prison a mere week ago. 'Maybe not just yet.'

Sophie nodded, then flashed a smile that didn't quite make it before she left Eva alone as Margaret entered.

Any hopes of talking to Zaccheo evaporated when she found herself at the doors of the chapel an hour later.

Catching sight of him for the first time since Monday, she felt her heart slam around her chest.

Romeo stood in the best-man position and Eva wondered again at the connection between the two men. Did Zaccheo have any friends? Or had he lost all of them when her family's actions had altered his fate?

The thought flitted out of her head as her gaze returned almost magnetically to Zaccheo.

He'd eschewed a morning coat in favour of a bespoke three-piece suit in the softest dove-grey silk. Against the snowy white shirt and white tie completing the ensemble, his long hair was at once dangerously primitive and yet so utterly captivating, her mouth dried as her pulse danced with a dark, decadent delight. His beard had been trimmed considerably and a part of her mourned its loss. Perhaps it was that altered look that made his eyes so overwhelmingly electrifying, or it was the fact that his face was set in almost brutal lines, but the effect was like lightning to her system the moment her eyes connected with his.

The music in the great hall of the cathedral he'd astonishingly managed to secure on such short notice disappeared, along with the chatter of the goggle-eyed guests who did nothing to hide their avid curiosity.

All she could see was him, the man who would be her husband in less than fifteen minutes.

She stumbled, then stopped. A murmur rose in the crowd. Eva felt her father's concerned stare, but she couldn't look away from Zaccheo.

His nostrils flared, his eyes narrowing in warning as fear clutched her, freezing her feet.

'Eva?' Her father's ragged whisper caught her consciousness.

'Why did you insist on walking me down the aisle?' she asked him, wanting in some way to know that she wasn't doing all of this to save a man who had very little regard for her.

'What? Because you're my daughter,' her father replied with a puzzled frown.

'So you're not doing it just to keep up appearances?'

His face creased with a trace of the vulnerability she'd glimpsed only once before, when her mother died, and her heart lurched. 'Eva, I haven't handled things well. I know that. I was brought up to put the family name above all else, and I took that responsibility a little too far. Despite our less than perfect marriage, your mother was the one who would pull me back to my senses when I went a little too far. Without her...' His voice roughened and his hand gripped hers. 'We might lose Penningtons, but I don't want to lose you and Sophie.'

Eva's throat clogged. 'Maybe you should tell her that? She needs to know you're proud of her, Father.'

Her father looked to where her sister stood, and he nodded. 'I will. And I'm proud of you, too. You're as beautiful as your mother was on our wedding day.'

Eva blinked back her tears as murmurs rose in the crowd.

She turned to find Zaccheo staring at her. Something dark, sinister, curled through his eyes and she swallowed as his mouth flattened.

I can't marry him without him knowing! He deserves to know that I can't give him the family he wants.

'My dear, you need to move now. It's time,' her father pleaded.

Torn by the need for Zaccheo to know the truth and the need to protect her father, she shook her head, her insides churning.

Churning turned into full-blown liquefying as Zaccheo stepped from the dais, his imposing body threatening to block out the light as he headed down the aisle.

She desperately sucked in a breath, the knowledge that Zaccheo would march her up the aisle himself if need be finally scraping her feet from the floor. He stopped halfway, his gaze unswerving, until she reached him.

He grasped her hand, his hold unbreakable as he turned and walked her to the altar.

Trembling at the hard, pitiless look in his eyes, she swallowed and tried to speak. 'Zaccheo—'

'No, Eva. No more excuses,' he growled.

The priest glanced between them, his expression benign but enquiring.

Zaccheo nodded.

The organ swelled. And sealed her fate.

CHAPTER ELEVEN

'Glaring at it won't make it disappear, unless you have superhero laser vision.'

Eva jumped at the mocking voice and curled her fingers into her lap, hiding the exquisite diamond-studded platinum ring that had joined her engagement ring three hours ago.

'I wasn't willing it away.' On the contrary, she'd been wondering how long it would stay on her finger once Zaccheo knew the truth.

The reception following the ceremony had been brief but intense. Six hundred people clamouring for attention and the chance to gawp at the intriguing couple could take a lot out of a girl. With Zaccheo's fingers laced through hers the whole time, tightening commandingly each time she so much as moved an inch away from him, Eva had been near-blubbering-wreck status by the time their limo had left the hall.

Once she'd stopped reeling from the shock of being married to Zaccheo Giordano, she'd taken a moment to take in her surroundings. The Great Hall in the Guildhall was usually booked for years in advance. That Zaccheo had managed to secure it in a week and thrown together a stunning reception was again testament that she'd married a man with enough power and clout to smash through any resistance.

Zaccheo, despite his spell in prison, remained a formidable man, one, she suspected, who didn't need her father's intervention to restore his damaged reputation. So why was he pursuing it so relentlessly? Throughout the reception, she'd watched him charm their guests with the sheer force of his charisma. By the time her father had got round to giving the edifying toast welcoming Zaccheo to the Pennington family, the effort had seemed redundant.

She watched Zaccheo now as the car raced them to the airport, and wondered if it was a good time to broach the subject burning a hole in her chest.

'Something on your mind?' he queried without raising his gaze from his tablet.

Her heart leapt into her throat. She started to speak but noticed the partition between them and Romeo, who sat in the front passenger seat, was open. Although she was sure Romeo knew the ins and outs of the document he'd been asked to witness yesterday, Eva wasn't prepared to discuss her devastating shortcomings in his presence.

So she opted for something else plaguing her. She smoothed her hands on her wedding dress. 'Do I have your assurance that you'll speak on my father's behalf once you hand over the documents to the authorities?'

He speared her with incisive grey eyes. 'You're so eager to see him let off the hook, aren't you?'

'Wouldn't you be, if it was your father?' she asked.

Eva was unprepared for the strange look that crossed his face. The mixture of anger, sadness, and bitterness hollowed out her stomach.

'My father wasn't interested in being let off the hook for his sins. He was happy to keep himself indebted to his betters because he thought that was his destiny.'

Her breath caught. 'What? That doesn't make sense.'

'Very little of my father's actions made sense to me, not when I was a child, and not as an adult.'

The unexpected insight into his life made her probe deeper. 'When did he die?'

'When I was thirteen years old.'

'I'm sorry.' When he inclined his head and continued to stare at her, she pressed her luck. 'How did he—?'

'Zaccheo,' Romeo's deep voice interrupted them. 'Perhaps this is not a subject for your wedding day?'

A look passed between the friends.

When Zaccheo looked at her again, that cool impassivity he'd worn since they'd left the reception to thunderous applause had returned.

'Your father has done his part adequately for now. Our lawyers will meet in a few days to discuss the best way forward. When my input is needed, I'll provide it. *Your* role, on the other hand, is just beginning.'

Before she could reply, the door opened. Eva gaped at the large private jet standing mere feet away. Beside the steps, two pilots and two stewardesses waited.

Zaccheo exited and took her hand. The shocking electricity of his touch and the awareness in his eyes had her scrambling to release her fingers, but he held on, and walked her to his crew, who extended their congratulations.

Eva was grappling with their conversation when she stepped into the unspeakable luxury of the plane. To the right, a sunken entertainment area held a semicircular cream sofa and a separate set of club chairs with enough gadgets to keep even the most attention-deficient passenger happy. In a separate area a short flight of stairs away, there was a conference table with four chairs and a bar area off a top-line galley.

Zaccheo stepped behind her and her body zapped to life, thrilling to his proximity. She suppressed a shiver when he let go of her fingers and cupped her shoulders in his warm hands.

'I have several conference calls to make once we take off. And you...' He paused, traced a thumb across her cheek. The contact stunned her, as did the gentle look in his eyes. 'You look worn out.'

'Is that a kind way of saying I look like hell?' She strove for a light tone and got a husky one instead.

That half-smile appeared, and Eva experienced something close to elation that the icy look had melted from his face. 'You could never look like hell, *cara*. A prickly and challenging puzzle that I look forward to unravelling, most definitely. But never like hell.'

The unexpected response startled her into gaping for several seconds before she recovered. 'Should I be wary that you're being nice to me?'

'I can be less…monstrous when I get my way.'

The reminder that he wouldn't be getting his way and the thought of his reaction once he found out brought a spike of anxiety, rendering her silent as he led her to a seat and handed her a flute of champagne from the stewardess's tray.

'Zaccheo…' She stopped when his thumb moved over her lips. Sensation sizzled along her nerve endings, setting her pulse racing as he brushed it back and forth. The heat erupting between her thighs had her pressing her legs together to soothe the desperate ache.

She hardly felt the plane take off. All she was aware of was the mesmerising look in Zaccheo's eyes.

'I haven't told you how stunning you look.' He leaned closer and replaced his thumb with his lips at the corner of her mouth.

Delicious flames warmed her blood. 'Thank you.' Her voice shook with the desire moving through her. More than anything, she was filled with the blind need to turn her head and meet his mouth with hers.

When his lips trailed to her jaw, then to the curve between her shoulder and neck, Eva let out a helpless moan, her heart racing with sudden, debilitating hunger.

His fingers linked hers and she found herself being led to the back of the plane. Eva couldn't summon a protest. Nor could she remind herself that she needed to come clean, sooner rather than later.

The master bedroom was equally stunning. Gold leaf threaded a thick cream coverlet on a king-sized bed and plush carpeting absorbed their footsteps as he shut the door.

'I intend us to have two uninterrupted weeks on the island. In order for that to happen, I need to work with Romeo to clear my plate work-wise. Rest now. Whatever's on your mind can wait for a few more hours.' Again there was no bite to his words, leaving her lost as to this new side of the man she'd married.

She stood, almost overpowered by the strength of her emotions, as he positioned himself behind her and slowly undid her buttons. The heavy dress pooled at her feet and she stood in only her white strapless bra, panties, and the garter and sheer stocking set that had accompanied her dress.

A rough, tortured sound echoed around the room. *'Stai mozzafiato,'* Zaccheo muttered thickly. 'You're breathtaking,' he translated when she glanced at him.

A fierce blush flared up. Eyes darkening, he circled her, tracing her high colour with a barest tip of his forefinger. Her gaze dropped to the sensual line of his mouth and she bit her own lip as need drowned her.

She gasped, completely enthralled, as he dropped to his knees and reached for her garter belt, eyes locked on hers. He pulled it off and tucked it deep in his inner pocket. When he stood, the hunger on his face stopped her breath, anticipation sparking like fireworks through her veins.

He lightly brushed her lips with his.

'Our first time won't be on a plane within listening distance of my staff.' He walked to the bed and pulled back the covers. He waited until she got in and tucked her in. About to walk away, he suddenly stopped. 'We will make this marriage work, Eva.'

Her mouth parted but, with no words to counter that unexpected vow, she slowly pressed her lips together as pain ripped through her.

'Sleep well, *dolcezza*,' he murmured, then left.

Despite her turmoil, she slept through the whole flight, rousing refreshed if unsettled as to what the future held.

Dressing in a light cotton sundress and open sandals, she left her hair loose, applied a touch of lip gloss and sunscreen and exited the plane.

They transferred from jet to high-speed boat with Romeo at the wheel. The noise from the engine made conversation impossible but, for the first time, the silence between Zaccheo and Eva felt less fraught. The strange but intense feeling that had engulfed them both as he'd undressed her on the plane continued to grip them as they raced towards their final destination. When she caught her hair for the umpteenth time to keep it from flying in the wind, he captured the strands in a tight grip at the base of her neck, then used the hold to pull her closer until she curved into his side. With his other arm sprawled along the back of their seat, he appeared the most at ease Eva had ever seen him.

Perhaps being forced to wait for a while to tell him hadn't been a bad thing.

She let the tension ooze out of her.

Despite the shades covering his eyes, he must have sensed her scrutiny, because he turned and stared down at her for endless minutes. She felt the power of that look to the tips of her toes and almost fell into him when he took her mouth in a voracious kiss.

He let her up for air when her lungs threatened to burst. Burying his face in her throat, he rasped for her ears only, 'I cannot wait to make you mine.'

By the time the boat slowed and pulled into a quiet inlet, Eva was a nervous wreck.

'Welcome to Casa do Paraíso,' he said once the engine died.

Enthralled, Eva looked around. Tropical trees and lush vegetation surrounded a spectacular hacienda made of timber and glass, the mid-morning sun casting vibrant shades of green, orange and blue on the breathtaking surroundings. Wide glass windows dominated the structure and, through them, Eva saw white walls and white furniture with splashes of colourful paintings on the walls perpetuated in an endless flow of rooms.

'It's huge,' she blurted.

Zaccheo jumped onto the sugary sand and grabbed her hand.

'The previous owner built it for his first wife and their eight children. She got it in the divorce, but hated the tropical heat so never visited. It was run-down by the time I bought the island from her, so I made substantial alterations.'

The mention of children ramped up the tension crawling through her belly and, despite her trying to shrug the feeling away, it lingered as she followed him up the wide front porch into the stunning living room.

A staff of four greeted them, then hurried out to where Romeo was securing the vessel. She gazed around in stunned awe, accepting that Zaccheo commanded the best when it came to the structures he put his stamp on, whether commercial or private.

'Come here, Eva.' The order was impatient.

She turned from admiring the structure to admire the man who'd created it. Tall, proud and intensely captivating, he stood at the base of a suspended staircase, his white-hot gaze gleaming dangerously, promising complete sexual oblivion.

Desire pulsed between them, a living thing that writhed, consumed with a hunger that demanded to be met, fulfilled.

Eva knew she should make time now they were here to tell him. Lay down the truth ticking away inside her like a bomb.

After years of struggling to forge a relationship with her father and sister, she'd finally laid the foundations of one today.

How could she live with herself if she continued to keep Zaccheo in the dark about the family he hoped for himself?

Her feet slapped against the large square tiles as she hurried across the room. His mouth lifted in a half-smile of satisfaction. She'd barely reached him when he swung her into his arms and stormed up the stairs.

And then the need to disclose her secret was suddenly no longer urgent. It'd been superseded by another, more pressing demand. One that every atom in her body urged her to assuage. *Now.* Before the opportunity was taken from her. Before her confession once again found her in the brutal wasteland of rejection.

His heat singed where they touched. Unable to resist, she sank her fingers into his hair and buried her face in his neck, eager to be closer to his rough primitiveness.

Feeling bold, she nipped at his skin.

His responding growl was intoxicating. As was the feeling of being pressed against the hard, masculine planes of his body when he slowly lowered her to her feet.

'I've waited so long to be inside you. I won't wait any longer,' he vowed, the words fierce, stamped with decadent intent.

Arms clamped around her waist, he walked her backwards to the vast white-sheeted bed. In one clean move, he pulled her dress over her head and dropped it. Her bra and panties swiftly followed.

Zaccheo stopped breathing as he stared down at her exposed curves.

As he'd done on the plane, he circled her body, this time trailing more fingers over her heated skin, creating a fiery path that arrowed straight between her thighs. She was swaying under the dizzying force of her arousal by the time he faced her again.

'Beautiful. So beautiful,' he murmured against her skin, then pulled her nipple into his mouth, surrounding the aching bud with heat and want.

Eva cried out and clutched his shoulders, her whole body gripped with a fever that shook her from head to toe. He moved his attention to her twin breast while his fingers teased the other, doubling the pleasure, doubling her agony.

'Zaccheo,' she groaned.

He straightened abruptly and reefed his black T-shirt over his head, exposing hard, smooth pecs and a muscle-ridged stomach. But as intensely delectable as his torso was, it wasn't what made her belly quiver. It was the intriguing tattooed band of Celtic knots linked by three slim lines that circled his upper arm. The artwork was flawless and beautiful, flowing gracefully when he moved. Reaching out, she touched the first knot. He paused and stared down at her.

It struck her hard in that moment just how much she didn't know about the man she'd married.

'You seem almost nervous, *dolcezza*.'

Eva struggled to think of a response that wouldn't make her sound gauche. 'Don't you feel nervous, even a little, your first time with a new lover?' she replied.

He froze and his lips compressed for a fraction of a second, as if she'd said something to displease him. Then his fingers went to his belt. 'Nerves, no. Anticipation that a long-held desire is about to be fulfilled? Most definitely.' He removed his remaining clothes in one swift move.

Perfection. It was the only word she could think of.

'Even when you've experienced it more than a few dozen times?'

She gasped when his fingers gripped hers in a tight hold. When he spoke, his voice held a bite that jarred. 'Perhaps we should refrain from the subject of past lovers.'

Hard, demanding lips slanted over hers, his tongue sliding into her mouth, fracturing the last of her senses. She clung to him, her body once again aflame from the ferocious power of his.

Cool sheets met her back and Zaccheo sprawled beside her. After an eternity of kissing, he raised his head.

'There are so many ways I wish to take you I don't know where to begin.'

Heat burst beneath her skin and he laughed softly.

'You blush with the ease of an innocent.' He trailed his hand down her throat, lingering at her racing pulse, before it curved around one breast. 'It's almost enough to make me forget that you're not.' Again that bite, but less ferocious this time, his accent growing thicker as he bent his head and tongued her pulse.

She jerked against him, her fingers gliding over his warm skin of their own accord. 'On what basis do you form the opinion that I'm not?' she blurted before she lost her nerve.

He stilled, grey eyes turning that rare gunmetal shade that announced a dangerously heightened emotional state. His hand abandoned her breast and curled around her nape in an iron grip. 'What are you saying, Eva?' His voice was a hoarse rumble.

She licked nervous lips. 'That I don't want to be treated like I'm fragile...but I don't wish my first time to be without mercy either.'

He sucked in a stunned breath. 'Your *first*... *Madre di Dio*.' His gaze searched hers, his breathing growing increasingly erratic.

Slowly, he drew back from her, scouring her body from head to toe as if seeing her for the first time. He parted her thighs and she moved restlessly, helplessly, as his eyes lingered at her centre. Stilling her with one hand, he lowered his head and kissed her eyes, her mouth, her throat. Then lower until he reached her belly. He licked at her navel, then rained kisses on her quivering skin. Firm hands held her open, then his shoulders took over the job. Reading his intention, she raised her head from the pillow.

'Zaccheo.' She wasn't sure whether she was pleading for or rejecting what was coming.

He reared up for a second, his hands going to his hair to twist the long strands into an expert knot at the back of his head. The act was so unbelievably hot, her body threatened to melt into a useless puddle. Then he was back, broad shoulders easily holding her legs apart as he kissed his way down her inner thighs.

'I know what I crave most,' he muttered thickly. 'A taste of you.'

The first touch of his mouth at her core elicited a long, helpless groan from her. Her spine arched off the bed, her thighs shaking as fire roared through her body. He held her down and feasted on her, the varying friction from his mouth and beard adding an almost unholy pleasure that sent her soaring until a scream ripped from her throat and she fell off the edge of the universe.

She surfaced to feel his mouth on her belly, his hands trailing up her sides. That gunmetal shade of grey reflected deep possession as he rose above her and kissed her long and deep.

'Now, *il mio angelo*. Now I make you mine.'

He captured her hands above her head with one hand. The other reached between her thighs, gently massaging her core before he slid one finger inside her tight sheath. His groan echoed hers. Removing his finger, he probed her sex with his thick shaft, murmuring soft, soothing words as he pushed himself inside her.

'Easy, *dolcezza*.'

Another inch increased the burn, but the hunger rushing through her wouldn't be denied. Her fingers dug into his back, making him growl. 'Zaccheo, please.'

'*Sì*, let me please you.' He uttered a word that sounded like an apology, a plea.

Then he pushed inside her. The dart of pain engulfed her, lingered for a moment. Tears filled her eyes. Zaccheo cursed, then kissed them away, murmuring softly in Italian.

He thrust deeper, slowly filling her. Eva saw the strain etched on his face.

'Zaccheo?'

'I want this to be perfect for you.'

'It won't be unless you move, I suspect.'

That half-smile twitched, then stretched into a full, heart-stopping smile. Eva's eyes widened at the giddy dance her heart performed on seeing the wave of pleasure transform his face. Her own mouth curved in response and a feeling unfurled inside her, stealing her breath with its awesome power. Shakily, she raised her hand and touched his face, slid her fingers over his sensual mouth.

He moved. Withdrew and thrust again.

She gasped, her body caught in a maelstrom of sensation so turbulent, she feared she wouldn't emerge whole.

Slowly his smile disappeared, replaced by a wild, predatory hunger. He quickened the pace and her hands moved to his hair, slipping the knot free and burying her fingers in the thick, luxurious tresses. When her hips moved of their own accord, meeting him in an instinctive dance, he groaned deep and sucked one nipple into his mouth. Drowning in sensation, she felt her world begin to crumble. The moment he captured her twin nipple, a deep tremor started inside her. It built and built, then exploded in a shower of lights.

'*Perfetto.*'

Zaccheo sank his fingers into Eva's wild, silky hair, curbing the desire to let loose the primitive roar bubbling within him.

Mine. Finally, completely mine.

Instead he held her close until her breathing started to return to normal, then he flipped their positions and arranged her on top of him.

He was hard to the point of bursting, but he was determined to make this experience unforgettable for her. Seeing his ring on her finger, that primitive response rose again, stunning him with the strength of his desire to claim her.

His words on the plane slashed through his mind.

Sì, he *did* want this to work. Perhaps Eva had been right. Perhaps there was still time to salvage a piece of his soul...

Her eyes met his and a sensual smile curled her luscious mouth. Before he could instruct her, she moved, taking him deeper inside her before she rose. Knowing he was fast losing the ability to think, he met her second thrust. Her eyes widened, her skin flushing that alluring shade of pink as she chased the heady sensation. Within minutes, they were both panting.

Reaching down, he teased her with his thumb and watched

her erupt in bliss. Zaccheo followed her, his shout announcing the most ferocious release he'd experienced in his life.

Long after Eva had collapsed on top of him, and slipped into an exhausted sleep, he lay awake.

Wondering why his world hadn't righted itself.

Wondering what the hell this meant for him.

CHAPTER TWELVE

Eva came awake to find herself splayed on top of Zaccheo's body.

The sun remained high in the sky so she knew she hadn't slept for more than an hour or two. Nevertheless, the thought that she'd dropped into a coma straight after sex made her cringe.

She risked a glance and found grey eyes examining her with that half-smile she was growing to like a little more than she deemed wise.

He brushed a curl from her cheek and tucked it behind her ear. The gentleness in the act fractured her breathing.

'Ciao, dolcezza.'

'I didn't mean to fall asleep on you,' she said, then immediately felt gauche for not knowing the right after-sex etiquette.

He quirked a brow. 'Oh? Who did you mean to fall asleep on?' he asked.

She jerked up. 'No, that's not what I meant…' she started to protest, then stopped when she saw the teasing light in his eyes.

She started to settle back down, caught a glimpse of his chiselled pecs and immediately heat built inside her. A little wary of how quickly she was growing addicted to his body, she attempted to slide off him.

He stopped her with one hand at her nape, the other on her hip. The action flexed his arm and Eva's gaze was drawn to the tattoo banding his upper arm.

'Does this have a special meaning?'

His smile grew a little stiffer. 'It's a reminder not to accept less than I'm worth or compromise on what's important to me. And a reminder that, contrary to what the privileged would have us believe, all men are born equal. It's power that is wielded unequally.'

Eva thought of the circumstances that had brought her to this place, of the failings of her own family and the sadness she'd carried for so long, but now hoped to let go of.

'You wield more than enough share of power. Men cower before you.'

A frown twitched his forehead. 'If they do, it is their weakness, not mine.'

She gave an incredulous laugh. 'Are you saying you don't know you intimidate people with just a glance?'

His frown cleared. 'You're immune to this intimidation you speak of. To my memory, you've been disagreeable more often than not.'

She traced the outline of the tattoo, revelling in the smooth warmth of his skin. 'I've never been good at heeding bellowed commands.'

The hand on her hip tightened. 'I do not bellow.'

'Maybe not. But sometimes the effect is the same.'

She found herself flipped over onto her back, Zaccheo crouched over her like a lethal bird of prey. 'Is that why you hesitated as you walked down the aisle?' he asked in a harsh whisper. The look in his eyes was one of almost...hurt.

Quickly she shook her head. 'No, it wasn't.'

'Then what was it? You thought that I wasn't good enough, perhaps?' he pressed. And again she glimpsed a hint of vulnerability in his eyes that caught at a weak place in her heart.

She opened her mouth to *finally* tell him. To lay herself bare to the scathing rejection that would surely follow her confession.

The words stuck in her throat.

What she'd experienced in Zaccheo's bed had given her a taste that was unlike anything she'd ever felt before. The need to hold on to that for just a little while longer slammed into her, knocking aside her good intentions.

Eva knew she was playing with volcanic fire, that the eventual eruption would be devastating. But for once in her life, she wanted to be selfish, to experience a few moments of unfettered abandon. She could have that.

She'd sacrificed herself for this marriage, but in doing so she'd also been handed a say in when it ended.

And it would be sooner rather than later, because she couldn't stand in the way of what he wanted...what he'd been deprived of his whole life...a proper family of his own.

She also knew Zaccheo would want nothing to do with her once he knew the truth. Sure, he wasn't as monstrous as he would have others believe, but that didn't mean he would shackle himself to a wife who couldn't give him what he wanted.

She squashed the voice that cautioned she was naively burying her head in the sand.

Was it really so wrong if she chose to do it just for a little while?

Could she not live in bliss for a few days? Gather whatever memories she could and hang on to them for when the going got tough?

'Eva?'

'I had a father-daughter moment, plus bridal nerves,' she blurted. He raised a sceptical eyebrow and she smiled. 'Every woman is entitled to have a moment. Mine was thirty seconds of hesitation.'

'You remained frozen for five *minutes*,' he countered.

'Just time enough for anyone who'd been dozing off to wake up,' she responded, wide-eyed.

The tension slowly eased out of his body and his crooked smile returned. Relief poured through her and she fell into the punishing kiss he delivered to assert his displeasure at her hesitation.

She was clinging to him by the time he pulled away, and Eva was ready to protest when he swung out of bed. Her protest died when she got her first glimpse of his impressive manhood, and the full effect of the man attached to it.

Dry-mouthed and heart racing, she stared. And curled her fingers into the sheets to keep from reaching for him.

'If you keep looking at me like that, our shower will have to be postponed. And our lunch will go cold.'

A blush stormed up her face.

He laughed and scooped her up. 'But I'm glad that my body is not displeasing to you.'

She rolled her eyes. *As if.* 'False humility isn't an attractive trait, Zaccheo,' she chided as he walked them through a wide door and onto an outdoor bamboo-floored shower. Despite the rustic effects, the amenities were of the highest quality, an extra-wide marble bath sitting opposite a multi-jet shower, with a shelf holding rows upon rows of luxury bath oils and gels.

Above their heads, a group of macaws warbled throatily, then flew from one tree to the next, their stunning colours streaking through the branches.

As tropical paradises went, Eva was already sure this couldn't be topped, and she had yet to see the rest of it.

Zaccheo set her down and grabbed a soft washcloth. 'Complete compatibility in bed isn't a common thing, despite what magazines would have you believe,' he said.

'I wouldn't know.' There was no point pretending otherwise. He had first-hand knowledge of her innocence.

His eyes flared with possession as he turned on the jets and pulled her close.

'No, you wouldn't. And if that knowledge pleases me to the point of being labelled a caveman, then so be it.'

They ate a sumptuous lunch of locally caught fish served with pine-nut sauce and avocado salad followed by a serving of fruit and cheeses.

After lunch, Zaccheo showed her the rest of the house and the three-square-kilometre island. They finished the trek on the white sandy beach where a picnic had been laid out with champagne chilling in a silver bucket.

Eva popped a piece of papaya in her mouth and sighed at the beauty of the setting sun casting orange and purple streaks across the aquamarine water. 'I don't know how you can ever bear to leave this place.'

'I learned not to grow attached to things at an early age.'

The crisp reply had her glancing over at him. His shades were back in place so she couldn't read his eyes, but his body showed no signs of the usual forbidding *do not disturb* signs so she braved the question. 'Why?'

'Because it was better that way.'

She toyed with the stem of her champagne flute. 'But it's also a lonely existence.'

Broad shoulders lifted in an easy shrug. 'I had a choice of being lonely or just…solitary. I chose the latter.'

Her heart lurched at the deliberate absence of emotion from his voice. 'Zaccheo—'

He reared up from where he'd been lounging on his elbows, his mouth set in a grim line. 'Don't waste your time feeling sorry for me, *dolcezza*,' he said, his voice a hard snap that would've intimidated her, had she allowed it.

'I wasn't,' she replied. 'I'm not naive enough to imagine everyone has a rosy childhood. I know I didn't.'

'You mean the exclusive country-club memberships, the top boarding schools, the winters in Verbier weren't enough?' Despite the lack of contempt in his voice this time round, Eva felt sad that they were back in this place again.

'Don't twist my words. Those were just *things*, Zaccheo. And before you accuse me of being privileged, yes, I was. My childhood was hard, too, but I couldn't help the family I was born into any more than you could.'

'Was that why you moved out of Pennington Manor?'

'After my mother died, yes. Two against one became unbearable.'

'And the father-daughter moment you spoke of? Did that help?' he asked, watching her with a probing look.

A tiny bit of hope blossomed. 'Time will tell, I guess. Will you try the same with your mother and stepfather?'

'No. My mother didn't think I was worth anything. My stepfather agreed.'

Her heart twisted. 'Yet you've achieved success beyond most people's wildest dreams. Surely the lessons of your childhood should make you proud of who you are now, despite hating some aspects of your upbringing?'

'I detested all of mine,' he said with harsh finality. 'I wouldn't wish it on my worst enemy.'

The savage edge of pain in his voice made her shiver. She opened her mouth to ask him, but he surged to his feet.

'I don't wish to dwell in the past.' That half-smile flashed on and off. 'Not when I have a sunset as stunning as this and a wife to rival its beauty.' He plucked the glass from her hand and pulled her up.

Tucking her head beneath his chin, he enfolded her in his arms, one around her waist and the other across her shoulders. Eva knew it was a signal to drop the subject, but she couldn't let it go. Not just yet.

She removed his shades and stared into his slate-coloured eyes. 'For what it's worth, I gave away my country-club membership to my best friend, I hated boarding school, and I couldn't ski to save my life so I didn't even try after I turned ten. I didn't care about my pedigree, or who I was seen with. Singing and a family who cared for me were the only things that mattered. One helped me get through the other. So, you see, sometimes the grass *may* look greener on the other side, but most of the time it's just a trick of the light.'

Several emotions shifted within his eyes. Surprise. Shock. A hint of confusion. Then the deep arrogance of Zaccheo Giordano slid back into place.

'The sunset, *dolcezza*,' he said gruffly. 'You're missing it.'

* * *

The feeling of his world tilting out of control was escalating. And it spun harder out of sync the more he fought it.

Zaccheo had been certain he knew what drove Eva and her family. He'd been sure it was the same greed for power and prestige that had sent his father to a vicious and premature death. It was what had made his mother abandon her homeland to seek a rich husband, turn herself inside out for a man who looked down his nose at her son and ultimately made Clara Giordano pack her bags and move to the other side of the world.

But right from the start Eva had challenged him, forced him to confront his long-held beliefs. He hadn't needed to, of course. Oscar Pennington's actions had proven him right. Eva's own willingness to marry Fairfield for the sake of her family had cemented Zaccheo's belief.

And didn't you do the same thing?

He stared unseeing at the vivid orange horizon, his thoughts in turmoil.

He couldn't deny that the discovery of her innocence in bed had thrown him for a loop. Unsettled him in a way he hadn't been for a long time.

For as long as he could remember, his goal had been a fixed, tangible certainty. To place himself in a position where he erased any hint of neediness from his life, while delivering an abject lesson to those who thought themselves entitled and therefore could treat him as if he were common. A spineless fool who would prostrate himself for scraps from the high table.

He'd proven conclusively yesterday at his wedding reception that he'd succeeded beyond his wildest dreams. He'd watched blue-blooded aristocrats fall over themselves to win his favour.

And yet he'd found himself unsatisfied. Left with a hollow, bewildering feeling inside, as if he'd finally grasped the brass ring, only to find it was made of plastic.

It had left Zaccheo with the bitter introspection of whether a different, deeper goal lay behind the burning need to prove himself above the petty grasp for power and prestige.

The loneliness he'd so offhandedly dismissed had in fact eaten away at him far more effectively than his mother's rejection and the callous disregard his father had afforded him when he was alive.

Impatiently, he dismissed his jumbled feelings. He didn't do *feelings*. He *achieved*. He *bested*. And he *triumphed*.

One miscalculation didn't mean a setback. Finding out Eva had had no previous lovers had granted him an almost primitive satisfaction he wasn't going to bother to deny.

And if something came of this union sooner rather than later... His heart kicked hard.

Sliding a hand through her silky hair, he angled her face to his. Her beauty was undeniable. But he wouldn't be risking any more heart-to-hearts. She was getting too close, sliding under his skin to a place he preferred to keep out of bounds. A place he'd only examined when the cold damp of his prison cell had eroded his guard.

He was free, both physically and in guilt. He wouldn't return to that place. And he wouldn't allow her to probe further. Satisfied with his resolution, he kissed her sexy, tempting mouth until the need to breathe forced him to stop.

The sun had disappeared. Lights strung through the trees flickered on and he nodded to the member of staff who hovered nearby, ready to pack up their picnic.

He caught the glazed, flushed look on his wife's face and came to a sudden, extremely pleasing decision.

'Tonight, *il mio angelo*, we'll have an early night.'

The first week flew by in a dizzy haze of sun, sea, exquisite food, and making love. Lots and lots of making love.

Zaccheo was a fierce and demanding lover, but he gave so much more in return. And Eva was so greedy for everything he had to give, she wondered whether she was turning into a sex addict. She'd certainly acted like one this morning, when she'd initiated sex while Zaccheo had been barely awake. That her initiative had seemed to please him had been beside the point.

She'd examined her behaviour afterwards when Zaccheo had been summoned to an urgent phone call by Romeo.

This was supposed to be a moment out of time, a brief dalliance, which would end the moment she spilled her secret to him. And yet with each surrender of her body, she slid down a steeper slope, one she suspected would be difficult to climb back up. Because it turned out that, for her, sex wasn't a simple exchange of physical pleasure. With each act, she handed over a piece of herself to him that she feared she'd never reclaim.

And that more than anything made her fear for herself when this was over.

A breeze blew through an open window and Eva clutched the thin sarong she'd thrown over her bikini. Dark clouds were forming ominously over the island. Shivering, she watched the storm gather, wondering if it was a premonition for her own situation.

Lightning flashed, and she jumped.

'Don't worry, Mrs Eva.' Zaccheo's housekeeper smiled as she entered and turned on table lamps around the living room. 'The storm passes very quickly. The sun will be back out in no time.'

Eva smiled and nodded, but she couldn't shake the feeling that *her* storm wouldn't pass so quickly.

As intense rain pounded the roof she went in search of Zaccheo. Not finding him in his study, she climbed the stairs, her pulse already racing in anticipation as she went down the hallway.

She entered their dressing room and froze.

'What are you doing?' she blurted.

'I would've thought it was obvious, *dolcezza*.' He held clippers inches from his face.

'I can see what you're doing but...*why*?' she snapped. 'You already got rid of most of it for the wedding.' Her voice was clipped, a feeling she couldn't decipher moving through her.

Zaccheo raised an eyebrow, amusement mingled with something else as he watched her. 'I take it this look works for you?'

She swallowed twice before she could speak. When she finally deciphered the feeling coursing through her, she was so shocked and so afraid he would read her feelings, she glanced over his head.

'Yes. I prefer it,' she replied.

For several seconds he didn't speak. Her skin burned at his compelling stare. Schooling her features, she glanced into his eyes.

'Then it will remain untouched.' He set the clippers down and faced her.

Neither of them moved for several minutes. The storm raged outside, beating against the windows and causing the timber to creak.

'Come here, Eva.' Softly spoken, but a command nonetheless.

'I'm beginning to think those are your three favourite words.'

'They are only when you comply.'

She rolled her eyes, but moved towards him. He swivelled in his chair and pulled her closer, parting his thighs to situate her between them.

'Was that very hard to admit?' he rasped.

Her skin grew tight, awareness that she stood on a precipice whose depths she couldn't quite fathom shivering over her. 'No.'

He laughed. 'You're a pathetic liar. But I appreciate you finding the courage to ask for what you want.'

'An insult and a compliment?' she said lightly.

'I wouldn't want you to think me soft.' He caught her hands and placed them on his shoulders. 'You realise that

I'll require a reward for keeping myself this way for your pleasure?'

The way he mouthed *pleasure* made hot need sting between her thighs. Several weeks ago, she would've fought it. But Eva was fast learning it was no use. Her body was his slave to command as and when he wished. 'You got your stylists to prod and primp me into the image you wanted. I've earned the right to do the same to you.' Her fingers curled into the hair she would've wept to see shorn.

He smiled and relaxed in the chair. 'I thought being primped and plucked to perfection was every woman's wish?'

'You thought wrong. I was happy with the way I looked before.'

That wasn't exactly true. Although she'd loved her thick and wild hair, she had to admit it was much easier to tend now the wildness had been tamed a little. And she loved that she could brush the tresses without giving herself a headache. As for the luxurious body creams she'd been provided with, she marvelled at how soft and silky her skin felt now compared to before.

But she kept all of it to herself as he untied the knot in her sarong and let it fall away. 'You were perfect before. You're perfect now. And mine,' he breathed.

Within seconds, Eva was naked and craving what only he could give her, her eventual screams as loud as the storm raging outside.

CHAPTER THIRTEEN

'Come on, we're taking the boat out today. As much as I'd like to keep you to myself, I think we need to see something of Rio before we leave tomorrow.'

Eva stopped tweaking the chorus of the melody she'd been composing and looked up as Zaccheo entered the living room.

The perverse hope that he would grow less breathtaking with each day was hopelessly thwarted. Dressed in khaki linen trousers and a tight white T-shirt with his hair loose around his shoulders, Zaccheo was so visually captivating, she felt the punch to her system each time she stared at him.

He noticed her staring and raised an eyebrow. Blushing, she averted her gaze to her tablet.

'Where are we going?' She tried for a light tone and breathed an inward sigh of relief when she succeeded.

'To Ilha São Gabriel, three islands away. It's a tourist hotspot, but there are some interesting sights to see there.' He crouched before her, his gaze going to the tablet. Reaching out, he scrolled through her compositions, his eyes widening at the three dozen songs contained in the file.

'You wrote all these?' he asked.

She nodded, feeling self-conscious as he paused at a particularly soul-baring ballad about unrequited love and rejection. She'd written that one a week after Zaccheo had gone to prison. 'I've been composing since I was sixteen.'

His eyes narrowed on her face. 'You've had two million pounds in your bank account for over a year and a half, which I'm guessing is your shareholder dividend from your father's deal on my building?'

Warily, she nodded.

'That would've been more than enough money to pursue your music career without needing to work. So why didn't you use it?' he queried.

She tried to shrug the question away, but he caught her chin in his hand. 'Tell me,' he said.

'I suspected deep down that the deal was tainted. I hated doubting my father's integrity, but I could never bring myself to use the money. It didn't feel right.' Being proved right had brought nothing but hurt.

He watched her for a long time, a puzzled look on his face before he finally nodded. 'How was your session with Ziggy Preston?' he asked.

She saw nothing of the sour expression he'd sported that night in the club. 'Surprisingly good, considering I'd thought he'd have me on the blacklist of every music producer after your behaviour.'

An arrogant smile stretched his lips. 'They'd have had to answer to me had they chosen that unfortunate path. You're seeing him again?'

She nodded. 'When we get back.'

'Bene.' He rose and held out his hand.

She slipped her feet into one of the many stylish sandals now gracing her wardrobe and he led her outside to the jetty.

Climbing on board, he placed her in front of the wheel and stood behind her. She looked around, expecting Zaccheo's right-hand man to be travelling with them. 'Isn't Romeo coming?'

'He had business to take care of in Rio. He'll meet us there.'

The trip took twenty-five minutes, and Eva understood why the Ilha São Gabriel was so popular when she saw it. The island held a mountain, on top of which a smaller version of the Cristo Redentor in Rio had been erected. Beneath the statue, bars, restaurants, parks and churches flowed right down to the edge of a mile-long beach.

Zaccheo directed her to motor past the busy beach and round the island to a quieter quay where they moored the boat. 'We're starting our tour up there.' He pointed to a quaint little building set into the side of a hill about a quarter of a mile up a steep path.

She nodded and started to walk up when she noticed Romeo a short distance away. He nodded a greeting but didn't join them as they headed up. The other man's watchfulness made Eva frown.

'Something on your mind?' Zaccheo asked.

'I was just wondering…what's the deal with Romeo?'

'He's many things.'

'That's not really an answer.'

Zaccheo shrugged. 'We work together, but I guess he's a confidant.'

'How long have you known him?'

When Zaccheo pulled his shades from the V of his T-shirt and placed them on, she wondered whether she'd strayed into forbidden territory. But he answered, 'We met when I was thirteen years old.'

Her eyes rounded in surprise. 'In London?'

'In Palermo.'

'So he's your oldest friend?'

Zaccheo hesitated for a second. 'Our relationship is complicated. Romeo sees himself as my protector. A role I've tried to dissuade him from to no avail.'

Her heart caught. 'Protector from what?'

His mouth twitched. 'He seems to think you're a handful that he needs to keep an eye on.'

She looked over her shoulder at the quiet, brooding man.

'My father worked for his father,' he finally answered.

'In what capacity?'

'As whatever he wanted him to be. My father didn't discriminate as long as he was recognised for doing the job. He would do anything from carrying out the trash to kneecapping a rival gang's members to claiming another man's bastard child so his boss didn't have to. No job was too small or large,' he said with dry bitterness.

The blood drained from her face. 'Your father worked for the *Mafia*?'

His jaw clenched before he jerked out a nod. 'Romeo's father was a *don* and my father one of his minions. His role was little more than drudge work, but he acted as if he was serving the Pope himself.'

She glanced over her shoulder at Romeo, her stomach dredging with intense emotions she recognised as anguish—even without knowing what Zaccheo was about to divulge.

'That bastard child you mentioned…'

He nodded. 'Romeo. His father had an affair with one of his many mistresses. His mother kept him until he became too much of a burden. When he was thirteen, she dumped him on his father. He didn't want the child, so he asked my father to *dispose* of him. My father, eager to attain recognition at all costs, brought the child home to my mother. She refused but my father wouldn't budge. They fought every day for a month until she ended up in hospital. It turned out she was pregnant. After that she became even more adamant about having another woman's child under her roof. When she lost her baby, she blamed my father and threatened to leave. My father, probably for the only time in his life, decided to place someone else's needs above his ambition. He tried to return Romeo to his father, who took grave offence. He had my father beaten to death. And I…' his face tightened '…I went from having a friend, a mother and father, and a brother or sister on the way, to having nothing.'

Eva frowned. 'But your mother—'

'Had hated being the wife of a mere gofer. My father's death bought her the fresh start she craved, but she had to contend with a child who reminded her of a past she detested. She moved to England a month after he died and married a man who hated the sight of me, who judged me because of who my father was and believed my common blood was an affront to his distinguished name.' The words were snapped out in a staccato narrative, but she felt the anguished intensity behind them.

Eva swallowed hard. Stepping close, she laid her head on his chest. 'I'm so sorry, Zaccheo.'

His arms tightened around her for a heartbeat before he pulled away and carried on up the steps. 'I thought Romeo had died that night, too, until he found me six years ago.'

She glanced at Romeo and her heart twisted for the pain the unfortunate friends had gone through.

They continued up the hill in silence until they reached the building.

They entered the cool but dim interior and as her eyes adjusted to the dark she was confronted by a stunning collection of statues. Most were made of marble, but one or two were sculpted in white stone.

'Wow, these are magnificent.'

'A local artist sculpted all the patron saints and donated them to the island over fifty years ago.'

They drifted from statue to statue, each work more striking than the last. When they walked through an arch, he laced his fingers with hers. 'Come, I'll show you the most impressive one. According to the history, the artist sculpted them in one day.'

Smiling, she let him tug her forward. She gasped at the double-figured display of St Anne and St Gerard. 'Patron saints of motherhood and fertility…' She stopped reading as her heart dropped to her stomach.

Zaccheo traced a forefinger down her cheek. 'I can't wait to feel our child kick in your belly,' he murmured.

A vice gripped her heart, squeezed until it threatened to stop beating. 'Zaccheo—'

His finger stopped her. 'I meant what I said, Eva. We can make this work. And we may not have had the best of role models in parents, but we know which mistakes to avoid. That's a good basis for our children, *sì*?' he asked, his tone gentle, almost hopeful.

She opened her mouth, but no words formed. Because the truth she'd been hiding from suddenly reared up and slapped her in the face.

Zaccheo wanted children, not as a tool for revenge, but for himself. The man who'd known no love growing up wanted a family of his own.

And she'd led him on, letting him believe he could have it with her. The enormity of her actions rocked her to the core, robbing her of breath.

'Eva? What's wrong?' he asked with a frown.

She shook her head, her eyes darting frantically around the room.

'You're as pale as a ghost, *dolcezza*. Talk to me!'

Eva struggled to speak around the misery clogging her throat. 'I...I'm okay.'

His frown intensified. 'You don't look okay. Do you want to leave?'

She grasped the lifeline. 'Yes.'

'Okay, let's go.'

They emerged into bright sunlight. Eva took a deep breath, which did absolutely nothing to restore the chaos fracturing her mind.

The urge to confess *now*, spill her secret right then and there, powered through her. But it was neither the time nor the place. A group of tourist students had entered the room and the place was getting busier by the second.

Zaccheo led her down the steps. He didn't speak, but his concerned gaze probed her.

The island seemed twice as crowded by the time they descended the hill. The midday sun blazed high and sweat trickled down her neck as they navigated human traffic on the main promenade. When Zaccheo steered her to a restaurant advertising fresh seafood, Eva didn't complain.

Samba music blared from the speakers, thankfully negating the need for conversation. Sadly it didn't free her from her thoughts, not even when, after ordering their food, Zaccheo moved his chair closer, tugged her into his side and trailed his hand soothingly through her hair.

It was their last day in Rio. Possibly their last as husband and wife. Her soul mourned what she shouldn't have craved.

Unbearable agony ripped through her. She'd been living in a fool's paradise. Especially since she'd told herself it wouldn't matter how much time passed without her telling Zaccheo.

It mattered very much. She'd heard his pain when he'd recounted his bleak childhood. With each day that had passed without her telling him she couldn't help him realise his dream, she'd eroded any hope that he would understand why she'd kept her secret from him.

A moan ripped from her throat and she swayed in her seat. Zaccheo tilted her face to his and she read the worry in his eyes.

'Do you feel better?'

'Yes, much better.'

'*Bene*, then perhaps you'd like to tell me what's going on?' he asked.

She jerked away, her heart hammering. 'I got a little lightheaded, that's all.'

His frown returned and Eva held her breath. She was saved when Romeo entered. 'Everything all right?' he asked.

Romeo's glance darted to her. The knowledge in his eyes froze her insides, but he said nothing, directing his gaze back to his friend.

Zaccheo nodded. '*Sì*. We'll see you back at Paraíso.'

The moment he left, Zaccheo lowered his head and kissed her, not the hungry devouring that tended to overtake them whenever they were this close, but a gentle, reverent kiss.

In that moment, Eva knew she'd fallen in love with him.

And that she would lose the will to live the moment she walked away from him.

Their food arrived and they ate. She refused coffee and the slice of *chocotorta* the waiter temptingly offered. Zaccheo ordered an espresso, shooting her another concerned glance. Praying he wouldn't press her to reveal what was wrong just yet, she laid her head on his shoulder and buried her face in his throat, selfishly relishing the moment. She would never get a moment like this once they returned to Casa do Paraíso. He placed a gentle kiss on her forehead and agony moved through her like a living entity.

You brought this on yourself. No use crying now.

She started as the group they'd met on their exit from the museum entered the restaurant. Within minutes, someone had started the karaoke machine. The first attempt, sung atrociously to loud jeers, finished as the waiter returned with Zaccheo's espresso.

Eva straightened in her seat, watching the group absently as each member refused to take the mic. The leader cast his eyes around the room, met Eva's gaze and made a beeline for her.

'No.' She shook her head when he reached her and offered the mic.

He clasped his hands together. *'Por favor,'* he pleaded.

She opened her mouth to refuse, then found herself swallowing her rebuttal. She glanced at Zaccheo. He regarded her steadily, his face impassive. And yet she sensed something behind his eyes, as if he didn't know what to make of her mood.

She searched his face harder, wanting him to say something, *anything*, that would give her even the tiniest hope that what she had to tell him wouldn't break the magic they'd found on his island. Wouldn't break *her*.

In a way it was worse when he offered her that half-smile. Recently his half-smiles had grown genuine, were often a precursor to the blinding smiles that stole her breath...made her heart swell to bursting.

The thought that they would soon become a thing of the past had her surging to her feet, blindly striding for the stage to a round of applause she didn't want.

All Eva wanted in that moment was to drown in the oblivion of music.

She searched through the selection until she found a song she knew by heart, one that had spoken to her the moment she'd heard it on the radio.

She sang the first verse with her eyes shut, yearning for the impossible. She opened her eyes for the second verse. She could never tell Zaccheo how she felt about him, but she could sing it to him. Her eyes found his as she sang the last line.

His gaze grew hot. Intense. Her pulse hammered as she sang the third verse, offering her heart, her life to him, all the while knowing he would reject it once he knew.

She stifled a sob as the machine clicked to an end. She started to step off the stage, but the group begged for another song.

Zaccheo rose and moved towards her. They stared at each other as the clamouring grew louder. Her breath caught when the emotion in his eyes altered, morphing into that darker hue that held a deeper meaning.

He wasn't angry. Or ruthlessly commanding her to bend to his will. Or even bitter and hurt, as he'd been on the hill.

There was none of that in his expression. This ferocity was different, one that made her world stop.

Until she shook herself back to reality. She was grasping at straws, stalling with excuses and foolish, reckless hope. She might have fallen in love with Zaccheo, but nothing he'd said or done had indicated he returned even an iota of what she felt. Their relationship had changed from what it'd been in the beginning, but she couldn't lose sight of *why* it'd begun in the first place. Or why she couldn't let it continue.

Heavy-hearted, she turned back to the machine. She'd seen the song earlier and bypassed it, because she hadn't been ready to say goodbye.

But it was time to end this. Time to accept that there was no hope.

Something was wrong. It'd been since they'd walked down the hill.

But for once in his life, he was afraid to confront a problem head-on because he was terrified the results would be unwelcome. So he played worst-case scenarios in his head.

Had he said or done something to incite this troubled look on Eva's face? Had his confession on the hill reminded her that he wasn't the man she would've chosen for herself? A wave of something close to desolation rushed over him. He clenched his jaw against the feeling. Would it really be the end of the world if Eva decided she didn't want him? The affirmative answer echoing through him made him swallow hard.

He discarded that line of thought and chose another, dissecting each moment he'd spent with her this afternoon.

He'd laid himself bare, something he'd never done until recently. She hadn't shown pity or disgust for the debasing crimes his father had committed, or for the desperately lonely child he'd been. Yet again she'd only showed compassion. Pain for the toll his jagged upbringing had taken on him.

And the songs...what had they meant, especially the second one, the one about saying *goodbye*? He'd witnessed the agony in her eyes while she'd sung that one. As if her heart was broken—

A knock came at his study door, where he'd retreated to pace after they'd returned and Eva had expressed the need for a shower. Alone.

'Zaccheo?'

He steeled himself to turn around, hoping against hope that the look on her face would be different. That she would smile and everything would return to how it was before they'd gone on that blasted trip.

But it wasn't. And her next words ripped through him with the lethal effect of a vicious blade.

'Zaccheo, we need to talk.'

CHAPTER FOURTEEN

EVERY WORD SHE'D practised in the shower fled her head as Eva faced him. Of course, her muffled sobs had taken up a greater part of the shower so maybe she hadn't got as much practice in as she'd thought.

'I...' Her heart sank into her stomach when a forbidding look tightened his face. 'I can't stay married to you.'

For a moment he looked as if she'd punched him hard in the solar plexus, then ripped his heart out while he struggled to breathe. Gradually his face lost every trace of pain and distress. Hands shoved deep in his pockets, he strolled to where she stood, frozen inside the doorway.

'Was this your plan all along?' he bit out, his eyes arctic. 'To wait until I'd spoken on your father's behalf and he was safe from prosecution before you asked for a divorce?'

She gasped. 'You did that? When?' she asked, but his eyes poured scorn on her question.

'Is being married to me that abhorrent to you, Eva? So much so you couldn't even wait until we were back in London?'

'No! Believe me, Zaccheo, that's not it.'

'*Believe* you? Why should I? When you're not even prepared to give us a chance?' He veered sharply away from her and strode across the room, his fingers spiking through his hair before he reversed course and stopped in front of her once more. 'What I don't understand is why. Did I do something? Say something to make you think I wouldn't want this relationship to work?'

The confirmation that this marriage meant more to him was almost too hard to bear.

'Zaccheo, please listen to me. It's not you, it's—'

His harsh laughter echoed around the room. 'Are you *seriously* giving me that line?'

Her fists balled. 'For once in your life, just shut up and listen! I can't have children,' she blurted.

'You've already used that one, *dolcezza*, but you signed along the dotted line agreeing to my clause, remember? So try again.'

Misery quivered through her stomach. 'It's true I signed the agreement, but I lied to you. I *can't* have children, Zaccheo. I'm infertile.'

He sucked in a hoarse breath and reeled backwards on his heels. 'Excuse me?'

'I tried to tell you when I first saw the clause, but you wouldn't listen. You'd made up your mind that I'd use any excuse not to marry you because I didn't want you.'

The stunned look morphed into censure. 'Then you should've put me straight.'

'How? Would you have believed me if I'd told you about my condition? Without evidence to back it up? Or perhaps I should've told Romeo or your PA since they had more access to you than I did in the week before the wedding?'

He looked at her coldly. 'If your conscience stung you so deeply the first time round, why did you change your mind?'

Her emotions were raw enough for her to instinctively want to protect herself. But what did she have to lose? Zaccheo would condemn her actions regardless of whether she kept her innermost feelings to herself or not. And really, how much worse could this situation get? Her heart was already in shreds.

She met his gaze head on. 'You know I lost my mother to cancer when I was eighteen. She was diagnosed when I was sixteen. For two years we waited, hoping for the best, fearing the worst through each round of chemo. With each treatment that didn't work we knew her time was growing shorter. Knowing it was coming didn't make it any easier. Her death ripped me apart.' She stopped and gathered her courage. 'My father has been suffering stress attacks in the last couple of months.' She risked a glance and saw his brows clamped in a forbidding frown. 'He collapsed on Friday after you called to tell him the wedding was off.'

Zaccheo's mouth compressed, but a trace of compassion flashed through his eyes. 'And you blame me? Is that what this is all about?'

'No, I don't. We both know that the blame for our current circumstances lies firmly with my father.' She stopped and licked her lips. 'He may have brought this on himself, but the stress was killing him, Zaccheo. I've watched one parent die, helpless to do anything but watch them fade away. Condemn me all you want, but I wasn't going to stand by and let my father worry himself to death over what he'd done. And I didn't do it for my family name or my blasted *pedigree*. I did it because that's what you do for the people you love.'

'Even when they don't love you back?' he sneered, his voice indicating hers was a foolish feeling. 'Even when they treat you like an afterthought for most of your life?'

Sadness engulfed her. 'You can't help who you love. Or choose who will love you back.'

His eyes met hers for a charged second, before his nostrils flared. 'But you can choose to tell the truth no matter how tough the telling of it is. You can choose *not* to start a marriage based on lies.'

Regret crawled across her skin. 'Yes. And I'm sorry—'

His hand slashed through air, killing off her apology. Walking around her, he slammed the door shut and jerked his chin towards the sofa. He waited until she'd sat down, then prowled in front of her.

'Tell me of this condition you have.'

Eva stared at her clasped hands because watching his face had grown unbearable. 'It's called endometriosis.' She gave him the bare facts, unwilling to linger on the subject and prolong her heartache. 'It started just before I went to university, but, with everything going on with my mother, I didn't pay enough attention to it. I thought it was just something that would right itself eventually. But the pain got worse. One day I collapsed and was rushed to hospital. The diagnosis was made.' She stopped, then made herself go on. 'The doctor said the...scarring was too extensive...that I would never conceive naturally.'

She raised her head and saw that he'd stopped prowling and taken a seat opposite her with his elbows on his knees. 'Go on,' he bit out.

Eva shrugged. 'What else is there to add?' She gave a hollow laugh. 'I never thought I'd be in a position where the one thing I couldn't give would be the difference between having the future I want and the one I'd have to settle for. You accused me of starting this marriage based on lies, but I didn't know you wanted a real marriage. You did all this to get back at my father, remember?'

'So you never sought a second opinion?' he asked stonily, as if she hadn't mentioned the shifted parameters of their marriage.

'Why would I? I'd known something was wrong. Having the doctor confirm it merely affirmed what I already suspected. What was the point of putting myself through further grief?'

Zaccheo jerked to his feet and began prowling again. The set of his shoulders told her he was holding himself on a tight leash.

Minutes ticked by and he said nothing. The tension increased until she couldn't stand it any more. 'You can do whatever you want with me, but I want your word that you won't go after my family because of what I've done.'

He froze, his eyes narrowing to thin shards of ice. 'You think I want you to martyr yourself on some noble pyre for my sick satisfaction?'

She jumped to her feet. 'I don't know! You're normally so quick to lay down your demands. Or throw out orders and expect them to be followed. So tell me what you want.'

That chilling half-smile returned with a vengeance. 'What I want is to leave this place. There's really no point staying, is there, since the honeymoon is well and truly over?'

The flight back was markedly different from the outbound journey. The moment Zaccheo immersed himself in his work, she grabbed her tablet and locked herself in the bedroom.

She threw herself on the bed and sobbed long and hard into the pillow. By the time the plane landed in London, she was completely wrung out. Exhaustion seeped into her very bones and all she wanted was to curl into a foetal position and wish the world away.

She sank further into grey gloom when she descended the steps of the aircraft to find Zaccheo's limo waiting on the tarmac, along with a black SUV.

Zaccheo, wearing a black and navy pinstriped suit, stopped next to her, his expression remote and unfriendly.

'I'm heading to the office. Romeo will drive you to the penthouse.'

He strode to the SUV and drove off.

Eva realised then that throughout their conversation on the island, she'd made the same mistake as when she'd foolishly disclosed her condition before. She'd allowed herself to *hope* that the condition fate had bestowed on her wouldn't matter to that one *special person*. That somehow *love* would find a way.

A sob bubbled up her chest and she angrily swallowed it down.

Grow up, Eva. You're letting the lyrics of your songs cloud your judgement.

'Eva?' Romeo waited with the car door open.

She hastily averted her gaze from the censure in his eyes and slid in.

The penthouse hadn't changed, and yet Eva felt as if she'd lived a lifetime since she was last here.

After unpacking and showering, she trailed from room to room, feeling as if some tether she hadn't known she was tied to had been severed. When she rushed to the door for the third time, imagining she'd heard the keycard activate, she grabbed her tablet and forced herself to work on her compositions.

But her heart wasn't in it. Her mood grew bleaker when Romeo found her curled on the sofa and announced that Zaccheo wouldn't be home for dinner either tonight or the next two weeks, because he'd returned to Oman.

The days bled together in a dull grey jumble. Determined not to mope—because after all she'd been here before—Eva returned to work.

She took every spare shift available and offered herself for overtime without pay.

But she refused to sing.

Music had ceased to be the balm she'd come to rely on. Her heart only yearned for one thing. Or *one man*. And he'd made it abundantly clear that he didn't want her.

Because two weeks stretched to four, then six with no word from Zaccheo, and no answer to her phone calls.

At her lowest times, Eva hated herself for her lethargy, for not moving out of the penthouse. For sitting around, wishing for a miracle that would never materialise.

But the thought of flat-hunting, or, worse, moving back to Pennington Manor, filled her with a desperate heartache that nothing seemed to ease.

Romeo had brought her coffee this morning at the breakfast table. The pitying look he'd cast her had been the final straw.

'If you have something to say, just say it, Romeo.'

'You're not a weak woman. One of you has to take the situation in hand sooner or later,' he'd replied.

'Fine, but he won't return my calls so give him a message from me, will you?'

He'd nodded in that solemn way of his. 'Of course.'

'Tell him I'm fast reaching my tolerance level for his stupid silence. He can stay in Oman for the rest of his life for all I care. But he shouldn't expect to find me here when he deigns to return.'

That outburst had been strangely cathartic. She'd called her ex-landlady and discovered her flat was still unlet. After receiving a hefty payday from Zaccheo, the old woman hadn't been in a hurry to interview new tenants. She'd invited Eva to move back whenever she wanted.

Curiously, that announcement hadn't made her feel better—

'You've been cleaning that same spot for the last five minutes.'

Eva started and glanced down. 'Oh.'

Sybil, Siren's unflappable manageress, eyed her. 'Time for a break.'

'I don't need a—'

'Sorry, love,' Sybil said firmly. 'Orders from above. The new owner was very insistent. You take a break now or I get docked a week's wages.'

Eva frowned. 'Are you serious? Do we know who this new owner is?'

Sybil's eyes widened. 'You don't know?' When she shook her head, the manageress shrugged. 'Well, I'm not one to spread gossip. Shoo! Go put your feet up for a bit. I'll finish up here.'

Eva reluctantly handed over the cleaning supplies. She turned and stopped as the doors swung open and Ziggy Preston walked in.

The smile she tried for failed miserably. 'Ziggy, hello.'

He smiled. 'I heard you were back in town.'

She couldn't summon the curiosity to ask how he knew. 'Oh?'

'You were supposed to call when you got back. I hope that doesn't mean you've signed up with someone else? Because that'd devastate me,' he joked.

Eva tried for another smile. Failed again. 'I didn't sign with anyone, and I don't think I will.'

His face fell. 'Why not?'

She had a thousand and one reasons. But only one that mattered. And she wasn't about to divulge it to another soul. 'I've decided to give the music thing a break for a while.' Or for ever, depending on whether she felt anything but numb again.

Ziggy shoved his hands into his coat pocket, his features pensive.

'Listen, I was supposed to do a session with one of my artists tomorrow afternoon, but they cancelled. Come to the studio, hang out for a while. You don't have to sing if you don't want to. But come anyway.'

She started to shake her head, then stopped. It was her day off tomorrow. The extra shift she'd hoped to cover had suddenly been filled. She could either occupy herself at Ziggy's studio or wander Zaccheo's penthouse like a lost wraith, pining for what she could never have. 'Okay.'

'Great!' He handed her another business card, this one with his private number scribbled on the back, and left.

A couple of months ago, being pursued by a top music producer would've been a dream come true. And yet, Eva could barely summon the enthusiasm to dress the next day, especially when Romeo confirmed he'd given Zaccheo her message but had no reply for her.

Jaw clenched, she pulled on her jeans and sweater, determined not to succumb to the unending bouts of anguish that had made her throw up this morning after her conversation with Romeo.

She wasn't a pearl-clutching Victorian maiden, for heaven's sake!

Her life might *feel* as if it were over, but she'd been through the wringer more than once in her life. She'd survived her diagnosis. She'd survived her mother's death. Despite the odds, she'd mended fences with her father and sister.

Surely she could survive decimating her heart on a love that had been doomed from the start?

Deliberately putting a spring in her step, she arrived at Ziggy's studio in a different frame of mind. Looking around, she repeated to herself that *this* was a tangible dream. Something she could hang on to once Zaccheo returned and she permanently severed the ties that had so very briefly bound them.

Eva was sure she was failing in her pep talk to herself when Ziggy gave up after a third attempt to get her to sample an upbeat pop tune.

'Okay, shall we try one of yours?' he suggested with a wry smile.

Half-heartedly, she sifted through her list, then paused, her heart picking up its sluggish beat as she stared at the lyrics to the song she'd composed that last morning on the island.

'This one,' she murmured.

At Ziggy's nod, she sang the first line.

His eyes widened. 'Wow.' Nodding to the sound booth, he said, 'I'd love to hear the whole thing if you're up to it?'

Eva thought of the raw lyrics, how they offered love, pleaded for for ever and accepted any risks necessary, and breathed deeply.

If this was what it took to start healing herself, then so be it. 'Sure.'

She was singing the final notes when an electrifying wave of awareness swept over her. Her gaze snapped up to the viewing gallery above the booth, where she knew music moguls sometimes listened in on artists. Although the mirrored glass prevented her from seeing who occupied it, she swore she could smell Zaccheo's unique scent.

'Are you okay?' Ziggy asked.

She nodded absently, her gaze still on the gallery window. 'Can you sing the last two lines again?'

'Umm...yes,' she mumbled.

She really was losing it. If she couldn't sing a song she'd written with Zaccheo in mind without imagining she could feel him, smell him, she was in deep trouble. Because as she worked through the other songs Ziggy encouraged her to record, Eva realised all her songs were somehow to do with the man who'd taken her heart prisoner.

She left the studio in a daze and got into the waiting limo. Physically and emotionally drained, she couldn't connect two thoughts together. When she finally accepted what she needed to do, she turned to Romeo.

'Can you take me to Zaccheo's office, please?'

He looked up from the laptop he'd been working on. After a few probing seconds, he nodded.

A wave of dizziness hit her as they waited for the lift at GWI. She ignored the curious glances, and concentrated on staying upright, putting one foot in front of the other as she made her way down the plushly decorated corridor to Zaccheo's office.

Anyetta's coolly professional demeanour visibly altered when she saw Eva, then turned to shock as her gaze travelled from her head to her toes.

Eva wanted to laugh, but she couldn't be sure she wouldn't dissolve into hysteria. When Anyetta stood, Eva waved her away.

'I know he's not in. I was hoping *you* would email him for me.'

'But—'

'It won't take long, I promise.'

The tall brunette looked briefly bewildered, but her features settled back into serene composure and she sat down.

'Mark it *urgent*. Presumably, you can tell when he opens emails from you?' Eva asked.

Warily, Zaccheo's PA nodded.

'Good.' Eva approached, pushing back the errant curls obscuring her vision. She folded her arms around her middle and prayed for just a few more minutes of strength.

Anyetta's elegant fingers settled on the keyboard.
Eva cleared her throat.

Zaccheo.
Since you refuse to engage with me, I can only conclude that I'm free of my obligations to you. To that end, I'd be grateful if you would take the appropriate steps to end this marriage forthwith. My family lawyers will be on standby when you're ready, but I'd be obliged if you didn't leave it too late. I refuse to put my life on hold for you, so take action or I will.
For the record, I won't be accepting any of the monetary compensation offered, nor will I be seeking anything from you, except my freedom. If you choose to pursue my family, then you'll do so without my involvement, because I've done my duty to my family and I'm moving on. I won't let you use me as a pawn in your vendetta against my father.
You're aware of the state of my father's health, so I hope you'll choose mercy over retribution.
Regardless of your decision, I'll be moving out of the penthouse tomorrow.
Please don't contact me.
Eva.

'Send it, please,' she said.

Anyetta clicked the button, then looked up. 'He just opened it.'

Eva nodded jerkily. 'Thank you.'

She walked out with scalding tears filling her eyes. A solid presence registered beside her and when Romeo took her arm, Eva didn't protest.

At the penthouse, she dropped her bag in the hallway, tugged off her boots and coat as her vision greyed. She made it into bed as her legs gave way and she curled, fully clothed, into a tight ball. Her last thought before blessed oblivion claimed her was that she'd done it.

She'd survived her first hour with a heart broken into a million tiny pieces. If there was any justice, she might just make it through the rest of her life with a shredded heart.

CHAPTER FIFTEEN

IN THE SPLIT SECOND before wakefulness hit, Eva buried her nose in the pillow that smelled so much like Zaccheo she groaned with pure, incandescent happiness.

Reality arrived with searing pain so acute, she cried out.

'Eva.'

She jolted upright at the sound of her name. Jagged thoughts pierced her foggy brain like shards of bright light through glass.

She was no longer in her own suite, but in Zaccheo's.

Her clothes were gone, and she was stripped down to her bra and panties.

Zaccheo was sitting in an armchair next to the bed, his eyes trained on her.

And he was clean-shaven.

His thick stubble was gone, his hair trimmed into a short, neat style that left his nape bare.

Despite his altered appearance, his living, breathing presence was far too much to bear. She jerked her head away, stared down at the covers she clutched like a lifeline.

'What are you doing here?' she asked.

'You summoned me. So here I am,' he stated.

She shook her head. 'Please. Don't make it sound as if I have any power over your actions. If I did you would've answered my numerous phone calls like a normal person. And that email wasn't a summons. It was a statement of intent, hardly demanding your presence.'

'Nevertheless, since you went to so much trouble to make sure it reached me, I thought it only polite to answer it in person.'

'Well, you needn't have bothered,' she threw back hotly,

'especially since we both know you don't have a polite bone in your body. Things like *consideration* and *courtesy* are alien concepts to you.'

He looked perturbed by her outburst. Which made her want to laugh. And cry. And scream. 'Are you going to sit there with that insulting look that implies I'm out of my mind?'

'You must forgive me if that's what my expression implies. I meant to wear a look that says I was hoping for a civilised conversation.'

She threw out her hands. 'You have a damned nerve, do you know that? I...' She stopped, her eyes widening in alarm as an unpleasant scent hit her nostrils. Swivelling, she saw the breakfast tray containing scrambled eggs, smoked pancetta, coffee, and the buttered brioche she loved.

Correction. She'd *once* loved.

Shoving the covers aside, she lunged for the bathroom, uncaring that she was half-naked and looked like a bedraggled freak. All she cared about was making it to the porcelain bowl in time.

She vomited until she collapsed against the shower stall, desperately catching her breath. When Zaccheo crouched at her side, she shut her eyes. 'Please, Zaccheo. Go away.'

He pressed a cool towel to her forehead, her eyelids, her cheeks. 'A lesser man might be decimated at the thought that his presence makes you physically ill,' he murmured gravely.

Her snort grated her throat. 'But you're not a lesser man, of course.'

He shrugged. 'I'm saved by Romeo's report that you've been feeling under the weather recently.'

Eva opened her eyes, looked at him, then immediately wished she hadn't. She'd thought his beard and long mane made him gloriously beautiful, but the sight of his chiselled jaw, the cut of his cheekbones, and the fully displayed sensual lips was almost blinding.

'I can't do this.' She tried to stand and collapsed back against the stall.

With a muttered oath, he scooped her up in his arms and strode to the vanity. Setting her down, he handed her a toothbrush and watched as she cleaned her teeth.

Eva told herself the peculiar look turning his eyes that gunmetal shade meant nothing. Zaccheo had probably come to ensure she vacated his penthouse before succumbing to whatever was ailing her.

Steeling her spine, she rinsed her mouth. He reached for her as she moved away from the vanity, but she sidestepped him, her heart banging against her ribs. 'I can walk on my own two feet.'

Zaccheo watched her go, her hips swaying in that impertinent, yet utterly sexy way that struck pure fire to his libido.

He slowly followed, paused in the doorway and watched her pace the bedroom.

Although he'd primed himself for her appearance, he hadn't been quite prepared for when he'd finally returned to the penthouse last night and found her asleep in her suite. All the excuses he'd given himself for staying away had crumbled to dust.

As he'd stood over her, his racing heart had only been able to acknowledge one thing—that he'd missed her more than his brain could accurately fathom. He'd thought the daily reports on her movements would be enough. He'd thought buying Siren and ensuring she didn't overwork herself, or silently watching her from the gallery at Preston's studio yesterday, listening to her incredible voice, would be enough.

It wasn't until he'd received her email that his world had stopped, and he'd forced himself to face the truth.

He was nothing without her.

For the last six weeks he'd woken to a tormenting existence each morning. Each time, something had broken inside him. Something that would probably slot neatly under the banner of heartache. It had nothing to do with the loneliness that had plagued his childhood and led him to believe he needed a family to soothe the ache. It had nothing to do with the retribution he was no longer interested in exacting from Oscar Pennington.

It had everything to do with Eva. Flashes of her had struck him at the most inappropriate times—like the brightness of her smile when he was involved in tense negotiation. The feeling of being deep inside her when he was teetering on the edge of a platform three hundred metres above ground, with no net to catch him should he fall. And everywhere he'd gone, he'd imagined the faintest trace of her perfume in the air.

Nothing had stopped him from reaching out for her in the dead of the night, when his guard was at its lowest and all he could feel was *need*. Ferocious, all-consuming need.

Even the air of sadness that hung around her now wasn't enough to make him *not* yearn for her.

His heart kicked into his stomach, knowing it was his fault she wore that look.

Her throat worked to find the words she needed. He forced himself to remain still, to erect a force field against anything she might say.

'Let's end this now, Zaccheo. Divorce me. Surely you'd prefer that to this mockery of a marriage?'

He'd expected it. Hell, her email had left him in no doubt as to her state of mind.

Yet the words punched him in the gut...*hard*. Zaccheo uttered an imprecation that wasn't fit for polite company.

Give her what she wants. Stop this endless misery and be done with it.

It was the selfless thing to do. And if he needed to have learned anything from the stunning, brave woman in front of him, it was selflessness. She'd sacrificed herself for her family and turned over her innermost secrets when she could've just kept quiet and reaped untold wealth. She'd continued to stay under his roof, continued to seek him out, when fear had sent *him* running.

He *needed* to be selfless for her.

But he couldn't. He walked stiffly to the side table and poured a coffee he didn't want.

'There will be no divorce.'

She glared at him. 'You do realise that I don't need your permission?'

He knew that. He'd lived with that fear ever since she'd announced back in Rio that she didn't want to be married to him any more.

'*Sì,*' he replied gruffly. 'You can do whatever you want. The same way I can choose to tie you up in endless red tape for the next twenty years.'

Her mouth dropped open, then she shut her beautiful, pain-filled eyes. 'Why would you do that, Zaccheo?'

'Why indeed?'

She shook her head, and her hair fluttered over her shoulders. 'Surely you can't want this? You deserve a family.'

There it was again. That selflessness that cut him to the core, that forced him to let go, to be a better man. *Dio mio*, but he wanted her to be selfish for once. To claim what she wanted. To claim him!

'How very noble of you to think of me. But I don't need a family.'

Shock widened her eyes. 'What did you say?'

'I don't need a family, *il mio cuore*. I don't need anything, or anyone, if I have you.' *She* was all he wanted. He'd prostrate himself at her feet if that was what it took.

She stared at him for so long, Zaccheo felt as if he'd turned to stone. He knew that any movement would see him shatter into useless pieces.

But he had to take the leap. The same leap she'd taken on the island, when she'd shared something deeply private and heartbreaking with him.

'If you have *me*?'

He risked taking a breath. 'Yes. I love you, Eva. I've been racking my brain for weeks, trying to find a way to make you stay, convince you to stay my wife—'

'You didn't think to just *ask* me?'

'After walking away from you like a coward?' He shook his head. 'You've no idea how many times I picked up the phone, how many times I summoned my pilot to bring me back to you. But I couldn't face the possibility of you saying no.' He gave a hollow laugh. 'Believe it or not, I convinced myself I'd rather spend the rest of my life living in another country but still married to you, than face the prospect of never having even the tiniest piece of you.'

Her face crumbled and he nearly roared in pain. 'That's no life at all, Zaccheo.'

'It was a reason for me to *breathe*. A selfish but *necessary* reason for me to keep functioning, knowing I had a piece of you even if it was your name next to mine on a marriage certificate.'

'Oh, God!' Tears filled her eyes and he cursed. He wanted to take her in his arms. But he had no right. He'd lost all rights when he'd forced her into marriage and then condemned her for trying to protect herself from his monstrous actions.

He clenched his fists against the agony ripping through him. 'But that's no life for you. If you wish for a divorce, then I'll grant you one.'

'What?' Her face lost all colour. She started to reach for him, but faltered. 'Zaccheo...'

A different sort of fear scythed through him as she started to crumple.

'Eva!'

By the time he caught her she was unconscious.

Muted voices pulled her back to consciousness. The blinds in the strange room were drawn but there was enough light to work out that she was no longer in Zaccheo's penthouse. The drip in her right arm confirmed her worst fears.

'What...happened?' she croaked.

Shadowy figures turned, and Sophie rushed to her side.

'You fainted. Zaccheo brought you to the hospital,' Sophie said.

'Zaccheo...' Memory rushed back. Zaccheo telling her he loved her. Then telling her he would divorce her...

No!

She tried to sit up.

The nurse stopped her. 'The doctors are running tests. We should have the results back shortly. In the meantime, you're on a rehydrating drip.'

Eva touched her throbbing head, wishing she'd stop talking for a moment so she could—

She stared at her bare fingers in horror. 'Where are my rings?' she cried.

The nurse frowned. 'I don't know.'

'No...please. I need...' She couldn't catch her breath. Or take her eyes off her bare fingers. Had Zaccheo done it so quickly? While she'd been unconscious?

But he'd said he loved her. Did he not love her enough? Tears brimmed her eyes and fell down her cheeks.

'It's okay, I'll go and find out.' The nurse hurried out.

Sophie approached. Eva forced her pain back and looked at her.

'I hope you don't mind me being here? You didn't call when you got back so I assume you don't want to speak to me, but when Zaccheo called—'

Eva shook her head, her thoughts racing, her insides shredding all over again. 'You're my family, Sophie. It may take a while to get back to where we were before, but I don't hate you. I've just been a little...preoccupied.' Her gaze went to the empty doorway. 'Is...Zaccheo still here?'

Sophie smiled wryly. 'He was enraged that you didn't have a team of doctors monitoring your every breath. He went to find the head of the trauma unit.'

Zaccheo walked into the room at that moment, and Sophie

hastily excused herself. The gunmetal shade of his eyes and the self-loathing on his face made Eva's heart thud slowly as she waited for the death blow.

He walked forward like a man facing his worst nightmare.

Just before she'd fainted, she'd told herself she would fight for him, as she'd fought for her sister and father. Seeing the look on his face, she accepted that nothing she did would change things. Her bare fingers spoke their own truth.

'Zaccheo, I know you said…you loved me, but if it's not enough for you—'

Astonishment transformed his face. 'Not enough for *me*?'

'You agreed to divorce me…'

Anguish twisted his face. 'Only because it was what *you* wanted.'

She sucked in a breath when he perched on the edge of the bed. His fingers lightly brushed the back of her hand, over and over, as if he couldn't help himself.

'You know what I did last night before I came home?'

She shook her head.

'I went to see your father. I had no idea where I was headed until I landed on the lawn at Pennington Manor. Somewhere along the line, I entertained the idea that I would sway your feelings if I smoothed my relationship with your father. Instead I asked him for your hand in marriage.'

'You did what?'

He grimaced. 'Our wedding was a pompous exhibition from start to finish. I wanted to show everyone who'd dared to look down on me how high I'd risen.'

Her heart lurched. 'Because of what your mother and stepfather did?'

He sighed. 'I hated my mother for choosing her aristocrat husband over me. Like you, I didn't understand why it had to be an either-or choice. Why couldn't she love me *and* her husband? Then I began to hate everything he stood for. The need to understand why consumed me. My stepfather was easy to break. Your father was a little more cunning.

He used you. From the moment we met, I couldn't see beyond you. He saw that. I don't know if I'll ever be able to forgive that, but he brought us together.' He breathed deep and shoved a hand through his short hair. 'Possessing you blinded me to what he was doing. And I blamed you for it, right along with him when the blame lay with me and my obsession to get back at you when I should've directed my anger elsewhere.'

'You were trying to understand why you'd been rejected. I tried for years to understand why my father couldn't be satisfied with what he had. Why he pushed his family obsession onto his children. He fought with my mother over it, and it ripped us apart. Everything stopped when she got sick. Perversely, I hoped her illness would change things for the better. For a while it did. But after she died, he reverted to type, and I couldn't take it any more.' She glanced at him. 'Hearing you tell that newspaper tycoon that I was merely a means to an end brought everything back to me.'

Zaccheo shut his eyes in regret. He lifted her hand and pressed it against his cheek. 'He was drunk, prying into my feelings towards you. I was grappling with them myself and said the first idiotic thing that popped into my head. I don't deny that it was probably what I'd been telling myself.'

'But afterwards, when I asked you...'

'I'd just found out about the charges. I knew your father was behind it. You were right there, his flesh and blood, a target for my wrath. I regretted it the moment I said it, but you were gone before I got the chance to take it back.' He brought her hand to his mouth and kissed it, then her palm before laying it over his heart. *'Mi dispiace molto, il mio cuore.'*

His heart beat steady beneath her hand. But her fingers were bare.

'Zaccheo, what you said before I fainted...'

Pain ravaged his face before he nodded solemnly. 'I meant it. I'll let you go if that's what you want. Your happiness means everything to me. Even if it's without me.'

She shook her head. 'No, not that. What you said before.'

He looked deep into her eyes, his gaze steady and true. 'I love you, Eva. More than my life, more than everything I've ever dared to dream of. You helped me redeem my soul when I thought it was lost.'

'You touched mine, made me love deeper, purer. You taught me to take a risk again instead of living in fear of rejection.'

He took a sharp breath. 'Eva, what are you saying?'

'That I love you too. And it tears me apart that I won't be able to give you children—'

His kiss stopped her words. 'Prison was hell, I won't deny it. In my lowest times, I thought having children would be the answer. But you're the only family I need, *amore mio*.'

Zaccheo was rocking her, crooning softly to comfort her when the doctor walked in.

'Right, Mrs Giordano. You'll be happy to hear we've got to the bottom of your fainting spell. There's nothing to worry about besides—'

'Dehydration and the need to eat better?' she asked with a sniff.

'Well, yes, there's that.'

'Okay, I promise I will.'

'I'll make sure she keeps to it,' Zaccheo added with a mock frown. He settled her back in the bed and stood. 'I'll go get the car.'

The doctor shook his head. 'No, I'm afraid you can't leave yet. You need to rest for at least twenty-four hours while we monitor you and make sure everything's fine.'

Zaccheo tensed and caught her hand in his. 'What do you mean? Didn't you say you'd got to the bottom of what ails her?' His eyes met hers, and Eva read the anxiety there.

'Zaccheo…'

'Mr Giordano, no need to panic. The only thing that should ail your wife is a short bout of morning sickness and perhaps a little bed rest towards the end.'

Zaccheo paled and visibly trembled. 'The *end*?'

Eva's heart stopped. 'Doctor, what are you saying?' she whispered.

'I'm saying you're pregnant. With twins.'

EPILOGUE

ZACCHEO EMERGED FROM the bedroom where he'd gone to change his shirt—the second of the day due to his eldest son throwing up on him—to find Eva cross-legged on the floor before the coffee table, their children cradled in her arms as she crooned Italian nursery rhymes she'd insisted he teach her.

On the screen via a video channel, Romeo leaned in closer to get a better look at the babies.

Zaccheo skirted the sofa and sat behind his wife, cradling her and their children in his arms.

'Do you think you'll make it for Christmas?' she asked Romeo. Zaccheo didn't need to lean over to see that his wife was giving his friend her best puppy-dog look.

'*Sì*, I'll do my best to be there tomorrow.'

Eva shook her head. 'That's not good enough, Romeo. I know Brunetti International is a huge company, and you're a super busy tycoon, but it's your godsons' first Christmas. They picked out your present all by themselves. The least you can do is turn up and open it.'

Zaccheo laughed silently and watched his friend squirm until he realised denying his wife anything her heart desired was a futile exercise.

'If that's what you wish, *principessa*, then I'll be there.'

Eva beamed. Zaccheo spread his fingers through her hair, resisting the urge to smother her cheek and mouth in kisses because she thought it made Romeo uncomfortable.

The moment Romeo signed off, Zaccheo claimed his kiss, not lifting his head until he was marginally satisfied.

'What was that for?' she murmured in that dazed voice that was like a drug to his blood.

'Because you're my heart, *dolcezza*. I cannot go long without it. Without you.'

Eva's heart melted as Zaccheo relieved her of their youngest son, Rafa, and tucked his tiny body against his shoulder. Then he held out his hand and helped her up with Carlo, their eldest by four minutes.

Zaccheo pulled them close until they stood in a loose circle, his arms around her. Then, as he'd taken to doing, he started swaying to the soft Christmas carols playing in the background.

Eva closed her eyes to stem the happy tears forming. She'd said a prayer every day of her pregnancy as they'd faced hurdles because of her endometriosis. When the doctors had prescribed bed rest at five months, Zaccheo had immediately stepped back from GWI and handed over the day-to-day running of the company to his new second-in-command.

Their sons had still arrived two weeks early but had both been completely healthy, much to the joy and relief of their parents. Relations were still a little strained with her father and sister, but Oscar doted on his grandsons, and Sophie had fallen in love with her nephews at first sight. But no one loved their gorgeous boys more than Zaccheo. The love and adoration in his eyes when he cradled his sons often made her cry.

And knowing that love ran just as deep for her filled her heart with so much happiness, she feared she would burst from it.

'You've stopped dancing,' he murmured.

She began to sway again, her free hand rising to his chest. She caught sight of her new rings—the engagement ring belonging to his grandmother, which he'd kept but not given her because the circumstances hadn't been right, and the new wedding band he'd let her pick out for their second, family-only wedding—and her thoughts turned pensive. 'I was thinking about your mother.'

Zaccheo tensed slightly. She caressed her hand over his heart until the tension eased out of him. 'What were you thinking?' he asked grudgingly.

'I sent her pictures of the boys yesterday.'

A noise rumbled from Zaccheo's chest. 'She's been asking for one since the day they were born.'

She leaned back and looked into her husband's eyes. 'I know. I also know you've agreed to see her at Easter after my first album comes out.'

Tension remained between mother and son, but when his mother had reached out, Zaccheo hadn't turned her away.

Standing on tiptoe, Eva caressed the stubble she insisted he grow again, and kissed him. 'I'm very proud of you.'

'No, Eva. Everything good in my life is because of *you*.' He sealed her lips with another kiss. A deeper, more demanding kiss.

By mutual agreement, they pulled away and headed for the nursery. After bestowing kisses on their sleeping sons, Zaccheo took her hand and led her to the bedroom.

Their lovemaking was slow, worshipful, with loving words blanketing them as they reached fulfilment and fell asleep in each other's arms.

When midnight and Christmas rolled around, Zaccheo woke her and made love to her all over again. Afterwards, sated and happy, he spread his fingers through her hair and brought her face to his.

'Buon Natale, amore mio,' he said. 'You're the only thing I want under my Christmas tree, from now until eternity.'

'Merry Christmas, Zaccheo. You make my heart sing every day and my soul soar every night. You're everything I ever wished for.'

He touched his forehead to hers and breathed deep. *'Ti amero per sempre, dolcezza mia.'*

* * * * *